THE
GRAND
Rise

THE GRAND RISE

LANCE & SCARLET - PART TWO

JC HAWKE

To the angels who read The Grand Ruin in April 2023,
knowing I'd take my time with part two.
This happy ever after is for you.

Playlist

Welcome Home, Son - Radical Face.

Happy Ending - MIKA.

You're Somebody Else - Flora Cash.

Rescue -Lauren Daigle.

More Than Life -Whitley.

Keeping your Head Up - Birdy.

Rome - Dermot Kennedy.

Lose You Again - Acoustic - Tom Odell.

I Will Wait - Mumford & Son.

Thank God I Do - Lauren Daigle.

To Build A Home - The Cinematic Orchestra, Patrick Watson

All I Want - Kodaline.

We'll Be Fine - Acoustic, Luz.

Wait - M83.

There She Goes - The La's.

PROLOGUE

Mason

I climb from my Bentley and look up at the home I grew up in. Stare at the curved terrace I ran around and around as a boy. At the ivy creeping over the granite walls. Before I think too much about it, before I let the memories send me in the other direction, I make my way up the steps, stealing a full breath into my lungs as I walk inside.

The house is veiled in darkness, and a shiver snakes down my spine as I reach blindly for the switch in the main entrance, lighting up the grand sweeping staircase.

"Scar?" I call out cowardly, hoping she'll hear and come to the door.

She's never liked the dark, and yet the heavy gloom filling the corridors of our childhood home seems to reflect our reality too well.

I swallow thickly and walk to the stairs, knowing she's not on the lower level.

My hand skims over the handrail, memories not just of a boy coming back to me, but memories from only a couple of weeks ago, when we were all here, together at the ball.

It was the first time I truly believed Nina and I could make it back to one another. I danced with her to no music that night, and no matter how hard it had been to be back here in this house, right now, with Nina lay in a hospital bed, I'd give anything to go back to that night—barefoot at three a.m.

I make my way down the west wing, crossing to Scarlet's bedroom. There's a chance she's not home, but with the way she left the hospital looking so utterly lost, I can't imagine she'd go anyplace else.

As I reach her room, I see the soft glow of light gleaming from inside. I push on the closed door and find her. Exactly where I thought she'd be. And maybe it's the lack of sleep or the fact I almost lost my fiancée this week, but as I take in my sister's sleeping form, I'm hit with so many emotions all at once. I lose myself to them.

I frown, then shake my head.

Scarlet is curled up on the bed, the covers pulled tight around her, the material clutched in her fists. And behind her, lay atop the bed sheets with a thin throw covering his lower body, Charlie Aldridge sleeps.

He must sense my presence and awakens, lifting his head and catching me in the doorway.

"Fuck," he mutters, rubbing at his eyes with one hand.

Scarlet rouses, rolling over slightly before she sits up in a rush, looking at me then at Charlie and then back to me again. "Is it Nina? Is she okay?"

I nod quickly, feeling like I've swallowed the necessary words. "She's great. Just sleepy still. Luce is with her."

Our friends haven't slept in days, and I know what happened has hit them all hard.

Scarlet's shoulders drop, and then she looks down at the man at her side, giving him a small sad smile. "You should get home. You don't have to stay."

Charlie stares back at her, something—a question or assessment of some kind passing between them.

My friend looks up at me with not an ounce of judgement in his eyes and asks, "Are you staying the night?"

I open my mouth to speak, but—

"He'll need to get back to Nina," Scarlet answers for me.

Charlie eases off the bed, giving me a nod. "I'm staying the night," he tells me.

He reaches for his phone on the nightstand and stops as he passes me, grasping me on the back. "She's okay?"

I try to clear my throat but end up nodding in answer.

He sighs and gives me a small victory smile.

Once Charlie's gone, I bring my eyes back to Scarlet. She drops her head, looking at the bed to avoid my gaze. "Are things really that bad?" she whispers.

I frown, clenching my jaw until my teeth ache.

"You're here," she adds when I don't answer, and I know if she put any grit behind it, her voice would've cracked. "It's really that bad, Mase, isn't it?" She covers her face and cries.

I go to her, wrapping her in my arms and holding her. "I'm sorry."

When I arrived at Nina's apartment and found Scarlet covered in her blood, as I sat opposite her in the hospital room and watched thoughtlessly as Elliot pulled his sweatshirt over her head to cover Nina *and* Joey's blood, my mind wasn't with her. It was with Nina and whether she'd make it back to me.

I've always known my sister is a fighter, but the way she fought for Nina and Joey's lives isn't something I'll ever forget.

I'm not sure it's something she'll ever forget either.

"I'm sorry," I tell her again, forcing the barrage of emotion building in my throat back down. "I'm so sorry."

She cries in my arms, not saying a word and not asking for a single thing from me. After a while, she leans back an inch, finally lifting her eyes to mine. And the raw pain I find in them sends my heart sailing down the centre of my chest.

Lance.

"Did he hurt you?"

She tries to mask the emotion, but it eventually wins out and screws up her face in sadness. She shakes her head and whispers, "God, no."

I let out a shaky breath, holding her tighter. "What happened, Scar?"

"We didn't tell you," she says into my sweater. "I kept asking him to wait, or the time wouldn't be right, and he'd put it off."

I frown, piecing together the parts I have. The way Lance looked at her. The way he did what he did for her. "The two of you are together?"

"He saved me, Mase. When there was no one left to pull me out of this place, he saved me."

He saved her?

"And now he's not here, and I don't know what to do."

"You know, your sister once told me that when you're carrying all that you can in your hands, you can't allow yourself to feel guilty about anything that spills over."

"When did she tell you that?"

"A long time ago."

I close my eyes, sucking in a breath as realisation dawns. "Lance saved you?"

"In more ways than he'll ever know."

"Lance," I repeat, almost tasting the sound of his name on my tongue as he becomes someone else entirely to me.

"I love him," Scarlet mutters, her eyes filling again. "I'm pretty sure he's the only person I'll ever love."

As he becomes someone my baby sister loves.

It wasn't until Scarlet left the hospital that I thought about everything that had unfolded. I kept coming back to the moment Lance's eyes met hers when the police arrived. The apology. The tears.

It was as if I knew all at once. As if it made sense. And yet it didn't.

Because why wouldn't he tell me?

He saved me, Mase.

He saved her... while I saved myself.

If I didn't owe Lance Sullivan enough already, he made sure I'd owe him the world.

I take my sister's chin and lift her face up, dropping my forehead to hers. "I never saved you, Scar. When Mum and Dad died. When you were alone after. When a man came at you with a knife." I screw my eyes tightly together at the memory. "Never in my thirty-four years have I saved *you.*

You deserved to be saved ten times over, and if Lance ends up not being able to save you this time, if he has to go away for a while, I'll be here in his place." A tear lines my cheek as she crumbles in my hold, dropping her head to my chest. "You won't be alone this time, Scar."

And she won't be.

Because I won't let her.

ONE

Lance

I took a life once. A single gunshot wound to the chest, and I managed to destroy not only my life but the lives of everyone I loved most. Not a day goes by where I don't regret my actions that morning seven years ago. And although they now call me a free man, I don't believe I'll ever escape the guilt and shame that slowly, year after year, has embedded within me.

I wear it now. Too afraid to take it off at the risk of feeling something I shouldn't.

I found a semblance of peace in my mistakes. My wrong-doings. And the only reason I decided to make the ride out to Lowerwick Estate today is to make sure that she found hers.

I pick up speed as each memory flashes in my mind. Memories that probably should've faded—details lost and jaded at the edges—yet never did.

I remember every second of time spent with Scarlet

Lowell. Maybe even imagined my memories so often, so desperately in moments of fear, they transpired into something else entirely.

It was love.

I don't doubt it was love.

No amount of time or delusion can convince me otherwise.

My bike roars as I cross the cattle grid and take to the lane, the trees a blur as I pass. I swallow the tightness in my throat, keeping my eyes forward, knowing I can't let myself look. Can't let myself see the meadow or the hill or the trees lining the boundary. I know they've grown. A reminder of time lost that I can't bear to think about, let alone see.

Seven years isn't just a long time—her love taught me that —it's birthdays, adventures, graduations, *love*, and pain. It's freedom—all missed.

The trees in the meadow won't be the only thing that's changed, and no matter how much it felt like the world started and ended with Scarlet, it didn't. It kept spinning.

The sun slowly sets on the horizon, casting a pink glare beyond my visor. As I break through the trees, and the house comes into view, I steady my jaw and pray to anyone listening that I have the guts to follow through with this.

Pray to anyone who's fucking listening that she's happy.

Like a beacon, Scarlet stands atop the terrace watching me, her hand clenched to her chest as if she's in pain. My body seems to fight the urge to breathe, my next breath caught, suppressing the emotions swelling in my throat.

Her hand lifts to shield her eyes from the sun, and I

frown, wondering if this is a mistake. If maybe seeing me is the last thing she wants or needs.

If maybe seeing her is the last thing I really want or need.

Pain, a deep crippling ache, uproots my veins and pumps through my entire body, all the way to the tips of my fingers.

She's everything.

She's fucking everything and all I've ever known, and I can't take my eyes off her as I roll to a stop on the gravel.

I've dreamed of this moment. How I'd see her, take in every detail of her face, and never let myself forget again.

I watch as her mouth parts to say something and realise even after seven years, it's still there, that wild thump of my heart that only she has ever given me.

She's wearing a look of shock, but the anger, pain—hate even—it's all there. And I expected it.

Snapping out of my trance, I remove my helmet and get off the bike. Her eyes don't leave me, making my mouth go dry. I work on a swallow and frown up at her on the terrace.

"Scarlet..."

Her eyes close, her face screwing up. And it hits me again —the roaring ache inside of me. "Why are you here?" she asks.

With my focus solely on her, I take a step forward. My legs tremble as I stand, trying to say what needs to be said. "I felt maybe we needed some closure."

She goes to say something but snaps her mouth closed before she can utter the words. She's mad. Eyes wild. I frown as I watch her. I can't help but think about the last time I was here. The way I held her in my arms as we said goodbye. The way she begged me not to leave. The way I felt at that moment...

"Closure." Her voice cracks, and I flinch, that emotion I kept at bay flaring with my sharp inhale. "You think we need..."

Her unforgiving stare doesn't leave me, and I resist looking away to escape it.

"I know I never called—"

She shakes her head. "You should leave."

"Scar—"

"No!" She covers her mouth and takes two steps back before changing her mind and marching forward, taking the steps until she's a foot from reach.

My light, one step away.

"Nothing you say to me..." She pauses, and I freeze, trying to steady my breathing. My body. My fucking heart. She's so close I could touch her. "There is nothing you could say to me that will ever give me closure."

There is nothing you could say to me that will ever give me closure.

I take in every inch of her three times over, realising I never should've come here. I should have left it be. "I'm sorry, Scarlet."

"Yeah." She nods, and I die a little inside as a lone tear slips down her cheek. "But I'm not the one you should be saying it to. Your apologies don't mean a thing to me anymore."

I try for the right words. "I didn't come here to hurt you, but it felt wrong not to. I don't expect anything from you—I don't want anything from you. I'm going to stay in the city, see Mum—"

"You'll come back tomorrow," she tells me. "No... Friday. You'll come back on Friday."

A frown creases my brow, not expecting her to invite me back again. Maybe I should've told her I was coming out today. I knew Charlie would let her know I'd been released, and if there were any lingering thoughts because of it, I wanted to make sure she could move past them right away. "I just told you I'm going back to the city. I won't be around here."

She stares me down, her brown eyes gleaming with emotion. "*You're* selfish, did you know that? Probably the most selfish person I've ever known."

It would hurt less if she slapped me.

"You'll come back on Friday." She turns and runs up the steps.

"Scar."

She doesn't stop, and as the large wooden door slams shut behind her, I tilt my head back to the sky above and let out a long sigh.

She has every right to be angry at me, but it doesn't make it any easier to stand here and take.

I sit on the steps for over twenty minutes, considering how stupid it would be of me to knock on the door and try again. To try and get the words right.

Eventually, I decide she deserves better.

I remove her letters from my bike as planned and carry them up the steps, leaving them on the mat below the front door.

Closure.

And then I head back into the city, far away from the only thing that's ever felt like home.

Scarlet

I feel my brother's eyes on me long before he knocks on Ellis's bedroom door, and I'm in no hurry as I twist my head and look at him, waiting for him to say whatever it is he has to say.

Eventually, I give in. "You could help me, you know."

He shrugs, a contemplative harshness on his face as he leans against the door frame. "And you could leave my son's sheets to me or his mum to change."

"Jackass," I huff, reaching for the edge of the fitted sheet and tucking it under Ellis's mattress.

I move around the bed and start on the other side. After a moment, I'm bumped to the side, and Mason bends to take my place, tucking in the last corner himself. He picks up the quilt and lays it across the bed, smoothing out the creases.

"Have you heard anything?"

I pull my lip between my teeth and shake my head.

Mason's nostrils flare as he plants his hands on his hips. I cut him off before he can speak. "He didn't want to hear from me when he was in prison, Mase. We were fools to think it would be any different now."

"He doesn't get to do this to you."

I sigh and drop down to the bed, sitting on the edge. "I need you to stay out of this." I look up at my brother, a small, helpless smile forming as I catch the hard mask he's pulled into place. "He's going to need you, Mase. I don't think this works otherwise. Let me and Charlie handle the messy stuff, and you just be there for your friend."

Lance didn't show up on Friday. It's now Monday, and I know that Mason is on the verge of exploding. I also know that I'm on the verge of exploding, but I don't dare tell my brother that.

Mason's been back at Lowerwick for nearly seven years now. He turned up one day with Nina and his family and told me exactly how it was going to go. He was home and had no plans of ever leaving again.

I needed my brother, and he was here. Within a heartbeat.

That wasn't—hasn't been—easy for him.

"He's a fucking fool. I'm going over there."

"Mase," I warn.

"How can you be so calm, Scarlet?"

I huff out a laugh and drop my eyes to the ground, tamping down the fire growing inside me. "Don't do that," I tell him. "It's not fair when you know how hard this is for me —for all of us. I understand you're mad, and despite how I might be handling things right now, I can promise you I'm far from calm. But getting angry and doing something stupid isn't going to help."

His jaw ticks, and then he lets out a long exhale, scrubbing at his face. "I don't even know what I'd say to him."

"Exactly." I stand and gather up the dirty sheets from the floor, knowing I have no idea what I'd say to Lance either. I said all I had to say in my letters.

The letters that lay unopened on my doormat when I eventually stepped outside on Wednesday.

"Promise me you won't go over there," I say, loosing a breath and steeling myself all over again when a flicker of pain ebbs through me.

And I know my brother doesn't catch it.

At some point, I guess the pain became a part of me. It goes where I go now. Laces my every breath. Speaks for me in some moments and keeps me quiet in others. It's my constant in a world of unknowns. A pain that flows so deep within, just a spark of it has me reaching out a hand, desperate to hold on to it so that I can be reminded that it's still in there somewhere and that so am I. I'm unsure of the woman I am without it anymore, and if I'm honest with myself, that terrifies me.

Mason tucks his hands behind his back, nodding. "I promise."

I shake my head and turn to walk out of the room, grabbing up the washing basket as I go. "I know you just crossed your fingers, asshole."

"He has until the weekend," he calls after me.

I pause for a moment and then swallow, staring through the window at the end of the hallway and across the meadow.

I nod despite Mason not being able to see.

TWO

Lance

I should go and see my mum. She is, after all, the third person on my list of people I need to apologise to. But something stopped me from making the drive out to my childhood home this afternoon, and now I'm three beers deep at the bar closest to Elliot's house.

Elliot's house. Not mine.

Charlie Aldridge stuck to his word. Everything was taken care of whilst I was away. He even sold my penthouse and purchased Elliot's home when he bought a new place for his wife and kids. I say purchased, but I haven't paid a penny for the five-bedroom, gated home.

I also don't know the details of the wife. I certainly never thought I'd see the day Elliot Montgomery settled down.

The idea of missing that for him—Charlie and Mase, too... It's not a thought I let linger as I lift the beer bottle to my mouth and take a swig.

Charlie was waiting for me as I stepped out from the prison doors. I didn't know what to say to him at first. Felt sick the entire walk across the car park at the thought of him saying something that might not be what I wanted to hear. And then, he simply rounded the car and climbed inside. He didn't speak to me on the drive home, and I didn't speak to him either, reading the silence and accepting it.

I accepted the consequences of cutting them off years ago. The prison was a two-hour drive away. I couldn't sit back week after week and have them travel to see me.

And I couldn't have Scarlet wait for me.

I never expected them to understand that choice.

Plenty of men had few or no visits inside; I wasn't the only one. And as they came and went, each seeking their freedom, somewhere throughout the years the questions stopped.

I was Lance. A murderer with no family on the outside.

I even convinced myself it was true on the days I questioned my motives for not wanting to see them. The days I'd find myself slipping.

I didn't cry for the entirety of my time inside, no matter how fucking hard it was, and yet as my once best friend tossed me the keys to the sprawling house, told me it was mine and that Elliot now lives with his wife and kids out near Rosestone, and then left, well it was only then that something seemed to break inside of me. I felt nothing and everything as my shoulders finally sagged after seven long years, and I bawled like a child on the foyer floor.

"You want another?" the barman asks, lifting his chin toward the near-empty bottle in my hand.

My eyes cast over the slightly peeled-back label as I think

about the unpacked boxes I left stacked in Elliot's foyer, that list of people I need to apologise to...

"Sure," I say instead.

"Come on, fella." I lift my head as a solid hand claps me on my shoulder. The barman is wiping down the bar top beside me, and I swiftly drag my body up and wipe at my face. "We're closing up. You have a way home?"

I frown at his words—or that word in particular—then nod, standing from the stool.

"I can give you a lift if you're close by."

My body feels like a lead weight, but I'm not pissed enough to need looking after. Or to want to be looked after. "The fresh air will do me good." I pull my wallet from my back pocket and hand him the cash tucked inside. "Will that cover my tab?"

The guy watches me closely before flicking his eyes to the cash. He sifts through it before handing back half. "Take it steady, lad. The world doesn't wait for you to be okay before it fucks you."

"You can say that again." I pull on my jacket and push my hands into my jeans pockets as I step outside.

It's a short walk back to Elliot's house, and I opt to take the longer route through the park. The sky is clear, and as I tip my head back and inhale a deep breath of fresh air, listening to the gentle flow of the river in the distance, looking at the moon and stars that taunt me from above, I only think of Scarlet.

I wonder if maybe she's looking at them, too.

If maybe she looks at them sometimes and thinks about me.

I make it back to the house a little while later and stand motionless in the foyer, surveying the house I practically lived in once.

We spent our late teens and early twenties in this place. It's where Elliot and Mason lived during university, and when Mase bought the penthouse, Elliot decided to stay.

It's a place I know and once, a long time ago, felt somewhat at home in. So, it doesn't surprise me that the guys thought it was a good fit for me.

Only it isn't.

It's too big.

"Too fucking quiet," I murmur.

It reminds me of the home I grew up in. Fit for a family.

I kick off my shoes and walk to the kitchen, stopping in the doorway as I gaze around the huge space. My stomach growls, and I know I should eat, but the cupboards are empty. When I drove to the shops this afternoon and realised my bank card was out of date and invalid, I turned around and came all the way back, found the cash in the safe Charlie had mentioned, and then went to the pub.

Nothing feels quite like it did before I left. It's as if the people around me know something I don't, and yet nothing has really changed.

I head for the bedrooms upstairs, walking toward the room that was once mine. When I arrived last week, the main bedroom was dressed and made for me, and yet as I'd lain on the super-king bed and tried to sleep, the vast open room around me feeling hollow and cold, my entire body began to shake.

My old room is smaller and, apparently, the perfect place for Elliot to store his shit. I spent the day emptying it and then setting up my things.

I guess it was always the joke between us. Charlie had the third nicest room when we'd stay over, and I took the "closet room." I never minded it, always used to taking the lesser when growing up with three sisters like Nessa-Anne, Molly, and Chloe, and the room is hardly small.

I close the bedroom door behind me and lock it, then go to the en suite and clean my teeth in silence.

Just the whoosh and scratch from the bristles of my toothbrush against my teeth.

Nothing to say, and no one to listen.

When I'm done, I pull my sweatshirt over my head and strip down to my boxer briefs. With little thought to the why, and like every other night I've been here, I drag the covers back from the bed and pull them to the small two-seater sofa in the corner of the room, chucking down a pillow at one end.

Then I check the door's locked—twice—slip between the cushions and plush quilt, and lie in the silence of the house.

"Sullivan!"

I wake with a start as a fist hammers on the wooden door. My chest heaves, my heart thumping against my ribcage as I'm instantly on alert.

"The door's locked."

"You don't think he'd do anything, do you?"

I let the voices outside the door settle around the fog, telling myself that it's my friends and that I'm safe.

You're at Elliot's.

You're at Elliot's.

"Fuck," I breathe out.

Pulling in a harsh inhale, I grab up the quilt and toss it onto the bed along with the pillow.

"Lance?"

I swallow and clear my throat. "Just a minute."

I don't miss the collective sigh as I unlatch the lock and wrench open the door. "Sorry," I mutter, stepping aside to let them in.

The three of them stand shoulder to shoulder as they look into the boxy room and frown. Charlie is the first to step inside, and it's not until they're all over the threshold that I realise how stupid I must look inviting them into the room when we have a whole house beyond my bedroom's four walls.

"You took the closet room," Elliot remarks, eyeing the old room.

"Not many closets have en suites and double beds," I reply, chuckling awkwardly as I let my gaze move over them. They're all a little bit different, yet the same, with smile lines from what I can only hope are years of laughing.

I don't know what to expect as they stare back at me, thoughtful, hard looks on all of their faces. But then Elliot grins. "You're aging like wine, my friend." He pulls me in for a hug, and it's so unexpected, I stand stock still, unable to do anything as his arms wrap around my shoulders.

And fuck if I don't want him to let me go.

"You reek of stale beer," he groans, pulling away and brushing his hands together as if I'm dirty. "Get in the shower, and we'll grab breakfast." He nods, giving me a reassuring look. Mason and Charlie don't say a word.

When they turn to head out of the room, I clear my throat and say, "You don't have to do this for me. I'm fine—I'll be fine."

Charlie and Mason continue out the door, and it's Elliot who stops and looks at me straight-faced, a hint of the emotion my two best friends bore moments ago now creeping over his features as he replies, "We're not just doing it for you, Lance."

The sound of their voices echoes through the empty halls as I make my way to the kitchen, reminding myself that the stack of boxes inside the foyer needs to be unpacked.

Maybe I'll do that today.

"There wasn't any need for it. He could have taken the offer and kept the contract."

"It's a personal thing, Lowell. You'd have done the same."

"I might be fucking stubborn at times, but I'm not stupid enough to land my company in the shit."

"You are," I hear Elliot add. "But you also have Aldridge to wipe your ass and save your sorry soul so..."

"Fuck you."

"I see some things don't change." I huff out a bitter laugh as I round the doorway, finding them dotted around the kitchen. Charlie is at the hob, and he eyes me over his shoulder, pausing whatever it is he's cooking.

I breathe in and then out, letting the warm feeling in my chest spread with each inhale.

I've missed my friends so fucking much.

Mason stands with his hands resting on the kitchen island, his face hardening as he takes me in. "Plenty's changed," he says before pointedly flicking his stare to one of the stools. "Come eat."

I run my tongue over my teeth, knowing I should sit down, hating how it makes me feel to be told to.

"Thank you," I tell them, noticing the food scattered over the countertops. "I was going to go shopping today—"

"Lance..." Mason stops himself, the spatula in Charlie's hand dropping to the counter a moment later. "You're my friend first, Lance. Before anything else, you're my friend. But until I say what I need to say, it's hard to even look at you right now."

I swallow and nod, ready for whatever he needs to throw at me.

I hurt her.

His baby sister.

Scarlet.

"You never showed up last Friday. Why?" Mason asks.

"At the estate?"

Their eyes are trained on me, and with the tension in the room, the thought of her and what I've done... my jaw goes taut.

"Scarlet asked you to come back. Did you?" Elliot asks when Mason doesn't continue.

"No." I shake my head resolutely. "I didn't. I don't expect you to understand, but for the same reasons I kept you all at bay for the last seven years, things won't be changing."

"They fucking will—"

"Charles," Elliot sighs.

"And fast. They'll be changing fast."

My eyes dart between them all, my insides already burning with the question on the tip of my tongue. I look at Mason. Wanting to ask. Needing to know. I told myself I'd wait, that I wouldn't...

I shouldn't ask.

I shouldn't, but...

"Did she..." I clench my jaw, swallowing down the ache that distorts my voice. "Did she ever move on?"

They stare through me, all three of them, as if they're imagining what her moving on might look like.

I could give them the exact vision they're looking for if they asked. Multiple ways. Multiple endings. She's happy in my head. Married to a good man with kids, doing something she loves. A doctor—she's definitely a doctor.

She has to be.

"I plan to go and see my mum this morning," I lie, needing all the time I can get before going back to the estate. "If you think it's what Scarlet needs, I'll head out there during the week to see her."

"Your mum?"

I flick my gaze to Charlie, the disdain in his voice making me flinch as raw pain cracks my chest in two. "I owe her an—"

"No. You owe that woman nothing. You—" He cuts himself off, his chest working as he fights for calm.

"Stop doing that," I snap, the fire in my gut lashing its way up and across my tongue. I've known Charlie for over fifteen years and never once have I seen him so pent up. "Say what you need to say, Charlie."

"There's not a lot I have to say right now," he grits out, eyes livid. "But I'll tell you that while you chose to keep me, and Scar, and all of the people who loved you waiting and wondering and fucking worrying for seven years, that woman you call your mother and are so desperate to crawl back to didn't show up once. Didn't call you once. You might think you did us all a favour by cutting yourself from our lives, but you didn't. You hurt the people you should have protected worse than you'll ever know because you weren't here."

My nostrils flare as he throws the pan into the sink and leaves the house, the front door slamming shut as he goes.

After a couple of minutes of silence, Elliot stands from the kitchen island. "Don't take it too personally. His lady is out of town, and he gets a little... sensitive."

I frown, wondering who Charlie's *lady* is. "Who did you marry?" I ask Elliot, not bothering to clear the rasp from my throat.

A slow smile creeps across his face as if he can't control it. "Luce, obviously."

My brows lift as he slips past me and out of the kitchen.

Mason pushes off the counter next, stopping when he's at my shoulder. I stare straight ahead, a coward unable to look him in the eye. I feel his lingering gaze and then hear, "Go and see her, Lance."

THREE

Lance

I lift my hand and knock on the door to the house, knowing it's likely unlocked. Once, a long time ago, I'd have walked straight in, kicked off my shoes and searched for her.

"Baby Lowell..."

"Hmm."

I smile into her neck, loving the way her voice vibrates against my skin. "You didn't say it today."

"Didn't say what?"

I run my hand up her back, knowing that she knows. "That you love me."

I feel her smile. "Are you sure?"

"Certain of it."

"I think you're wrong."

"Impossible." I grin.

She draws her head back to look at me, rolling her eyes.

"This smile—it's yours. The reason I went out and planted those dafs—you."

"Me?" I frown, my smile not wavering.

"You told me it was your nan's favourite."

"That's why you planted them?"

She shakes her head as if I should already know. "The song I sang whilst cooking dinner—you. The dress I picked out to wear this morning—you." She reaches up and dusts her finger over my lips. "The way my heart rages on every single day. You. Everything is always you." She kisses me. "I might not say it with words some days, Lance, but you're in everything that I do."

Ever since I came here last week, I've seen nothing but her face when I close my eyes at night. And while she doesn't bring sleep, she does bring a calm I've not felt in years. Even being here now, standing on these steps, it brings me a feeling I know I'll never find anywhere else.

It's probably my favourite place in the entire world.

I pause as I hear screaming and shouting from the distance, then frown, realising it's getting closer.

I take a couple of steps to the left of the front door, following the terrace around to the west wing of the house. Just as I breach the corner, I run into a horde of kids. They come to a screeching halt when they see me, the taller, oldest-looking boy of them all crashing into my stomach.

"Shit."

"Ellis!" one of them scolds.

I step back, letting the boy, Ellis, go.

Holy shit.

Mason and Elliot's kids.

I scan them quickly, a slight shake of my head as I count all five of them. Ellis has to be around eight now. He's tall, too, his frame blocking his mousy-haired sister who he pulls in tight to his back. She has a garland of wildflowers sitting on her head, no doubt courtesy of her auntie. "Let me guess... Lowell." I point at Ellis. "Lowell." I nod at the girl now peeking out from behind his back. "Montgomery," I say to the small, sandy-haired boy. "Lowell." I chuckle, staring down at another mini Mase. "And you're a Montgomery." I smile at the little girl who looks exactly like Lucy.

Shit.

I rub my chest as I smile down at them all.

This. This is what I've missed.

"What are you doing here?" Ellis demands.

I blink as if I've forgotten the reason. "I came to see your auntie Scarlet."

He narrows his eyes on me, his stare not faltering. "She's working."

Shit. I scratch my brow. "Do you know what time she'll be back?"

"No. Leave, or I'll get my mum."

"Ellis," the mousy-haired girl warns, gripping his hand tighter.

"Don't speak, Ave."

"It's alright," I say, not wanting to upset them. "I'll leave. Could you tell Scarlet that Lance Sullivan stopped by and that I'll be back tomorrow? I'm an old friend of hers." I nod, smirking at Ellis before I turn and head across the terrace. "Boy's a tyrant," I mutter to myself as I jog down the steps.

"We know who you are, you big idiot."

I shift to look up at the terrace. Only two of them stand at the top now. Ellis and the little boy who's the split of Mase.

"I'd appreciate it if you'd let her know I popped by, Ellis." I try a half-smile, not wanting to get into it with a child. I turn and carry on toward my bike.

"I bet you would."

I pause, twisting my head to look at him over my shoulder.

"Why do you keep stopping, I told you to go."

I pop a brow.

"Best hope I'm not around when you come back."

With a shake of my head, I climb onto my bike and peel off out of the drive.

Me, too, Ellis. Me, too.

Scarlet

"Is it just me, or has this shift been the longest in history?"

I smile into my fist as I peer over the desk at Mia. "It's because it's a Sunday."

"You're right, it is. We should be at home... reading."

I screw up my face. "Or eating roast dinner and sleeping."

"Right, sorry. I forget you don't read," Mia sighs. "You're missing out on worlds far superior to this one. One day you'll cave."

"Maybe," I say, not bothering to tell her about the books I used to read.

"Here, you," Annie interjects with a smile. "Take bay

three. He's an outlier and far nicer than eight. And you've been an angel today."

"Thank you," I say, taking the file she hands me and backing away as I grin at my friends.

Annie is a registrar—very nearly a consultant—and my favourite superior to answer to. She's also a very good friend. Mia and I met in our foundation year here at the hospital. We were both lucky enough to get our first choice of rotations and crossed every hurdle we faced during them together. Both women have picked me up on bad days as I have them. Our bond was formed over a love of fixing people—and also our shared experience in love and loss.

They're both as broken as I am and oddly, I liked that.

I push aside the curtain and smile at the gentleman in bay three. "Hello, Alfred. I'm Dr Lowell."

The man grips the sheets in his hands and nods his head. "Hello."

"Could you explain your symptoms to me? I can see you were seen by one of us on Friday night. You're having trouble urinating?"

"Yes," he croaks, pain lacing his words.

I'm instantly around the bed and grasping his arm in a soothing hold. "Okay, let's get this sorted. When was the last time you were able to pass urine?"

"Days." He winces. "It's been days since I've been able to go properly."

I frown and read the chart further. "And you were given antibiotics. They're treating it as a UTI," I realise. "And yet your urine test was negative."

I note that he's had a bladder scan and needs a catheter.

"It's very painful. I can feel a lot of pressure."

"Am I able to check your abdomen?"

He nods, and I assist him as he moves down the bed. The first thing I notice is his swollen lower abdomen, and then my hands make contact with the hard mass beneath, and my eyes widen.

His bladder is full and...

I step toward the curtain and poke my head out, knowing I'm out of my depth and should ask for help. "Dr Harlow, could I borrow you for a moment?"

"Sure," Annie replies, handing Mia the folder she's busy reading.

"Alfred was in with us two days ago and was treated for a suspected UTI. Could you take a look at his abdomen for me, please?"

"Of course. You'll have to excuse me, Alfred. Dr Lowell's hands are notoriously warmer than my own."

"It's fine," he says politely.

I give him a warm smile and stand at his side, resting my hand on his forearm.

When Annie lifts back the sheet, she pauses for just a moment before her eyes lift to mine.

"I'd like to get a catheter in as soon as possible," I tell her.

"Agreed."

I opt to insert the catheter myself. It's one of my least favourite jobs, and yet the relief I know Alfred will feel once it's in will be monumental.

"Oh, gosh," he groans after a minute, sinking back into the bed.

"Is that feeling a little better, Alfred?" Annie asks.

"Yes." He smiles, eyes still closed. "Yes, it is... and you can call me Fred." He looks up, looking for me, still somewhat in distress. "Thank you, Dr Lowell."

"You're welcome, Fred." I feel my brow crease and flick my gaze to Annie again.

She gives me a sad smile and looks at the elderly man. "Fred, once we're done here. I'd like to get you up to urology for further testing."

"Why?"

"Unfortunately, I don't believe you have an infection at all. And I'd like to test the mass on your abdomen right away."

"Oh."

"Is there anyone we can call? Someone who can come upstairs with you?"

"Umm, no. Sorry, there isn't."

My heart sinks.

"You don't need to apologise," Annie tells him.

"Dr Harlow, if you could find someone to cover me, I would be happy to go up. I'd love the opportunity to see this through to discharge."

Annie gives me a knowing half-smile and nods. "I'm sure I can find someone." She steps away from the bed and goes to leave, pausing at my side as she rubs my shoulder. "Good work, Scar."

I stare at the numbers on the wall of the elevator as it carries me down to my floor, each level seemingly passing slower and slower with each second.

As the doors peel open and I step forward with a heavy sigh, feet throbbing, I pause.

"Annie, you're still here."

She eyes me over her shoulder, flashing me a faint smirk before continuing with her paperwork. "So are you."

I walk around the desk and drop down into the chair. My body feels about ready to give up.

"Need to talk about it?"

I shake my head. "Cancer."

Annie doesn't flinch. We both knew. "Head home, Scar. It's been a long one today," she tells me, not looking up from the notes she's making.

"Are you leaving soon?"

"Yep. Once I'm done here, I'll be right behind you."

I eye the five files stacked under the one she's working on. "Here, give me three."

"Nope. Mia tried this crap, too. You have a whole shit show waiting for you at home if what you alluded to in the coffee line this morning is true. Go... I don't know... fix it." She waves me off.

After a moment, she pauses her writing and looks up at me.

I pop a brow and tilt my head.

"I'll give you one," she relents, handing me a folder.

"Two, and I'll buy you lunch for a week."

"That bad?"

"Bad enough I'd rather stay here and check over these than go home and answer questions I don't have the answers to."

She gives me a sympathetic grimace. "Alright. Two, and you're done."

"Deal."

I take the folders and sit back on the chair.

We work in silence for a while, both of us lost to the words and numbers on the pages. It's not until we're finished and in the staff room collecting our belongings that Annie speaks.

"You can tell me about it if it will help."

I think back to Lance standing on the driveway. His bike. The way I've not slept since seeing him again. I've been busy today and tried desperately to not think about him, but the more hours that have passed, the harder it's been to shut him out of my mind. "I don't think it would," I reply with a smile, grateful that she cares enough to ask.

"That's fine. If you need to take some time over the next few weeks or months, just tell me. We'll figure something out. Don't struggle alone if we can help."

When I first met Annie, she was alone inside of a stock cupboard—in the dark—with tears brimming in her eyes.

I learnt two things about Annie that day.

One: she was a braver woman than me.

And two: she'd never let those tears fall. Even locked away in a store cupboard where no one could see, she'd never give into them.

She'd lost her husband the day before.

"I couldn't be without this job, Annie. It's the only thing that's kept me sane."

She eyes me sceptically, and I chuckle.

"It's my escape."

"I get that."

We make our way through the hospital and head for the main exit. "God, I have so much to do when I get home," she sighs, dropping her head to my shoulder as we walk. "This place doesn't give you a moment to think sometimes. The second I leave through those doors, it's like a floodgate opens to reality."

I swallow, slightly missing a step as the knot in my gut pulls tighter. "Want to know a secret, Annie?"

"Hmm?"

"Sometimes I'll go over paperwork I've already done, paperwork I know is right, just to stay a little longer."

Annie sniggers, linking our arms as we approach the automatic doors. "Don't tell anyone, but me too."

FOUR

Lance

When your word is all you have left, it's important to keep it. That's what I tell myself anyway as I round the circular drive at Lowerwick Estate.

There's no way of ever winning Scarlet back regardless of what my friends think. It's not why I'm here today either. The pain I put her through, along with all that she's endured in life, is enough for me to stay the hell away.

I'll make sure she's okay. Ask her if she's okay this time—instead of just staring at her like an idiot, telling her I want closure.

I came across as a dick, but seeing her again after so much time, having her so damn close I could touch her, it upended all rational thought. Everything I thought, everything I planned to say, it all seemed stupid, pointless compared to her.

It's late, and a dark veil slowly falls over the grounds,

making the house and the two headstones nestled in the small garden on the west side of the house seem even more morbid than normal.

I wonder what Anthony must be thinking, watching me turn up here now. He'd likely hate me. He definitely wouldn't have given me his blessing all those years ago if he knew what was to come.

If he knew what I was capable of.

I sigh and pull my helmet from my head, shaking out my hair. As I ease back, ready to climb off, Scarlet steps from the house, firmly closing the door behind her.

She stares at me for a moment, her face expressionless. And tired—she looks completely shattered.

I swallow and go to speak.

"Walk with me," she says. No grit, no anger, no nothing. *Walk with me.*

I ease my leg over my bike and place my helmet on the seat. When she gets to the bottom of the steps, I take my place beside her, keeping a good space between our shoulders.

She starts toward the lane, directing us away from the house.

"Mason's here." I tip my head toward the Bentley on the drive, his private plate letting me know it's his.

She wraps her cardigan around her, her gaze trained on the horizon. "He lives here."

Surprise flashes on my face, but she doesn't catch it. She doesn't acknowledge me. "He moved home?" My brow quirks. *I knew it.* "You must love having them here."

She nods. "It's been what we all needed."

Silence stretches between us, and it's not until I notice her hands shaking slightly as she pulls her cardigan even tighter, that I decide I need to talk.

"I'll be honest, Scarlet, I don't know where to start." I stare at the side of her head, willing her to look at me. "It's hard having to do this with you. To have these conversations as if I never knew you at all."

She finally looks up at me, a fire burning behind her dark eyes. "If you wanted to know where to start, you should've read my letters."

I shake my head without even meaning to, knowing deep down in my gut that what she's saying is impossible. "I couldn't. If I did..." I stare at her, her lavender hair tied in a messy knot on her head. Her eyes, big and brown and glassy. I wonder if her skin is as soft as I remember. If it would still pebble under my touch. "If I read those letters, I'd never have let you go. It would've killed me. Your words to me."

She comes to a stop, barely out of the driveway. "And it didn't matter what I wanted? What I needed? You just thought you'd decide what was best for you, and that was that?"

"It wasn't like that at all. It was better for *you* this way. I couldn't—"

"That's exactly how it was. Don't you dare stand there and moan about feeling awkward over questions you'd never need to ask if you'd just read the letters. You don't get to presume how this has been for me." Her voice rises with her anger, but she softens it when she adds, "Or how you did it for me. If anything, that's worse than doing it for yourself."

"It wasn't for myself. Nothing was for me. I understand

you didn't want that, and you don't accept it now, but I can't change it. I did what I thought was best at the time for all of you."

She stares at me, readying herself to go again, to unleash everything she's not been able to say for the last seven years.

And I'm ready for it.

I need it—maybe as much as she does.

But then pain flashes on her face, and she lets out a shaky breath. She pulls her shoulders back. "After you left, I... I found..." Her eyes fill with tears while I stand waiting, letting the pounding of my heart consume me. I prepare myself for what I know is to come. "I found—"

"You found someone else," I finish for her.

"What?" she slings back, voice tight and disbelieving.

"I'm sorry, I thought... it's none of my business."

A tear runs down her cheek, and she swipes it away angrily, her shoulders sagging as she shakes her head. "This situation deserves more," she rasps, face tight.

"Your brother told me to come here, Scarlet. I don't want to hurt you."

"You think you're hurting me now? You think these tears are for you?" I watch helplessly as her temper rises. "God. You have no idea! You have no idea because you chose yourself. You chose you. And the only reason you're here now is because you can't stand the idea of not knowing if it was the right decision. You want me to be happy and okay and perfect so that you won't feel the guilt that came with choosing to protect yourself."

Something deep inside of me jars at her words. The truth in them. I shake my head and step toward her.

"Stay away from me," she warns, turning and stalking away. She runs up the steps, passing Mason and Nina, who are now watching on from the terrace.

I pause at the bottom of the steps, looking up at the two of them. Mason's face is like thunder, and as his gaze moves to Nina, his wife, she gives him a sad pained look back before she nods once.

"No," Scarlet snaps, stepping through the doors and halting Mason as he takes the first step toward me. "He doesn't get your words. He doesn't get it sugarcoated." She stops when she reaches the top step.

My eyes widen as her arm pulls back, and then I flinch as something hurtles toward me.

Whatever it is cracks against my temple, and I stagger back.

I hear Nina gasp, and then I blink twice. Three times. Four.

Fuck.

I lift my eyes to the terrace, finding Scarlet and Nina wide-eyed and Mason nodding with a satisfied look on his face.

"I didn't... oh my god, I didn't mean to hit you." Scarlet frowns, conflicted. "I... I'm so sorry." She turns and rushes back inside the house.

Mason turns and follows her.

I feel a trickle of something on my eye and reach up to swipe at it, finding blood smeared on my finger.

"I think it looks worse than it is," Nina says, bending and picking up the stack of letters at my feet. "I can get you some-thing." She gestures to my eye, but I shake my head.

"It's fine."

She looks up at me, something like sympathy in her inquisitive gaze. "Are you okay, Lance?"

Of all the people I thought would ask me that... "It doesn't matter if I'm okay."

Nina nods then eyes the letters that have somehow found their way back into my hands. "You'll find a lot of answers in there..." She frowns a little, her throat visibly working. "You need to read them. Don't wait, okay?"

"What good will it do?" I ask, my cheeks reddening at the way my voice wavers. "It's been seven years, Nina. Why would she even want me to read them after so much time?"

Something flashes in her eyes, a realisation that quickly turns into pity as her head tilts. "She's not looking for a do-over..." Her shoulders drop. "You need to leave now. And call ahead next time. I'll have Mason send over the house number. She can't come home from work to this. It's not fair."

"I won't be back." I turn away from her, placing the letters inside the seat of my bike.

"Lance," she says in a bid to stop me.

I climb on my bike, eventually looking up as I pull on my helmet.

I tip my chin at her.

"I forgive you." My hands drop to the bed of my bike as she visibly swallows. *Breathe, Lance.* "For everything. All of it. And if you need us, you just call me or Mase."

I don't dare blink as she turns in a rush and walks up the steps to the house.

There are many things I regret. So much I'll never be able to take back. It's why I have so many apologies to make. And yet I never expected forgiveness from any of them, least not Nina.

She was the fifth person on my list.

When I arrive back at Elliot's home an hour later, I take my time to climb from my bike, wanting to draw out every second before I have to close the door behind me. There's a sad quiet about the house that I can't stand. Being here feels wrong, and yet this is supposedly *home* now.

It's technically all I have to my name.

I opt for a shower before I make something to eat. My mind is too busy playing a show reel of Scarlet's face as she stood on the gravel in front of me to allow me to consider how hungry I am.

For a long time, I dreamt about how seeing her again might go. At first, it was happy. She'd run for me, and I'd grab her, lifting her in my arms and hauling her to my body. I'd get lost in her. She'd love me. We'd be perfect again.

It wasn't until a couple of years had passed that I found myself letting go of that dream.

Because maybe time can heal all wounds, but Scarlet Lowell wasn't a wound that needed to be healed. She was, and is, the only woman I have, and will, ever love.

She changed me.

She fixed me.

She made me better.

And if she taught me anything, it's that it's okay to be afraid of the darkness, the tears in our souls, because when the sun comes up we can choose to be okay.

We can be broken, and we can be okay.

I eventually leave my shower and pull on a T-shirt and jeans before I head downstairs to the kitchen. With minimal options for a hot meal, I take the leftover pasta from last night out of the fridge and eat it cold. I wash up the few dishes from this morning and the bowl I've used, and then I stand at the kitchen island, hands spread out on the cool marble countertop as I stare down at the stack of letters in front of me.

I scratch at the scruff coating my jaw, my gaze unwavering.

There's nothing in those letters that will do *me* any good. And the only reason I'm contemplating opening them is because it seems to be what she needs.

I never wanted to hear what she had to say—I couldn't.

I love you.

I need you.

I miss you.

I'll wait for you.

"God. You have no idea! You have no idea because you chose yourself. You chose you."

She was right before. I did choose myself, and I do need her to be okay. I need to know that I made the right choice. That it was what was best for her as well as me. For all of them.

"Fuck." I push off the counter and walk to the fridge, pulling it open and reaching for a beer.

I place it on the countertop harder than intended and watch as froth seeps down the bottle's neck.

I pull my bottom lip between my teeth, heart racing.

Just one.

"I'll open one."

My hand reaches for the thick stack, reminding me of the thin cut on my brow.

I lift the rubber band and ease out the first letter, the top one, and the one I presume was sent first.

As I flip it over and see my name in her handwriting, the prison address and stamp dated years back, I know, deep down, that whatever I'm about to read will tear another hole in my chest.

Lance,

I came to visit you today, and you turned me away. It's important you know that I'm not mad. I'm not angry. And I understand.

When Dad died, I felt such guilt, pain and fear. I was so scared. Mostly of pulling you in and then losing you like I lost him. I didn't have Mum for long, but I know she makes up the patchwork of some of my messiest flaws, too. And then there's Mase. It all drove me to that moment I told you to leave me that day in the kitchen, and if there's anything about our love that I'll never forget, it is the way you loved me even in the moments I didn't deserve it. Especially in those moments after I pushed you away. I know I've never told you this before, but I think you knew. I mean, you didn't give up.

So, it's okay. It's going to be okay. I'm going to be here when you're ready to see me again. I won't give up.

I'm sorry it's hard.
I'm sorry this happened.
And I love you.
Don't bear this guilt, pain, and fear alone for longer than you need to, Lance. Share it with me.
Being apart makes me feel empty inside, but you, your love, our memories... all make me open my eyes and see the very same stars that you do.
Your sunshine, Lance. Always. x

I drop the letter to the counter and run my hands through my hair, pulling at the roots.

"Fuck."

I read it again.

Again.

Again.

And then I tear into the next.

Lance,
I miss the sound of your voice today. The feel of your chest under my cheek and the laugh that vibrates from beneath it. The smell of my sheets after you leave. The way you'd wrap me in your arms and just hold me without knowing I needed it after a long day. Our time together wasn't long enough, and I'm desperately trying to hold on to everything we did have. It can't be undone—our love was so much more than that—but somehow things fade.

I can't feel you. I can't see you. And you've never been so quiet.
I don't know if you're okay and that kills me a little inside every day.
Speak to someone, Lance. Please.
Your sunshine, always. x

I can't stop myself as I reach for the next.

Lance,
If this is how it's going to go, then forgive me for anything I say that might not make sense.
You've been gone for two months, and yet it feels like a lifetime.
I can only imagine how you might be feeling, and as I lie in bed at night, all I can think about is how badly you likely need to be held. I'd give anything for a hug.
I can't imagine the food is very good, but I can promise you everything I'm currently eating tastes like crap. Even cheese. I feel empty without you, as if a piece of me is missing.
I have everyone around me, making sure I'm okay. You saw how Mase was at the trial. He's not mad at you. He loves you. He understands why you did what you did, and if anything, no matter how tragic it was, he's grateful you loved me enough to protect me that day.
I wish you'd let us make sure you're okay. I think the

guys are losing their minds over the fact you haven't let them see you. And this isn't to make you feel bad or to sway you into seeing them before you're ready, but I think it's hurting them. Charlie isn't himself. He's driving out to the prison daily and causing all sorts of issues for himself trying to see you. They won't let him in.

They didn't know about us, Lance. You were left alone with a responsibility bigger than they ever knew. Especially Mase.

You don't owe anyone anything. Always remember that. But if you need your friends or happen to think about reaching out, know that they need you just as much. You're a void that no one could ever replace in this world, and you're mine. Remember that you are mine, Lance Sullivan, and you are not alone.

Your sunshine, always. x

I set down the letter and stare out through the kitchen window, tears lining my cheeks as they fall in streams.

I never wanted to hurt them. I didn't think it would. All I wanted was for them to move on.

I never—

My eyes drop to the next letter.

I open it.

I open it for them.

Lance,

I can't do this without you.

I'm exhausted. I'm broken, and it hurts, and I'm not okay.
I need you.
Please. x

"Baby, no." I rub my hand over my chest, reading her words over and over. "No."

The paper tears as I fight the next letter from the envelope.

Lance,
I wish there were an easier way. A different one where you take me somewhere special on the back of that bike, and I tell you something that would heal the broken parts of us both. Maybe that's expecting too much, but everything you gave me of you, everything you taught me about myself, showed me the man that you are.
The father you'd be.
So... I think you'd take me somewhere special on the back of that bike, and I'd tell you that I'm three months pregnant with our child, and you'd come alive all at once. You'd smile, Lance, and you'd be happy and silly and stupid. And then you'd hold me and tell me how incredible I am. You'd make sure I know it, too. You'd kiss me until it hurts, and we'd not leave that special place until the sun went down.
And we wouldn't be afraid.
I wouldn't be afraid with you by my side.

We would mend those broken parts together.
I need you to let me in now.
Please, Lance.
I can pretend and dream and write these letters for
a lifetime, but I need you to tell me it's okay, and
that I don't need to be afraid. Because I'm terrified
of doing this alone.
Just tell me it's going to be okay.
I love you.
Your sunshine. xx

The letter drifts to the counter.

I swallow, shaking my head as I step back. On autopilot, I run through the house, up the stairs, and into my room. I frown at my trembling hands as I search the pockets of my jeans for the keys to my bike, the tips of them feeling numb.

When I reach the front door, I grab my helmet, my mind running, confused—lost, as I pull it over my head and fumble to secure the clasp under my chin. "Fuck!"

My shoe connects with the stones underfoot, sending them spraying over my bike. Even in the early evening dusk, I can see the imperfections in the black paint.

Throwing my leg over the seat, I quickly take off out of the drive, not bothering or caring to lock up or close the gates behind me.

I don't feel the roaring of my engine as it vibrates beneath my thighs. I'm not sure I can even feel my hands anymore. The only thing I can feel is the thundering beat of my heart.

You'd take me somewhere special on the back of that bike, and I'd tell you I'm three months pregnant with our child.

I shake my head, picking up speed and skipping a light as I head out of the city. "There's no way—no."

It can't be true.

It can't.

I need you to tell me it's okay, and that I don't need to be afraid. Because I'm terrified of doing this alone. Just tell me it's going to be okay.

Tears blur my vision as I pull onto the back roads.

I blink them away.

The father you'd be.

The father you'd be.

"No." I hit the side of my head. "No, no, no, no." My voice roars in the confines of my helmet as everything I am, everything I wanted to be as a man, shatters into a million broken pieces.

I take another winding bend in the road, and my back wheel loses its grip, the bike weaving as I correct it. I grit my teeth and go faster.

I have to be there.

I need to be there.

I pick up my speed, the trees flashing past, the tarmac burning as I hold firm on the throttle.

And we wouldn't be afraid.

I wouldn't be afraid with you by my side.

"Fuck." I slam my closed fist down onto the bed of my bike. "I'm sorry," I cry out, knowing it'll never be enough. "Let me take it back." I suck in a breath, trying to fill my lungs as they're squeezed tight. "Let me take it all back. Please. Pleas—"

A flash of light blinds me. I reach for my brake, desperate in that final second to pull back a shred of control, but nothing can stop it from slipping away from me.

I see the lights coming and swerve. I feel myself fall, the bike sliding out from under me.

I feel nothing when it hits me.

FIVE

Scarlet

"Two plaits."

"It's late, baby. Let's put it in a ponytail, and then I'll plait it before school in the morning. You should be asleep already."

"Fine," she sighs, climbing onto my bed.

I smile at the back of her head and gently pull the brush through her soft waves. "What did you do today? Did Ralph and Elsie come over?"

"Yeah. We just played."

"*What* did you play?" I chuckle, wondering for the millionth time how my sweet and innocent seven-year-old grew up overnight.

"It was that game you, Uncle Mase, and Uncle Elliot used to play."

"In the meadow?"

She nods.

"Sleeping lions," I muse, smiling.

"Ellis made Sammy cry. He kept chasing him."

"Well, I'd say Sammy gives as good as he gets, wouldn't you?"

Her shoulders bristle, and I can sense her own smile. "Yeah."

"All done," I tell her, finishing off the last loop of the hair band. I quickly reach for her, sliding my arms under her legs as I lift her into my lap.

"Mum," she groans, pretending not to need me.

"I need a cuddle, Ave. Just one."

She twists in my arms, leaning up to wrap her arms around my neck. I close my eyes as she sinks into me.

"I missed you today, baby."

"I missed you, too."

"Scar."

I open my eyes and find Nina in the doorway of my room, her face... Ave turns in my arms to see her auntie. My heart seems to beat twice as fast. "What is it?" I frown.

She shakes her head as if in apology. "It's Lance."

My feet don't feel like my own as I run through the hospital carpark. I know that Mason is behind me. I know that Elliot is on his way. And I know that Charlie is already here.

"Lance Sullivan. Please. Where is he?" I say in a rush the second I reach the main desk.

"Scarlet?" Nick frowns at me.

Mason grasps my arm and steps around me, his breath short from keeping up with me. "Could you please direct us to Lance Sullivan. He was brought into the hospital a little over an hour ago after an accident."

My eyes dart around the entrance of the hospital as Mason reels off Lance's date of birth. The doors swish open and closed over and over. Nurses, doctors, patients stepping out for fresh air, loved ones heading home for the night.

"Lance Sullivan..."

I turn, catching Nick scanning the screen.

"He was taken to trauma... now on ward twelve E."

Ortho.

I take off through the hospital, taking stairwell after stairwell until I reach the correct floor. I pull open the double doors and look left toward Orthopaedics.

"Scarlet."

I immediately turn at the sound of my friend's voice. "Annie." I meet her at the double doors leading to the next ward. "It's Lance."

"I know."

"Have you seen him?"

She nods, looking over my tear-streaked face. "Come with me."

I follow her through the doors, glancing back to see Mason behind me. "Annie, please," I beg.

"He's okay," she tells me, face solemn. "Not great. Broken bones mostly, but he's okay."

My feet seem to slow, knees swaying, and then I stop, tipping my head back. "Oh my god."

"Keep walking with me," she urges.

Mason wraps an arm around my waist and guides me, directing me down the corridor.

He's okay.

He's okay.

"I need to see him." We reach the waiting room, and Annie turns on me, an apologetic look on her face. I shake my head, disbelieving, desperate. "I'm going in, Annie."

"You're on the other side of the line now. We have rules for a reason."

I shake my head as panic claws at my throat. "No. No, I need to be in there with him."

Her eyes blaze, letting me see more than she'd normally allow whilst at work. "Mia is chasing results, and I'm going in now. We won't leave his side. I promise." She nods at Mason, then turns and walks away.

"Come on, Scar," Mason tries.

"Annie?" My voice cracks. "Annie, please."

She doesn't look back.

Lance

The first thing I feel as I come around is a deep throbbing ache in my right leg. It takes seconds more, my head inching to the left, before I feel the ache spread throughout my entire body. I tense as it passes through muscles I've never felt before, turning my stomach and making it hard to breathe.

I grit my teeth and groan, willing it to stop.

"Lance?" I hear someone shift at my side and crack open my eyes, forcing them open despite the blinding lights. Mason sits in the chair beside me, his body braced on the very edge of the leather, knee bouncing. "What do you need?"

I remember then.

All of it.

The letters.

I look away, unable to hold his stare. Unable to ask for a single thing.

"Lance," he murmurs, standing. "Can you hear me?"

I nod once, flexing my fingers. The skin feels tight, and I think it cracks. "I can hear you."

Mason sighs, running a hand through his hair. "You scared the shit out of us, mate."

So, I think you'd take me somewhere special on the back of that bike, and I'd tell you that I'm three months pregnant with our child.

I lie motionless, the words paralysing me.

"I'll get a doctor."

I reach for him and wince, gripping his forearm.

He stops, stepping back to the bed. "Talk to me, Lance."

"Just give me a minute." I look up at him and swallow, my eyes blurring before I can blink. "And don't leave."

"I'm not going anywhere," he reassures me, sitting back down in the seat.

I lie in the quiet of the room for a while, only allowing myself to focus on the pain.

I can't do this without you.

I'm exhausted. I'm broken, and it hurts, and I'm not okay.

I need you.

Please.

"I never told you about me and Scar," I try, my voice a

whisper. I ease my head to the side to look at my best friend, pain shooting down my ribs. Mason's eyes are already fixed on me. "It's one of my biggest regrets, and if I could go back and change things, I would."

"Lance—"

"It wouldn't be telling you about the two of us, though. It would be me staying away. She wasn't ever supposed to get hurt, and she was entirely too good for me." I proved that ten times over. "But the only way I ever saw myself leaving her was in a body bag. I loved her. Too much at times. And I never imagined..." I clear my throat, settling my head deeper into the pillow as if it might smother my emotions. "It was shit. And I'm sorry that I hurt her. That I hurt all of you."

Mase works his jaw, his eyes glistening. "We don't need to do this now. You need to focus on getting back on your feet."

"I'll be fine."

"You were lucky, Lance. You were so fucking lucky."

I shift my gaze away from him, not being able to bear the look in his eyes. And yet I come face-to-face with something far, far worse.

"He's right." Scarlet leans in the doorway, arms crossed over her waist. "Your helmet saved your life."

You saved me.

"You have some broken bones. Your leg is pretty bad, but the surgeon doesn't think you'll need further operations. The bruising will fade—eventually." She doesn't break eye contact, and I don't dare look away. "How are you feeling?"

I feel the words leave my mouth without thinking about them. "I feel fine."

Mason chuckles, breaking me from my trance. "He needs something for the pain."

"We can get you something a little stronger."

"I'm going to go and tell the others you're awake."

"The others?"

Mason looks at me and frowns as if it's obvious who the others are. "The gang."

Scarlet lets him past and then follows him out of the room. She returns a moment later with a tray.

My eyes track her as she rounds my bed and sets the things down on the side.

She checks the machine set back against the wall, then reaches for a control that's attached to the trolley. "You know how one of these works?"

I tip my chin up, continuing to watch her.

She carefully reaches for my hand, her eyes focused on the cannula attached to my fist as she inspects it.

"Is this hurting you at all?"

I flex my fingers around hers and look down at her hand under mine, noticing the cuts and scrapes on my knuckles and the way my heart roars to life in my chest. "Not even a little bit."

She lifts her eyes to mine, and I'm pretty sure the world stops spinning.

"You were on your way to the estate," she says quietly, dropping my hand.

I steady myself and tell her, "I read your letter."

Her eyes fix on me, as if staring through me might keep the tears forming in her eyes from falling.

"Why aren't you angry at me, Scarlet?"

Sadness sweeps over her face, and she dips her head. "I had a long time to be angry." She chances a look up at me. "I should have just told you. If I thought something like this would've happened—"

"This isn't your fault."

"I was being stubborn. You deserved to know the moment I saw you that first day. I don't know why I didn't say it... I guess I couldn't."

"This isn't on you," I repeat.

She nods, and I see the flash of anger and frustration still lurking in her eyes. "I know."

I swallow, not knowing how or what or if I should even ask. I don't know how this goes. I don't know how to—

"She's beautiful," Scarlet says, a sad smile showing through her tears. "She's beautiful, and she can't wait to meet you."

My brow screws up tightly, my body going rigid as I tilt my neck back, looking to the ceiling.

"I'm sorry," she sniffs.

I shake my head, unable to comprehend her words as a tear falls down my face.

"She knows exactly who you are."

I can't do this.

I can't listen to this.

"I made sure she knew."

"Scar."

"I know," she whispers. "I know this is hard."

"I don't know what to say." I lift my head, finding her face as distraught as I feel. "I have a daughter?" I rasp.

"She's seven years old. Worries more about the girls in

her class liking her hair every day than her schoolwork, and
yet she's smarter than me and you put together. *She's the shit
with numbers.*"

I chuckle, but something in my chest catches; I fist my
hands at the slight whimpering sound that leaves me. Scarlet
just watches on, allowing me the time to process.

"I called you selfish... that day on the terrace." She wipes
her face clean of her tears, pulling herself together. "I knew I
didn't mean it the moment the words left my mouth. I was
hurt—a little shocked to see you. I said anything I could in
that moment to make it not hurt me, and likely hurt you in
the process. I'm sorry for that."

I go to speak, but she stops me.

"You're going to need some time." She looks toward my
body. "And so am I. I know this is hard to process, and I know
you'll need my understanding, too. I have a therapist that I
see, she stays and chats to Ave after my sessions sometimes."
She shakes her head. "Nothing too heavy, but I've found it
hard to help her understand her emotions surrounding you
throughout the years. She knows this will take a while to
figure out."

My breathing goes shallow as a hole opens up in my chest
and then seemingly fills itself back in again. "*Ave?*"

Scarlet's mouth slackens as she stands to her full height.
"I'm sorry. I was going to wait."

"Why would you wait to tell me her name?"

"Because I didn't want to hurt you any more than you
already are."

I frown, not understanding.

"Her name... her name is Waverley."

SIX

Scarlet

I knew it hurt him. The moment her name was in the air between us, I saw it destroy him and make him within the blink of an eye. Knew that the knowledge of having his daughter's name tattooed on his body whilst he had no idea she existed hurt more than any love ever would.

Somewhere deep inside of me, I long to shut off all emotions linked to him. To cut all ties between my head and my heart where he's concerned.

Only I don't look at Lance and see a patient, or even a man. I look at him and see the love I lost.

"He keeps asking if you're in."

I don't look at Mia as she walks into our small office and settles in the chair beside me. She pulls out her lunch, and I decide that I can't ignore her completely. "Who?"

I feel her eyes on me and take a hefty bite of my wrap.

"You don't want to know how he's doing?"

I drop the food into the foil on my lap and face her, swallowing my mouthful. "How is he doing?"

"He might need an operation."

My brow flickers.

"They think they'll need to pin his leg after all."

"What?" I mutter, sitting up a little straighter in the seat.

"Your brother was here before. He said he had to get back, and you were busy."

Between Mason, Nina, and Elliot, someone has been to see Lance every day. I've not been in since I told him about Ave, and I don't plan to go in for a while.

He needs time to process everything, and so do I.

"When will they operate if they do?"

"By the end of the week."

I thought he'd be long gone by the end of the week, not stuck in the same hospital as me while potentially healing from another operation.

I sigh and nod. "Okay."

"Does he have family, somewhere he can go when he leaves? If they choose to put him in a cast, he might be okay, but to be honest he's got to be in a whole world of pain with the other breaks. And if they do opt to operate... I can't help but think he's struggling mentally. He's very quiet. Is that normal?"

I swallow, dropping my eyes to my lap. I think about his mum and Elliot and Luce. Charlie, who although would never say no to helping, has not even been in to see Lance yet. "It's not something you should be asking me about."

Her eyes widen guiltily. "Right. I'm so sorry. With—"

"Don't apologise, Mia. *I'm* sorry. It's just really hard right now."

"Of course it is." She nods, and I know she understands. "How's Ave handing it all?"

"She doesn't understand why she can't meet him." I scrub at my face, already knowing I've given up on my lunch. "I think it's best to wait until he can go home. Or at least until he's visibly better. I can't have her meet him here. Can I?"

I watch as Mia thinks on it. "I guess it depends how long he's here for. It's not like he'll be magically better when he goes home. He's going to have some nasty bruising for a while." She gives me a sympathetic smile. "It might even perk him up a little bit."

She's right. Lance won't be magically better when he leaves this place. Physically or mentally.

"I need to think about it some more."

She watches me, trying to gauge my mood and maybe my thoughts. "You have time off at the end of next month. Didn't you say you might get away? Why don't you? You probably need a good break."

Ave would jump at the chance to head out to the lodges. It's hard being a single mum to a seven-year-old when you're trying to balance a career. I work long hours, sometimes seven days a week, meaning my days off fall on weekdays when she's at school. I love my job, and I know that Ave is doing just fine, but mum guilt is impossible to ignore at times. "I'll think about it," I tell Mia.

Lance

"Morning."

I look up as the blonde-haired girl steps into the room, her smile pinched but there. Mia, I think her name is. She walks to the end of my bed and picks up the folder there, checking everything over. It's all they seem to do at the moment.

The last couple of days have passed in a blur. I've felt pain I never knew was possible to feel and have barely slept more than five minutes at a time. I feel trapped in the hospital room, unable to even get out of bed to use the toilet.

"How are you feeling today?"

Like shit. "Mostly the same."

"We don't mind the same." She smiles, not looking up. I watch her and wait, wondering if she'll shed any light on Scarlet after I asked about her days ago. "Are you managing to get any sleep?"

I shake my head.

"Well, I have some good news for you. The surgeon had a look at your x-rays from yesterday and, providing your leg heals as it currently is, you'll be able to head home by the end of the week. Monday at the latest."

"No second operation?"

She shakes her head. "Nope."

That is good news. The idea of getting out of this room. This bed.

They've not been telling me a lot, probably to avoid getting my hopes up when the chance of a second operation was highly likely.

"I want to get you down for another chest x-ray this afternoon. It will depend on how the day goes."

I sigh and sit back in the bed. "Sure."

"Fed up?" she asks, placing the folder back.

Fed up isn't the word I'd use. "Is Scarlet in today?"

"No. She's covering for one of the girls so will be working nights for the rest of the week."

"She'll be here later?"

She pauses, watching me intently before answering. "Uh-huh."

"Who will be taking your place tonight?"

"The same person who took my place last night. Emma, wasn't it?"

"Can you make it so that it's Scarlet?"

Her eyes tighten on me. "No."

"Do you know someone who could?"

"Yes."

"You do?"

"Mr Sullivan—"

"It's Lance."

Her cheeks flame. "Lance... my job is to fix you, not to play the mediator between you and Scarlet." Her face softens somewhat. "Look, she's a very good friend to me. If she decides to pop in here, it isn't going to be because I told her to. Give her some space, okay."

"Knock knock." I drag my eyes away from Mia and toward the woman walking into the room. I remember her from the night I was brought in. She'd looked at me, heard my name, and then immediately asked me if I knew a Scarlet Lowell. "I thought I'd pop in and see how we're getting on."

"He's doing great," Mia answers.

"You're certainly looking a little better than the last time I saw you." She walks to my bedside, getting a good look at my face. She smiles. "My name's Dr Annie Harlow. I was the doctor who spoke to you when you were first brought in. How are you feeling?"

I wish they'd stop asking me that.

"Don't answer that." She chuckles. "I can understand how infuriating it can get being stuck in one of these beds for days on end. You're allowed to tell us to bugger off when we get to be too much."

She pulls something from her pocket and reaches for my forehead, pulling open my eye and shining a light directly inside.

"Jesus," I mutter, trying not to squint.

"Unless I'm doing my job," she adds, seemingly enjoying watching me squirm. "Any news on the leg?" she asks Mia.

"Daya doesn't think surgery will be needed."

"Music to my ears. So, what's the plan of action today?"

"I want to get another chest x-ray to check that fluid on his lungs. And then I have two discharges to do."

"Sounds like you have time for a coffee."

Mia grins.

"Would you like a coffee, Lance?" Dr Harlow asks.

I shake my head, closing my eyes.

Sleep doesn't come.

"He's way bigger than the picture, Daddy."

"Of course he is. He's a real person."

I open my eyes to see Elliot standing in the doorway, a little boy at his side and a girl on his hip.

"Lance. Good to see you awake."

I inch up in the bed, trying to hide the wince that comes with the movement. "Sorry. It's all the pills." I don't know why I lie, but I do. I wasn't asleep at all.

"We're not allowed to touch pills. They're for adults only."

Elliot smiles down at his son and then urges him forward with their joined hands. "Lance, meet my tribe. Elsie." He looks to the little girl in his arms, but she throws her face into his neck. He chuckles and smooths a hand up her back. I don't miss his wedding band glinting under the glaring hospital light. "And this handsome chap is Ralph."

"Can I sit on your bed?" Ralph asks.

I smile for the first time in days—years maybe. "Sure."

"You broke like eight bones," he says as he fights his way up onto the bed.

"Careful. Uncle Lance broke like eight bones, remember."

"Room for two more?"

Something warm spreads through my chest as I look around Ralph and find Lucy standing outside my room. She doesn't look like she's aged a day. Her blonde hair is curled and pulled over one shoulder, she wears the most genuine smile, and in her arms, a baby lies nestled into her warmth.

"Hi, Lance," she whispers, her eyes filling with tears. She walks to the side of my bed and leans in to kiss my cheek. "God, I missed your face."

"He looks not as dark as he did in the picture. Why is your face a different colour?"

Lucy chuckles, wiping at the corner of her eyes with one hand as Ralph leans closer to me, inspecting my face.

"It's because I've spent a lot of time indoors recently."

"Auntie Scarlet tells us we'll turn into turnips if we spend too much time inside watching TV."

"Do I look like a turnip?" I ask, my chest on fire.

Ralph shakes his head, smiling.

I look around at my friends, their family—the picture of perfection. It doesn't surprise me one bit. "What's this one called?" I peer over Lucy's arm.

"Her name is Thea. She's six weeks old."

"Wow," I whisper, taking in her little face.

"Rumour has it you're heading home this week," Elliot says.

Elsie seems to turn in his lap and peek over at me.

"Maybe." I nod, sighing as I relax back into the bed. "They're still x-raying me five thousand times a day at the minute."

"Well, we'll be around when you get home," Lucy promises. "I said to Elliot we could head back to yours for a few weeks, or maybe you can come to us. Either way works."

"I'll be fine. You guys don't need to worry about me."

"I can assure you she'll worry regardless," Elliot chimes in, grinning fondly at his wife from the other side of the bed before he looks back at me. "Whatever you need, alright? No pressure."

"I appreciate that."

Elliot and Lucy stay for over an hour, and it's not until the last ten minutes that Elsie climbs from her dad's lap and walks to the side of my bed, just staring intently up at me. I smile, not wanting to say too much and scare her.

I've never been around children and having Elsie and

Ralph visit me today only reinforces that I've missed the very years Elliot's children are currently living with my own daughter. She was a four-year-old like them once. A five-year-old. Six. And yet I know nothing of her. Nothing about her. I don't even know the colour of her hair.

I wonder if the stack of letters I left scattered on the kitchen island holds the answers. Scarlet said they did.

I have so many questions, and yet I can't find it in me to get angry at her for not being here to tell me the answers.

Scarlet

Night shifts are my preferred working hours. It's the only time I can be here guilt free. The only time when the most important people in my life rest their heads on pillows, and I can stop worrying. The hospital never stops. It's always here waiting for me, always pure chaos. And when it isn't, you can find it. Seek it out or wait. It comes. Every time.

"So, I'm waiting on blood work for the patient in bay three. Five came down from recovery around two hours ago and is managing with the pain fab for now. We have a new patient in two. She's likely to be on the schedule for surgery first thing so nil by mouth from midnight."

"Perfect," I say, finishing off jotting down the information Deanna has given me for handover. "I don't suppose you know how the guy in room three is doing?"

"Room three." She frowns, scribbling something on her list. "The guy who came off the bike?"

"Yeah." I school my features in a bid to seem as interested as I would be in any other patient.

"He's doing good from what I know. I think Annie has been keeping an eye on him for most of today."

"Annie?"

"Yeah. She mentioned he'll be discharged by the end of the week."

"Already?" So, they won't be operating.

Deanna doesn't say anything more as she disappears down the corridor and toward our office to collect her things.

I just sit and stare toward his room.

I can't help but think he's struggling mentally. He's very quiet. Is that normal?

I swallow down the nervous energy stirring at the base of my throat.

There's always that one patient. Every ward has them, and every ward dreads them. Tonight, my one patient, the man yelling at me not to come near him while gripping the rails of his bed in tight fists, his name is Mick.

"Mr Evelly, please calm down so that I can speak to you."

"Get out."

I take a step backward, knowing there's a fine line between respecting his personal space and the chances of him tearing his stitches if he doesn't calm down. All was fine when I left the ward for my break, and yet when I came back, I found the FY2 doctor with a nasty gouge down her arm and Mick in his bed yelling at anyone that tried to get close.

"I'll leave if you can promise me you'll stop thrashing

around in that bed. You're pulling on your stitches and risking opening your wound. Calm down, Mr Evelly, and let us help you."

He looks to his forearm, his eyes narrowed on the covered wound. His body gradually stills.

"I'll give you a minute," I tell him. "You can call us in if you need us."

I step out of his bay and drag the curtain around, instantly locking eyes with the shocked woman in the bay opposite.

"Are you okay?" I ask, refraining from blowing out the sigh I want to. I walk to the lady's bay. "Would you prefer your curtain to be pulled around for a little while?"

"No, no, that's okay, my love." She looks around me at Mick's bay. "Is that young doctor okay?"

"She'll be fine," I reassure her.

"He grabbed her. She was only checking his arm, and he reacted as if she'd been the one to put him in that bed." She looks up at me, her face sad. "You wonder what did put him in the bed with a temper like that."

I grimace and look behind me. The silence from the other side of the curtain is deafening. "Why don't you get some sleep while it's quiet. I'll be around if you need me before Dr Bondry comes back."

The lady nods, grasping her hands tightly on her chest and settling into the bed.

I take a moment at the desk and pull up Mick's information. He's not my patient, but I already know that his doctor won't have any issue with handing him over to someone else.

Around an hour later, I decide to check on him, hoping the time alone might've helped relax him.

"Mr Evelly," I say, waiting outside of the bay.

"Yes," he replies after a moment, a slight reluctance in his tone.

I ease back the curtain enough that the lady opposite can see inside, then stand at the end of the bed. "We need to continue with your observations now. I think Dr Bondry was fixing you up with some pain medication. I will need to insert a needle into the top of your hand." I make a fist and show him the top of it. "About here. It should only take me a couple of minutes tops. Would that be okay?"

He tips his chin at me to say that it is.

"Fab."

I turn and walk out of his bay with a smile, throwing the lady opposite a victory wink as I pass.

"Scarlet, thank you so much for taking five for me. You ended up giving him the morphine yourself?"

"Once he calmed down and listened to me, it felt wrong to put on the nurses. Are you okay?"

"No, it's a good call and the reason I chose to do it myself, too. We need to keep an eye on him." She looks down at her arm. "I ended up catching myself with the needle."

I wince. "Yikes."

She steps around the desk and pulls out her list. "Can you take room three for me tonight? I'm a million miles behind and need to chase down these results. He's not getting a lot of sleep, and I think it's because he's feeling a little stuck.

Can you try getting him up and on crutches for me? The last thing that man needs is a DVT because he's not moving. And no point putting it off 'til morning if it's what's keeping him awake. He's got them in the room ready to go."

"Room three?"

She smiles and steps closer, hushing her voice to a light whisper. "I know, polar opposite of bay five. He's gorgeous." Her smile gets wider. "If you can look past all the war wounds."

"I—"

She must miss my attempt to protest and eases off down the corridor toward the exit. I stare after her, my eyes slowly drifting back to the door on my left... Lance's room.

SEVEN

Scarlet

As I push against the door to room three, I tell myself that the man lying in the bed is just another patient who needs my help. He's not Ave's father, not my brother's best friend, and not the man I once loved.

Lance's eyes widen when he sees who's entering his room, and I watch as a small bit of hope tugs at the corner of his mouth. "Scarlet?"

A question.

Why are you here?

Where have you been?

"Hi... I was sent in to help out a colleague. They want you up and out of the bed." One question down. The other can wait... for now.

"Tonight?" he asks with a frown.

"You're not going to get out of this place until you're up and safe on your feet." I let my eyes roam his face, my toes curling in my trainers as I fight to get a grip on my reaction to even locking eyes with him. "You're not sleeping," I add.

And it's obvious. From the dark circles under his eyes to the way his body screams its exhaustion at me.

I can feel it.

Him.

As if he's all around me.

"When was the last time you got some sleep?"

He just looks at me as if waiting for me to come closer.

"I tend to get five minutes here and there."

I nod, rolling my lips. "Well, that's something."

It's not. It's completely inadequate and not considered normal based on the amount of pain medication he's on. I inhale a deep breath, wondering if I'm going to continue to do my job terribly the entire time I'm in his presence.

"Do you feel like getting up? They want you to use the crutches."

"I want out of this bed." He braces his hand on the bed and sits up a little straighter. "So yes."

The obvious pain he's in seems to set me into motion, and I walk to his bedside, moving the pillow at his back.

"What's your pain at?" I ask, waiting for him to sit back again.

"A five maybe."

I take in the fresh bruises dancing up his neck and jaw before he turns his head to look at me, his face entirely too close. "I can work with a five," I force out, leaving the pillow and turning away. I bring the crutches to rest against the bed. "I want you to take your time. Bring yourself to the edge of the mattress and slowly ease yourself to the ground. Use the bed to support yourself."

"Alright."

He slowly moves to the edge of the bed, dropping his feet to the floor. His right leg is in a brace, and I know it's hurting him because I can see the colour leaving his face.

I hand him the crutches.

"I only want one," he tells me, face hard.

"You've been given two."

He reaches for one and puts it on his right side. "Thank you."

I shake my head, not saying a word. I'd be lying if I said seeing him be a complete stubborn ass doesn't ease the twisted knot in my gut.

He bears down on his left leg, and even I wince. "Steady," I tell him.

I can't imagine how much pain he must be in. The bruising on his arms, legs, and face is nasty, and I know he has five broken ribs hidden under his T-shirt.

"Take your time."

I look up at his face as a groan leaves him and find he's holding his breath. I take a half step closer. "Breathe. You need to breathe."

He shakes his head, his face turning pale.

"Lance."

His head lifts the second I mutter his name, the breath he's holding slowly sagging out of him as he stares at me as if it's the first time all over again. "Yeah?"

I frown. "Breathe."

But he is breathing now, his chest gently expanding with each inhale. And I can't take my eyes off him.

I itch to reach out and smooth my hand over his bruised jaw. To dust my fingers up his neck and face and into his hair. I know how badly he needs it, too. Know how badly it would help.

"Will you tell me something about her?"

I blink twice, shaking off my thoughts. "Ave?"

"Waverley," he corrects with a nod. "There are things I want to know. Things I'm dying to ask. I'm just not sure I deserve the answers..." He looks to the ground between us, and I can see it tearing him up inside. "Maybe I shouldn't have asked at all. I'm sorry. You don't owe me answers, and I lost the right to ask questions about her when—"

"What do you want to know?"

We're too close.

I should step back.

"Her eyes?"

"Green."

His brows twitch. "Hair?"

"Brown. More my natural colour than your dark."

A thoughtful smile. "What's her favourite food?"

"Pizza."

"Pizza," he repeats, his mind storing away every tiny piece. "And yours? Has it changed?"

An ache rattles through my chest, and I sigh, tilting my head. "Does it matter what my favourite food is?"

His jaw goes rigid, and then I lose his eyes to the ground between us again. "It's always going to matter, Scar."

I watch him, my heart in my throat. It shouldn't hurt this

much. I broke a long time ago and put myself back together all on my own. I worked so damn hard, and it takes nothing—a look, a comment, a single word, and everything I stuffed down inside, everything I faced and fixed, breaks open and rattles me to my core.

A love like ours is a once in a lifetime thing—I'd never survive it a second time. And I don't want to.

Falling in love with a person, a friend, a job, or even the world we live in, it's unappealing to me. It feels like a risk. I fell in love with my baby nine months after giving birth to her.

It took me nine months.

Before that, I could barely even look at her. Too afraid of what I'd find. Too afraid of what I could lose.

"Scarlet."

I snap my eyes to his face, the ache in my throat still raging and threatening to break.

"Where did you go?"

To the very bottom... beyond the dust at my feet and then even deeper than that. "It doesn't matter."

I step up beside him and wait for him to take his first step forward. Wait for him to stop staring at the side of my head and get on with it before I stand here and cry like I want to.

It can't be like this.

I'm at work. I don't want to be sad. I want to make this work and move on from the bad stuff. The pain. That ache in my chest that's never fully gone away since the day I lost Dad. I want it gone.

I want to be full of warmth and excitement and happiness.

I want my peace.

"Are you okay?"

I ignore him, not letting his words penetrate. "How does that feel? Can you take a step?"

There's a brief pause, and then he takes a step forward. His body sways a little, but he recovers, using his crutch to take his weight. "Jesus Christ, my back."

"It's hurting?"

He nods.

"You've been stuck in bed, it's normal. Take a second."

He takes another step.

"Slow."

Another step.

I swipe my sweaty palms over my thighs. "How's that?"

"Feels... good. Fine."

"Good. That's good. Let's get to the door and then come back to the bed."

He makes his way around the room and past the door.

"Okay, now back to the bed." I follow behind him, my arms braced and ready to take his weight if needed. "Lance."

He stops, twisting his head over his shoulder. Pain mars his brow, but his sole focus is on me. "Hmm?"

"Back to the bed."

He carries on toward the bathroom in his room. "I'll be taking a piss in the toilet from now on, if that's okay."

I follow him. "Please, be careful." I stop on the threshold of the bathroom and watch as he twists, not using the crutch and balancing on one leg, his body swaying so heavily, he has to reach for the wall. "Jesus shit," I cringe.

"It's fine," he reassures me, pushing the door closed in my face.

I run my hands through my hair and take a moment.

Am I being unprofessional with him?

I'd never swear in front of a patient. Ever. I shouldn't even be in here. I should go find a nurse—or his actual doctor. He needs his doctor and his friends and his family, not me.

"Scarlet, I need you a sec."

"Shit." I close my eyes and step toward the door. "What with?"

"I'm bleeding a little bit."

I reach for the handle and open the door, finding him standing in the middle of the bathroom with a towel held against his hand.

"What happened?"

"The cannula came out, and I tried sticking it back in, and it started bleeding."

"You..." I walk to where he's standing (with no damn crutch near him) and reach for his hand. "Let me see."

He pulls back the towel to show me, and I instantly look up, his tall frame towering over me, his face set in a *I didn't do anything* expression.

"You've butchered that."

He watches me with tired eyes, so heavy, yet unwavering. I see the desperation in them, the fear even. He's scared. I peer down at his hand, trying to ignore the way his thumb brushes down the centre of my palm.

His chest fills then drops, his entire body relaxing.

I quickly pull my hand away. "You need to get back in bed."

He goes to reach for his crutch, but I grab it first, handing it to him. I wait as he wraps the towel around his hand, knowing I should do it for him, and then slowly follow him to his bed.

Once he's back up on the bed he drops his head to the pillow, staring at the ceiling in what I can only call defeat.

I begin cleaning up his hand. "You did good. The nurses will likely keep trying, and I'm happy to tell Dr Bondry that you're okay to get around yourself. Just don't do too much too soon."

He doesn't reply to me, his body spent. I bin the towel and the few wipes I've used and then stand at the end of his bed, unsure what to say or do or even think as he seems to shrink away from the world into another place.

My palm tingles from the reminder of his touch, and I fist it, readying to leave. "Try to get some sleep tonight, okay."

I turn and walk toward the door, pulling it open and slipping through, already knowing I won't want to come back. It's too hard.

I gently pull the door closed.

"Leave it."

I pause, pushing inside an inch. "Sorry?"

"Can you leave the door open?" he mutters, barely a whisper. "I can't..." I see his nostrils flare from across the room, and then he shifts in the bed, still staring at the ceiling. "I can't hear your voice when it's closed."

I watch him, knowing he can feel my stare. Knowing I should leave.

I've seen so many of the people I love at their most vulnerable selves. My dad, Mason, Nina, and Charlie.

And yet nothing could have prepared me to see Lance Sullivan at his.

"Sure," I tell him, backing away.

I leave the door wide open.

My eyes are heavy as I walk the meadow with Ave clung to my side. I finished work at eight o'clock this morning and came home and slept until one this afternoon. She'd never wake me, but I always set an alarm so that the day isn't completely lost.

I need this time with her.

It's worth more than any sleep I could ever get.

"Can we go? Please!"

"You want to?" I ask, smiling at her glee.

"Yes! We can get Uncle Mase and everyone to come."

"I don't know if they'll all be able to. We'd have to see."

"Please, please, I want to."

We've holidayed at our lodges in Bora Bora for the last five years. It took me a while before I even wanted to go after having Ave, but once I was ready, I discovered the pure sentiment that comes with sharing the most precious parts of my childhood with her. "We'll see, Ave."

"I'll do the dishes. And I'll even clean your car."

"Don't do it, Scar. I've still got the scratches on the Porsche to prove what a terrible job she does."

"Uncle Charlie!"

I chuckle as she slips from my side and turns, rushing for him as Daisy and Luna leave his side and prance over to me.

Charlie lifts Ave up from under the arms and pulls her to him, spinning her around.

"You've been gone for weeks."

He makes a face as she clings to his neck. "It's been a couple days, you giant queen."

"We're going to the lodges," Ave tells him.

"When?" he asks, looking toward me with a frown.

I shrug, smoothing my hand over Luna's snout when she nudges me. "I have some time off at the end of next month. I thought maybe it's what we need."

He looks at Ave and smiles. "Are you coming?"

She nods, her smile even bigger than his.

"Hmm. I might have to pass then." He tickles her sides, and she wiggles in his hold.

"I'm the *only* reason you'd come," she squeals, effectively making the man-child (who's only a man-child for my child) tickle her even more.

"Enough, you two. It'll only end in tears."

Charlie lets Ave down then takes her hand, walking to where I'm standing. "A good day?"

"So so," I say, letting him pull me in for a hug I didn't know I needed. "I worked the night shift."

"Mase said. Do you need me to take Ave out this afternoon? I'm in the mood to be verbally violated by a seven-year-old today."

"I greedily want to say no," I tell him.

"What if we take Bear, Daisy, and Luna to the Pennell Trail? Ave can take her bike."

"I want to do that. Can I go, Mummy?"

I look from Charlie to Ave, knowing I'll be spoiling their fun if I say no. "Sure."

"Yes!" I watch as she fist pumps the air. "Thank you! We can have breakfast before you go to bed tomorrow, and Auntie Nina said she's cooking dinner for when you wake up."

"It's okay, baby." I bend to kiss her head, getting to her level. "Go enjoy yourself."

"I'll get my bike."

I watch as she runs from the meadow, her shadow bounding along behind her.

When I glance back at Charlie, I find him watching me watch her. He tips his chin, and I slip under his arm as we slowly walk back toward the house.

"You've not been to see him," I say into our comfortable quiet as we make it to the first gate.

"I actually considered going this week until Mason told me he was going home."

"He's doing good. He was up walking in the night."

Charlie just nods, his eyes on the house.

"You can't avoid him forever, you know."

"I'm not avoiding him."

"No?"

He shifts his gaze to me, knowing I can see right through him. "I don't know how you do it. After everything you went through with Ave, how you can stand at his bedside and be okay—"

"I'm far from okay." I snigger. "I'm doing my job by standing at his bedside. It doesn't mean I forgive him—"

"Mummy!"

I cut myself off as Waverley comes flying toward us on her bike.

"This," she shouts, waving something above her head.

"Two hands, Ave!" I yell, watching her wheels buckle on the uneven ground.

She reaches us and sets down her bike, coming to stand in front of me. "Can you give this to my dad? It's my picture."

I open my mouth, then close it, taking the crumpled card from her hand.

"I know what he looks like, and I thought maybe he'd want to see what I look like, too. Just until we can meet each other properly."

I stare at the picture, my heart in my mouth as I try to blink back the tears gathering.

"Is it a bad idea? I thought it might make him want to see me faster."

"I... I..."

"It's a great idea, Ave," Charlie reassures her. "He's going to love it. And you."

"You really think so?"

"I know so."

She beams up at him, her small shoulders bunching. "Can we go?"

Charlie gives her a subtle nod, and she rushes me, throwing her arms around my middle. I pick her up and cuddle her extra tight. "You're so special, Waverley Sullivan. Remember that always, okay?"

She pulls back and climbs from my arms, desperate to get away and onto her bike. Charlie promises to have her back by bedtime—a lie I've never dared to police.

It's not until they're gone and I'm walking through the door to the house that I notice the words scribbled on the back of the photograph.

"He stole her from me, didn't he?"

I hear my brother's voice, but his silhouette is lost in a blur of tears.

"Scar?"

I hold out the picture, letting him see.

To my dad.

My name is Waverley Sullivan. I am seven and a half years old and go to Roseladden Primary School with my cousins. I like writing in my books and swimming the most. I am happy to get to meet you soon.

"Do you think you should give this to him?" Mason asks.

"How can I not?" I take it back and wipe my face. "She asked me to."

"Is he ready for it? Ready for her?"

"Honestly," I rasp, forcing the words. "It's not my concern."

His jaw goes taut, and he tilts his head.

I walk through the house and into the kitchen, finding Nina at the island pouring a glass of wine.

I instantly wish I didn't have to go to work.

"He's not himself, Scar. I mean, it's been years. I get it things will be different, but he isn't sleeping. He was camped out in that boxy room at Elliot's place when we went over last week. Didn't even have any food in the place. He's a mess—"

"Mase," I snap, cutting him off. I feel Nina's eyes on us. "Please don't do that. I can't."

"I'm just saying. If he leaves the hospital and goes home, is he really in the right headspace to deal with this?"

"You're talking about Ave?" Nina asks.

Mason nods.

"It's up to them. Stay out of it, bossman."

My nostrils flare as everything Ave went through as a baby, as a toddler, and as a little girl whirls through my mind. "He's your friend, Mase, and Ave is my daughter. She needs her dad, and maybe he'll need you because of that. It's not on me to make sure he's okay. I have one priority here."

My brother sighs, rounding the island and dropping down at the counter. "I'm sorry."

I slide the picture into my back pocket. "There's nothing to be sorry for."

EIGHT

Scarlet

"You're in early."

I don't say a word as I bypass Mia and Annie and head for the locker room, just giving them a smile which they return with a shake of the head. Once my things are in my locker, and I have on my scrubs, I head back to the desk, sliding in next to them so that I can check the results I'd been waiting on before I left to go home this morning.

"Did you come in early to see Lance?" Mia asks as if they'd discussed the possible options and that one seemed the more viable.

"I have no reason to worry myself with room three, Mia."

"Room three..." I can hear the smile in Annie's voice. "Is that what we're calling him now?"

I sigh and stand. "My child was whisked away by Charlie Aldridge this afternoon." I reach into our coffee fund jar and pluck out enough for three coffees. "Are you sad, broken bitches coming or what?"

"Charlie Aldridge," Annie sings. "Do you say his full name just to make our knees weak?" She smiles.

Mia hums in agreement. "If he were ever a patient, I'd put him in bed M1 A."

Annie chuckles. "And when I'd move him, I'd say... Excuse me, sir, could you please hold the bed RAIL for ME."

Mia bursts out laughing while I stare at them wide-eyed.

"And you ladies wonder why you're single," I whisper before turning and walking away.

After a moment I feel their shoulders brush mine as they catch up. I smile as we head toward the canteen.

"So, you helped him get up and about on his crutches. It doesn't mean anything," Mia reassures me. "It's your job."

Annie sighs. "I'd prefer it if you didn't work with him to be honest, Scar. It's never a good idea in my experience." She gives me a grimace. "It's not life or death, but past situations have taught me to keep the lines firm."

"I know. And I'm not going to go in again."

Last night was too hard. Being so close to him with so much to say. Seeing him struggle—physically and mentally. The spark I once knew in his eyes isn't there anymore, and if I let myself get close, let myself witness his pain, I know I'll fight against what's right for *me* to fix him.

I felt things being in his room. Feelings planted firmly enough I know they'll always be there. No matter the time or circumstance.

"You won't go back in with Ave?" Mia frowns.

"Not until he's at home." I swallow down the guilt-ridden lump forming in my throat. "I'll tell Waverley how it is. Make sure she understands it's me wanting to wait and not him."

Neither of them says a word, and I drop my cup to the table. "Go on."

They stare at one another briefly before looking back at me.

"It's okay to care about him," Annie tells me. "We wouldn't think less of you. You know that, right?"

I shake my head. "Of course I care. It's just..." I drop my eyes to the table. "I can't and won't ever go back to that... to..."

"To the woman crying and broken on the shower floor?"

I shift my gaze to Mia and nod, knowing she understands —knowing that both of these women understand after all they've been through.

"I think my brother and friends think it's all going to work out and be okay between us eventually, as if I've been holding out all these years for *him*. But I can't do that. I wouldn't do that again." I stare at my coffee cup, wondering how ridiculous I must sound. "He's Ave's dad. But that's all he'll ever be."

It's all he can be.

It is.

It's all he can ever be.

No matter how wrong that feels to say out loud. To think. To feel. It's the truth.

It *has* to be.

"Does it make me a bad person? To not want to fix it for Ave?"

"Not at all," Annie says quickly, giving me a soft smile.

Mia shrugs. "We can't be sad, broken bitches if you're happy." A playful grin slowly dances across her mouth, apologetic yet knowing.

I chuckle. "I guess that's true."

"Hey." Annie grasps my hand on the table, giving me her reassurance. "Let us deal with room three."

Lance

"And sleep... any improvement?"

I look up as Mia's question pulls me from my trance. I frown. "Why are you back in here?"

"I'm covering for your doctor," she tells me, but I sense there are other reasons. Considering she's not been in all day and should be finishing her shift soon. "Sleep? Any? None?"

I check the clock on the wall.

Eight more minutes.

"I'll go with none."

"I slept last night," I tell her and then watch as her face twists up in thought as she lowers the folder in her hands.

"You did?" She shakes her head as if confused. "After Dr Lowell got you up on your crutches?"

I wet my lips and move my eyes to the door, warmth spreading through my chest. A rarity these days. "Yeah."

Six.

"Hmm." She jots something down. "Did you sleep for long?"

"A couple hours." Until I woke up and couldn't hear her.

"Good. Great actually. Have you been up and about today?"

"Twice."

"Twice? That's... why haven't they had you up more?"

I shrug.

"Are the crutches not feeling right?"

"They're fine."

"You can't be in bed all day. You'll cause yourself more problems than a broken leg. I'm sorry no one's been in." She lowers the bed rail. "I want you up tonight, okay? Before you sleep."

"Hmm."

Her sigh pulls my attention from the clock. She looks fed up with me.

"When can I go home?"

She lowers her folder. "As soon as I see you out of this bed and able to get around safely."

"I can do that now," I huff before catching the snappiness in my tone and dropping my gaze. "I'm fine to go home on my own," I add. "I just need out of these four walls."

"Lance," she says after a beat, and I lift my eyes. "If your x-ray comes back good through the night, I'll have you discharged first thing tomorrow morning when I get in."

I nod, glancing back to the clock as she turns to leave.

Three minutes.

"Mia?"

She glances over her shoulder.

"Leave the door."

. . .

"Good evening, Tilly. You're looking much better tonight."

"I'm feeling better," the lady replies to Scarlet. "Did you manage that run?"

I hear Scarlet laugh, not completely genuine but not fake either. It's nothing to anyone else, but to me, it's everything. "I didn't. And that's the last time I tell you my over ambitious plans."

"Oh, I'm sorry." The lady chuckles. "I'm living vicariously through you whilst stuck in this bed."

"I promise it won't be long, Tilly, and you'll be back out doing what you love. I tell my daughter every day—"

I let my eyes drift closed, my body going slack.

"It could be better, and it could be worse, but anything in between is a starting point for you to grow."

Such a Scarlet thing to say.

"That's lovely, and so true. How old is your daughter?"

"She's seven." And as if she can't help it, she adds, "Her name's Waverley."

"Oh, what a beautiful name. Where did you find it?"

A smile pulls at my lips, but then that same heaviness I felt in my body last night starts to seep through to my bones.

"Uh..." Don't tell her, Scar. It's ours. Just ours. "I found it online. One of those unique baby name websites."

"Waverley. It's so pretty."

"You're wild, Lance Sullivan. Completely and utterly wild."

"You love me wild."

"I do, you know."

"You do what?"

I try to lift my hand off the bed, but I can't, my body—my mind—drifting away someplace safe.

"Love you."

"I love you, Lance."

It's ours.

"Messy, crazed love capable of tearing me apart."

"I've known it for a while now."

Just ours, Scar.

I don't know what time it is, but as Scarlet's raised voice echoes throughout the ward, my eyes snap open.

"Calm down. Please."

I pull back the covers, my foot barely meeting the cold hospital floor before I bear down on my broken leg and rush from the room. I frown, the roaring pain in my right leg—

"Mr Evelly, please. Let me go."

I look from left to right down the corridor, still disorientated from sleep. "Scarlet," I mutter, barely a whisper. "Scar."

"Dr Lowell, security is on their way. Mr Evelly—"

"Get back!"

My blood turns to ice as the baritone voice snarls. I follow the sound, rounding the desk and limping toward the cubicle at the far end of the ward.

"Call for Grant. Call for Grant now."

I grasp the curtain and drag it back, my eyes snapping straight to her.

"I told you, girl—"

Rage unlike anything I've ever known stills my entire body, a chilling calm spreading under my skin as I take in his towering form. He has Scarlet pinned to the bed, one of his hands locked on her throat, and his other on her wrist.

I catch the light shake of her head as I near, the useless plea in her fearful eyes.

I'm pretty sure adrenaline is the only thing keeping me on my feet.

Without thinking, without care for anyone else, I lunge at the man, grabbing his shoulders to twist his body away.

"Get off of me!" He blindly swings with his right hand, cracking me in the jaw. I groan and drag him back and away from Scarlet's small frame, but as I go to shove him further, forcing him back a step with my hand just below his throat, he grabs my T-shirt, then my waist.

A flash of pain radiates throughout my ribs, and I stagger. We crash into something at his back, taking it to the ground with us as we fall.

Crushing my leg in the process.

"Lance," Scarlet shouts, and it's all I can hear past the searing pain in my lower leg.

"Fuck." Stars. I see fucking stars.

I hear the curtain that's caught snag under the weight of whatever is on top of me, and then it tears from the railing, settling over me.

A commotion seems to happen then, people rushing the room, the guy beside me... my nostrils flare, and I turn, twisting my leg awkwardly but not caring. I grip his face, bringing it closer to mine and looking him dead in the eye. "Do not try me," I whisper, deathly quiet. "You think you can touch her? You think you can fucking touch her?"

"Get it off of them!"

I grip his face harder, keeping my voice hushed. "Do not try me. Not when it comes to her."

I feel the weight being lifted from my body, and then the curtain is dragged away, letting those glaring hospital lights blind me.

Scarlet kneels at my side, her hand resting above my knee. "He has a compound fracture in his lower leg. We need a bed, Jenny, can you please get us a bed?" she mutters to someone.

I finally let my mind focus on it—the pain, and it sucks the air right out of my lungs.

I feel the colour drain from my face.

"Get me a bowl," Scarlet says in a panic, and then she has the cardboard bowl on the ground beside me. I turn my head just in time to be sick into it.

"Fuck," I rasp, shifting my upper body as my face screws up. My vision blurs, the pain blinding. "Scar," I grit out, feeling myself go lightheaded from the searing burn in my leg.

"I know." She places a mask over my nose and mouth, her eyes glassy as everyone seems to rush around behind her. "Breathe."

I feel someone insert something into my hand, the tip of a needle followed by a heaviness that seems to chase the pain away. I look up at Scarlet, my vision still distorted as I take her in.

She's safe. She's safe. She's... I track the purpling marks on her throat, her torn tunic, and the cut on her jaw. *The motherfucker.* I force my hand up, reaching for the bruised skin. Everything fades at the feel of her beneath my fingertips. Everything. "Scarlet," I try.

She shakes her head but doesn't remove my hand, her gaze darting to my leg again. "Lance, what have you done?"

Scarlet

"They've pinned it," I say on autopilot, staring at my brother's chest, completely lost. "He's looking at three to six months recovery and will need someone to stay with him while he heals. They said he's awake and asking for me."

"Scar."

"You can go in and see him now. He won't want to be alone."

"Come here," Mason mutters, pulling me in for a hug. I cave to the warmth and safety of his arms, sinking into him. "I'm sorry, Scar."

"It was awful, Mase."

"Shh. Don't think about it. Think about Ave. About the lake and the trees and the meadow."

I squeeze my brother's back.

After a moment his mouth settles on my head, his voice a gentle whisper. "I'm taking some time off to stay at the house with him. We'll get a physiotherapist. Whatever he needs to get back on his feet."

"What about Nina and the kids?" I feel emotion building in the back of my throat and swallow it down.

"It's Nina. She has the girls and you. She'll be fine." He sighs, leaning back to look down at me with narrowed eyes. "He needs me."

My face goes hard, and I fight back the tears, knowing exactly what he needs.

"Come in with me."

"Does he have anything in place at home? Family who can take care of him?"

I shake my head at my brother, still replaying the surgeon's words over and over in my mind. "No." My chin wobbles. "They've sent me home for the night."

He steps back, squeezing my hand before he drops it. "Alright. I'll see you back there, okay?"

I hold it together the entire way to my locker, removing my things before walking through the hospital and to my car.

When they told me to finish my shift early and to head home, I'd been gutted, but I agreed. I knew I couldn't carry on through the night after what happened with Mick, and my mind was completely lost to Lance.

Just as he takes one step forward, he's knocked ten steps back.

It's not until I get to my car and pull my phone from my pocket that the tears come.

"Hello?" Nina answers.

I sniffle, clearing my throat to speak, but it's too heavy, too much.

"Oh, Scar. Where are you?"

"In my car," I croak.

"Talk to me."

"He asked..." I try to breathe through my nose, my words breathy and ragged. "He asked me to leave the door open," I tell her, holding my chest as my heart throbs at the memory. "He hadn't slept in days, and he asked me to leave it open because he couldn't hear my voice, and then when I went back to his room at the end of my shift, he was asleep."

I hear her blow out a heavy rush of air.

"I don't think I can leave him alone in this, Nina. I can't watch him struggle alone."

"So, then what do you want to do?" she asks as if knowing I have the answer and promising not to judge me for it.

"I don't know," I lie.

"Mason said he'd go and stay with him. Do you think that's something you need to do instead?"

"No. I don't want to leave Ave."

"Could she go with you?"

No. No way. "Lowerwick is her home. It's close to school and... it's where *I* need to be."

She goes quiet on the phone, just letting me be while I sit in my car and cry.

"I'm scared, Nina," I eventually say, staring through my windshield and not daring to blink as my eyes continue to fill. "I'm scared of falling all over again. For him, and then the rest of the way down." I shake my head. "I can't go back to the person I was when he left."

"You won't—"

"I already did."

"Bring him home, Scar," Nina says softly.

I cover my mouth as a sob creeps up my throat. "I'm scared," I manage, the words barely audible.

"I know. But you're also strong." I hear her voice waver before she clears it. "And I believe you'll do what's right for you, Ave, *and* Lance because of that strength. You're not the type of person to put yourself before anyone else—and sometimes that's impossible to watch, but you know what you want and need to do here. I know you do."

I suck in a breath, letting it out on a shaky exhale. "What if I fall?"

"We won't let you fall."

I slump forward in my seat, everything I've buried deep inside since Lance was released hitting me all at once.

"Do whatever it is you need to do," she tells me. "And know that I'll be doing the same. I won't let you lose yourself again. I promise."

I drop my head back to the rest, my face wet with my now silent tears. I want to speak, want to say thank you, to tell her no, and that she's wrong.

But I can't.

I can't because I can hardly breathe.

"I'm here," she whispers. "I'm right here, Scar."

NINE

Scarlet

When I was a child, my brother would sneak out of his room and come into mine. It didn't happen often, but when it did, he'd tell me it was because he knew I was afraid of the dark, and he didn't want me to be alone. He did that until he was ten.

He wasn't always the hard-ass he grew up to be.

I smile from the doorway to Waverley's room, the shadow at my back looming. "Do you think they'll always be this inseparable?" I whisper to Mason.

Waverley isn't in her bed. She's curled up in her secret nook, the stable-like doors thrown open wide and her night lights set in a deep purple hue. Ellis is flat out at her side.

Mason doesn't reply, presumably watching them sleep with the same warmth and contentment in his chest as I hold in mine.

Or maybe he's thinking about those nights when we were kids, too.

"Is it a stupid idea?" I ask, not bothering to turn toward him. He knows I'm talking about Lance staying here.

"It's not stupid," he mutters straight back, as if annoyed I've even considered it might be.

We stand in silence for a while simply watching Waverley and Ellis sleep.

"You're going to have to put yourself first one day, Scar."

My face turns hard as walls form around me just as quickly as they fall.

"You'll regret it. I know I do. But putting up boundaries so that you can fix yourself, no matter how much you'll hate yourself for it, it's not wrong. It's not as selfish as you think it is. And if anything, it makes the things you miss—the things I'm lucky enough to have now—even better."

"I already put myself first," I say after a minute.

"When?"

I look over my shoulder at him. "I work, don't I? I spend more time at the hospital some weeks than I do with Ave."

His head tilts to the side. "Maybe you're owed a little more than that. A little more than you going off and saving people's lives for a living."

I cross my arms and look away again. "You're being dramatic."

He chuckles, and then I smile when his lips meet the crown of my head. "It's not stupid."

I take his word for it and step into the room, knowing it's wrong to wake them but also knowing I can't resist or put it off. I kneel at the edge of the nook, peering in at the two of them.

Waverley stirs first, and then I feel Mase at my back, reaching in to tap Ellis on the leg. "Leave him," I tell him.

"Mummy," Ave croaks, a slow sleepy smile spreading across her lips. "Is it morning?"

I shake my head, waiting as she sits herself up. Ellis stirs awake and pushes up onto his elbows. "What time is it?" he asks, his voice too loud for the sleeping house.

"Shh," Mase soothes. "Everyone's asleep, mate."

"I was sent home from work after an incident at the hospital," I explain to them.

"What happened?" Ave asks.

"A patient got upset and hurt me."

"Are you okay now?" Ellis asks, looking me over, his eyes catching on my jaw.

"I'm fine," I say with a chuckle, twisting my neck to see Mase. He's leaning against the nook door, his head ducked to see inside. He gives me a warm, encouraging smile. I take a second to find my words. "Your dad hurt himself, though, Ave."

"I know that already. He fell off his bike."

I shake my head. "No, baby, he hurt himself tonight. He came to find me when I was calling out for help and damaged his leg worse than before. He needed surgery."

"But I thought he was coming home soon... so that... so that I could go to Uncle Elliot's old house and meet him." She looks up at Mason, tears filling her eyes. "You said I'd be able to redecorate a room there, too."

"You still can," I promise. "You'll be able to do all of those things, okay?" She looks back at me, face sad. "I wanted to ask you if it would be okay for your dad to stay here while he gets better. He needs someone to look after him and make sure he can recover fully—"

Her eyes widen. "Here?"

I nod. "If that's okay with you. He'd stay until he's able to get around and look after himself." I take her hand, needing her to listen. To understand the best she can. "Once he's better, he'll go back to his new house. I don't want to confuse you, Ave. He'd only be here for a little while, and then he'd be back in the city where you'd visit."

"My dad is going to come and stay here?" She beams.

I sigh, giving her the best fake smile I can muster. "Yeah."

"Thank you!" she tells me, pushing up onto her knees to cuddle me. She pulls back and holds my face in her small hands, her nose brushing mine. "Just like Papa Lowell."

"What—what do you mean?" I frown.

"When he was sick and needed you. You're going to help my dad like you did Papa Lowell." She kisses my forehead. "You're the best mummy in the whole wide world."

I open my mouth to speak, to say something, anything. But the words I need are tangled and lodged with the lump in my throat.

"She is the best," Mason whispers. "You're lucky, sweet Ave." He smooths his hand over her soft brown hair. "Ellis, up, mate. You have school in the morning."

Ellis shuffles past us and out of the nook. I can tell he's feeling a little put out at the news. He's more than a little protective of his cousin.

I take Ellis's place on the makeshift bed and lie on my back next to Ave, staring up at the lights.

"Where will he sleep? And when is he coming home? Can I come with you to get him?"

I chuckle and take her hand, pulling her to lie in the crook of my arm. "We'll figure it all out in the morning, okay?"

"He can sleep in here."

I sigh and hold her tighter. "He'll have his own room. You can help me get it ready if you want."

She nods. "What's his favourite colour? We can get paint and new bed covers."

I want to tell her all the things. Everything I know. But the churning ache in my gut tells me to wait. To let them figure it out on their own. "When you meet him, you can ask him."

"Tomorrow?" she asks hopefully.

"Not tomorrow. But because of his surgery, they'll let him come home sooner this time. It's not like before when they didn't know if he'd need an operation."

Her teeth peek out from a stretched smile. "I'm a little nervous."

I close my eyes, letting her settle all around me. "Me, too, baby. But we're going to be just fine."

Lance

"Any luck?"

I shake my head, running my tongue over my teeth in pure frustration. "What happens from here?"

"Well…" Mia looks down, clearly debating what she's about to say. "Your friend Mason was pretty clear you'd be leaving with him today. That you'd be able to go home and that he'd be coming with you."

"It's not a possibility for him," I tell her again, holding her stare in the hope she gets it this time. There's no way I'd have Mason live away from his family. I was the cause of it once before, and I won't be it again. "I'll try finding my mum's number. If not, I'll be going home alone. I'll sign whatever it is you need me to sign to allow it."

"Lance, there's no way you'll be able to go home alone."

I grit my teeth and stare at my leg.

Charlie told me that my mum hadn't called me once while I was away, and while I didn't expect her to care, I can't lie and say I wasn't disappointed that she didn't.

I don't even have my mother's phone number anymore.

"We can give it another couple of days, see how you are—"

I shake my head, annoyance getting the better of me. I feel ready to explode. I can't take much more of this room. This bed. The quiet and the not knowing about Waverley and—

"Hey."

I flick my eyes up at the sound of her voice, quickly righting my slumped form in the bed and running my hand through my hair, smoothing it out the best I can. "Scarlet."

"Hey! What are you doing here?" I look to Mia just in

time to catch her frown. Scarlet is meant to be on leave after being attacked. I've not seen her all week.

She tries to pretend it's nothing. Tries to. Her eyes meet mine, and she forces a shaky smile. "I'm here to pick Lance up."

I tilt my head, not understanding and feeling stupid for having to explain that I have no one to look after me at home.

"Lance isn't able to leave," Mia answers for me. "He doesn't have aid at home. He'll be in for another couple of days until he's at least able to get around."

"He has aid," Scarlet confirms, the words firm, as if she's telling herself.

Mia seems to frown harder, a little taken aback. "What aid? He's refusing to have your brother stay."

She doesn't look at me. Won't look at me. "He has me. He's coming home with me."

Home.

Did she just say home?

"With you?" Mia gives Scarlet a look that says *Have you lost your mind?*

"With me," Scarlet says, her eyes darting everywhere but the bed.

"Right. Well then... I'll go and get you a chair." Mia leaves the room.

I sit and watch as Scarlet looks toward my things on the recliner. "Do you have anything in the bathroom to pack?"

No.

It's not right. No.

"Lance."

"No."

"It's all in here?" she mutters, fastening the strap and testing the weight.

"*No*, I'm not coming home with you."

She finally lifts her eyes to mine, one brow raised. "No?"

"I'm not—" I tilt my head back, my nostrils flaring as a rush of air leaves me. "You're not doing this for me."

"I am."

"Scarlet—"

"You have a line of other people queuing up someplace I don't know about?"

"I can't have you look after me."

She stares at me, hurt marring her beautiful face. "Why?" she eventually asks.

"Because. I..." *Fuck.*

Her face is hard, daring, waiting for a reason good enough.

"Scarlet."

"Why, Lance?"

"Because I can't have you save me," I say resolutely. "I can't and won't let you do this—I don't deserve it. You think I don't see that look in your eyes. That I don't know how badly I broke you. If I could take it all back, I would, but I can't. I have a choice here. I can walk away this time."

I can do the right thing.

For once, I can do what's best for her.

I have to.

I wait for her to speak, to find her words. She simply, too calmly, reaches down and picks up my bag, placing the strap on her shoulder. "Waverley thinks you're coming home. Maybe that's on me, and I should've discussed it with you first. If you choose not to, I'll have her come visit here so that the two of you can finally meet. You can tell her yourself that you won't be coming back to the estate with us."

She continues toward the door before stopping and turning again.

"Water under the bridge, Lance." She shrugs, and instantly, I know I've hurt her. "But if you knew me at all, if anything ever meant what I thought it did, you'd know the lengths I was willing to go to. Yes, I might have fallen apart when you left—maybe I'm still a little bit broken now, but there wasn't—isn't—a second of *us* I'd ever take back."

She pulls something from her back pocket and places it on the bed—a picture. Once she leaves the room, I lean down and pick it up, my chest caving in as my eyes scan the image.

A picture of something, someone, I just told her I'd take back.

TEN

Lance

Lowerwick Estate is over an hour's drive from the hospital, and yet as we take the tree-lined lane toward the circular drive, a lump grows in my throat, and the drive is suddenly not long enough. The house comes in to view too quickly for me to fully prepare myself. To be ready.

"I saw her."

I feel Scarlet's eyes shift toward me.

"I came out to see you, and she was with Ellis. He hid her behind him, but I saw her and didn't know who she was." My fingers flatten out the creases in the photograph. "I couldn't remember what she looked like. I didn't know I needed to remember."

I don't expect Scarlet to say anything, she hasn't spoken to me the entire drive home, still hurt from what I said back at the hospital. But I wish that she would.

I wish she'd talk to me now.

I can see the figures on the terrace. The two of them. At first, I presumed it was Mason, but now that we're closer, I can see it's Charlie. The ache in my chest somehow grows impossibly worse.

"He's been good to you?" I ask, not taking my eyes off them.

Charlie sits on the terrace steps, Waverley tucked at his side, waiting.

Scarlet nods, and I know her silence isn't out of anger anymore.

She tightens her hands on the steering wheel and sucks in a deep breath. "He wasn't the only one. All of them." She finally pulls her gaze away and looks at me. "I wasn't okay for a while, Lance." Her brow creases as if she's trapped in a memory. I can't help but want to steal it. To know it. The fact I know nothing of a time when she wasn't okay, let alone it existing, makes me feel fucking feral inside.

There was a time when I thought I'd never not know this woman. A time when I loved her so deeply, I knew nothing but her. And now it's as if I know nothing.

"You're shaking," she whispers, her gaze now on my hands.

"I'm fine," I tell her, tipping my head toward the terrace as we roll the last few metres into the drive. "What do I say to her?"

She twists her head and looks out of her window, her smile widening when Waverley stands and starts to wave.

And the second I see her smile, the way she looks at Scar, my entire chest caves in. Scarlet reaches for the handle, and I snap out my hand, grabbing her arm. "Scarlet."

I wonder if she can hear it, see it even, as my heart seems to pound so hard, I feel echoes of it in my fingertips.

She twists in the seat, her gaze rolling over me. Her face falls, and then without holding my eyes, her head dropping, she slides her hand over the top of mine on her arm. She'll never know what it does to me. What it does *for* me. "I don't know how this feels," she tells me honestly. "I don't know what you should say or do or think. But I do know that she's going to adore you, Lance."

"Can I get the door?" I hear her voice call out, the glass making it muffled.

Time seems to stand still as Scarlet looks up with watery eyes and smiles at me.

A reassuring smile.

I steel myself and sit back in my seat, knowing what's coming the second I turn my head to look out of the window.

Although nothing could prepare me for what greets me.

Waverley pulls on the handle, but it doesn't open. Charlie steps up behind her a second later to swiftly pull open the door.

She beams at me, *my daughter*, her smile nervous and yet sure. "Hi."

She's beautiful.

She's so fucking beautiful.

"Hello, Waverley."

I can't take my eyes off her.

Charlie places his hands on her shoulders and shuffles her back a step, his smile warm and focused on her. "Why don't you let him out of the car before you go full creeper on him."

"Shut up," she says, smiling over her shoulder before pushing him back playfully.

I slide from the car, resting my weight on the door.

I know I'm frowning.

I know I should smile.

But as I sink to the ground on my good leg in front of her, I can't help but stare.

She shuffles forward when Charlie steps away.

"Hi again." She giggles and then shrugs. "You can call me Ave if you want to. Waverley is a mouthful."

My heart feels like it's too big. Too full. Too fast. "Would you mind if I called you Waverley?"

She turns and looks at where Scarlet watches us, then back at me again. "No one really calls me Waverley, so..."

"Okay." I nod, scanning her face. Her eyes are big and greener than the picture showed, framed by long, dark lashes. She's the split of Scarlet. "You're very beautiful, Waverley."

Her dark brows wiggle as she laughs. "You said you'd call me Ave."

I focus on her words and not on her face, realising my mistake. "I'm sorry. I'm a little nervous."

"I was nervous about meeting you, too. Mrs Penny taught me the five-finger thing."

"What's that?" I ask, wondering if she's even real.

"Hold up five fingers."

I do.

She reaches out, using her pointer finger to trace the outside of my thumb. I stare at her in awe, the feel of her soft skin grazing my rough. "Breathe in," she tells me. I swallow and breathe in until she reaches the top of my thumbnail.

"Then when I go back down here, you breathe it out." She glides her finger down the skin between my thumb and pointer. "Then keep going. In." She traces back up the next finger. "Out." And down again.

She repeats it on the last two fingers then pulls her hand back slightly. "Better?"

A spark flares in my chest, a small part of me rousing awake, as if coming alive again. And she has no idea. "Much."

She flattens her hand against mine carefully, spreading her fingers wide. "You have huge hands!"

I smile, shaking my head as I watch her. "Yeah."

"Do you want to see your room? They told me you might be hurting and to take things slow, but—" she cuts herself off abruptly, as if remembering something. "Can I call you Dad? If—" She looks to Scarlet again, unsure. "If I let you call me Waverley, can I call you Dad?"

The spark in my chest explodes, burning through me until I feel it in the backs of my eyes. "Yeah—" I clear the rasp from my throat, my words coming out barely a whisper. I see Scarlet turn away out of the corner of my eye. "That would actually make me really happy."

The nervous look on her face transforms, and she grins, glancing over at Charlie with pure confidence.

My heart sinks. I can't help but wonder how long it will take for her to look at me that way. They've had her for seven years more than me. It's hard not to question how I'll ever live up to the mother Scarlet is. The man I know Charlie is.

I've missed too much.

Too much that I can't get back.

"Ave, go and help your mum inside with the bags," Charlie mutters.

"Okay!" Waverley rushes around the car, and I drop my head, letting my eyes fall closed.

I hear the car door open and close, the gravel crunching under his shoes. And then Charlie's arms slip underneath mine, his body straining as he helps me to my feet.

I blink open my eyes, not bothering to wipe away the tear that's fallen.

My friend's face is a poignant mask of sorrow, his throat working on a swallow behind his top button. "It's not about what you missed anymore, Sullivan. It's about everything that follows."

I stare at him, a little fucked on the inside. "I don't know how to be a dad," I admit. "She deserves—"

"She'll make it easy." His jaw clenches, his eyes darting around my face as if he has more to say but can't. Or isn't ready to. "Come on." He hands me the crutches he got from the car, and then waits as I put my arms through each one, slowly making my way around the car and toward the front steps.

I'm nearly at the door when a muddy dog flies past me, inches from my broken leg, and skids through the hallway.

ELEVEN

Scarlet

"Bear, no!"

"Oh no," Waverley squeals. "Oh no, I'm in trouble." I watch as she looks up at Lance, her gaze still a little awestruck. "I was supposed to get a towel," she tells him.

"Ave," I sigh. "What have I told you about that dog?"

"I couldn't find him before. I thought he was at Nana Frey's."

"Bear?" Lance mutters, his face now pale from climbing the steps.

Shit. Trust everything to come barrelling at us all at once. "Yeah. We have Bear now. I'm so sorry I never said, with everything—"

"Bear? As in...?"

We lock eyes. I nod, swallowing around the uneasiness in my throat. I should've warned him. He's just met Ave for the first time, and now I'm shoving his mother's dog in his face.

"Shower. Now, Bear. Come on." I cringe as he bounds on skittering paws up the stairs.

"I'll take him," Charlie tells me, smiling wide as he follows a sheepish Ave up the stairs.

I look down at the muddy path left behind and shake my head. I scrub at my face, wondering how Lance must feel after everything that's just unfolded in the last five minutes.

"You said Mason lives here?" Lance questions.

"Yeah," I sigh, dropping my hands. I feel utterly drained. "Yeah, he does."

"I thought he was allergic to dogs."

I can't help the smile that taints my mouth. Of all the questions I thought he'd have, that wasn't the one I expected. "He gets an allergy shot. They keep a wide berth, and it seems to do the trick."

"I see."

There's a heaviness in Lance's eyes, one that I can't seem to ignore. I know he's tired. I know he's barely eaten the food at the hospital and that today has been a lot. But the spark I saw ignite out on that terrace... If nothing else feels okay right now, bringing him here does.

It was the right thing to do.

"I'm about to get dinner on," I say, thumbing toward the kitchen. "You can get comfortable in the sitting room if you'd like. Get that leg up."

I watch him lift his gaze to the high ceiling, the curved staircase, the rooms darting off to the sitting room and different wings.

And I know that it was the right thing to do.

"Thank you," he says, looking back at me with something

like awe in his stare. "Thank you, Scar."

"You're welcome." I give him a small smile and walk into the kitchen, knowing I should help him get comfortable, but sensing he needs a minute alone more.

It's half an hour later when Charlie walks into the kitchen with a soaked towel clutched in his fist. "That dog is a complete dick sometimes."

I chuckle, continuing to egg wash the pie. "Thank you for bathing him. Where's Ave?"

He disappears into the washroom to discard the towel, then comes to stand opposite me at the kitchen island. "She's in with Lance."

I arch a brow at him, knowing he knows how Ave can be when she gets talking.

"I told her to go easy on him tonight," he says. "She's just excited."

"She looked so happy out on that terrace." I pull open the oven, lift the steak pie, and slide it in. "I know it wasn't my doing, but I felt guilty watching them together. She's been deprived of so much time with him I can't even fully comprehend it, and yet I've lived it."

"She was happy," Charlie agrees. "And they've both been deprived of each other. I was here for Ave, but watching something that should have been that hasn't played out in front of us like that..." He shakes his head, his face grim. "You did the right thing, you know. I wasn't sure when you first told me, but it's exactly what they need."

I nod, smiling softly but still feeling a little defeated. "I know."

"Mummy, where's your phone?"

I narrow my gaze on Ave as she appears in the kitchen doorway. "Why do you need my phone?"

"I want to show my dad the video of the waterslide we built." She walks around the kitchen island, patting my dungaree pockets before looking around the worktops.

"It's probably up in my room, Ave."

Her shoulders drop.

I glance at Charlie and shake my head. "Will you be staying for tea?" I ask him.

"Of course he is," Ave answers for him. "It's steak pie."

"I'm actually not tonight." He squats down to level with her. "I've got an important call with an important lady that I can't miss tonight."

A slow smile spreads over Ave's mouth. "Aunt Lissie?"

Charlie smiles back. "Can I make it up to you another time? I'll pick you up from school next week, and we can get ice cream."

"With the others, too?"

He lifts one dark brow. "All of them?"

Her eyes seem to widen at the idea. "Even baby Thea."

I chuckle. "I think Luce will have a thing or two to say about that."

"Maybe not baby Thea," Charlie tells her, picking her up and giving her a tight hug. "But I promise I'll come get you and your cousins in the mum bus so we can go for ice cream."

"Deal!" She wraps her arms around his neck, finally squeezing him back. "My dad can come, too! You can be friends again." She wiggles down and runs from the room.

Charlie stands, staring after her. "Did she just play me?"

"You're only now figuring that out?"

"I don't like that she's so aware."

"About you and Lance?"

He nods. "I don't want her worrying."

"You could talk to him. Take the weight off the seven-year-old's shoulders."

He narrows his eyes at me. "Are you working together?"

I shrug, grinning. "Nina, Ave, and I may have hatched a plan while walking Bear this morning. As always, Ave has zero chill and veered off course fast."

"Jesus, she's savage," he mutters, but I know he'd do anything for my child, no matter how much she likes to conspire to bring him to his knees. "You should check on Lance before he runs for the hills," he deadpans.

I give him a look. "You could do that for me on your way out."

He holds up his phone, Lissie's name flashing on the screen as if he had her call right at that second on purpose. "Have you seen my wife?"

I chuckle. "You know what I'm excited for, Mr Charlie Aldridge?"

"You have about a second to tell me."

"I'm excited for you to get phone fucked by your wife tonight so that tomorrow we can get the less grumpy—"

"Lis." He stares me down in disbelief, his eyes darkening within a second.

I'll never understand, nor want to understand, the primal need Charlie Aldridge has for his wife. Lissie is the sweetest, funniest person I've ever met, and to look at her, you'd never believe she'd be the woman to wield as much power as she does over him.

It's hot as much as it is dangerous.

"I'm now leaving Lowerwick. Half an hour?"

"Half an hour is too fast," I mutter.

"I won't drive too fast," he huffs to his wife, clearly frustrated with the both of us.

"Hi, Lis!" I call out.

"No, you can't talk to her," Charlie tells Lissie, the tension in his shoulders getting visibly thicker. "You'll see her in a couple of weeks anyway."

"Give me the phone," I tell him, reaching across the island.

"Cut it out, both of you," he snaps.

"Charles!" I playfully scold.

"Lis," he groans, listening. "Fine."

He hands the phone to me, his face like thunder. I turn my back to him. "Hey!" I grin into the phone.

"I feel like we have three minutes before he self-destructs."

I look over my shoulder at her husband, steam practically flowing from his ears. "You're not wrong. You're going to have your work cut out tonight."

"Can he hear us?"

"No," I say a little quieter. "Why?"

"I'm at home."

"What?" I snap, my eyes widening. "But..."

"I'm not due home for another three weeks, I know. Mum and Dad came with me."

"Oh." I grimace, wondering about the semantics of that...

"They're renting a place while they're here obviously," she clarifies. "There's no way I could have them stay with us.

And I was excited to see my beautiful brute of a man tonight, but now I'm nervous as shit. He's pent up?"

I look over my shoulder again and find Charlie, hands on hips, glowering at me. "I think you should *extend* your trip, Lis. I'd run for the hills."

"Give me the phone," Charlie demands, reaching forward and taking it from my hand.

"Bye, Lissie!" I shout. "I'll be praying for you."

"You're thirty-eight years old," he accuses, pocketing his phone. "What is wrong with you women?"

"Lissie brings out my fun. She's still a baby."

"Don't blame Lis. It's the girls."

"Nina, Luce, and Megs?" I question, feigning hurt.

"I heard my name. Am I in trouble?" Nina questions, slipping into the kitchen and dropping her bag to the floor. I hear the house come alive as her children disperse. "Charles." She leans in to quickly kiss his cheek. "Looking extra scrumptious tonight, if I do say so myself." She's wearing her dance tights and a leotard, her shorts pulled up over the top. She looks at me. "We having a bitch?"

Charlie sighs when I laugh. "I'm not even going to attempt it with you two tonight." He heads toward the door.

Nina grins at his back. "Don't be a spoilsport."

"Goodbye, girls."

Nina shoves her bag under the counter with the back of her foot, then moves around the kitchen, snatching the chilled bottle of rosé from the fridge. "I saw Lance set up in the lounge..." She walks to where our wine glasses hang. "How'd that go?"

"I'd love one," I tell her, and she takes down two glasses.

"And it went better than I could have hoped. I cried. Everyone got a little teary, actually. But it was... okay."

"I told you it would be." She pours the two glasses of wine and then slips onto the stool at the island. "That pie smells incredible," she hums.

"Mase in with Ave and Lance?"

"Yep. We're trying to talk Ellis into not choking Lance out WWE-style. Thought it would be good to introduce them formally before we sit them at the dinner table and put a fork in his hand."

"Hmm." I brush it off, sipping the wine she hands me. "I can't help but root for Ellis's hostility. He gets away with everything I can't as a mature adult woman." I give her a sarcastic smile.

"You want to off him with a fork?"

My face screws up. "Off him is a bit strong."

"Make him bleed a little bit?"

I let my eyes light up. "Exactly."

"I get that. Sometimes Mase will breathe wrong, and I'm just like, *die*."

We both start laughing at the same time, Nina's glass lifting first before I clink mine against it.

I love that she gets me.

"Feel better?" she asks through her laughter, a slight frown creasing her brow as she observes me. I know she's worried. They're all worried.

"Yes. I didn't realise I needed to laugh so badly until I spoke to Lissie on the phone just now. I miss..."

"The lightness."

I nod. "I wished those seven years away for the sake of

them both. I never truly thought about how heavy everything would hit when the time came."

She gives me a sad smile, just listening.

"I don't think I know where to start with him. I don't know what to say."

"He probably feels the same," she offers. "I can only imagine how lost he's likely feeling after being stuck in one place, no contact with us or his family, for seven years. I get it was his choice, but..."

"I know." My shoulders drop, that weight pulling me right back down. "I can't tell you how badly I need to see him be him again, you know. To say something Lance-like."

"Mase would say the same thing whenever he'd get back from visiting the hospital. We'll keep an eye on him. He's here now and..." She pauses, the children's shouting and laughter ensuing from somewhere deep in the house. "I mean, if that can't fix a person, I don't know what will."

"Time," I tell her.

She nods, smiling as she stands and does a stupid little shuffle around the kitchen, slipping her arms around my waist and cuddling me. "Time. Definitely time. And also, in case you forgot today, I'm so stinking proud of you. Mase, too."

"Thank you, Nina."

"Always always."

"Can I have five more minutes?" Ave begs, her hands plastered together and held tight to her chin. "Please, Mummy."

"You have school in the morning, Ave. One more day, and then it'll be the weekend. You can have a later night then. It's already nine o'clock."

"He said." She runs to keep up, following me toward her bedroom. "He said I could come see him after Uncle Mase helped him in the shower."

I walk into her room and find her clean pyjamas, setting them out on the bed. I turn, looking down at her. "Pjs, teeth, bed."

"Fine," she groans, taking her pyjamas off the bed and changing into them. When she goes to the bathroom to clean her teeth, I riffle through her bookcase, searching for her favourite.

I wait for over five minutes for her to come back, my trust and confidence in her dwindling with each second passed. Eventually I give up, making my way down the landing toward Lance's room. I find her sat on the end of his bed with her legs crossed, the two of them both chuckling.

I swallow the bitter lump forming in my throat, knowing it's silly. I shouldn't be jealous of the two of them. I've wanted this for too long to let my ego get in the way.

"Knock knock," I announce, stepping fully through the door.

Lance is sat up in the bed, a clean T-shirt covering his broad chest. I quickly drop my eyes, wondering how they managed in the shower. There's no way Lance let Mason help him like he should have.

"Did we get lost on the way back from the bathroom, Miss Sullivan?" I ask, raising my eyebrows at her.

I hear Lance's intake of breath as her name passes my

lips, but choose to ignore it, knowing he likely didn't want me to catch the reaction.

"I didn't mean to," Waverley tries.

Lance clears his throat. "It is a big old house."

"See," Waverley adds.

"Here." I walk to the bed. "If you're not too tired," I say to Lance, catching his gaze and regretting it. The air is knocked from my lungs as I take in his damp hair and freshly trimmed beard, his eyes somehow clear of the shadows that lurked before. And the smell. The smell of his fresh soap, of him, all but knocks me on my ass as I'm taken back years, to a time when he was mine, and I was his, and there was no doubt or question or pain.

Ave swipes the book I have held out in my hand. "I can read in here?"

I try to process her words, still lost somewhere else.

Someplace I've missed very much.

"Mum?"

"Just a few pages tonight." I tear my gaze away and step back, doing all I can to put one foot behind the other and not stumble.

"You can stay, too, Mum. Come sit with me."

"Not tonight. I'm sorry," I mutter, not daring another glance in Lance's direction as I leave the room in a rush.

Once outside, I put my back to the wall and slide to the ground, my heart still pounding—wild.

And then I listen, as my sweet baby gets to read to her dad.

TWELVE

Scarlet

Scarlet: I'm on the struggle bus this morning

Megan: I'm on the way to New Zealand

Scarlet: Lie to me

Megan: What's going on

Scarlet: Lance is home

Nina: Lance is home home*

Megan: At the estate?

Scarlet: Yes

Megan: I've missed a chapter somewhere

Lucy: We need a group facetime. You're not home for weeks Megs :(

Megan: I'm living, laughing and loving life. Don't worry about me

Nina: If England lose I want you to get that tattooed on your ass

Megan: Done.

Megan: Miles said if we win you have to

Lucy: LOL

Nina: No

Scarlet: I sent Mia to the estate to make sure Lance is okay

Lucy: I thought you were on leave from work?

Scarlet: I had a wobble last night

Nina: You're at work?

Scarlet: No, I went and put flowers on Joey's grave and now I'm in the coffee shop.

Scarlet: On my fourth cup.

> Megan: Can we call in a few days? We're boarding soon so will message when we land. I have absolutely no idea what's going on, Scar.

> Lucy: Be safe Megs! Love you.

> Scarlet: We'll catch you up once you land

My phone starts to vibrate in my hand, Nina's name flashing on the screen. "Hey," I answer.

"Let me add Luce, hold on."

I wait, glancing around the quiet little coffee shop. There are two other women in the café and one elderly gentleman. I lower the volume on my phone and turn on my camera so that the girls can see me.

Seconds later they fill my screen in two split boxes.

"You sent Mia?" Nina asks.

"She said she didn't mind. I couldn't be there alone with him today. It's a lot." I watch as Nina grimaces, noticing the office in the background behind her. "Are you at the Montwell?"

"Briefly," she says, waving me off. "Mia was Lance's doctor at the hospital, wasn't she?"

"For a time. It depends who's on shift."

"It makes sense to send her. I get it," Lucy tells me.

"She has work tonight." I cringe. "I'm such a shit human being."

"You're not," Nina argues, "but maybe you should figure

out exactly what's causing your 'wobbles' so that you can get back there this afternoon and relieve her."

I look up through the café window, sighing deeply. "It's so stupid."

They both wait as I find my words.

"I can't even look at him, girls," I admit. "When we met that summer, I fell for the person he was. Yes, he was gorgeous. But the man inside that no one else seemed to know. The way he treated me. It was always more than just lust." I roll my lips, knowing there's no way they'll have the answers I'm looking for. "I don't know how to look at him and not remember it all. And the way he looks at me tells me he hasn't forgotten a thing."

"Does it make you mad?" Nina asks.

I shake my head. "Not that I remember everything from before, but I think I'm still holding on to the fact he cut me off. I don't think I can just forget it." I run my tongue over the front of my teeth. "Last night I went into his room and found Ave on the end of his bed. He'd come home a couple of hours before, and they hit it off straight away. Ave made it so easy for him. And it's not that I want it to be hard, but..."

"It wasn't quick for you. Or easy," Nina mutters.

I shake my head. "And then I looked up at him, and the second our eyes locked, it was as if everything faded, and we were back to that summer seven years ago. Just like it used to be."

"When I went to see him in the hospital, I was shocked at how emotional I felt just seeing his face again. I know I'm eight weeks postpartum, but I was a mess," Lucy tells me. "I can't imagine how it must feel after everything you've shared together."

"It's confusing. I look at him and get overwhelmed by all these feelings."

"Can I tell you what I think?" Nina asks.

"Yes. But don't make me cry."

"I think he's wearing one hell of a brave face right now. He's hurting. We all know that, but Ave is Ave. She's a chatterbox and the most loving of kids. I know they made it look easy, but I can guarantee you it's not. And with regards to how it makes you feel seeing it happen so naturally, I think you need to tell him."

"Tell him?" I frown.

"About Ave's birth. Everything after."

I'm shaking my head before she can finish.

"But do you not think some of the anger you're feeling is down to the fact he never read your letters?" she cuts in. "He doesn't know what you went through, and now he's back and circumstance puts him right there with Ave. Under your roof. Personally, I think you have every right to tell him what you need to in order to move forward yourself."

Lucy gazes guiltily into the phone. "You have to make this situation work for you, too."

"I said I'd be here for you," Nina continues. "I get why you're doing this for him and think you're incredible for it. But you can't bottle up the emotions that come with him being back. You went through so much, Scar."

She's right. If I ignore the things that hurt me just to save him from his shadows, I'll end up right back where I was. In my own darkness.

"I think having a conversation—about anything, could help break that barrier and make it clear to both of you what this is going to be going forward."

"It can't be anything," I correct.

"You're Ave's parents. You'll be something for the rest of your lives. I mean a friendship... maybe," she adds. "When you're ready, obviously."

I sit for a minute contemplating that. Friends. A friendship with Lance.

"Can I ask you something?" Lucy pipes up.

I nod.

"When you think about him, or say, if someone says his name, how do you feel?"

I drift back into my contemplating hole of confusion.

Not because I don't know what I feel at the sound of Lance's name but because the idea of the answer scares me shitless.

Lance

She bailed on me.

Day one, and Scarlet was gone before I could get my ass to the toilet and take a piss.

When Mia came and found me in the gym, telling me she'd be helping around the house for the day, I knew it was because Scarlet had panicked last night and was avoiding me now.

The way she looked at me as she handed the book to Waverley last night was unexpected. She gave me everything in that moment, completely bared, and with our daughter sitting at my feet, being here in this house, and around the table with my friends, my wounds all but crawled back together and fused right then and there.

Later, when Waverley's cheeks pinked, and she told me that she still sleeps with her night light on and that so does Scarlet, I knew that the open wounds inside of me may have temporarily touched, but they'd never heal and scar.

They're too deep.

"You surprised me today," Mia tells me. "You absolutely shouldn't have weightlifting on the brain, but the fact you got yourself out of bed and down two flights of stairs is impressive."

"Amazing what a little bit of pain relief can do," I mutter, continuing up the stairs to the room that Mason showed me to last night. My leg was killing me when I tried to get up this morning. I needed help, truthfully. But then I realised there wasn't anyone here and an overwhelming need to see this place in all its glory had me pulling back the covers.

I always knew Scarlet wanted to renovate the basement level. The dusty gym, library, and wine cellar hidden below. And with the obvious renovations on the upper levels, I presumed downstairs would be completed, too.

I was right.

The gym is now top of the line with a swimming pool littered with inflatables and a sauna—big enough for a football team.

Mason designed it. I knew it without needing to ask anyone.

I searched further for a while, passing the glass double

doors that restrict access to a wine cellar. And another door which, when I pushed it open, gave way to a dance studio.

A pang of something heavy settled on my chest after that, the idea that the library was just gone, after all the memories we'd had in there and knowing how important it was to Scarlet.

"Do you know where the library is now?" I ask Mia as I reach the top step on my ascent back up the stairs. Mia told me she was great friends with Scarlet. She must know.

"I don't. I'm not sure there even is one. Scarlet doesn't read."

I pause, giving my leg a second to just hang mid-air as I rest on my crutches. And to process the bullshit Mia just spouted. "Yes, she does."

"She doesn't."

"Well, she did. And she had a library once, too." She has one now. There's no way she doesn't.

She'd need somewhere to put her mother's books. Her own collection wasn't small.

"She never mentioned it," Mia mutters, carrying on down the corridor toward my room. "You should shower and get your leg elevated. I get the need to not sit around, but you have to give it time to heal." She waits for me to reach the door, a friendly smile on her face. "I already know you're going to be a nightmare patient."

With Mia's reluctant help fetching me three different weights when I asked, I managed to complete fifteen bicep curls before spots invaded my vision, and she took them from me.

My ribs and chest are screaming at me for it now.

"What would you like for lunch?" Mia asks as I make my way into my room.

I feel her at my back, following me. "Nothing. I'm not hungry."

"But you've—"

"And I can shower just fine alone."

"Well, I'll grab you a towel and be gone then," she confirms.

"Thank you," I tell her, knowing I sound ungrateful. It's bad enough having my friends and Scarlet see me unable to do basic, everyday tasks, let alone random people I don't even know.

When we reach the en suite, she walks past me and into the bathroom. "Oh, I have a waterproof boot bag in the car. I'll go grab it quick."

I shake my head, resting a crutch against the wall. Reaching behind my neck, I tug on my T-shirt, fighting it up my back and over my shoulders. "I was fine last night. I just kept it out of the spray," I tell her, feeling myself sway as a flash of pain slashes across my ribs.

"Sit," she mutters, her hands grabbing my raised arms and directing me to the edge of the bathtub.

For fuck's sake.

She pulls my top the rest of the way off. "You have to be more careful than that."

"I'm fine," I tell her, frustration getting the better of me.

I can't stand this.

"You're fine? I just watched you almost bear your weight. It was hard enough watching you get up two flights of stairs." She eyes my ribs and winces. "You're impossible."

"He's always been a little bit impossible." We both turn at the sound of Scarlet's voice.

She's standing in the doorway, her lavender hair pinned atop her head in some kind of bun, her flyaways making it clear she's been outside walking or sitting in a breeze.

She's perfect.

"I was working from the café this morning, but I thought you might want to head out for a walk or something after you're done here."

My brows rise in surprise.

"He's not stopped all day." *Shut the fuck up, Mia.* "I recommended rest for this afternoon. He's been—"

"I'd love a walk."

Scarlet's mouth twists up, as if she finds it amusing to watch Mia go up against me. "Did you bring the chair, Mia?" she asks her friend.

Mia nods. "He wouldn't use it."

"I am here," I say, shaking my head.

The two women smile at one another. "Get home. You have work tonight, and I already stole your entire morning."

They seem to communicate in that way only women know how to communicate without words. With a look.

"It's fine," Scarlet reassures her. "Can you leave the chair outside?"

"Yeah, of course." I watch as Mia smirks, dropping my T-shirt beside the sink as she passes Scarlet.

I stay sitting on the edge of the bathtub as she leaves, my eyes too busy lingering on Scarlet. She's wearing a floral print summer dress, and for the first time in seven long years, I let my gaze roam the length of her. With her hair pulled up I can see the full length of her neck, her skin sun-kissed and glowing despite the bruises covering it. Her body is as I remember it, the swell of her breasts and dip of her waist bottle necking to her hips. I let my eyes travel down her legs, smooth and long. God, she's beautiful.

"Do you need anything before I head downstairs?"

I bring my gaze up, finding her watching me. When I don't reply right away, I wonder if I missed more than what I caught her saying.

She bends to pick up my T-shirt. I use it as a chance to rearrange the completely inappropriate erection that's growing in my shorts. "That's..." She cringes, throwing it into the wash basket outside the door. "Sweaty."

"I used your gym."

Her brows rise, her feet carrying her back into the room. "You did what?"

"Nothing heavy. I couldn't."

She stares at me, her expression somewhere between wanting to kill me and wanting to check if I'm okay. "How is your leg feeling now?" She sighs, dropping her eyes to try to get a better look at my side. "Your ribs—"

I bring my arm to settle across my lap, concealing the heavy bruising. "I'm fine."

Uneasiness settles across her face, and I get the feeling she wants to check for herself.

"Could you get me a towel?" I point behind her, knowing giving her something to do will make her feel like she's helping in some way.

I stand while she reaches into the rack for a fresh towel, letting my leg hang. It's throbbing. As I lift my head up, I find her staring at me, her eyes travelling from my loose shorts to my exposed chest and torso.

"Your ribs are hurting you," she eventually says, her face pinched as if it's her who's in agony.

"I took some painkillers," I tell her.

"You need to be more careful." Her eyes lift to meet mine. "Please be careful, Lance."

Every time she says my name, something inside of me erupts. It's uncontrollable and renders me stupid each and every time.

I nod. "Okay."

She stares at me, seeing too fucking much with how deep her eyes go, and I almost think she's lost her nerve, but then she steps forward. "Let me get the shower for you. It's cold at first, and I don't want you jarring your leg."

I step back slightly as she nears, leaving enough room for her to lean in around the shower. Only as she leans in, her right leg lifts, gliding between the two of mine until her calf meets my thigh. I lean in, letting her leg rise higher, my chest a hair's width from her back. *Fuck.* I close my eyes, feeling her body heat against my chest. She's so close, so fucking close I can almost—

She staggers back when the water comes through, thumping into my chest. "Shit!" She turns, looking down. "Did that hurt you? Did I catch your leg?"

"You didn't hurt me."

She breathes a sigh of relief, carefully leaning back in to test the temperature of the water, keeping her feet firmly on the ground. When she turns around again, I wonder if the blush visible beneath her makeup is as obvious as my straining cock in my shorts. "That's better. You can get in on your own I presume? With Mase did you..."

Lie.

Lie, you son of a bitch.

"I can get myself into the shower, Scarlet." And I can. It's a struggle, and I'll have to fight to pull my shorts over my leg and foot, but I refuse to be bared to this woman whilst I'm battered and broken.

"Good. That's good."

Dare I say, I sense a touch of disappointment...

"I'll go get the chair and come back in a bit. If you're struggling just stop and shout for me."

"I'll be fine."

She becomes flustered, her face blushing further. "Perfect. Great."

I stare after her as she disappears from the room.

THIRTEEN

Scarlet

You'd think there would come a time when I'd grow out of blushing. The utter lack of control after thirty-eight years on this earth, my cheeks a flame of betrayal.

Maybe it's because in seven long years, the only bare chest or half naked male I've dared to pay attention to have been those of my brother or friends.

"Can I ask you a question?" Lance asks, thankfully keeping his gaze forward as I walk at his side. He wouldn't use the chair, and after feeling a little flustered leaving him in the shower, I wasn't about to pick a fight.

"I guess."

I sense his smile without needing to look up. "Where's your library?"

Of course he'd want to know that. "I don't have one currently," I tell him honestly.

"But your books."

No one has asked me about my books since I emptied the library and made way for the renovations. Even then it was a question of getting rid of them or storing them away. Mason seems to have little to no knowledge of the value in a book. "They're in baskets stored under my bed."

Lance doesn't reply right away, but I know he's frowning. "Why?"

We reach the bench that's nestled between two of my mother's trees. I wait for Lance to sit down, watching as he holds his thigh up, lowering his foot to the ground.

I take a seat beside him. "I didn't have anywhere to put them when we redesigned downstairs. I wanted them to be kept safe and not just dumped in an empty room."

"But you read still?"

I finally look up at him, finding him watching me. "Sometimes," I lie.

His head tilts and I feel my pulse quicken.

"What?" I ask.

He darts his tongue out to wet his bottom lip, the pouty skin shining. "What was the last book you read?"

Shit.

Shit. What was the last book I read? It's been years. "A classic of Mum's."

He gives me an upside-down smile and then turns to gaze around the meadow.

It's been a long time since I picked up a book and read a story about someone falling in love. I did try. For months I'd grab book after book from the bookstore in the hopes something would pull me from the slump I was in. Nothing worked. And something tells me it's more to do with me than the books I was picking.

The words are just that. Words. They don't resonate or touch me or even penetrate my mind in a way that makes them mean anything.

"Why don't you read anymore, Scarlet?"

I continue to stare ahead, wondering how and when I became so transparent. "You know, you once called me a presumptuous witch for asking such questions."

He sniggers, and I catch the slight nod of his head as he lets it go. "Waverley reads," he tells me.

I give him my attention, thankful for the change in direction. "Every day," I say softly. "What else did she tell you?"

A smile spreads across his mouth as he repositions his leg on the ground. And seeing that smile, knowing it's for her, after all the days, months, and years I spent telling her how much he'd love her, how much she'd make him happy, seeing that smile on his face at the mere mention of her name, it makes all those really shitty days worthwhile. "I'd say every thought that passed her mind left her mouth."

I shake my head and match his smile. "She waited patiently to tell you those things. She'd write them down some days. Anything she didn't want to forget."

"She's nothing like what I expected," he mutters, rubbing at his chest. "I was terrified," he admits, his eyes meeting mine and holding. "I'm not sure how I say thank you for raising—"

"You don't need to thank me for raising our child, Lance."

His dark brows gather. "You did it alone."

"I had plenty of help. You know that."

"But I should have been here." His throat bobs, eyes searing through me.

I can't argue with that. He should have been here. Because as much as I believe in justice, I've not known injustice quite like seeing my daughter blow out her birthday candles, wishing for her dad to be home, year on year.

"You've done incredible. With her, the house, your job. I'm not shocked, but to see it—"

I look away, hating the way my chest blooms at his praise. Hating how it makes me feel like a fraud. "I did the best I could." Which was nowhere near *incredible*.

"Scarlet."

I grit my teeth, my feet slipping on the mental grip I've learnt to cling on to. Nina told me to speak to him, to tell him, but I can't. I can't tell him all the ways I failed her, no matter how hard it is to sit and listen to him tell me what he thinks he knows. How incredible I am.

"Scar," he tries, and the need that one word carries makes my heart physically ache. I turn to face him. "I don't want to make you sad. I'm sorry."

I shrug, staring down at the wood separating us. "I'm not sad. I'm just... confused. I feel reluctant to tell you things you deserve to know, and I don't know why."

"You don't owe me a thing."

That's not true. "You deserve to know her," I correct. "At the very least."

"And I'll get to know her," he assures me. "So long as that doesn't cross any boundaries for you."

I sigh, wishing everything could be a little simpler. I swallow past the rising lump in my throat, asking it to hold off, to let me have a second to say what I need to say. "Ave is everything that I am. All I have. Giving you the parts of her I've experienced—no matter what I think you deserve to know—feels like I'm opening up parts of myself I left in the past. And I can't give you any of those parts right now."

I tried for the truth, not overthinking the words as they fumbled past my lips but... "I sound like a bitch."

"No, you don't."

"I put a lot in the letters," I tell him, offering him something. "If you want to know anything, I'd start there. Just, please... please don't tell me I'm incredible, or that Ave is perfect—which she is, she's beyond perfect. But that's not on me." I frown at my thoughts. The harshness of them. "You've known her for a day. I don't expect you to get it all yet, but please don't put me on a pedestal and thank me. You just... you have no idea."

"I don't," he mutters, the trees gently rustling at his back. And something passes between us then. An understanding, maybe. A silent conversation where I tell him I'm falling apart at the seams, and he tells me he knows, and that it's okay and that so is he. That we can be something. Not friends, not lovers—but something. For Ave.

His head drops to his shoulder as he stares over at me. "I'm sorry for being a presumptuous witch."

I close my eyes, desperately wanting to disappear. And then I chuckle. "No, I'm sorry." When I open my eyes again, they burn a little. "I've left you with nothing."

"Not completely true."

"No?"

His eyes drop to my hands, and I frown, glancing down. I

catch myself and freeze, my fingertips featherlight against the pale purple stone on my right ring finger.

He shakes his head. "No... I have a question. If that's okay."

I try to control my heart, slowly slipping my left hand over my right to cover the ring. He saw it, there's no way he didn't. "What's that?" I ask, pretending he didn't.

Vulnerability seems to fill his chest with a deep inhale. I tilt my head, forgetting about his ring on my finger as he asks, "Did she really not call? My mum."

My heart sinks, the lump in my throat getting impossibly thicker. "No. But I've been in touch—"

"She knows about Waverley?"

I nod, pinching my lips into a thin line as I contemplate how I explain this to him.

His jaw locks tight, eyes fixed on the house in the distance.

"She's working. The girls, too."

"I don't care."

I keep quiet, sensing his pain, feeling it for him, deep down in the tips of my toes.

"Do they see her?"

"They've been to see her."

"When?"

I avert my own gaze. "They haven't missed a birthday," I eventually say, knowing it'll tell him enough—that they care for her. Maybe not as much as I'd like them to care, but enough not to forget her birthday.

And I know that fact will hurt him. I don't say it for that reason, I'd never intentionally hurt him, not when I know how much his mum's let him down already, but he deserves the truth.

"You didn't have to make an effort with them," he tells me after a while. "Thank you for that."

"I didn't do it—"

"No," he cuts me off. "I know you didn't. You did it for Ave."

I give him a half smile.

He stares at me before chuckling. "Can you remember up on the balcony? It was the first night we spent together here. I said something..." I watch him ponder it while I pretend I haven't thought about that night, him, all that came after, and every word he ever uttered to me, over and over, every day since he left. "I said something like... sometimes we're allowed to presume someone is good."

"You called me incredible."

His eyes spark. "And I barely even knew you."

Why did I say that?

I will myself to shut up as heat roars under my makeup.

"I just knew." He smiles at me. "I'll happily wear being a presumptuous witch, Scarlet, because I'm *certain* you've done an incredible job raising our daughter."

My legs drag along the dirt underfoot, my body an unpredictable ball of energy. What do I even say to that?

"I don't think we have to know everything to see that someone is good. Sometimes we're allowed to presume—that was it."

I shake my head, looking at my now dust-covered sandal. "Maybe."

"You're incredible," he mutters, almost hopefully, and my heart all but stops.

I go to open my mouth and close it, not trusting my words. Knowing I should shut my damn mouth because... "You said that already."

He twists his head away, but I know he's smiling, and damn me for playing into this game.

I wait, wondering, yet knowing the words that will come.

"I'm just making sure you believe it."

Word for word.

Seven years later. And he remembers. Word for word.

"I know I have a lot to put right." I meet his eyes, panic flaring in my chest at the way the conversation is going. "I know you don't trust me. That I did the one thing I promised you I wouldn't when I left, and then I cut you off." A shiver snakes down my spine, the hairs on my arms standing on end. "But I'll put it right. I'll make it right somehow. For both of you."

I want to tell him it's fine. I want to tell him there's nothing to be sorry for and that I forgive him.

But I don't.

Seven years ago, I'd have rolled over and told him it was okay. I'd have done anything to take his guilt away—just like I always did with Mase and my dad. But I'm not that girl anymore. I'm a woman. A doctor. A mother.

And I deserve to have the wrongs righted.

"I need to pick Ave up from school. The others, too," I say, standing and changing the subject.

Lance watches me, his gaze unforgiving. "I'll walk back in a while, if that's okay."

"Of course," I tell him quickly, desperately needing to be alone. Or just... away from whatever this is.

I brought him here to help him heal. But this, him apologising and making promises... I'm not ready for it.

I'm not interested in it.

"Why can't you sleep?" I ask before I walk away, knowing if I can help him sleep, I can heal him quicker. "In the hospital, you struggled, and Mason said you weren't sleeping before at Elliot's... I was just curious why?"

His jaw goes taut, eyes glazing over as he drops his stare to my feet. I see him contemplate telling me and realise the mistake I made asking him at all. "Inside, I had the four walls of my cell, a shitty little mattress, and a blue door I'd stare at for hours on end. It was my safe space from everything going on around me." His eyes travel back to me, back to the now. "I'd spend my day looking over my shoulder, making sure..." He locks his jaw again and frowns, the words dying off before he can utter them. "There was no sunshine," he eventually says. "And I had to learn to sleep without the moon and stars. I guess no matter how fucked it was, I got used to that cell enough to now miss the escape it gave me."

But I'm your sunshine, when all you can see is the moon and stars.

My heart thrashes in my chest, my eyes wide. "I..."

He shakes his head, cutting me off. "You don't have to find answers to make it better, Scarlet. It's going to take time to adjust."

I nod. "Here... do you sleep here?"

He takes a second too long to reply, and I know. "I get sleep."

A lie. He's lying.

"You'll be late," he tells me, gesturing toward the house.

I turn wordlessly and walk back across the meadow to the first gate.

I feel his eyes on me the entire walk home.

Lance

My smile isn't fake, but as Waverley hops out of Scarlet's car, her ponytail swishing from shoulder to shoulder, I have to fight to keep it on my face.

"Daddy!"

I surrender the internal battle in an instant, laying down my shields at her feet. And it's not just my smile that falters. My heart, the world around me, it all seems to slow as she clocks me on the steps and rushes for me.

Daddy.

"Did you know that the Mona Lisa has no eyebrows? Some guy cleaned her so much that they rubbed off!"

I try with everything in me to shake off the initial surprise. Waverley isn't even aware of what she's said, or if she is, she doesn't know. Doesn't understand.

Pulling myself together, I sit back on the stone step and pat the granite beside me. "I didn't know that."

She settles close at my side, her full focus on me. "Once you see it, you can't unsee it. They are gone."

A small smile tugs at my mouth. "Did you have a good day at school?" I ask.

"It was okay. I just wanted to be here. Mum wouldn't let me in your room this morning because you were sleeping."

I wasn't sleeping, but I'm not about to undermine Scarlet by telling Waverley that. "I'll try to wake up a little earlier next week, maybe I can help you get ready."

She shakes her head, as if telling me no need. "Mummy sets an alarm before everyone else. She gets everything ready for me. You can help me feed Bear, though. That's my job. And I have to walk him, but he walks himself. I just follow."

I smile, a warm feeling spreading throughout my chest. "Where is Bear?" I ask, wondering why I've not seen the dog around all day.

"He goes to Freya and Glen's when everyone is at work. He ate one of Uncle Mase's shoes once—just this one time—and he wasn't allowed to be left alone after that."

I stare down at her as she looks up at me, her heart-shaped face flushed from the sun, freckles smattering across her delicate nose.

It shouldn't hurt this much to look at her. Each and every glance threatens to break me.

How?

How did I miss so much?

How can I not know her when she's half of me?

"You think too hard," she says, her grin lighting up her whole face. "Let's do something fun tonight!" She looks away from me, and I finally turn my attention to Scarlet and the other children.

My eyes widen.

Ellis is stood beside the car, his arms crossed as he

watches the two of us. Scarlet has Elsie in her arms, her small body limp in her slumber. "Come on, Ralph, out of the car."

"No."

"Please," Scarlet sings. "We can go inside and get some ice cream."

"I want Daddy."

"He'll be here soon. Come on."

And then there's Sammy, who's currently beating the ground with a stick held in his outstretched hand as he yells, "DIE."

"Ellis, get your cousin out of the car for me, please," Scarlet mutters, giving me a small smile as she passes me on the steps, carrying Elsie into the house.

"I'll get him!" Waverley tells Ellis, skipping back down the steps to the open car door. I follow her, peering into the car as she tries to coax him out.

"I thought you couldn't walk," Ellis asks, narrowing his gaze on me.

"The crutches," I tell him. "They help me."

He eyes them, then my leg. "Does it hurt?"

"Yes."

He seems satisfied with my answer and moves his attention to the car. "Do you want to play on my Xbox, Ralph?"

Ralph's eyes light up, and he nods, his tears evaporating almost immediately.

Ellis leans past Waverley, picking up his cousin and placing him on the ground. "Sammy," he yells. When the little guy peers up at his brother, I expect him to tell him to cut it out or to stop beating the ground, but he smiles like a complete psychopath instead. "Did you get it?"

Sammy nods, chucking down the stick and running up the steps and into the house.

I look down at Waverley once everyone is inside, my eyes slightly widened. "Is it always this chaotic?"

"Yup. But Mummy says it's perfect chaos, that she'd never go back to before."

"Before?"

"Before me," she clarifies. "She was alone here before I was born. Did you not know that?"

"No, I did know that. I—"

"Because you were here. You used to live here, didn't you?"

"I didn't live here," I correct her, closing the car door and letting her lead the way up the steps. "But I spent a lot of time on the estate with your mum."

"You knew my papa Lowell."

I smile. "I did."

"Mummy always says how much he'd have loved to meet me. All of us."

"I think so, too. He'd have loved your chaos."

"Do you like it?" she asks, a slight trepidation in the way she gazes up at me.

I stop on the steps and bend down, desperately wanting to pull her in for a hug. "I think it might be the best thing I've ever seen."

"Really?"

"Really," I promise.

Her face transforms. She rubs her stomach. "I had butterflies."

"Can I tell you a secret, Waverley?"

She nods, getting closer. "I get butterflies, too. Every time I think about being your daddy." I swallow, loving and hating and dying a little inside at the way that word makes me feel. "But then you show up, like you did in my room last night when you read to me or just now when you got here, telling me about your day, and I forget all about the butterflies."

"I don't know what you mean." She chuckles, leaning back.

Of course she doesn't. I smile with her. "You make me really happy."

Without a moment's hesitation, she leans up and cuddles my neck. I close my eyes, dropping my right crutch and wrapping my arm around her. It's the first hug she's ever given me.

And fuck, I'd give anything to lift her into my arms and hold her properly.

"If you stay this time," she mutters into my ear. "I can try to do that forever."

I pull back, looking into her eyes. "I'm not going to go anywhere. Not now. I won't disap—"

I cut myself off, knowing I've made promises like that before and failed in meeting every single one of them.

Failed them both.

"I want to make you happy, too," I say instead, knowing it's all that matters.

And I will. The moment she ran down those steps that first day and pulled on the car door to get to me, I knew that I'd spend the rest of my life rebuilding everything I took from her.

"Can I show you my bird?"

"You have a bird?" I frown.

She grins, stalking up the steps to the house. "Wait here. The nest is around the back of the house, and I have to change out of my uniform, or Mum gets mad." She pauses, as if remembering something, stepping back toward me. "And don't tell her about Mingo—she doesn't know."

"Who's Mingo?" I frown.

"My bird!"

"Why is it called Mingo?"

"You'll see."

FOURTEEN

Lance

I did, in fact, see. Mingo is a tiny little thing, likely a newborn swallow if what Waverley has told me is true. He's pink and featherless with a long neck and a head that he can barely hold up.

"He fell from the nest. Ellis thinks he was pushed, but look at this thing. His brothers and sisters wouldn't have the muscles if they're anything like him."

"And he's called Mingo because..."

"He looks like a baby flamingo," she confirms. "I need to find him some worms."

"I don't think you should be feeding it, Waverley." I watch as she stands, the small bird limp in her hand. "Or touching it."

"We can't just leave it to die." She continues on, lifting the chipped, broken plant pots to peer under them. "Ahh!

This one. It's a little worm." She turns her head to look at me, at my leg. "Can you help?"

I make my way to her, my crutches catching in the overgrown grass. My leg is throbbing, and I know I've well and truly overdone it for the day.

When I reach Waverley, I lean down, taking hold of the tilted plant pot.

"Mingo, look at this baby!"

My eyes widen in mortification as she picks up the worm. "Waverley, put that down."

She dangles it near the bird's large yellow beak, and before I can reach for her to knock it from her hand, the little thing opens its mouth and takes it from her.

"Good god."

"He loves them," Waverley says, watching the baby bird with intense fascination. "I watched for an entire hour after finding him on the ground, but his mother never came back. I put him in his nest, but it was empty and cold when I came out the next morning."

"How long have you been coming out here and feeding it?"

"Three days. Please don't tell Mum. She'll call someone to come take care of it."

I contemplate whether that would be the right thing to do.

"I googled it. If the parents don't come back, I can hand raise him until he can fly. I'll just need a cage to keep him in."

"I think your mum might notice a cage."

"You're going to tell her?" she says sadly, her happiness fizzling out.

"No," I counter quickly, watching as her eyes light back up. "I won't tell her."

She hugs my waist one-handed, careful not to hurt the bird in her hand. "Thank you!"

I sigh in relief, the idea of upsetting her spearing me right in the chest. I wait as she climbs the small hedge to place the bird back into its nest that's wedged in the depths of a low but thick tree branch.

"A couple more days, and I'll bring him in," she says resolutely, dusting her hands together to clean them.

"You need to wash those properly when we get in." I grimace as I look down at her hands, the underside of her fingernails filled with dirt. "You're as wild as your mother."

She grins at that.

So do I.

We walk side by side as we round the side of the house, past Ellis and Anthony's graves, and toward the terrace.

"Where have you two been?" Scarlet asks, appearing at the top of the steps.

I don't panic, not at all. That is until I look at my daughter, who for the first time in two days, has gone mute. I pop a brow at her and twist back around to look at Scarlet. "Waverley was showing me the birds."

"The birds?"

"The birds," I confirm.

Scarlet seems to shake off her questions, the day visibly wearing thin on her. "I've just woken up your cousin," she tells Waverley. "Will you please go and play with her until Uncle Elliot gets here? I need to start dinner."

Scarlet lets her eyes scan me before she walks off ahead of us.

I feel Waverley's eyes on me and shift my gaze to her. She winks. "Uncle Charlie once told me that half-truths are told by the wicked," she whispers.

I hold a finger to my lips to shush her.

She chuckles, running ahead of me and toward her mum. "My dad is wicked!"

Scarlet slows at that, allowing me to catch up. "Wicked?"

I wince, the pain in my leg getting worse. "You don't want to know."

"Did you rest your leg at all while I was gone?"

"Briefly."

"You've done too much too soon. We normally don't recommend being up for more than a couple of hours a day at first."

"I needed to be out of bed." I side-eye her, knowing she's looking at me. I don't need to tell her how fed up I am of being stuck. She's always been intuitive. She'll know.

Inside, Scarlet heads straight for the kitchen. I follow her, sliding onto a stool at the island.

After a minute, she places down four pills and a glass of water.

I take them silently, at ease just watching as she moves around the kitchen, gathering vegetables and an array of pans for dinner.

Lots and lots of pans.

The amount you'd need to feed a whole family.

My heart warms, a smile pulling at the corners of my lips as I watch her, my mind drifting to a memory.

"I have this dream."

I let my fingers tangle in hers, her body already entwined with mine. My head twists to face her. "Tell me."

She smiles, and I kiss her cheek. "It's a lot of noise. Christmas maybe—but I see the dining table full. Mason, Nina, and Ellis. Charles, Ell, the girls. Everyone. Drinking and laughing and just living. I used to try imagining it, but it was impossible. I didn't have the girls. The guys never really showed up like they did after Dad died." She pauses, her eyes thoughtful. "We grew up loud. We weren't told to be quiet. That age-old saying children should be seen and not heard. Well here, in this house, and at Glen and Frey's, if we were quiet, that's when they came looking for us. For so long this house has been silent, and I crave having that noise again more than anything. Mase doesn't see it. He doesn't even want it. I don't think he knows what he's missing," she mutters sadly. "But recently, since the memorial ball and having the girls come around more, it feels like it's touchable. Like maybe in a few years' time, we'll all be around the dinner table—happy. There'll be noise and laughter and life here again."

I swallow down the rest of my water as I watch her, my heart thrashing in my chest. The memory is bittersweet.

Scarlet got her happy.

Her house full of noise and life.

But as if in some cruel twist of fate, I wasn't in it.

"Dinner will be a while if you want to go for a lie-down," she tells me, her eyes barely holding on me before they're back on her task.

I can't seem to look away. "I think I'm afraid I'll miss

something," I say honestly, not even meaning to speak the words out loud.

She immediately stops chopping the veg, looking at me with a frayed understanding. "With Ave?"

I nod. *And with you.* "I can't get back the years I've missed. I can't risk missing a second more. It's probably another thing that's messing with my sleep."

"You'll heal quicker if you rest," she pleads, gingerly slicing a carrot. "She doesn't stop. Ever. You'll burn out if you run in her shoes."

"She's a lot like you then?"

Scarlet rolls her eyes, as if she's been told it a million times before. "Ave's more like you than you think."

I tilt my head in question.

"I'm not going to give you all the answers," she says, her smile genuine. I smile with her, transfixed, desperately wanting to remember the look on her face.

This simple moment while she stands at the kitchen counter, happily cutting up veg.

"I suppose I deserve to work for it."

She pops a brow, trying in vain to hide her smile as it grows bigger.

Fuck, that feels good to see. And although I do deserve to work for it, I also want the answers. The missed moments and little pieces of them I'll never get back, I want them injected into my brain as if they've never been lost.

"What time does Mason finish work today?" I ask.

"He should be leaving the office around now. Why's that?"

I stand, rearranging my crutches. "I just need a favour. I'm going to go for a lie-down."

Scarlet watches me, as if she has something to say. "Sure. I'll send someone up once dinner is ready."

I leave the kitchen and make my way up the stairs, my leg still throbbing. A little while longer and the pain meds will hit. It'll see me through dinner, at least.

In my room, I walk to my bed, picking up my phone from the sideboard.

I call Mason.

"Sullivan?"

I chuckle at the familiarity my last name brings after so much time. "Yeah, it's me. Have you left the office yet?"

"I'm in the car waiting on Nina. Is everything okay?"

"Everything's fine. I was wondering, the letters Scarlet wrote to me, are they still at Elliot's place?"

There's quiet on the other end of the line, and I pull the phone away from my ear, wondering if he's hung up on me.

After the fuss about me reading them—granted it was important as fuck—I don't expect pushback from him now on it.

"I'll stop by on the way home. And, Lance?"

"What?"

"It's not Elliot's place anymore. It's yours."

I run my hand through my hair, not realising what I've even said. "Right, yeah, of course."

My place.

I end the call and toss the phone down on the bed, followed by my body. I prop my leg up under two pillows, the ache still pulsing like a second heartbeat.

I feel broken, every muscle in my body desperate for rest.

Closing my eyes, I sink into the soft duvet, not hopeful that sleep will come.

The sound of a fist pounding flesh echoes through the walls.

Thuds.

Grunts.

The guards.

Doors.

Doors banging and banging.

Screaming.

Shouting.

Crying.

"Fuck," I grit out, fisting my hand at my sides.

Stop.

Stop.

Please, stop.

It doesn't. Even confined behind the locked door, it doesn't go away. There's no way to block it out. No way to escape it.

Another door bangs, and I flinch, my heart jarring in my chest. Sweat forms on my brow, the sound of the guards shuffling outside my door.

I swipe at my forehead, frustration at my inability to not let it affect me. That bang. It makes me feel sick to my stomach every damn time.

Stop.

Please.

You're safe.

You're—

I hear the lock unlatch and bolt up in my bed, my eyes wide as I search for the door.

The blue door.

Instead, I find Scarlet, her smile falling from her lips as she runs her eyes over me.

My heart pounds so hard in my chest I can feel it in my shoulders, like a drum beating throughout my entire body. I open my mouth, sucking in a rush of air.

I snap my eyes to the window, finding it light outside.

A bead of sweat runs down my slick back, my hair sticking to my temples.

"Lance?"

I shake my head, covering my face in my cupped hands.

No.

No. No. No.

I hear her come closer and drag my hands away, turning on the bed and climbing from the opposite side before she can settle on the mattress. I stagger on my leg, but I don't feel it. I don't feel a thing but the inability to breathe. "I'm fine."

She watches me like I'm a skittish animal ready to bolt.

"I'm fine. I just need a minute," I repeat, the words ragged.

"You want me to go?"

I stare at her. Searching for the answer I know I should give.

Tell her yes.

Tell her to go.

"Let me get the shower." She sets off around the room, keeping a wide berth this time.

I stand stock still as I try to control my breathing, my lungs feeling five times smaller than they should be.

Lifting my hand, I see it trembling. I shake it out, clenching my fists in an effort to hide it.

I need her gone.

Far, far away from me.

I can't have her see me like this.

I know my body is betraying me, my knees threatening to give.

I don't dare take a step toward the bathroom.

I can't.

How do I even hide that from her?

Why is she in here?

"Lance." I look up, finding her standing in front of me. "Should I go?"

I manage a nod. "Go."

She steps back, uncertainty making her feet featherlight against the floorboards. "If you need me... just get one of us, okay?" Her eyes are riveted on me, assessing—terrified.

I've scared her.

I let my eyes drift closed as she turns and walks from the room.

Scarlet

Every step around the kitchen feels forced, my whole chest screaming at me to go to him. To check on him.

He told me to leave him.

He wanted to be alone.

What could I have even done for him if I had stayed?

"Is the table laid?" Mason asks.

I turn, finding him removing the now warm plates from the oven.

Should I send Mase up?

"Scar?"

I blink, focusing back on Mason. "I'm not sure. Nina might have..." I should go back up there. I have to.

"You okay?"

I nod, toying with the ring on my right hand. "Everyone's home?"

"Elliot just turned up." He eyes me warily, but I step past him.

"I'll bring the food out." Then I can check on Lance. Give him time then go back up.

I remove the food from the oven and call everyone to the table. Mason is just finishing laying down the cutlery as I carry in the jugs of juice for the children.

My brows rise in surprise when I find Lance sitting at the table.

He's talking to Ave, his smile... full.

I stand in the middle of the room, holding the jugs, watching as they interact. I can't hear what they're saying, but I see the way Ave laughs at whatever he's saying. The way she shuffles impossibly closer. The need to know one another. There's no other feeling quite like the feeling in my heart. It's not happy or sad or angry or jealous. It's... I don't know what it is. But watching them, seeing his smile after the way I found him just now... Ave can heal him.

The realisation hits me like a slap to the face.

Lance doesn't need me.

"Auntie Scar," Ellis calls, and I drag my gaze to him. He holds up his cup, gesturing toward the jugs of juice in my hands.

Shaking myself out of my trance, I walk the rest of the way to the table, reaching over to fill Ellis's cup. My hand shakes, the juice splashing over his wrist and then the tablecloth.

"Shit," I mutter. I look up into Ellis's surprised face. "Sorry, Ellis."

"I can do that," Mason tells me, taking the jug from my hands. "Go and sit down," he adds so gently no one else hears.

There's a seat at the end of the table, right beside Ave, and I make my way to it, doing my best to calm down and ease my trembling hands.

As I pull my chair in, I look up and lock eyes with Lance. He's watching me, his face questioning but soft.

A silent plea. *Are you okay?*

It's the only tell that he'd been the way he was upstairs half an hour ago, and no one else at the dinner table would even know it.

Nina said he was putting on a brave face, but this, this is more than that. So much more.

I can't help but wonder if giving him more of Ave, the parts he missed, would maybe help him heal. Could it distract him? Give him something to think about away from his time in prison?

He could have damaged his leg tonight jumping out of the bed.

God, he had no recollection of where he was when I pushed open the bedroom door. His face was so pale, so lost. He was somewhere else.

How often does this happen?

"Mummy, you aren't eating."

I shift my gaze from Ave to my empty plate, and then to everyone else's full ones. I reach forward and scoop up the chicken, not making eye contact with a single person at the table.

Still, I feel every eye in the room on me.

FIFTEEN

Lance

"The letters," Mason tells me, coming to stand beside me at the bottom of the stairs where I sit, waiting for Waverley.

She disappeared moments ago to get her welly boots so we can feed Mingo.

She told Scarlet we were going to visit her nana and papa's graves after dessert, and I prepared myself to betray my child, knowing I couldn't outright lie to Scarlet's face, but she barely even nodded in reply, gently bending down to kiss the top of Waverley's head.

If I thought she'd let me pull her into a hug right there in the kitchen and tell her everything is okay, I would've. Before the blood in my veins could reach my heart and beat.

The nightmares always rocked me. It normally took me hours to get myself back from the shaking, trembling mess to a semblance of a man again. Today was quicker. Maybe because it was cut short before it could get as bad as they have in the past. Or maybe because I had a table of people waiting for me downstairs.

People, who after all I've put them through, are still here.

The idea that Waverley, my flesh and blood, was waiting on me... it gave me a place to be. A reason to pull myself together.

Seeing Scarlet so visibly affected wasn't something I anticipated when I sat down at the table. Her face was deathly pale, her eyes unwilling to hold on a single person in the room.

She was deep in her own mind and still is now.

Because of me.

I take the letters from Mason. "Thank you for getting these."

"Of course. We were passing anyway."

My fingers curl around the thick stack, desperate to tear into them, to inhale every word, every detail. I can't help but wonder how much of what Scarlet can't tell me is currently held in my hands.

To think I had them all that time.

I could have known Waverley had I just let them in.

"I have a question," Mason says, watching me with a wary gaze. "It's been years, so you might not remember. But back before... before—"

"Before I went to prison," I say for him.

He nods. "I gave you the deeds to this place. The documents signing the estate over to Scarlet."

"You did," I confirm, narrowing my gaze on him.

He stares back, a hint of shame tainting his face. "Where are they?"

I twist my head around the banister. Scarlet and Nina are in the kitchen, their chatter carrying through the house. "They're in a safe place," I say, quietly enough no one will hear. "I can get them for you."

His jaw clenches and unclenches. I can't decide if he's mad and is about to hit me, or if he's ready to burst into tears. I pray for the former. "Why didn't you give them to Aldridge?"

I roll my lips, wondering how honest I want to be. I decide the whole truth is the fairest option, considering the sensitivity of the topic. "Because I couldn't, and wouldn't, see her hurt any more than she already was. She'd just lost your dad. It wasn't the time to take more names from the house—from her. If I hadn't been there that night in your office, and you gave those documents to her... you'd have lost her, Mase. And I don't like to think what that might've meant for our friendship."

He drops his eyes, staring at his feet.

"And I knew..." I wait for him to meet my eyes again, Waverley's feet thundering down the stairs at my back. Mason frowns down at me, a pained look on his face. "I knew you'd come home."

His nostrils flare, and I take it as my cue to get up.

Waverley grasps my hand as she passes, pulling me with her. "Crutches," I groan, wincing as I stand.

She sighs. "I forget you're slow."

"I could be even slower and go tell your mum about Mingo."

Her eyes widen, hurt painting her face. "You can't!"

I smile wide and tip my chin. "Go find some worms, Scamp. I'm coming."

She bolts out the door, her grin full and perfect. I stare after her, listening as her feet echo faintly across the terrace.

I eventually look back at Mason, his focus already on me.

He holds out his hand. I stare down at it suspiciously before taking it. And then he pulls me in for a hug. "Thank you, Lance. For everything."

My brows lift, not expecting it from him.

I pull back, squeezing his shoulder in response. "I'm glad you're here," I tell him, stepping around him and out the door.

It's still early when I make my way up the stairs to my bedroom. My leg is throbbing, a sick feeling sitting heavy in my gut. I did too much today. Scarlet told me more than once to put my leg up, but I didn't, too afraid I'd miss something.

I fall heavy onto the bed, pulling a pillow from behind my head and wedging it under my leg. The second my leg settles, I close my eyes, the pain only getting worse as I finally relax it.

"Shit."

I'm not due any more painkillers for another two hours.

I scrub at my face and rest back against the headboard, willing my brain to take me somewhere else, away from the burning sensation in my leg.

I think about my mum and the fact she knows who Waverley is.

That was a shock to me.

Why do I care so much about her still?

She didn't call.

Not once.

If there was a switch, I'd flick it. Without hesitation.

I thought time might change things. That maybe she'd need me one day and want to see me. But I've been out of prison for weeks, and there's not been a peep from her or the girls.

"Daddy?"

My eyes flicker open. I lift my head, smiling when I find Waverley standing at the end of my bed. Bear follows behind, knocking her hand for attention. "I thought you were supposed to be going to sleep," I ask.

"I am. I brushed my teeth and gave Mummy a cuddle and kiss." She looks around my room and then back to me. "Can I give you a cuddle good night, too?"

My child—this beautiful, smart, sweet girl—will never know what it is, how much it aches, to not know the feel of her mother's arms. Of my arms.

Because I already know I'm going to spend the rest of my life giving her everything I never had.

I tip my chin for her to come closer. As she nears the side of the bed, I lift her, grunting as I pull her to lie on the mattress next to me. She snuggles into my side, her arm wrapping around my waist.

Bear hops up on the other side, huffing as he curls up at her feet.

"I used to wonder what your cuddles would be like," she says, voice tired. "I thought they'd be like Uncle Mason's."

Every bit of pain in my body is worth it. Just for this one moment.

"Are they?" I ask, making sure to hold her a little tighter. I dip my nose to her hair, inhaling the smell of her coconut shampoo.

"No. Uncle Mason is too rough. He's always tickling or squeezing me. He never just snuggles me like this. Uncle Charlie is better. He'll snuggle occasionally."

Jealousy spreads through me like wildfire, but I refrain from voicing anything that could let Waverley know it.

No matter how much it kills me inside, I can't help but feel relief that she had Charles these last seven years.

There's no one better.

"You snuggle the best."

I smile. "You're the best snuggler, too."

"Better than Mum?"

Pain shudders through me. Because I miss it. And because I can't quite remember how it feels to hold her. I can picture her lay in my arms, staring up at me. But I can't remember the feel of her skin on mine or the smell of her shampoo.

"Did you not snuggle?" Waverley eventually asks.

"No, we did. We used to snuggle all the time."

"I think if you asked her nicely, she'd let you snuggle her again."

"I don't know about that, Scamp."

"Why will you call me Scamp but not Ave? I googled what it meant earlier, and I had to remember that I'm trying to make you like me and not to get offended."

I chuckle, desperately trying to commit her, this moment,

the feel of her snuggled in close, and the smell of her shampoo, to memory. "It's not a bad thing. And..." I lean across, lifting her chin to look at me. "I already like you very much." I swallow around the lie, dousing down the love I have for this little girl. "And I'll call you whatever you want me to call you."

"You used to call Mummy sunshine."

Fuck.

I take a breath, let out a shaky exhale, then force a smile. "Who told you all my secrets?"

Waverley grins. "She did."

I tut sarcastically. "What else did she tell you?"

She thinks for a second. "She told me that you loved your bike. Did you know it's nearly fixed? I'm going to ride on it when it's better."

Scarlet's fixing it? Again? "You are?"

"Yep. And those letters." She leans over my chest, pointing to them on the bedside table. "She wrote those out every month for six years, but you never replied. I even wrote in some of them."

"You wrote to me?"

She nods. "I have messy handwriting, but I've almost got my pen licence, so just you wait. Then I'll write new ones for you."

I didn't think I could regret not reading the letters any more than I already did. Not after finding out they held the truth about Waverley. And yet lying here now, I feel ready to tear into my own flesh and bone for being so fucking stupid. For missing so much of her life.

"I'm sorry, Waverley. I didn't know you'd written to me,

but I promise if I'd known, I'd have read your letters every single day over and over while I was away."

"You'd have tried." She grins. "My handwriting was really bad in some of them."

I smile at her sense of humour.

How can Scarlet not take credit for raising her?

She's incredible.

Just like her.

"Have you read them?" Waverley asks.

I look over at the stack of letters. "Not yet. Do you think I should?"

"Yes. You missed so much, and Mum told you all about it when she'd write. The weddings." She rolls her eyes. "And Christmas days. My school stuff, like parents' evening. Oh, and the day I got Bear. You have lots to read about."

I *do* need to read them. Immediately. "What's so bad about the weddings?"

"I only remember Uncle Charlie and Lissie's, but they kissed, and then Uncle Charlie left me for two whole months to go on a honeymoon. He only called me two times."

"Two times a *week*, Ave. You're going to have to let that go eventually." I move my gaze to where Scarlet is standing in the bedroom doorway. "Come on. Back to bed," she says softly.

Waverley sighs, giving me one last squeeze before she sits up. "Can we walk Bear together tomorrow?"

"For sure," I promise her.

She climbs from the bed, Bear instantly getting up to follow. "Good night, Dad."

"Good night, Waverley."

"I..." She looks at Scarlet, her expression unsure. "Will you come, Mummy? To walk Bear. Just the three of us."

I see Scarlet working around a swallow, her mouth opening and closing as Waverley and I seem to wait on whatever her reply might be. "We'll see, okay? Go get into bed. I'll come tuck you in."

She disappears out of the room, but Scarlet hovers, her smile forced as she glances back over at me. "You're in pain."

Not a question.

I nod, deciding not to lie. "A little."

"You need rest tomorrow. She'll be okay with Bear for another day. If you don't rest, you won't heal."

"I overdid it today. I can admit that. But I can manage a walk."

She watches me, her eyes hesitant as they flutter around my face. I know she's thinking about what happened before dinner. How she found me. "Are you okay?"

"I'm fine."

She rolls her lips and nods. "Do you get them often?"

"Not often enough for it to be a problem. Normally just when I get tired."

"Out in the meadow today, you said you get sleep here." She drops her eyes momentarily before looking back up, bringing with them an apology in the depths. "You were lying."

"I'm fine, Scarlet."

"That wasn't..." She trails off, her brows drawing together, but then she nods. "Sorry. It's not... It's not my business. I'll leave you to rest."

Before I can stop her. Before I can tell her it'll only ever be her business, she leaves, shutting the door gently behind her.

I sigh, dropping my head back to the pillow.

After a while, I give in and reach over to pull the next envelope from the stack of letters.

Lance,

My thoughts are scattered today. I find myself thinking about you without realising it at times, and then I end up in this deep void of darkness that I can't seem to crawl out of. I remember the day we lost Joey. Not all of it—I seem to pick and choose the parts of that morning. Maybe that's a good thing. But the one thing I can't forget, that seems to live with me through every new step through this life, is the moment it was clear you were going to be taken from me.

It's incredibly selfish, isn't it?

I think it's your fault, though. I've never met anyone who's loved me as fully, as attentively, as honestly as you did.

For that time, that summer, I felt like I was your world, Lance. As if I was all that you saw.

I remember being happy when we met. Life was a certain kind of way for me, and I couldn't change that. I wanted to be here for Dad. I was happy. I was happy before you.

But then I met you, and that happiness I felt paled in comparison. It was insignificant compared to the way you made me feel. What you brought to me in such a short space of time was beyond anything I could have dreamed.

I said I wanted it to hurt, that if it wasn't painful, messy, crazed love, then I didn't want it. And I meant it. With every breath that passed with those words, I meant it, but, Lance, this is unbearable.

I'm walking around with a you-shaped hole in my heart, and I'm so broken, so lost and afraid, I find myself avoiding anything that could risk healing it.

Not every day is like this. I don't want you to think I'm mopey. It's just a bad week. I just felt a little lonely today and knew speaking to you, even if you don't get to read this, would help.

I still write to Mum. She gets the other "why won't Lance let me love him" letters.

I guess I'm tired. And overworked. And I know I need to eat something more than ginger biscuits (it's all I can keep down).

God, I miss you. Your voice. Your face. Your mind.

It's weird because to everyone else you're just a some-body. To speak about our time out loud to anyone else, you're that guy who I fell for that one summer. No one cares. No one gets it. But to me, you're the some-body. The somebody I woke up to everyday. The some-body I'd think about whilst walking the meadow. The somebody who'd be waiting for me at the end of a day. The somebody I showed my deepest and darkest parts to. The somebody I knew would be there—no matter what. You told me yes, and no, and to do what felt right, or to smile, and then you'd hold me when I'd cry.

Is love really wanting to stand on the highest point on earth and scream at everyone below that you're not just a somebody, you're the somebody?

My somebody.

You really did a number on me, asshole.

Maybe I'm crazy. But I know that there will never be another one for me if there is a you.

I definitely feel less alone with my pen on paper. Maybe I should write more. It would help if I knew whether you are reading my letters.

I have a scan next week, so I'll know more then, but so far everything is perfect. I'm still terrified but I'm doing my best to be the best for our baby. I promise. Maybe it will get easier to talk about soon.

I love you.

Your sunshine xx

I lie in the bed staring at the ceiling for hours after reading her letter. I should read more. I want to. But the coward in me has me contemplating how much it might hurt to read any more of her words. Even when she's not telling me something important, it feels like the most sacred thing I've ever heard.

Being in prison changed me. Day by day. Night after night. It fucked me up better than anything else ever has. To think I had her right there, so close, even if it was just ink on a page.

I wonder if she could've saved me.

If maybe letting her in instead of shutting her out would've been enough. If maybe I would've closed my eyes and seen her before the nightmares came.

"Lance."

I look up at the sound of her voice, surprised her interruption doesn't startle me as she pulls me from my thoughts.

It's got to be well past midnight.

I thought everyone was asleep.

"Is that..." She looks pointedly at my side, the paper scattered there.

"Your letters."

She looks around the room, pulling her dressing gown tighter. "You've not been to sleep yet?"

I frown and tilt my head, noticing the dark circles under her own eyes now she's free of her makeup. "Have you?"

"I work shifts. I don't sleep like I used to."

Me neither.

Our eyes settle into a knowing, forbidden stare. "Have you taken your pain medication?" she asks.

I glance down at my leg, having forgotten about the pain there. I rub at my chest. "Not yet. I'll head down—"

"I can get them."

She leaves the room without another word.

I fold up the letters and place them in the bedside drawer, then slump down in the bed, my hand running through my hair in what feels like defeat.

I need my leg to heal. I'll sleep better then, especially if I can burn off this frustration in the gym.

I miss that. Running on the treadmill when things got too much, forcing my heart to race in a rhythm that couldn't remember her name.

Anything to forget for a while.

Scarlet

He isn't sleeping.

I knew it.

I chew on the inside of my cheek as I stand in the kitchen, knowing I should take the water and pills back to his room and then go back to bed myself.

But he isn't sleeping.

When I walk back up the stairs and into Lance's room, I don't think past the tired, defeated look on his face as I set down his water and pills and walk to the window.

I pull back the curtain an inch, illuminating the room.

And then, I sink down into the chair below the now visible full moon and stars.

"Scarlet," Lance says with a frown, watching me.

I close my eyes, not wanting or needing to look at him. "Get some sleep. She'll be up at the ass crack of dawn to walk the dog."

Lance doesn't answer me, but I feel his eyes on me for a long time before my body relaxes into the chair, and I fall asleep.

SIXTEEN

Lance

Lance,

You're not reading my letters. I realised it weeks ago, knowing if you knew what was written in them, there's no way you'd ignore me. It's sad. I want you to read them in some ways, but then again, it feels freeing knowing you're not. Like I can write absolutely anything, like I do with Mum, because no one is going to see them.

I never had to be honest with you when you were here. You'd look at me and see anything heavy I'd dare try hiding from you. Every single time you'd pull me up by the straps of my dungarees and love me in that way you did. Everything always seemed to be okay by the time you'd ride off the next morning.

It's the same reason I know that you're afraid right

now. That you need me to move on with life and not wait for you.

It's love—the real kind. The kind I'm not sure every person gets to experience in life.

Why were we the lucky ones?

Without wanting to disappoint you, I can't move on. Because even though you're not here with me physically, there's this pit deep down in my soul that's so quiet in its certainty, I know it belongs to you.

It's why I'm not afraid of your silence.

It might be small, but it's all I have to hold on to right now. I'm not letting go.

Mason has been to the house nearly every week since I found out I was pregnant. He tried to have me go stay with him in the city, but I couldn't leave the estate. It felt wrong. He's trying. I can tell he wants to be better. I'm just not sure he's ready.

I'm twenty weeks pregnant today. It's why I wanted to write to you. I had a scan this morning, and I saw the baby's hands and feet. Little pieces of us, Lance.

I've not let myself think too much about it. I know what I need to do to stay healthy, and I'm following everything I should be, but I wasn't (still am not—maybe) ready to think about what's to come.

You'll be away for at least five years. Charlie thinks it'll be more like eight. He feels helpless. I'm not sure he even knows what he can do to get you home sooner. I think it scared him. Seeing you in that courtroom, knowing what you were about to face.

The idea of doing this without you for five whole years is terrifying.

I'm going to have to learn how to parent alone. Go through firsts that belong to you. Change every nappy and wipe every tear.

I have no idea how to be a parent. I only had Freya growing up, and I have Nina to follow now. She's incredible with Ellis. If I can do what she does, I think I'll be okay.

Why do I know that you'd be a natural?

I've added a scan photo in the envelope. You can see the fingers and toes!

Congratulations, Daddy.

I'm sorry you can't be here to experience this with me.

I love you.

Your sunshine, always. xx

I slip the small image from the envelope, holding it up in front of me. The sun's streaming in through the bedroom window, the double doors to the terrace are thrown wide open, and from my seated position on the bed, I can hear the children in the fields beyond. Only faintly, but I can hear them.

The image is hard to make out, and I squint, turning it upside down, trying to figure out what's fingers and what's toes.

"When I was pregnant with Samuel, I had to ask the sonographer to point out exactly what I was looking at." I lower the photo to find Nina in the doorway, her smile gentle. "You overdid it, didn't you?"

"Apparently so." I adjust in the bed, sitting up a little straighter. When I woke up this morning, Scarlet was awake and watching me. She quickly folded the blanket she'd covered herself with when I caught her, and then left.

Moments after, Waverley and Bear came like a tornado into the room, ready for their walk.

I climbed from the bed in agony. My leg throbbing and my torso tender even against my T-shirt. Scarlet reappeared with my tablets as quickly as she'd left.

"The kids are out on the lake today, so they won't disturb you," Nina tells me, coming to sit on the end of my bed. "Maybe make the most of it."

"They go out on the lake?"

"Hmm. Scarlet and Mase take them on the weekends that Scar has off from the hospital. It's kinda their thing. We all go sometimes, but we're in need of a bigger boat," she says with a chuckle. "With Elliot, Luce, and their family growing, and then when Megan visits, too, it's a lot." She looks me over. "Can I get you anything?"

I shake my head. "I'm fine. Just reading through these." I hold up the letter I just read.

Nina nods toward the scan photo. "May I?"

I hand it to her, her smile widening as she peers down at the image. "Ah, I saw this one." She shuffles closer. "This is the body. You can see the spine here. And then this is a hand, and that there is a foot. Can you see the toes?"

I take it back from her, looking more closely now, spotting everything she's pointed out. "Holy shit," I say as a smile forms.

"Incredible, isn't it."

I stare at it, amazed. "It sure is."

"The two of you seem to be bonding a million times quicker than we thought you would. Ave couldn't stop talking about your walk this morning. She's always been a happy little thing, but having you here makes it feel like she's got a Duracell battery strapped to her back with the way she's buzzing around the house."

"It feels like I've never been without her." I look at the letters on the bed and swallow. "Although I'm realising how much I've actually missed by reading these."

"Where are you at?"

"Scar was twenty weeks pregnant in this one."

"Ah, you're on the good bits. She found herself again as Ave grew, as she started to show. You can imagine how impossible she was about not doing as much around the estate, too."

I snigger. "Yeah, I can."

She looks at me thoughtfully, and I realise she didn't come in here to talk about Scarlet. "Mase told me about the deeds last night," she says a little quieter. "I didn't know before—back then. He never said."

"You were still fighting your way back to one another when he gave them to me," I clarify.

"I know. I wasn't mad that he didn't tell me. I was annoyed he'd put it on you instead of sorting it with Charlie himself. He didn't know about you and Scar, but the fact he was willing to leave it to you and Charlie to tell her that he didn't want this place..." She shakes her head, her disappointment clear. "I'd like to think he's grown from that point in time."

"I'd say he's come a pretty long way." I gesture to the house.

She gives me a gentle smile. "Yeah. And it's why I'm glad, backwardly, that he was too cowardly to go to Scarlet himself. I'm grateful that you made the decision you did." Her features tighten, her eyes sharpening as she focuses on me. "That you loved them both enough to go against your word. *Again.*"

My jaw locks tight.

"When you came to me that morning after the ball. You told me..." She sucks in a breath, giving me a knowing look. I just nod in understanding. "I should have known you were lying to me. You made it make sense for the most part, but then after everything that happened with Scarlet, the way you protected her. And then both of them by keeping the deeds. You know, I played that morning over and over in my head for years before I went to Vinny."

I stare at her, a chill spreading throughout my chest.

"I know about your sister and her boyfriend. They're still together by the way."

My heart thunders in my chest.

"I know that they played you, Lance. And I know that you even tried to stop it that night. I might not have all the details, but Vin got me enough."

"Nina—"

"I presume they threatened you," she says with untamed

anger. Not anger meant for me, but for them—my sister and Ben. "Which is why you told me it was you."

"It was me. I believed it was you, Nina. I told Ben to plan the entire thing."

"I've seen the texts, Lance. I've seen the fake statements. Vinny told me I could sue them both."

My eyes widen.

"I know," she sighs. "Because they *did* threaten you, didn't they?"

I shake my head, feeling my control of the situation slipping. "You deserved the truth," I say simply. "You deserved to know that Mason never did what you thought he did. The rest didn't matter. None of it."

"Lance, you deserved better," she says. "You deserved to have someone you could be honest with, unafraid of what that honesty meant for the people around you." She reaches for my hand, picking it up and squeezing it. "I'm so sorry they did that to you. I really am. I remember that year. The way you were different. Quieter. Walking around as if you were lost. The way you kept yourself from Scar." Her jaw locks, her eyes shining. "It all made so much more sense once I knew."

The need to reassure her, to let her know that I have it all under control... "If it ever came out—if Ben ever... I'd take Marcus's death as my own. I wouldn't let it come back on Mase."

"It's not going to come out. Vinny dealt with it—with all of it. Ben has more to lose by speaking than any of us." She looks toward the double doors, the sound of laughter carrying across the estate, stealing her attention. She smiles and looks back at me. "Mase still doesn't know. I stuck to my word."

I swallow the knot forming in my throat, wondering what I ever did to have the friends that I do. After everything I put them through. "Do you want to tell him?" I ask.

Nina looks at my hand in hers. She's changed since I left. She's softer now. A gentleness in her posture as if she's at one with herself and her life here. "No." She looks up at me. "No, I don't. I decided a long time ago that it wouldn't ever go beyond the two of us. Vinny wouldn't—"

"I know," I tell her.

"And you deserve my word." She stands, her hand squeezing mine once more before she steps away. "After everything you've been through and done for them, you deserve a chance to move forward. A chance at your own happy."

I shake my head and avert my gaze as it burns. "I am sorry, Nina," I force out. "For the time you lost with Mase and Ellis. I know you say you forgive me, but I'll never forget what I did. What I took from the three of you."

She stares at me for a moment, her head tilting. "You have to. You've got to let it all go now. Don't be bitter or angry or sad. Trust me, you'll only make life more painful if you carry it." She scans me, her eyes lingering on my leg. "You're not a criminal, Lance. You do know that, don't you? There's a reason you're sat here just seven years after... after what happened. It's because you don't know malice. I don't believe you know anything but love. Find me anyone who wouldn't have done what you did when faced with what you were. You lost more that day protecting Scar—Mason's baby sister—than

Mase lost in the six months the two of us were apart. And if *I* had let it go—the bitterness, anger, and pain—we'd have made it out of our mess long before Ellis was even born."

"You have changed," I say aloud.

She huffs a laugh. "I grew up. I learnt a lot along the way. Mase, too."

I never imagined Mason would be here by the time I got out. I knew he'd come home, but I always imagined it would be later in life when he was done with the company. To think he came back here, likely for the sake of Scarlet and Waverley.

"I buried the deeds." I look up at Nina as a small smile pulls at the corner of my lips. "They're under Ellis's trees in the meadow. The fifth one."

She gives me a quizzical look. "Why the fifth?"

"Ellis. His birthday."

Scarlet

"How long are you off work, Scar?"

I sit down in the chair between Elliot and Lance as Elliot bites into the slab of steak Mason has cooked and sliced up. We're in the garden having a BBQ. Elliot, Lucy, and the children are here as well as Charlie and Lissie.

"They told me to take two weeks to let the bruising settle down, and then they'll have me in to decide if I'm ready to come back. I have annual leave booked at the end of next month, so I think they'll wait until after that before having me in again."

He grins at me. "You must not know what to do with yourself. How long has it been since you had time off like that?"

"A long time," I agree. "Probably after Ave when I took my break."

"You took time off after you had her?" Lance asks.

He came down late this afternoon despite us telling him he didn't have to. He wanted to get out of the room, which is understandable. I can tell he's in pain still. The bruising on my neck is nothing compared to the bruising on his face and body, and this morning his leg was twice the size as it was yesterday.

"Just over a year. I knew it would be too difficult balancing both so soon after giving birth." I just had no idea how badly I'd need that time off when I planned it.

"And she wouldn't let us help her," Elliot adds.

"That's not true. I snapped your hands off once she was born and I realised I needed you all."

"It only took you seven months."

I turn away from him, rolling my eyes at Lance. "I was fine."

"You're always fine," he mutters, smiling as he looks down at the beer in his hands. "They let you do that, though. You took the year and then went back?"

"Yep. It was only my second year. After everything that happened and then being on placement whilst pregnant, I was ready for the break."

In hindsight, it was probably exactly what I needed at the time.

"When did you graduate?"

"Two years ago." I feel my cheeks widen as Lance's eyes spark. "I'm in my second foundation year now."

"Mase threw a huge party here on the estate with all her classmates," Elliot tells him. "Rivalled one of the fancy balls she puts on."

"It did." I chuckle, remembering the night. "I'll never forget it."

I turn my gaze on my brother, but he's not looking at me. I catch his nod, as if to say *No worries, don't sweat it, it was the least I could do.*

I don't look at Lance.

"I thought about moving the ball this year," I say. "I have the next few weeks off, so it seems silly to plan it once I'm back at work when I have the time now."

"How much sooner, Scar?" Nina asks from the other side of the table.

"Maybe next month. With the weather we're due to have, it's perfect."

"I thought we were going on holiday while you're off from work," Ave says from behind me.

I didn't know she was paying attention to the conversation.

"We can still go," I reassure her. "I haven't made any definite plans yet."

"I want us all to go. Can we?" She steps closer to the table, Ellis now listening, too. "Uncle Mase?"

Mason looks at me. "On your week off?"

I nod, and he focuses back on Ave.

"Please," she begs her uncle.

He chuckles, cocking his head for her to go to him. "We'll be there."

"Yes!" She wraps her arms around his neck, climbing onto his lap. "Uncle Charlie. Auntie Lissie?"

"I'd have to ask the boss," Lissie says, looking up at Charlie. "What do you say, Charlie boy?"

"He won't say no to me." Ave grins. "Uncle Elliot—"

"You've got a full house, Ave," he tells her before she can even finish.

"My dad, too?" She looks toward the two of us hopefully. "Will you come, Dad?"

I feel Lance's eyes on me and turn to meet his gaze.

"Would you like to come?" I ask quietly, knowing everyone is listening.

His brows lift in surprise, quickly focusing back on Ave.

Did he expect me to say no?

"I'd love to come."

Waverley grins wide.

Lance twists his head back to look at me again. "Thank you."

I search his face, feeling like he's not just thanking me for the invitation.

I stayed all night in his room. It was stupid. I should stay a million miles away from him and protect my heart. But he slept. *He slept.* I watched him for over an hour before he woke up and caught me. And the lack of darkness surrounding his eyes this morning told me he was asleep for longer than I watched.

I keep telling myself the more rest he gets, the quicker his body will heal, and the quicker he can go home.

Because that's what has to happen.

It's the plan.

"I'm all for moving the ball forward," Nina says. "There's something about having it in springtime that I love. They've always been the best in my opinion."

"I'd be free to help," Luce tells me. "And Megs will be back by then, too."

"She will. That's actually perfect timing," Nina agrees.

"And then a holiday will be needed after all this last-minute planning, right girls?" Lissie offers, smiling behind her wine glass.

I chuckle, looking between the three of them as they scheme. They'll help me. I know they will. "I'll make some calls, see what's available."

"You can't just have time off, can you?" Elliot says with a chuckle. "You're relentless."

"Can we play rounders?" Ellis asks, already swinging a bat in his hand.

"I'm going to start the dishes," Lucy says, standing and collecting up the empty plates.

"I'll come help." Lissie stands and starts to help clear the table.

"Mum, you can play, but you're not bowling today," Ellis tells Nina.

"Aww, thanks, mate," she sings sarcastically. "Why don't you put me into a position that suits you instead."

"Back stop," Ellis says without hesitation.

Mason chuckles. "I'll bowl, angel. You can get distracted by my face." He leans in and kisses her neck.

Ellis tuts and stomps off down the terrace.

"You don't have enough players for two teams," Lance says.

"It's a variation of rounders," I explain as everyone disappears from the table. "You bat until you're caught out. You catch them out, you bat."

"So not rounders."

"No, I guess not." I smile, sitting back down in the chair beside him, appreciating the last of the evening sun as the children play.

"You're not playing?" Lance asks.

I shake my head, grinning. "I'm as bad as Nina."

"I don't believe that."

"Well, I won't embarrass myself by proving it. The last time I joined in, I swung the bat so wide, I cracked Ellis in the ribs."

Lance chuckles, dropping his head back. "He spoke to me earlier, you know."

"That's progress," I manage, his infectious laugh making my words shaky.

He cringes, a lightness settling over him like the sun sinking behind the meadow's hilltop. "He told me if he were me, he wouldn't eat the burger I was about to eat."

I laugh harder, grabbing his arm, shaking my head to reassure him. "He's messing with you. He wouldn't dare do anything to it."

His eyes flick around my face, as if memorising parts of it. A furnace ignites behind my cheeks. "I know. I gave him some serious eye contact while I ate the entire thing."

As if on cue, Ellis passes us, heading toward the middle of the field, the bat swinging aimlessly. He walks to where

Waverley is sitting and drops down next to her. "He's fiercely protective of her," I say absentmindedly. When I turn to look at Lance, I find him already watching me. "He almost got suspended from school last year after getting into a fight with a boy two years older than them, just because he called Ave shrimp."

"Shrimp?"

"For being small. Kids are assholes sometimes. Ave is pretty tough, and it doesn't tend to bother her. Ellis is a little more sensitive about it."

Lance drags his eyes away to the garden below. "Hmm. Maybe Ellis and I will get along better than I thought."

"Probably." I keep my gaze on him, greedily watching him as he watches the kids.

When he came downstairs this afternoon, I could see the pain written across his face. He took his medication and seemed to be more relaxed during dinner, but I can't help but think he's still doing too much.

Sensing my stare, he brings his focus to me.

Our eyes meet and hold.

They're exactly as they were when he left. His face has aged like my own, small promises of wrinkles that now form with each fractured smile we exchange, but his eyes, they're as green, as vivid, as I remember them.

Catching myself, I drop my gaze, then look up and out across the estate. Anywhere but into his eyes.

"You must be happy. Having Mason and the children all out here on the estate."

I smile. "Hmm. I never believed it would happen."

Silence settles between us as I take a moment to be reminded of how much life has changed. How fortunate I am to have what I do. "It makes everything worth it."

He doesn't say anything, just waiting for me to finish.

"It felt like I'd be stuck in that quiet forever." I even accepted it after a while, knowing I'd likely be alone here without family eventually. "I used to tell myself and everyone else that I loved it, that I was happy with life back then. But I think I was just used to it."

"It was all you knew."

I cave, turning to look at him. I nod. "Having them here feels right. As it should be and always should've been."

His lips curl in a slow, easy way that makes my stomach flip. "I'm happy for you, Scar. Truly. You deserve this."

I smile and shrug. "Maybe."

"*No.* You do." His features harden, and I almost look away. Almost. But it's Lance. "In my eyes, there's no one else on earth who deserves all that you do."

I shake my head. "There are people who have lived, or are living, through far worse than me. You're—"

"I said in my eyes," he cuts in, his pinkie reaching out to brush mine.

Instinctively, I run my hand down my arm, the hairs standing on end. He follows the motion, his stare trailing so intensely, it's as if I can feel him there, gliding slowly across my skin.

He swallows and flicks his eyes back to mine. "Because there's no one else I see."

I roll my lips, desperately needing to look away.

I should look away.

"So," I say gently, fighting with everything in me not to fall at his feet. "I should add delusional to the list?"

He chuckles, caught off guard, the tension between us dancing away in those fine lines around his eyes. "The list. That thing's still going?"

"Indefinitely," I tell him, letting out a deep exhale as the moment fizzles out.

"Indefinitely..." He grins. "Fuck, that's a good word."

I laugh and elbow his bicep. "Stop smiling."

"I'm not allowed to smile?"

I try with all my might to conceal my own. "You're messing with me."

He nods. "Indefinitely."

I stand and shake my head, my cheeks aching. "Well, fuck you," I say hushed, walking toward the steps that lead to the garden. Once I reach the bottom, I turn and add a little louder, "Indefinitely."

SEVENTEEN

Scarlet

"Did you take me because you knew she'd give me shit?"

I turn my head and smile out of my car window. We're on our way back to the estate after a trip to the hospital.

Lance woke up in pain this morning. More pain than even the likes of him could keep off his face. I happened to be asleep on the chair and caught it before he could hide it from me.

"I took you because I knew you overdid it this week." I look across at him. "You're probably the worst patient I've ever had."

"That Annie is a bitch. I don't like her."

"She's the best of the best. She'll win all the medical awards one day."

"Better than you?"

"Yes. She's almost a consultant."

"I don't like her."

"Because she made you squeal like a pig or because she's better than me?"

I feel his eyes on me and grin. "I didn't squeal like a pig."

"Are you sure about that?"

He doesn't answer me, and I leave him to wallow in his shame. Annie did exactly what I needed her to do today.

She scared him.

Lance isn't listening to anyone when it comes to healing. Every day since coming home, he's pushed the boundaries, and then this morning when he woke up, leg still swollen, thinking he'd be walking Bear, I knew I needed backup.

"I know you don't want to miss anything with Ave, but you really need to listen to what Annie told you today. Your body's been through something horrific. Give it time to rest and heal. You'll be surprised how quickly it happens when you start looking after yourself."

"I feel like I'm letting her down whenever I miss something."

"You're not."

"I have. I did; whilst I was away."

"She's young, Lance. What do you remember of being a baby or a toddler?"

He frowns, pain flashing on his face.

I look back toward the road. "She's going to grow up and remember the time she had with you. Not the time she didn't." When he doesn't say anything, I glance at him. "Why not give it two weeks. Annie said half an hour at a time is all you should be up until the swelling's gone down, right?"

"Half an hour every two hours."

"Will you give me five days of sticking to that? If the swelling goes down, we can make it an hour. And maybe if your ribs are healed, you could try lifting some weights again."

He drops his head back to the rest, his eyes drifting closed. "Do I have a choice?"

"Of course you do. But there's no way I'll let you fly if you've got swelling like that." I point toward his leg. I don't tell him that Waverley wants him to come to Bora Bora because he already knows that. The gentle reminder that we're going away at the end of next month should be enough.

"I'll be there," he tells me.

"I know." I smile. "Because you're going to stop doing stupid shit and listen to me."

He cracks open an eye, peering down at me.

I just about catch the corner of his mouth twitch before he turns and looks out the window.

"Where's my dad?"

"He's gone upstairs for a lie-down." I turn to look at Waverley, her mousy hair pulled back from her face in two French braids. "He'll be down for dinner later."

She comes to stand next to me at the counter, carefully picking up a mason jar to examine the dried flowers inside. "Is he okay?"

"Not really. He's been doing a little too much too soon."

"Is it his leg?"

I nod, smoothing over her braids. "He wants to spend lots of time with you, and like you, doesn't know when to stop."

"You tell me it's my superpower."

"It is." I smile, then kiss her forehead as I step around her. "But your dad was recently hit by a car."

"Is there anything that could harm a bird in this?"

"Harm a bird?" I frown, turning to find her peering into the mason jar.

She nods, fingering through the jar and destroying the flowers.

"Why would it harm a bird? It's flowers."

"So... nothing's poisonous?"

"No." I chuckle. "But they won't eat dried flowers. There's bread in the bread bin if you want to feed them."

"Bread?" she retorts. "What kind of diet is bread for a bird?"

I place my hands on my hips and tilt my head as I watch her. "Coming from the girl who'd live off pizza and chips if I let her."

"Can I go see my dad?"

"No." I shake my head, narrowing my gaze on her. "What are you up to, Waverley Sullivan?"

She empties two mason jars of dried flowers into the pockets in her dress and then walks backward from the room. "Nothing."

Before dinner, I told Lance, Mason as my witness, that taking two of his new pain medication tablets along with the beer Nina slid across the worktop toward him was a bad idea. I didn't tell him not to. He's a fully grown man and doesn't need to be mothered. But I used my knowledge from the last eight years learning medicine to warn him against the idea.

"I really like that doctor friend of yours."

"You said that already," I tell him, following him up the last few steps with extra caution. He makes his way down the landing toward his room. "Are you okay getting into bed?"

"I need a shower."

I shake my head and chuckle.

"What?" he asks, turning to face me, his smile slow and relaxed. "I feel high as fuck."

"I did warn you."

"Warn me?" He drops one of his crutches and pulls at his T-shirt. "I feel great."

I bend to pick up the crutch. "You're not in pain?"

He gives up on his T-shirt, smiles down at me a little dazed, then kicks off his trainer. "I'm achy as hell, but for the first time in days, I don't feel like I've been hit by a bus."

"Well, I'm glad you're feeling better." I step around him. "Would you prefer a bath? Annie said—"

"You're glad?" He snorts. "I thought you'd hate me forever."

I pause just inside the en suite door, and he stumbles into my back. I glance up over my shoulder, his tall frame towering over me.

My body warms, as if wrapped up in a blanket.

His pupils are huge, and he blinks over and over. That lazy smile reminding me too much of nights I've long let go. "A bath sounds good," he mutters, his eyes flicking around my face.

I swallow and nod, turning away to run the bath. "I don't hate you, Lance. I've never hated you."

"Maybe you should. It would be easier if you did."

As the bath fills, I grab a fresh towel and place it on the side, close enough for him to reach once he's done in the bath. Lance watches me from his spot in the middle of the room.

He looks utterly knackered. "I knew those tablets would hit you hard. You're tired."

He shakes his head adamantly. "I've been sleeping because of you."

He has been. In fact, Lance has slept uninterrupted for the past week. Each night I sat in the chair, the curtain slightly pulled back.

"Your eyes are heavy. You're about five minutes from falling asleep." I already know the bath is a bad idea. "Here." I tap his arm for him to lift it.

A sly smirk drags up one side of his face. "You want me naked, Lowell?"

I give him an incredulous look.

His eyes don't leave me. "You always were the hornier of the two of us."

"I see we're letting our intrusive thoughts win tonight."

"They're not intrusive. It's factual information."

Lord, help me. I reach for his other crutch, but he pulls it out of reach.

"But... are you saying you have intrusive thoughts that you don't let win when you're around me?"

I sigh. "Anyone with any self-control has intrusive thoughts they don't let win. Do you want my help or not?"

"Are they about me?"

I pause and look up at him. "No."

He grins then winks. "Sure."

Fucking asshole.

And fuck Annie and her tablets. As if my life wasn't interesting enough without a spunky, off-his-face Lance to deal with.

"Are you going to stay? Keep me from drowning?"

"You have less chance of drowning if I leave."

I chuckle, but he frowns, his smile slowly dropping as he watches me with a slight shake to his head. "But the only time I feel like I can breathe is when you're around. Will you stay?"

My eyes drop to the tile, the vulnerability in his eyes not familiar. "Put your arms up so I can get your top off."

He moves his crutch to the side of the sink, then lifts his arms. As I pull his T-shirt over his head, I take in the bruising that decorates his chest and ribs properly for the first time. His entire right side is mottled in black, purple, and blue bruising.

"Lance."

"Shh." He rolls his shoulders. "Don't remind me."

It's one thing to know someone you... you care for is broken, but to see it. To see the physical marks in the aftermath hurts as much as the marks themselves.

Without thinking—following pure instinct—I reach out, letting my palm connect with his abdomen. Lance shudders, his head dropping back. I trail my fingers across his hard stomach, around to his side. My thumb strokes over the darkest part of the bruising. "A bath will help," I say, not knowing what else there is to say. "It'll ease the pain."

He brings his head up, looking down at me. My stomach coils tightly, and I gently let my fingers slip off his skin as he reaches for his waistband with one hand, his chest and abs rippling.

I wait with my heart in my mouth as he pushes his boxer briefs and shorts down his thighs, letting them drop past his knees to the floor. My eyes seem to flutter as I force myself to look anywhere but at him. I turn toward the door.

He's injured, Scarlet.

Battered, bruised, and broken.

Do not look at him.

I hear the water slosh then still. When I turn back around, I find him submerged deep in the water. His head rested on the rim of the tub as he watches me.

He smiles, a light chuckle leaving his chest.

I walk to the bath and sit down on the edge. "When was the last time you had a bath?"

"A long time ago," he tells me, closing his eyes as his entire body relaxes. "I think it was here, with you."

My stomach clenches even tighter. I don't remember the last time we bathed together, but I know that I've had many baths since.

"Scar, I know there are things you can't tell me. Things you don't want to tell me. But will you tell me something? Anything?" His eyes barely part as he looks up at me. "I want to hear your voice when you tell me the things you put in those letters."

"You're reading them?"

"Slowly."

I wonder how far he's got with them. If he's read about Waverley's birth and everything after.

"What about the memorial balls you hosted? Will you tell me about them?"

A part of me screams at me not to open up to him. That if I do, I'll leave myself open to more questions and with them, pain. But Lance knows I don't want to talk about Ave or us.

I can give him parts.

Or at least I can try.

I stand and move around the bath, kneeling at his head. "I've hosted one every year. In the rain, pregnant, and with Ave as a toddler." I reach for the showerhead that attaches to the floor standing taps, turning it on and directing the water flow over Lance's shoulders and neck. He sighs, sinking down a little deeper in the water. I start wetting his hair. "It grew bigger and became more well-known year after year until it got so big, I decided it wasn't what it once was, and I went right back to basics."

"What changed?"

"Everything. People came for the wrong reasons, knowing they'd make it into the tabloids come Monday morning."

"You had media?"

"Uh-huh. Megan comes with quite the entourage now." I smile softly at the memories. "The last one before I downsized was the worst event I've ever organised."

"I don't believe it could be that bad. You wouldn't let it be bad."

"It was a mess," I promise, gently smoothing my hand through his dark hair. He groans, leaning into my touch as my fingers skim the tops of his ears. "Ask the others. We had the clean-up of our lives the next day." I reach behind me for his shampoo, squeezing it into my palm. He lets out a long, heavy exhale as I begin massaging his scalp. "Nina was right earlier. The best ones were the ones we had in the spring—after that first one, of course. I'm not sure anything will ever beat the first. But November was always hit and miss with the weather. It became impossible to plan."

There's silence for a while, and it allows my attention to turn to the suds lathering in his hair. I knew what I was doing as I chatted my way into a sitting position at the head of the bath, making the choice to take care of him.

For seven years I had no idea how this man was. I didn't know if he was okay, if he missed me, if he needed us.

I was alone and needed him desperately, but I didn't know if he felt the same.

"Did you dance?"

I come back to the now. "Did I dance?"

"Did anyone ask you to dance?" he confirms, a little sharper.

His eyes are closed, his jaw now tense. "You mean with a man. Did any men ask me to dance?"

"Yes."

I shake my head, rolling my eyes. "There was this one guy."

"Who?" He frowns.

My heart flips. *Traitorous little bitch.* "He was gorgeous. Dark hair, tall—a clean-looking man."

"Clean? What's a clean-looking man?"

I slide my hand from his hair down across his jaw. "He didn't have all this scruff."

He goes to brush his lips to my hand, but I pull back, reaching for the shower head to wash out the shampoo. "What song?"

"It was years ago." I chuckle, even though I remember.

"Was it romantic?"

"In a way, yes."

His body jolts. "What was his name?"

I smooth my thumb over his forehead, swiping away the shampoo there. I decide to put him out of his misery. "Charles."

His shoulders settle. "Aldridge?"

"It's actually the only time I've danced at an event since the first we hosted. I didn't want to. But it was the end of the night. Everyone was on the dance floor, and he wouldn't let it be. He was drunk—Lissie was driving him wild at the time."

"They weren't together?"

"No. But they weren't nothing. He came up to me, blue eyes shining, and told me to close my eyes and pretend it was you."

Lance stills under my touch.

"I guess I always did a pretty shit job of hiding my feelings when it came to you. I mean, look at me now."

He swallows, brows pinching together. "Why? What do you feel now?"

Everything. I feel everything, and it's terrifying because I can't. I let Mason back in and with Mason came Nina.

Waverley is my entire world, my only reason. And now Lance is here, home, making me feel *everything*.

I sigh, carefully rinsing the shampoo from his hair. "I feel like I'm running toward the sun, afraid that at any minute it'll be knocked from the sky, leaving me in total darkness. Like there's nothing I can do to stop it or save them."

"Save them?"

I frown, staring deep into the water. "Mase, Nina, Ave. I can't keep them safe, and I know I wouldn't survive losing them."

"Why would you lose them?"

I look down at him, my smile barely forming as I try to pull back a little. "Everything disappears eventually, Lance. It's a part of being. The good gives way to the bad like the day gives way to night."

"They're not going to go anywhere. You're family. Mason and Nina. The kids."

I want to argue with him. I want to tell him that he's wrong because it's life, and it happens, and we can't change that.

"They're not going anywhere, Scarlet," he repeats.

I close my eyes in a bid to block him out, my fingers stroking lazy circles from his temples to the base of his neck. After a while he goes quiet, and I'm almost certain he's drifted off to sleep. I lean against the bath, my hand still passing through the short dark hair at his ears as I watch him.

I want to believe Lance. I want to wake up—to fall asleep —without the constant dread that something awful is going to happen every single day. But I've loved and lost and broken repeatedly throughout my life. I'm not sure there's ever been a time I've not lived through one of the three. And maybe it's messed up for me to wait for it, to look around corners to see it coming, but better that than to be naive to the way of the world. To the way it can so easily humble me.

I once allowed myself to love this man. Everything that he was. He took it all from me, including my heart, but I took his, too. I bundled it up in my arms clinging on so tight, never thinking I'd have to let go—never wanting to. I thought I deserved to be happy and in love for a little while, that it was my time.

I was naive and stupid to believe that because it was all taken away from me.

As the bath threatens to lose its warmth, I wake him.

"Lance," I whisper, my voice thick.

I'm tired.

Tired and confused.

"Lance," I try again.

I trace his brow, my hand smoothing over his jaw, not really wanting to wake him up at all. "Lance."

"Hmm."

An overwhelming burn rages in my throat, and I fight to swallow it down. *You don't love this man, Scar. You don't.* "You should go to bed."

His eyes part lazily, his neck twisting so he can look at me. His head rests in my palm, and as I go to pull back, he catches my wrist, bringing it to his mouth to kiss the centre. His nose dusts over where his lips touched, sending a shiver snaking down my spine.

God, I miss being in love with him, though.

I miss being in love with him more than I've ever missed anything.

His eyes flicker to mine as he effortlessly claws back the little pieces of us we lost. "If I could crawl inside of you and live there, I would," he whispers. "I'm pretty sure it's the safest place on earth."

EIGHTEEN

Lance

"**B**ear, you bastard, you better drop it."

I step left, but he goes right, his tail wagging as he pounces front to back on his paws, bounding around the garden.

You'd think he is a damn puppy.

I was taking my second sip of coffee this morning when a flash of beige caught my eye at the front door.

Scarlet is out, thankfully, taking Waverley to school.

Thankfully, because the flash of beige was Bear, and the trail that led me to him were twigs and mud from the bird's nest that's currently hanging from his muzzle.

"Bear!" I drag my hand through my hair. *Shit.* "Bear, drop!"

He stops, getting low with his feet planted, readying to bolt. I take a hesitant step toward him. "Bear—"

He takes off.

With the swelling in my leg only now easing, I'm not about to chase the shitting dog around the back garden. "Bear, damn it, you better drop it."

The nest starts to fall apart in his jaw as he pounces through the overgrown grass.

"Here. Now." I whistle, at a loss. "Bear!" I thunder.

He stops in his tracks, turning to me, and coming to my feet. I bend down and force his mouth open, pulling out the mangled nest.

Although it's not a nest anymore.

I close my eyes, sighing when I find it empty.

The feel of a wet snout nuzzling my hand draws my attention down. I open my eyes to look at him. "What did you do, mate?"

His mouth parts, a great big tongue hanging free as he pants.

I spend the next hour and a half scouring the grass for the baby bird, knowing Waverley will be devastated if he's gone.

With no luck, no sign of Scarlet, and my leg feeling like it has its own heartbeat, I head inside the house to find my phone.

I call the one person I know would do anything for my child, no matter how much he hates me.

"A fucking bird?" Charlie questions, looking in his mirrors as he pulls out from the narrow lane and onto the main road. "Where did she find it?"

"It was in the nest."

"The nest that Bear ate," he confirms. "Do you think he ate the bird?"

"No." I frown. "I don't think so."

"But it was gone."

"I couldn't find it," I tell him, running my hand over my face. "There's a rescue centre out by the old mill. I'll see if they have any we can buy."

"That's your plan? Replace it with another?"

"What else do I do? She left me in charge of it."

He looks at me and then back at the road. "They're not just going to give you a bird, Sullivan. It's a rescue centre not a pet shop."

"I'll talk to them."

"And say what? We found a bird, killed it, and now need another one for my dog to eat?"

I close my eyes, sighing.

"Yeah. I'm not coming inside. You're on your own."

"I called you because I thought you cared about Waverley enough to help me."

"And I'm here, aren't I?" he counters. "And Ave is smart. She'd think this is the stupidest idea in the world."

"Well, I'm not telling her he's dead. I'll see if I can get her the bird, and if not, I'll find a way around it."

"You could just say it flew off."

I shake my head. "It doesn't even have feathers."

He chuckles to himself. "She once rescued a squirrel. Did she tell you?"

"No."

"We'd just got back from the lodges. Vinny went to start the cars, just to make sure all was okay for the morning, and he found this baby squirrel. Ave caught it and brought it inside. Mangy looking thing. She kept it for over a month, hand feeding it, before she let it out into the wild. She thinks it comes back every year, but..." He looks over at me and smiles. And the fondness in that smile, the way I've never seen him smile that way, it tells me what I already knew. "I don't know. It could be any squirrel."

"She's so much like Scar," I say, chuckling.

"She is," he agrees, and the gentleness in his tone, it's confident, it's knowing. Because he made a promise to look after her, and he did.

"You went above and beyond for them." We don't look at one another, but I see the grip Charlie has on the steering wheel turn white-knuckled. "Scarlet wrote about you in her letters, told me how you travelled out to the prison every day. I haven't read many of them yet. I'm still trying to get my head around it all." I readjust in the seat, focusing on the road ahead. "I guess thank you feels... not enough."

"It's enough," he interjects.

I nod, swallowing around the guilt lodged in my throat. "How about I'm sorry?"

His cheek tics, the only tell he's pissed off with me. Or hurt. I'm pretty sure I hurt my friend.

"Aldridge, I could sit here and explain my reasoning, but what good is it to you now? I just want you to know that I'm aware of how badly I fucked up. That I know you were there for Scarlet when I shut her out. That you still showed up when I shut you out. And I'm sorry. I regret it more than anything. It's done, and I don't expect a thing from you or your friendship. The same as I don't expect a thing from Scarlet and Waverley." I crack my neck, my tongue swiping across my teeth. "I just need you to know that I've never taken your friendship for granted. I know it probably seemed like I didn't care and that it was easy for me to just block you all out, but—"

"Do you think I think that? That it was easy?"

I look toward him, not bothering to mask the emotion I know is painted across my face. "I don't know what you thought. You've barely muttered five words to me since I got out."

He sniggers and looks away again. "The number of nights I lay in my bed cursing you for not talking to us. Needing you to just pick up the phone if nothing else and explain that you wanted her to move on. I'd spend the day doing everything I could to see you and then go home and would have to tell Scarlet there was still nothing. I'd go over it constantly, trying to figure out what you were thinking. Why you were doing it. For a while, I was angry at you for hurting her, but you know what pissed me off more? What makes me want to clobber you in the face every time I look at you, even now?" He looks from me to the road. "It's the fact you did what you did to yourself. That you knew we'd be here for you, but you didn't know yourself well enough to see you deserved it."

I stare at him, my chest going tight.

"Years of friendship, of family, and you treated yourself no better than a fucking criminal."

His words cut deep. Too deep. "You'd have let me tell her to move on? You think she'd have even listened? I needed her to find a shred of happiness, Charlie. To come out the other side of the shitstorm that was hanging over her."

"And what about you?" he snaps, making my heart sink. "What about you, Lance? Are you unscathed? Scarlet had all of us. You knew that. You knew she was going to be okay because you knew she had me!" He shakes his head as he tries to compose himself. "I spent months watching her struggle after Ave was born. Watched her fight her way back to her feet, too," he rasps, lowering his tone. "But what about you? Who did you have?"

I clench my jaw, not having an answer.

"You had nobody. Because you couldn't bear the idea of burdening us, your family, with a life we'd long decided to walk with you." He turns into the old mill rescue centre and sits for a minute, just staring straight ahead. "Of course it's fucking enough." He nods toward the entrance. "Go get your bird."

The rescue centre doesn't give me a bird. I climb back into the car, feeling defeated and a little fucked physically and mentally.

"Did you tell them it was for a child?"

I side-eye Charlie, and he sighs. "I tried everything. It's against their *moral code*."

He passes me his phone. "Put that address into the navigation."

I run my hand through my hair and type in the address. "Wings Ridge Rescue."

He looks across at me and nods. "There's a list of at least fifty centres around the UK in my Notes app."

I check the address he's given me, noting the centre is an hour's drive. "But you've—"

"But nothing," Charlie interjects, glancing at me again. "Put in the address, Sullivan."

We don't find a bird at the first, second, or third shop we go to, and as we drive down the motorway, putting more and more tarmac between us and home, the hope to find a bird for Waverley seems to lessen with every mile covered.

I have my head rested against the seat, the fields whipping past one after another as I take in the views.

I've not been this far from home since getting out of prison. When I was inside, I'd fantasise about all the places I'd travel to once I was out, the places I'd go on my bike—the freedom I'd have. But now that I know about Waverley, and with my duffed-up leg, I can't help but not want to be anywhere but one place. On the estate.

It's the only place I've ever felt a sense of home.

Charlie's phone starts to ring through the car's speaker, and he reaches out to answer. "Lis. I'm not alone."

I hear her tut. "Who's the fun sponge today?"

Charlie glances across at me, his face stony. "Lance."

"Oh. Well, that's unexpectedly wonderful. Am I to add him to the Christmas card list after all?"

His lip twitches the slightest bit. "Not yet."

"Keeping it awkward and honest as always, Mr Aldridge. What time should I expect you home?"

"I'll be late." He checks the time. "Maybe eight-ish."

"Hmm. Make it eight fifteen with a bottle of our favourite, and I'll meet you in the tub."

Charlie readjusts in his seat, his smile creasing his eyes. "Deal."

"Lance," Lissie adds.

I glance at Charlie, and he shrugs.

I sit up a little in my seat. "Yes?"

"He's been like a lovesick puppy ever since you got home and not over me. Don't let his stubbornness fool you into thinking he doesn't love you. He's really good at that. I find flattery and a good push-up bra works wonders on the man."

I laugh out loud. "I'll keep that in mind, thank you."

I hear her chuckling. "I love you, Charles."

She hangs up before he can reply.

"Lissie Aldridge," I mutter into the silence, letting her name hang in the air between us as I continue to rest back in the seat.

I sense Charlie's smile without needing to look at him.

"How'd you two meet?"

"The club."

My brows rise as I drop my head to the side. "Really?"

"And the office."

"The office? A client?"

He shakes his head. "No. Of course she wasn't a client."

"Then what? She worked for you?" I ask, shocked. "Fuck, you broke rules."

He sniggers as if remembering that time. "All of them."

"Fuck," I say. "There was a time, if I'm being honest, when I didn't think you'd ever change."

"There was a time I knew I wouldn't change," he replies. "I still look back now and wonder how she did it."

I watch him, genuine happiness spreading through me at the idea of him finding his own happiness. "Happens without even realising it sometimes, doesn't it?"

Charlie turns to look at me, but I drop my eyes, thinking back.

"One day you're telling her you want to take her on a date, and the next, you're lying awake at night watching her sleep, wondering why a freckle on her cheek seems like the most sacred thing on earth."

Or the rise and fall of her chest, as I count each beat of her heart, curious—desperate—for it to know me.

"You still love her."

I lift my gaze to Charlie's. "Without reason," I tell him. "I mean, I can sit here and give you a million. But it's more than the person she is, you know. Or the way she makes me feel. It's more than words."

"But you questioned her." He gives me a hard look. "You asked her if she'd met someone else."

I clench my fists at the idea. "Charlie, I wouldn't know peace if she was with another man. But if she found hers, if she was truly happy... well then, I'd rot and wallow in the memories. In every freckle I memorised, every beat of her heart, and every fucking mason jar she'd fill with flowers for someone else. I'm pretty sure if she was happy—truly at peace, I'd be alright."

"You'd be alright... if she was with another man."

"Don't."

I hear him chuckle deep in his chest, his tall frame

shaking slightly in the seat. "Are you planning on getting her back? Mason said you've not tried a thing."

"She made it clear she didn't want that. I'm Dad now. That's it."

"But... but what about the freckles?"

"Fuck you."

He fights his smile. "I'm serious. What are you talking about *you're Dad, and that's it*? You're living in her house."

"Because I didn't have a single other fucker willing to help me."

He throws me a hard stare. "Sure. So, the two of you haven't had a single moment. A glance that's lasted a second too long?"

I swallow and cast my gaze away, focusing on the road ahead.

"When was the last time you spent time alone with her?"

My mind instantly goes back to this morning, but it gets chased away by memories of last night. She'd sat beside the bath, her hands on my face, my hair—fucking everything I needed—coaxing me to sleep. And then this morning, as she sat up in the chair, her eyes tired, she didn't so much as look at me as she slipped from the room before anyone would notice.

"She's still in love with you. You do know that, don't you?"

I frown, shaking my head instinctively. "How can she be after everything—even if she wanted to, I wouldn't blame her if she didn't. I've barely scratched the surface with her letters, but if the end is anything like the beginning, I'm pretty sure

I'll hate myself enough for the both of us by the time I'm done."

"You don't get to decide that. You've learnt nothing. Scarlet didn't wait for you, but she didn't move on either. She might've moved forward with life, her job and family, but she never left you behind. Not like you wanted."

"It's not what I wanted." Not even a little bit. "But what sort of person asks that of someone? She was locked up in that house for years away from the real world. No matter how much she says she did it for Anthony, I knew what she needed. I watched her come back to life that summer. Saw her for what she was."

"We all saw it," Charlie agrees.

"I couldn't have her go back to that. I needed her to live."

He nods. "You know, when she found out she was pregnant, she was on cloud nine. It was as if she found her sparkle again."

"When did she tell you?"

"Technically she didn't. Nina was worried and came to me. Scar was losing weight. She told Nina it was because she couldn't keep her food down. I think Nina knew before anybody else."

I would have noticed. If I was there, I'd have noticed. "Did anyone go with her to the appointments?"

"All of us at one point or another. Although it was Megan and Freya who somehow got bedside when Scar was taken into surgery for the birth."

"Megs?"

Charlie nods, his attention on the road. "They're all just

as close as they were. Nothing really changed with those girls."

That's good. She needed good friends. "Her and Mase figured things out, too."

"It definitely took time, but yeah, Mase really pulled his finger out."

I should be happy, but it never should've taken Mason the years it did to realise that his sister needed him.

"You want me to come in this time?" Charlie asks, pulling off the motorway and taking the turn to *Little Lo's Rescue.*

I shift to look at him, knowing it wasn't lost miles on the road today. The two of us needed this. "You think you can do a better job than me?"

His smirk is full of confidence. "Always, Sullivan. Always."

The second we step foot in the shop, I know that inviting Charlie inside was a dangerous game.

"Generous. So generous." The rescue centre owner slides her glasses back up her nose, smoothing out her greying hair that's pulled back in a loose plait. "Let me show you the rest of the centre. We have—"

"As much as we appreciate your time, Mrs Tessen, we need to hit the road to get back before dark."

"Of course." She nods, her eyes going wide as Charlie signs the cheque and slides it across the desk. "Wow."

"You have my details. If you have any issues banking it—"

"Thank you. Thank you so much. You don't know how much of a difference this will make here. We don't... we don't get donations like this." Her gaze slides to the baby bird that's securely nestled in the box I'm holding. It came in just days ago, and fortunately for us, it looks exactly like the bird Waverley found in the back garden. "Please, remember everything I told you."

"We'll take good care of it," Charlie promises, giving the lady a gentle nod before leaving the shop.

I follow, catching up with him at the car. "I'll pay you back."

"I don't want your money, Sullivan." He gets in swiftly and shuts his door.

I climb in, careful to not knock or jolt the bird. "I'm paying you back."

He pulls on his seat belt, then looks across at me. "You want to pay me back?"

"You just donated ten thousand pounds for a featherless bird. I think—"

"Make it right." He watches as I swallow down the rest of my words. "She loves you, Lance. If you don't use this opportunity to win her back, you're a fucking idiot."

My brows lift as I try to lighten the blow. "You think getting run over by a car is an opportunity?"

"I think meeting someone like Scarlet, someone who forgives and loves and cares like she does, is an opportunity." He starts the engine and turns the car around, heading for home. "You both deserve to be happy. So, make it right."

NINETEEN

Lance

Despite the fact I'm in agony and haven't taken any pain medication since this morning, I make my way up the stairs at Lowerwick on one crutch, with the biggest smile on my face, the baby bird safely secured in a cage in my other hand.

I didn't think we'd pull it off. Not with the resounding "no" we were given at every centre we tried.

But I did it.

I got her the bird.

I push open Waverley's bedroom door with a smile stretching my cheeks, knowing this will make her happy.

My smile drops when I find Scarlet sitting on Waverley's bed, a hair band hanging from between her lips as she plaits Waverley's hair.

I swing the small cage I bought at the pet shop behind my back.

"Hi," I say as Scarlet looks up at me.

"Where have you been?" she mumbles, quickly reaching up to take the band from her mouth. "You've been gone all day, and you missed dinner."

"Yeah, I'm starved," I tell her, using my crutch to work my way backward out of the room. Waverley will kill me if I give up the Mingo secret.

"There's pasta in the oven," Scarlet says, looking back down as she finishes the plait.

"What's that?" Waverley asks, wiping her face.

I shake my head to tell her to shut up immediately.

Scarlet looks up, down, and then up again. She frowns, peering behind my back. "What *is* that?"

"Uh, nothing."

They both wear matching *What the fuck* frowns.

Waverley sniffles as she scoots off the bed, and I notice the dried tears on her cheeks. I'm instantly down on my good knee in front of her. "Waverley."

She throws her arms around my neck, hugging me.

Shit. She knows. I close my eyes and wrap my arms around her. I knew it would break her heart finding out he was dead. If only I'd found the bird quicker or let her bring it inside sooner. "No, don't cry. Look, Mingo is fine. He's right here." I reach around and pick up the cage. "Here. Look. I took him on a little trip to get a cage."

"Is that another damn bird?" Scarlet asks, and I give her a look, telling her not to be so insensitive. She stands and moves to get a closer look.

"W-what?" Waverley croaks, pulling back. "That's not Mingo."

"Yes, it is. Look."

She looks up at me with teary eyes. "No, it isn't."

Fuck.

Of course she'd know it's not the same bird.

I close my eyes, gutted that I've completely fucked it.

"Waverley, please don't cry, baby. I thought I'd be able to get back before you noticed him missing. I'm so sorry."

"What are you talking about?" She kneels to get a closer look into the cage.

"When I went to check on Mingo this morning, I found him dead. Bear somehow got to his nest." I shake my head, devastated. "I knew it would upset you. I just wanted to replace him." I shrug, a sick feeling stirring in my gut as Waverley looks at me absolutely mortified. "I didn't think you'd notice, but I get how silly that was now."

I peer up at Scarlet, feeling like I've gone from dad of the year to a lying son of a bitch in three seconds flat.

Seeing Waverley so upset over this is like a spear to the heart, and I can only hope that the look I'm trying to convey to Scarlet shows I only wanted to make our daughter happy.

I shake my head at her, at a loss.

A chuckle slips past her lips, and my face goes slack, my eyes widening. "*Scarlet.*"

She covers her mouth, trying and failing to hide it. "Sorry."

I hear Waverley chuckle, too, and snap my gaze down to her.

My mouth opens and closes, but nothing comes out.

"You went and found me a new bird because Mingo was

dead?" Waverley asks, her shoulders shaking. *"That's* where you've been all day?"

I nod, rubbing at my chest as the ache starts to ebb away. "Your uncle Charlie drove me all the way down to Devon to find it."

She laughs harder.

Scarlet loses all control and snorts.

"What?" I say, a nervous laugh forcing its way out.

Waverley glances at her mum and then gets up, walking to her nook. She reaches in and pulls out a slightly larger cage next to the one at my feet. "Mingo isn't dead. I was crying because you were gone, and we didn't know where you were. I thought you left." She looks at Scarlet. "Mum caught me making a new home for Mingo with her dried flowers last night. She told me I should've told her right away after I found him and then took me to get him a new cage early this morning before school."

I stare at the cage in her hands. "Tell me that cage is empty," I mutter.

Scarlet continues to laugh, her hand on her stomach.

"It's definitely not empty, Dad." Waverley grins.

I scrub at my face, shaking my head. "I thought."

They both continue to laugh. "I thought he was dead."

"So, you..." Waverley chuckles. "So you drove all the way to Devon with Uncle Charlie to get another one?" Waverley bumps into Scarlet, both of them struggling for breath.

"It's not funny," I mutter, pulling at my hair.

"Oh, Lance," Scarlet croons, her eyes watering. "You're very sweet."

"The way he was pretending, though." Waverley holds

up the new cage. "*Look, Mingo is right here.*" She barely gets the last word out, setting Scarlet off all over again.

I drop my head back in defeat, listening to their laughter and letting it settle into my bones. My leg throbs, but all I can think about is how we drove for eight hours today to replace a bird that wasn't dead, and the fact I waited seven years to hear that laugh—her laugh—only to get the both of them like this.

My chest rumbles with my own laughter.

I right my head and take them in, feeling like the luckiest, lying son of a bitch in the world.

It's a good fucking feeling.

"*I took him on a little trip to get a cage,*" Waverley repeats, falling back to the bed in hysterics.

I shake my head, bending over as my laugh deepens so much, I can't stop, just as lost as they are. "Just wait," I try. "Just wait until you hear how much Charlie paid for it."

Their laughter goes silent as they lose complete control.

And I know that no matter how badly my body might be screaming at me, no matter how tired or out of pocket I am from travelling all day, the bird doesn't matter.

None of it matters.

Nothing but them and this moment right here.

It was never about the bird.

Scarlet

Lance is already on the landing when I leave my bedroom to make my way to his. It's past midnight, and the whole house is quiet, everyone long gone to bed.

There's a plethora of reasons I haven't gone to his room before now, the most obvious one being that I shouldn't. He's here to heal. To get better so that he can go home and build a new normal there.

Regardless of that fact, I've made this walk every night since I found Lance in the throes of that nightmare.

"I thought maybe you'd given up on me," he rasps, voice low.

I dip my head to my shoulder. "Trust me, I've tried."

His smile lights up his whole face. "You coming?" he asks, cocking his head toward his room.

I make my way to him, side-eyeing him as I reach him. When we get to his room, he pushes open the door with one hand, holding it open for me to pass. "You're extra smiley tonight," I tell him.

He chuckles, setting his crutch straight to follow me in. "I have plenty to smile about."

"You do?" I say, not helping my own smile.

"I do."

"You're not going to give me any more than that?"

He shrugs, watching me as I pick up the pillow and walk to the chair below the window. "I think it's pretty self-explanatory." A frown. "Sleep in the bed. I'll take the chair tonight."

I chuckle, sitting down. "We're long past gentlemanly gestures, Lance. I'm here so that you can heal quicker. And besides, I sleep better in this chair than I do in my own bed."

"Hmm. Because that has nothing to do with the lack of shift work you're currently doing?"

As observant as ever. "Maybe," I mutter, placing the pillow behind my head and leaning back in the chair. "You should get some sleep. I have the girls coming over tomorrow to start plans for the ball."

His head dips, and he nods. I narrow my eyes on him, instantly knowing he needs something. Maybe even needed something so badly, he was on his way to ask me for it. "What is it?" I ask.

He readjusts on his crutches, reaching up to rub the back of his neck. "I was going to ask you to read to me. It's late, though, you're right."

"Read to you?" I frown.

He stares at me, looking lost. "Like we used to." He drops his eyes, as if reminding me somehow takes him back. "I have your letters, and I'm making my way through them, but..."

I had to read my mother's diaries alone for years before I met him, and while I'm not sure how it would've felt to have my mum read her words aloud to me, the entries Lance did read, the ones we shared together, well, those were the ones I remember most. The ones that mean more.

"I'll read one," I tell him. "Where are they?"

His brows lift in surprise, and then he makes his way around the bed, pulling open the top drawer. I stand and walk to the bed, sitting back against the pillows.

He hands me the letters, the top few torn into.

Words he's already read.

"I'm not very far in. I tend to read one and need a while to digest."

I huff out a humourless laugh, looking up into his eyes. "I wish I had that luxury as I lived it."

"I know," he says sincerely. "Or at least I'm learning." He takes the letters, sliding out the ones he's read before handing the stack back to me. "You don't have to read them. I'm being a fucking coward."

I drop my gaze to the letters, my thumb dusting over the small tears in the paper. "You're not a coward, Lance."

He waits for me to focus back on him before he smirks and says, "I was on my way to get you just now."

I smile back, shaking my head. "And I was already halfway out the door." I close my eyes, debating whether I actually want to read the things I put in these letters out loud. I can barely remember the words, just the time. "It's been years."

"If going back is too painful, Scarlet—"

"Get comfy," I tell him, resting my head down on the pillow.

I pull out the letter on top and open it.

"*Lance,*

I'm on bed rest and losing my mind.

They won't let me work, Mason won't let me breathe without shitting himself, and Nina might as well move in. I feel coddled and trapped, and I'm mad at you because if you were here, they'd all leave me alone.

To say things have taken a turn since the last time I wrote is an understatement. I have preeclampsia, a condition that can affect women during pregnancy. I remember learning about it briefly last year, and yet I didn't pick up on the signs. It wasn't until a visit to my midwife where I told her about the headaches I've been getting that they tested me. She asked to see my hands and feet, and I knew, remembered instantly. They've been swollen for weeks.

The baby is okay. My blood pressure is still high, but they're monitoring us both. I'm trying my best to listen. It's hard when there's so much to do before the baby gets here, but everyone is here to help me.

I think I'm going to paint the baby's bedroom cream. Doesn't that sound awful?

I didn't want to find out the baby's sex. I know that Mum and Dad never knew with Mason and me, and she told me how special that was for them. She always went on about the day I have children, giving me all these tips and tricks, which seemed so typically her and her rambling. I never thought I'd need those words so soon.

I think part of the reason I didn't want to find out the sex was because even if I did, you wouldn't know. So, by not finding out, neither of us know. It feels like it's all we have between us right now. A secret.

I started planning the memorial ball this week. Nina has no idea, and I plan to book as much as I can before telling any of them. I'm almost certain Mason will shut the whole thing down when he finds out, but I can't lie here and not do anything. I have the resources to plan it from my bed, I even contacted the team you used last year who took everything away for us. I won't lift a finger.

I'm lying. I'll definitely make some sort of flower arrangements for the tables and grounds, but I swear that will be it.

Mum and Dad gave us so much. They deserve one night of the year dedicated to them.

I'll hate not having you here with us for it. It's still super weird coming home from work and not having you somewhere in the house. You belong here. I didn't see it before, but I think this house became just as much a home to you than your mother's ever was.

You were you here, and you were loved.

To me, that's a real home.

I have absolutely nothing to do, but if I don't stop writing, I won't ever stop.

I miss you a little bit more every day.

Just keep me busy, okay. Stay running around and around in my mind while I get through this.

Never forget how much I love you. It's an ungodly amount, and unfortunate at times, and infinite.

Infinite always,

Your sunshine."

I frown as I stop reading, my eyes rolling over the words as if seeing them for the first time all over again.

"Scar." Lance's thumb connects with my cheek, drawing my attention up to him. We're lay on the bed facing one another, the letter clutched in my hand. "You okay?"

"I forgot," I whisper.

"You got sick?"

My chest burns, my eyes filling with tears as my words play over and over. "I didn't listen. I went through with the ball that year."

Lance watches me, his gaze vivid and locked on me.

"Ave was born prematurely, Lance." I wet my lips, more tears falling as my guilt overwhelms me. "I didn't listen, and she almost died."

"Don't cry," he mutters, wiping away my tears. "She didn't die, Scar. She's here, and she's perfect."

I push his hand away. "It was bad. She was in hospital for months. I almost lost..." I shake my head, frowning. "I can't talk about it tonight, I'm sorry. I know you need to know, but... I can't... I—"

He takes my face in his hands, forcing my gaze to his. "You don't apologise. Do you hear me? *I'm* the one who's sorry." His thumb grazes my temple, his eyes sad. "You never should've gone through it alone. I should've been here. I had a choice, and I made the wrong one. I cut you off. I'll spend the rest of my life regretting that."

I take a deep breath and ease back until his hands leave my face.

I huff a laugh, sitting up on the bed, wiping my face myself. "And you said you were the coward. I can't even talk about this stuff without getting into a complete mess."

"We all have scars we can't talk about," he says, pulling himself up and resting against the headboard. "When you're ready—if you're ready, I'll be here to listen." He takes the letters back. "We don't have to read these."

I put a hand over his, stopping him. "Don't get rid of them."

He shakes his head. "I wouldn't."

There was a reason he kept the letters all those years. I can't help but wonder if him bringing them back here that day was about more than just closure. "I promise I'll give you everything there is of her. One day soon, I will."

"I know you will." He gives me a small smile, opening the

drawer and dropping them back inside. "You've already given me more than I deserve."

We stare at one another, so much left unsaid.

"Please sleep in the bed?" he eventually asks.

I drop his gaze and stand from the mattress. "No."

Grabbing my pillow, I hug it to my chest as I go and turn out the main light. Then, I settle back in the chair, looking up at the moon shining in through the window before letting my tired eyes drift closed.

"Scarlet," Lance says.

"Hmm," I mutter back.

"Infinite is a way better word than indefinitely."

I smile.

Because he's right.

It is.

TWENTY

Lance

My heart jolts with the thud of a door echoing into my sleep.

My eyes snap open.

I grip the sheets in my fists, quickly ripping them off my legs as I search the room, the door.

I blink and blink again.

Where's the—

I flinch, clenching my eyes closed as another door booms closed, the sound reverberating through the cells.

I can't... I can't get the sheet off my legs.

"Fuck. No. No, no."

They're coming.

I look up for the door but it's not there.

"Lance."

No. No. No. The door. Where's the door? Another door

crashes shut, and I kick at the sheets, desperately trying to get them off me.

"Lance!"

My eyes fly open.

"Lance, it's me. It's Scarlet. I'm here. I'm here."

I push her back, standing quickly when she stumbles. "Get away from me!"

"Lance. It's me. You're safe."

I look down at myself, my T-shirt stuck to me, dripping in sweat. "Fuck..." I can hardly breathe. "Leave—"

A large boom ripples over the house, my entire body recoiling as I tense.

"Thunder," Scarlet tells me in realisation. "Lance, it's just thunder."

Her eyes are wide, fixed on me, and the sorrow, the pain and pity. I fight to keep the bile rising in my throat from coming up.

She goes to step toward me, but I shake my head, telling her without words not to come any closer as my chest heaves.

Breath after ragged breath, I will my heart to slow. To just ease the slightest bit.

"Let me... I'll run the shower. Let me run the shower," she croaks.

My entire body trembles, and as Scarlet steps away from me, my knees threaten to give out.

Not again.

Not with her as a witness.

I hear the shower turn on, and my eyes drift closed.

A thunderous roar rages above the house, and I sway, the

ripples roving the floorboards underfoot and echoing throughout my entire body.

My breathing gets heavier.

My chest constricting.

I turn my head toward the bathroom. To where she disappeared. And as I do, Scarlet steps into the doorway, her stance hesitant as she watches me. Yet knowing swims in her eyes.

Something inside of me cracks. "I need—you."

Her feet move before I can fumble out all the words, as if she did know, and her mind was already made up. She runs to me without thought, and the moment she's close enough, I haul her against me, her small frame settling between my arms like a lost puzzle piece.

She looks up at me, her searching eyes desperate. "It's okay." A promise.

Another crack of thunder rattles the house, and I tighten my hold on her, my heart kick-starting all over again after barely slowing.

I clench my eyes tight, feeling sweat run down my jaw.

The warmth of her small hand seeps into my chest as she settles it against my skin, covering my heart. "Lance," she whispers. "Open your eyes, and look at me."

I do, finding her staring diligently up at me. Her other hand smooths across the side of my head, down over my jaw. "It's okay. I'm right here."

I shake my head, barely able to stand steady on my feet as my throat thickens. "Scar."

"It's okay." She keeps her hands skin to skin, her body pressed against mine. It's as if she's trying to shield me, protect me, from the fear I can't hide from her, no matter how hard I try.

More thunder rumbles, and I clench my eyes tight, agitation thinning my lips at the knee-jerk reaction. *Fuck.*

"Look. At. Me," Scarlet demands, grasping me by the back of the neck.

I want to look at her, need the warmth and safety and home I've only ever found in her eyes, but it terrifies me what she might find staring back.

I hear a cry from somewhere in the house, and my eyes immediately open. "Waverley," I panic.

"She's okay."

"But—"

"Ellis," she tells me. "She'll go to Ellis before me, always." She runs her hand from my shoulder to the centre of my chest. "Lance, you need to breathe. It's okay. You're safe."

I drop my head forward, but she catches it with her own, forcing it up. I stare into her eyes, this woman who, despite all life has thrown at her, will stand here now, steadying my feet to the ground.

"I don't deserve you," I utter. "I don't deserve to exist in this world whilst you walk it. I'll never understand how— why." I stand in the middle of the room trembling, desperately clinging to her. "Scarlet—"

"It's okay," she whispers again, her nose brushing mine. "Just let us be." My lips drag over her nose, her cheek, skirting too close to her mouth. "You're safe. Whatever you need, Lance."

I flex my hands as they flatten against her back, smoothing over soft skin.

"Let us be," she repeats.

I bring my hand up to cup her face, my fingers threading into the silky hair behind her ear. It's been seven years since I've held her this close. Something deep in my chest surges at the thought. Regardless of circumstance, she's here in my arms, dancing blindly with me tonight.

Charlie's words scuttle around my brain. *Make it right.*

I lower my lips to brush gently over hers, and she shudders, brown eyes flicking up to mine.

I do it again, slower, deliberate, and then I lay my forehead back on hers, swallowing thickly as my cock pulses in my boxer briefs.

When Scarlet steps back, my heart constricts, and I fight the urge to drop to my knees and beg her to forgive me right here and now, to love me like I never left, while I promise her I'll never hurt her again.

But she deserves more than a man at her feet, begging for forgiveness.

She deserves something I can't give her because undoing what I've done is impossible.

"Careful on your leg," she tells me gently as she pulls me by the hand into the bathroom. She doesn't bother switching on the light, the moon our guide as it looms beyond the window. The shower is already running, warm enough a thick steam starts to gather around us.

My heart thuds against my chest, sweat still running down my back, as Scarlet pulls her vest over her head, dropping it to the ground and then stepping out of her pyjama bottoms.

I'm fixated on her as she peels my T-shirt from my skin,

letting it gather at my ribs before tilting up her chin for me to lift my arms so that she can ease it over my head.

Silently, she kneels, removing my boxer briefs.

I fight the urge to cover my hard-on, wordlessly following her when she stands, relinks our fingers, and directs me to sit on the deep ledge in the shower.

I tip my head back, letting the water run over my face until she shadows the spray, droplets deflecting off her in rivulets and speckling my shoulders. She brings her body close, too close, until it's all I can do but lift my hands to the smooth skin at the backs of her thighs.

My cock strains at the feel of her pebbled skin against my fingertips. After so much time, after believing I'd never hold her like this, at all, again. "I'm sorry," I tell her, knowing she noticed my erection before. "It's been a while."

And you're too fucking perfect.

Her hands drag through my hair, forcing my head back so she can see me. She looks down at me, and it takes everything in me to keep my eyes on hers when her breasts sit heavy in my periphery. I wet my lips, locking our gaze.

She reaches between us, and my breath catches, her hand trailing my forearm around to her back where she takes my hand. She lifts it, placing it over her heart. "We don't apologise for this."

Her heart pounds beneath my splayed palm, a continuous, fierce, uninterrupted beat that I've missed. *Fuck*, I've missed this.

I drop my gaze, needing to see, but a frown pulls my brows when I notice the tattoo marked into her pale skin.

I sit forward.

Vines curve down and around her left breast. The pads of my fingers trail over the stem, over the leaves. Lower. And then they pause, my heart matching her erratic beat.

The tattoo is the exact same design as my own, but at the bottom, just disappearing on the underside of her left breast, *hopelessly fucking wild* is inked into her skin. "Scarlet..."

"Nobody's ever made my heart race quite like you do," she whispers, her eyes not leaving mine. "I'm sorry it chose tonight to remember you."

I drop my head forward to rest between her breasts, my hands gliding across soft skin to curl around the backs of her thighs again. She stands with her hands running through my hair, letting me unravel, unravelling herself.

My lips part, teasing the ink. "Sunshine," I rasp, not even certain she's real. "You'll never know how much I missed you." I kiss the underside of her breast.

I feel her shudder, and then she climbs onto my lap, her knees hugging my sides as she brings us chest to chest. She lifts her sad eyes to mine, tearing into my soul momentarily before she buries her face in my neck.

My hands roam from the top of her neck to the base of her spine, the tips of my fingers grazing her ass as I smooth down the length of her spread thighs, and back up again.

I can't get her close enough, can't touch enough of her skin.

"Lance," she whispers, her lips brushing my jaw as her head tilts back. I drop my chin, bringing our noses a hair's width apart. "I missed you, too."

I swallow thickly as my eyes trace every line of her face onto my heart. "I want to kiss you," I tell her.

Her lips quirk, and then she inches forward the slightest bit. "Then kiss me."

My lips skim hers. I shake my head. "I won't stop." *Not ever.*

Brown eyes flutter into focus, searching my own. "Then kiss me."

My chest rumbles as I seal my mouth over hers in a slow but deep kiss, our lips lingering as one for what feels like minutes. Her fingers run through my scalp, teasing the roots of my hair and pulling me impossibly closer as she slips her tongue past my lips to tangle with mine.

I groan into her mouth, my hands smoothing and squeezing my favourite parts of her body.

"Scarlet." She tugs my bottom lip between her teeth. My cock is hard and straining between our stomachs, her pussy resting at the base and impossible to ignore.

"Scarlet, I... I'm..."

She leans back, dragging her pussy up the length of my cock and moaning. "Please."

Did she just... I grab her hips to halt her. I'll come in seconds if she doesn't stop. "Scarlet," I hiss, her hips defying my pathetic hold and grinding up my length.

"You want me," she says, looking down at me with heavy eyes.

I reach up and pull her chest to mine, taking her mouth in another kiss. I shake my head as she pulls back. "No. I *need* you."

More than fucking air.

"You managed seven years without me."

I smooth her wet hair away from her face, trying anything

to distract myself from the feel of her grinding against my cock. "I managed seven years because of you, not despite you."

She smiles, wrapping her arm around my neck, our lips marrying in bursts of barely-there touches. "Then trust me to know what you need." She rolls her hips, and we both drop our heads to look down, our foreheads meeting.

I hold my breath as she rises on her knees. Her pussy drags up the length of my cock with ball-busting torture. When she reaches the head, she teases it against her clit. A moan passes her lips, and I roll our foreheads, catching the corner of her mouth with a kiss before she can grind slowly back down to the base.

"I'm not even inside of you, and I'm going to come."

Her reply comes in the form of another moan, her body trembling as she rubs herself over me. I close my eyes and feel her, letting her work herself to the place she wants to be while I try desperately to hold off.

My cock grows stiffer with each pass of her hips, the way she toys with the head, and the feel of her, of how wet she is as she coats me with her excitement.

I shift her closer, taking one of her nipples into my mouth, and she gasps, her fingers fisting in my hair. She's close. She's going to come just like this, grinding her pussy up the length of my cock.

Scarlet drags my head up, her lips capturing mine again. I open my eyes, finding hers barely parted.

I take her face in my hands and lick through her mouth.

"Lance." Her hips roll twice, and then she tenses, her clit pulsating against my cock as she comes around me.

I look down, my hands on her hips. I move her forward, and her body trembles, still riding out her orgasm. As her slick pussy slides back down my dick, she coats me, rolling her hips over and over until my toes curl on the tile, and my orgasm nears.

I tense, knowing I can't hold off any longer as my cock jerks and bobs. My cum releases in spurts, coating her pussy and dripping down the length of my dick.

Scarlet continues the up and down motion over me, gathering the sticky white substance at her clit with the head of my cock, and then smearing it down to my base.

It's one of the hottest things I've ever seen.

Her pussy wrapped around me, covered in our cum, and rippling for more.

Scarlet

> Lance: I could have sworn I fell asleep with you in my bed last night

I read the message twice, and then once more for no good reason, my heart doing a stupid little flip and sending a tidal wave crashing throughout my stomach.

> Lance: If you tell me it was all a dream, I might never recover

I chuckle, brushing three knuckles over my lips as I consider replying.

"Your smile."

I bring the phone to my chest, snapping my eyes up to Ave on the other side of the café table. "What?"

"It's gone now." Her inquisitive stare doesn't leave me as she slurps from her hot chocolate. "Who was it?"

Since she's been able to talk, I've taught my daughter never to lie. To always tell the truth no matter what. But... "Just someone from the hospital." Lance is technically still a patient.

"Hmm," she muses. "I've never seen you smile like that before."

"Of course you have." I wave her off. "There's no way I could smile wider than I do for you, Ave."

"It was a different smile. Not the one I get. It was more..." She shrugs her shoulders. "Different."

Wonderful. Not only did I completely lose all common sense last night, I'm now also as transparent as an ice cube in water. I school my features and try deflecting. "I have a surprise for you," I tell her.

Ave sits up in her seat, pointing her finger at me. "Is it a boy smile?"

My cheeks tingle with heat beneath my makeup. "What, no!" I lean in closer so that no one can hear. "*Ave!*"

"It's how Evie looks at Seb whenever he speaks to her on break."

"I was *not* smiling like an seven-year-old, thank you very much. Do you want to know the surprise or not?"

She grins. Just like an seven-year-old. "I'll find out who's liable."

I close my eyes and curse under my breath. "You spend far too much time with your uncle Charlie."

Pride glows across her cheeks. "How's my dad's leg?"

My phone vibrates on the table.

I lift my coffee and take a heavy gulp. "It's doing better, I think."

"You think." She frowns. "Are you not... helping him?"

My cheeks redden as images of us in the shower last night come barrelling to the forefront of my mind. "I've been trying, Ave." I pluck up the shop's laminated menu and lightly fan my face. "It's hot in here, isn't it."

"Not even a little bit." She giggles, giving me a cheeky look. "But we can pretend it is."

I roll my eyes and pick up my phone when she goes back to drinking her hot chocolate.

> Lance: Because I remember vividly the feel of you sliding over

I don't read the whole text, slamming my phone back to my chest. I close my eyes in mortification.

When I left Lance in bed this morning, I had no idea how everything would pan out. After changing the sheets last night, he climbed into the bed and told me to get in with him.

He didn't ask me like every other time.

He told me.

I climbed in next to him, my heart a puddle in his hands and my head a scrambled cloud of thoughts.

"It means whatever you need it to mean, Scarlet," he told me, smoothing my hair back from my face.

What he didn't—doesn't—realise is that I know exactly what it means. I'm just terrified of the consequences of it being true.

Scarlet: I'm out with Ave

Lance: Is she as beautiful as I remember?

I glance past my phone at Ave, her big eyes roaming the café.

Scarlet: What do you think?

Lance: When can I kiss you again?

God, the way he can make my stomach twist up in knots after all this time.

Lance: I'll earn every single one of them.

I bite my lip, staring at the message. Did I give in too easily? Too soon? I couldn't control myself being wrapped in his arms. The second he pulled me to him I was done for. In the moment, I needed him as much as he needed me.

Now it feels like there's no way back.

"Mum..."

I lift my head up to look at Ave.

Guilt spears me when I find her sweet face now confused and waiting on me. Guilt because this little girl has been with me through every second of pain I've faced, from the moment Lance left me to the moment he rode back in the lane. Ave knows it broke me. I didn't ever want that. I tried to hide it, hated that she witnessed it, but she did see. And she's the one who put me back together again when no one else knew how. Wordlessly, never complaining or questioning me.

No matter how good, how right it feels to be held by Lance again. To wake up in his arms and have his lips tangle with mine. I can't forget that for seven years he chose to do what we promised we'd get through together alone.

Ave deserves better than half.

She deserves to be the centre of all my smiles.

My eyes burn, and I drop them to the table along with my phone. "Ave, I'm sorry."

"What for?" she asks, shuffling in her seat.

A lot of things, baby. "Getting sucked into my phone."

She flicks her hair off her shoulders and leans forward, wise beyond her years. "What's my surprise?"

TWENTY-ONE

Lance

"Dad, look!" Waverley spins, her dress splaying wide. "Auntie Luce had it made for me. It's for Nana and Papa's ball. Mummy surprised me today."

I stand from my resting position at the kitchen island, using my crutches to make my way toward her in the hallway. "You look like a princess."

"I feel like a princess!" she sings gleefully. "You should see Mummy's dress. Your eyes will fall out of your head."

I chuckle, dropping my chin. *Oh, baby girl, you have no idea.* "Probably."

She looks over her shoulder and then motions me closer with her hand.

I drop to my good knee. "What?"

"Did you text her?"

I frown, recalling our conversation this morning. I'd asked Waverley if she knew her mother's phone number. She came back not five minutes later with it written out on a scrap of paper. "I said I was going to."

"But *did* you?" she says wide-eyed, desperate for my response.

"Yes, I texted her."

A smile transforms her face. "I knew it!"

"You knew it?" I ask.

"Uh-huh. She was *sweating.*"

"She was?"

Waverley nods, her grin still stretched. "What did you say to her?"

Sweet shit balls. "Uh... I—um..." I swallow, running a hand through my hair. "I told her how..." My brain misfires. I have nothing. "Waverley—"

"You told her what? Come on!"

"I told her I wanted to kiss her," I rush out.

Her mouth drops open.

"Crap," I mutter. "Don't tell anyone that."

"Did you at least say hi first?"

I shake my head. "What?"

"Did you just say I want to kiss you? Or did you say hi, Scarlet. I want to kiss you?"

I grin, looking down at her. "No, I didn't say hi first."

She rolls her eyes. "Mum hates bad manners. No wonder she was sweating."

"I'll remember that."

She nods, stepping back and twirling her dress from one side to the other. "You want to kiss her?"

I shrug, my blood roaring under my skin. "Maybe."

"I could speak to her—"

"No," I cut her off. "Don't say anything, you." I chuckle and scrub at my face. "Can we go get ice cream or something now?"

She nods, smiling. I stand and make my way into the kitchen.

Waverley gets the bowls while I fetch the ice cream from the freezer.

We're two bowls deep when Scarlet walks into the kitchen, two brown paper bags in her arms.

She must have gone down to the village.

Her eyes immediately meet mine and hold, paralysed in a shared memory of water droplets on feverish skin... stolen whimpers I now own—fuck, the sounds she made.

I see her cheeks flare, her attention flicking to Waverley. She walks to the counter and places down the bags, taking out two jars of jam. "Ice cream before dinner and in that dress, Ave? You know better."

"Sorry, Mummy."

I roll my lips, unsure if she regrets last night or is just as fucked up over it as I am and can't look at me.

Because me... I'm already halfway to hard in my shorts at the mere thought of it.

Waverley's foot connects with my brace, and I hiss, the air leaving my lungs like a sucker punch to the gut. I whip my head down to ask her what the hell, but her eyes are wide, a spoonful of ice cream hovering near her mouth. She flicks her head toward her mum at the counter pointedly.

I look between them, the pulse in my leg steadily easing.

Hooking a finger over the edge of Waverley's bowl, I drag it away from her and dump her ice cream into my own, giving her a look that says *If you weren't my kid, I'd throttle you.*

My gaze falls away from her, drifting to Scarlet again.

Feeling like a scolded child, I scratch my forehead and say, "Hi, Scarlet."

She freezes at the counter, the back that my hands roamed and clung on to only hours ago going rigid.

She eventually turns, barely able to look at me before eyeing Waverley, the lights, the door, the counter. Anything but me. "Hi," she says, as if we're strangers.

"Do you need a hand with dinner?" I ask when she goes back to putting the shopping away. "Waverley said we're having—"

"I've got it covered. You should rest your leg."

I've been resting my leg all day. "My leg feels great."

"Will you walk Bear with me, Dad? I said to Nana Frey and Papa Glen that I'd bring him down to see them soon."

Scarlet doesn't seem to acknowledge the fact I've spoken, slipping off into the pantry with the jars in her hands. I look down at Waverley, her big green eyes peering up at me. "Of course I'll come. Go get dressed, and I'll meet you outside."

She slides from her seat and skips off down the hallway. I watch her until she disappears around the staircase, her feet stomping up the stairs.

Leaving my crutches where they are, I make my way into the pantry. I stand in the doorway, watching as Scarlet empties the jars of jam into smaller reusable tubs. She goes from one task to the next, her focus on each feeling delicate and gentle.

I could stand here and watch her potter around all day.

"If I told you I'm not ready to talk about it yet, would you listen to me?"

I smile at her back before uncrossing my legs and gingerly walking to where she stands. It feels good to walk across a room without rubber burning the palms of my hands. Feels even better to walk to her. To stand this close again. So close I can feel her back against my chest.

Leaning down, I gather the hair covering her shoulder and ease it back. She side-eyes me but doesn't move. Doesn't stop me as I drop a kiss to the underside of her jaw. "I would." I see her pulse flutter and cover that, too, my lips gentle, greedy. "You could tell me you fucking hated me, Scarlet. That you never want to see me again, and I'd listen." The pale purple diamond on her right hand glints up at me, catching my attention. I take her hand in mine, lifting it to my mouth. Her neck twists, and she watches, eyes locked on mine, as I lick the sticky sweet jam from the length of her thumb. I place her hand on the counter and fist my own, bringing it between our bodies before taking both of her hands on the counter. I drag my nose up the length of her neck, distracting her. "I'd listen, sunshine. But we'd still be us, and I'd still fucking love you."

She lets out a shaky breath, her heart beating so hard I can feel it against my chest. I chuckle and step back, feeling like, for the first time in a long time, I might win her back. "I'll listen," I whisper before turning and leaving the pantry.

Scarlet

My thumb glints under the lights, the feel of his lips brushing the sensitive skin still lingering. Frowning, I flex my hands, realising... I look down at them, my heart wild, wondering how and when he switched my ring from my right ring finger to my left.

Lance

I intended to kiss her once and leave like she asked, but the second I saw my ring on her finger, I knew exactly what I wanted.

There was a time I let Scarlet slip through my fingers, a time when I let us drift for an entire year out of guilt over what I did to Mase. If I knew then what I know now—that our days were limited—I'd have loved her the way she deserved sooner. I'd have made sure she knew it, too.

I can't let her slip through my fingers again.

Lance: Are you awake?

After a couple of minutes, three dots bounce across the screen. I smile, but then they disappear.

Lance: Talk to me, Scar.

Scarlet: I don't know what to say to you

Lance: Well, you can tell me to stop texting you, and I'll leave you alone. You can ask me to come and get you, and I will.

Scarlet: And if I left it up to you?

I grin.

Lance: You're not ready for those truths

Three dots bounce and then stop, over and over.

Lance: Come on, Scar

Lance: You didn't come to my room tonight for a reason, but you're still awake at nearly three o'clock in the morning.

Lance: Talk to me, sunshine. Put me on the same page

Please.

Scarlet: You made me feel things I'm not sure I'm ready to feel. I don't regret last night, not one bit, but it's been on my mind all day and I've felt so off-centre ever since.

Three dots continue to bounce and then stop.

Lance: That's why you avoided me all day?

Scarlet: I didn't mean to avoid you. I was just scared of what this all means. What you'd think it means.

Lance: You're forgetting what I was willing to settle for before you brought me here

> Lance: To even be a thought that runs
> through your mind is more than enough

Lies.

Because if this woman will have me, I'm going to marry her.

> Lance: What do you need?

She doesn't reply to my message, and I lie staring at her words for over five minutes before tossing my phone and scrubbing at my face.

Was I too much? It didn't feel that way, not at all. She wanted it. She instigated it. And fuck if she wasn't right there with me.

I don't regret last night.

Her words rein in my racing heart.

Reminders of the night before sets it wild.

Reaching down, I palm my growing cock, the need to ease the ache overwhelming.

The feel of her spread over my lap.

Her pussy.

The way her lips felt against mine.

The way her heart beat beneath my palm.

I sear that memory into my mind over and over, wondering when the next time will be that I get to feel it.

There's a tap on the door, and I still, her silhouette a shadow in the darkness as she steps into the room. I swallow, and blink, my cock twitching as it fails to catch up.

Her breathing is fast, not chest-heaving, body-trembling fast, but quickened enough that I notice.

She walks to the empty side of the bed, pulls back the covers, and slides in.

Wordlessly, knowing, I reach over and flick on my bedside light, waiting in the dimly lit room for her breathing to even out before I close my eyes and relax into the pillow.

"I'm just scared," she whispers.

I open my eyes, finding her watching me with so much anguish, I'm rendered speechless.

"You terrify me, Lance."

I lean in and kiss her forehead, a piece of shit man who can't stay away.

Her hand flattens against my bare chest, telling me to stay close as her eyes close. The tips of her fingers brush through the fine hairs beneath them.

"Can I ask for time but not space? Is it awful of me to ask for that?"

I chuckle, lifting her hand on my chest to my lips, tentatively dusting my thumb over the diamond that's back on her right ring finger.

Not where I left it.

"Sunshine, you could ask me to bleed purple, and I'd find a way."

For a second today, I thought I got it all wrong. I thought I got her all wrong. I smile and bring her closer, holding her against me as I wrap her in my arms. "Sleep, Scar. We'll figure it out."

Turns out I'm still the luckiest fucker in the world.

TWENTY-TWO

Lance

"You ou want me to come in with you today?"

I hand Scarlet the parking ticket and make my way into the hospital with her by my side. "And have you and Annie laugh at me in pain?" I side-eye her. "No, I do not."

Scarlet's smile is full, has been for weeks. "We don't laugh at you."

"No, you do a shitty job of not laughing at me."

"It's an x-ray and check in. She isn't going to hurt you. She'll probably let you get rid of your crutches today. You seem pretty steady on your feet."

"I've not needed them for weeks."

"Not true." Her hand roams the length of my back and around to my side. She pushes up onto her tiptoes to place a kiss on my cheek. "But I love your enthusiasm. I'm going to go see Mia."

I watch from the waiting room door as she slips out of my

grasp, entranced by the way she moves through the hospital corridors as she does through life. Fully. Head up. Never missing a step.

The last few weeks have felt impossible, and yet, they've been the easiest of my life.

She's right there, always smiling and laughing and perfect. And I'm here, trying—fucking trying my hardest, to give her the time she needs.

We share a bed. We walk the meadow. We steal moments only we'll ever know about, and then share precious ones with our daughter that she'll never forget.

And we pretend every fucking day it's not a big deal. That I'm not already on my ass in love with her, and she's not tripping at my feet, falling.

I shake my head and push into the room, knowing I look like a fool staring after her.

When Annie eventually calls my name, I pick up my crutches in one hand and walk the distance to the examination room without aid.

"Look at you go." She whistles as I pass her. "Show off. I see Dr Lowell has done a stellar job looking after you."

"Coddled, that's what she's done to me." I fight the smile that threatens, knowing Scarlet would have my ass if she could hear me.

Annie grins, setting me up on the bed. "So, we're flying tomorrow. It's quite the distance, isn't it?"

"Two days of travel."

She nods. "You'll have some discomfort." She puts a hand on her chest. "I'd have discomfort. But you should be okay.

Let's get some x-rays done, and I'll see how well you can really pitch on that leg."

Annie takes me to x-ray herself, telling me she could use the walk. We're in and out before Scarlet can get back.

"It's looking good. I'm so glad they operated in the end, you know," she tells me without turning around. She nods at the x-ray on the screen. "I can see the callus growing around the break, and you seem to be pretty comfortable pitching on it."

I smirk. I told Scarlet I didn't need my crutches.

Annie spins on her chair, smile wide, victorious. "Do you think you could go home, try finding your feet back in your own space?"

My smile drops, and I frown, the room turning grey as I sit, wondering if Annie just said I could go home as if it's the greatest idea in the world. "Home?"

Her brows rise, panic washing out her glee. "Oh, sorry. I don't know why I thought Scarlet said you had a place of your own to go back to." She shakes her head. "I see so many families, Lance, you'll have to forgive me."

I stare at a spot on the ground, wondering at what point I lost sight of the goal. Wondering at what point I forgot I'd have to leave them again. "I have a place," I say absent-mindedly.

"You do?"

"Yeah," I mutter.

"Okay... we'll need—"

I tune her out.

I need more time. *She* needs more time. There are a million reasons I don't want to go home, Waverley being one of them, but Scarlet has walls that tower around her heart a mile high, and I'm so fucking close. I know I can tear them down—indefinitely.

But I can't do that from the city.

"Does that sound like a plan?" Annie says, pulling me out of my thoughts.

I scrub at my face, nodding with no idea what she's said to me. "Yeah. Yeah, that's great."

The walk through the hospital and to the car feels too short, the idea of leaving the estate to go back to that cold empty house making my insides twist up in knots.

Scarlet is, and will forever be, my good. I'd do ten life sentences if it meant having her for a single day. Her place in my world isn't a want, it's a need.

If I thought we'd make it, I'd go home happy. I'd go home with a fucking smile plastered on my face and wait for as long as she needed.

But I don't know that we will.

She isn't ready.

With my face to the sun, I lean back against her car and think of all the ways I could beg her to love me again—to let me stay.

There's fear there, I know that much. The way she shut down on me the day after my nightmare showed me that much. But these last few weeks, even if she hasn't given me anything more—I'm not stupid.

"You may have paid for that car, Sullivan, but it doesn't mean you get to rub your ass all over it."

I look over my shoulder and take her in as she approaches me. She's wearing a pretty dress today, leaving her legs, arms, and chest bare. She's glowing, her bruises all but gone.

When she's nearly to me, I twist my body, wondering how I'll ever go a day without seeing her face smiling up at me like this. "Did I tell you you look beautiful today?"

She bites on her bottom lip, brown eyes glinting at me from beneath her lashes. "No, but when I brought you your coffee this morning, I did spot your raging hard-on."

I look to the sky and laugh.

She pokes my ribs. "What did Annie say?"

Fuck, I need her.

I need her.

I can't do this without her—don't want to.

The idea of sleeping without her wrapped around me.

My leg might be healed, but I'm not.

We're not.

I swallow, focusing on the two freckles that are littered above the bow of her lips. It'll be the first and last lie I ever tell her. "It looks good, but the callus isn't growing as quickly as Annie would like. She wants me to take it easy still."

Her shoulders drop, and her obvious disappointment makes my heart sink. "I knew you'd been doing too much."

"Yeah," I say, running a hand through my hair. "Maybe."

"Can you fly? I presume it's fine, but—"

"Flying's fine. It's just keeping it in the brace a little while longer. I can still bear weight."

She gives me an upside-down smile, as if that's not the advice she'd give. "What about your crutches?"

Annie never mentioned the crutches. I just picked them up out of habit when I left... "Just the one for now."

"Well, *that's* progress, at least," she says, opening the car door and smiling up at me in some kind of way.

"What?" I eventually ask, hating that I've lied to her.

She frowns slightly, her eyes dropping to my lips. "Nothing. I'm just thinking about how happy Ave will be that you're coming with us."

I blow out a breath, remembering why I'm doing this. I step toward her, slipping between the open car door to stand at her front. "What about you? Are you happy I'm coming?"

She tilts her head to the side, my eyes dancing around her smiling face as she contemplates it. She is so close, so beautiful.

"Yeah. Yeah, I am."

"You got the all clear? We can go?" Waverley asks, jumping up and down on the steps at Lowerwick. She has a summer dress on, a sun hat, and a black pair of sunglasses covering her eyes.

I step out of the car and hobble toward her. "I got the all clear."

She rushes to me and hugs my waist. "Vinny just finished packing up all the cars. We're leaving in twenty minutes!" She runs back up the steps, passing Mason and Ellis on her way. Mason steals her hat, placing it on Ellis. Ellis pulls it off, rolling his eyes and giving it back to Waverley.

"They said you're good to fly?" Mason asks with a wide smile on his face.

I nod. "Just about."

"He still has some way to go," Scarlet corrects. "And they'd like him to use a crutch."

She passes it to me, and I slip my arm through the loop.

"The cars are packed up?" Scarlet asks.

"Yep. Everything that was in your rooms. Ave was snooping in your suitcase," Mason tells me. "I don't think she took anything out, but you're welcome to check. I'll get my tribe rounded—"

I follow his line of sight, his frown aimed over my shoulder. When I turn, I see the Audi rolling slowly in the lane. As it nears, my heart drops to my ass.

My mother sits behind the wheel.

"Did you know she was coming?" Mason asks.

I shake my head. "No, I did not."

As she steps from the car, I take in everything about her all at once. From the smile lines that make up her face, to the dyed, muddy brown hair she has chopped short at her shoulders. Not much has changed, if at all, and yet I can't help but hope that maybe it has. That maybe she'll come over and give me a cuddle and tell me she missed me.

"Sorry, I didn't call ahead. I did try your phone, Scarlet, but I couldn't get through."

I turn to look at Scarlet, not sure what to expect. She seems to be waiting, like I was, maybe for the same thing even.

"Hello, Lance. It's good to see you."

My brows rise in surprise. "It's good to see you, too. I didn't realise Scarlet had your number. I was trying to contact you whilst in the hospital."

She takes a half step back. "I've been working a lot. It's a busy couple of months in the hospitality industry, and with Dougie, Lois, and Poppy not in school, it's impossible to get away."

Regardless of the fact the school holidays started after I was released from hospital, my attention snags on the other part of her sentence. "Sorry... who?"

"Douglas, Lois, and Poppy," she repeats, a sliver of guilt shining in her eyes. "Nessa and Chloe's children."

The sound of my father's name passing her lips after so much time is like a shot to the heart.

I'm an uncle?

"Again, I'm sorry I couldn't get a hold of you, Scarlet. You know how it is." She smiles, stepping toward Scarlet. "I noticed on the last payment, there was a little more than normal. I hope you don't mind, but I popped into that little boutique that Waverley likes, the one on that side street, and picked out some new sandals."

Scarlet closes her eyes briefly before opening them and taking the bag my mother holds out to her. "Thank you, Vanessa, that was really kind of you."

"Of course. Is Waverley around?"

Heat fills my chest as I watch my mother look around me and up toward the house. I've never felt this woman's love. My father loved me. My mother tried. But it was always a whisper of a promise that never came through.

Scarlet stares at my mother, unblinking. "She's in the house."

"Can I?" She points to the bag Scarlet's now holding.

Scarlet hands it back to her. "Sure."

Silence lingers with every step she takes away from us.

Her words pass over and over in my mind, her lack of acknowledgement, the way she told me about Chloe and Nessa—their children.

It fucking hurts.

I lift my head up to look at Scarlet, Mason now standing by her side.

"What payments is she talking about?" I ask.

"Lance." She sighs, taking a step toward me. "I wasn't going to see her struggle. She's your mum."

I turn and make my way toward the fields, knowing if I stay and ask any more questions, I'll struggle to keep my head. "I need a minute."

Scarlet

I approach Lance from behind, his shoulders tense under his T-shirt as if he's ready to square off against the world. "I didn't like it at first either."

His jaw clenches beneath his stubble. "So then why is she here?"

I look out at the meadow and sigh, knowing I need a second before I tell him what I need to. What I've buried deep within me for the last seven years. "When I first found out about Ave, I was terrified. I didn't think I could do it without you, and I felt empty—completely empty and lost. But then she started to grow inside of me. Nina was here with Ellis a lot, and I felt like maybe it would be possible. I saw what she did effortlessly and thought that maybe I'd be able to do it, too. That I'd be an amazing mum," I say with a sad chuckle. "When Ave came early, they took her straight from me, put her inside this tiny see-through box, and told me I couldn't even touch her." I shake my head, not able to look at Lance. "That fear of failing, of being alone in something I felt so unprepared for, it swallowed me whole." I roll my lips, guilt burning my throat. "I kept telling myself that once Ave was back with me again, and I could hold her, once she could open her eyes and see me, I'd feel better." I look up at him as a tear slides down my cheek. "I felt nothing, Lance. I was her mum, her guardian, and protector, and I felt nothing when they finally placed her in my arms."

"Scarlet."

I shake my head. "Everyone was walking on eggshells around me. They didn't want to upset me, but I wasn't me. I was lost, and I knew it. I knew I needed help but asking for it seemed like I was failing her. Failing you." I don't dare to look at him as my voice cracks. "I knew you'd be amazing if you could've been here. I just—" A knot forms in my throat, and I cover my mouth. "I just knew she needed you, and that you would make me better."

He blows out a shaky breath, his eyes filled with tears.

"Nina slept in my bed for two months while I recovered. She forced me to hold Ave some days, on the darkest ones, and I hated her for it." I wipe at my face and pull my shoulders back. "Without her I don't know if I'd have ever got better. But I did. It took time." I nod, feeling my throat closing up again. "And I'm sorry for that. I am. If I could have been what she needed sooner, I would have given it to her within a heartbeat." My words strain barely audible. "I just didn't know how."

"It's all my fault."

"Ave deserved to be loved by everyone who wanted to love her," I finally say. "We didn't always get that for ourselves, Lance, but she can. There was no decision-making when I let your mother in. She loves her. It's all that matters."

"You gave her money?"

"Charlie said you'd stopped. When I found out she was struggling, I couldn't not. It's what I thought you'd have done."

With something like gratitude in his eyes, Lance pulls me by the neck to him, tucking me under his chin. I smooth my hands up his back, relishing his warmth.

"I'm so sorry, Scarlet."

With the lake spread wide below us, I snuggle deeper into his chest. "This isn't something to be sorry for." I tip my chin up to look at him, knowing there's an apology he'll never get that I can give him. "I'm sorry your mum hurt you."

His jaw tics. "I'm a clown to think she'd change."

"In some ways, I think she has. I didn't know her well before, but over the years, I've noticed a difference."

He lets out a humourless laugh, looking down his nose at me. "Scar, I knew from the second her cold eyes landed on me nothing has changed." He smooths a hand up my back, his face relaxing a little. "I trust your judgement, though. If you think she should be a part of Waverley's life, I'll respect that."

"Ave's smart. If she wants to see your mum, she can."

He nods, letting his eyes dance around my face. "I'll pay you back every penny."

I bury my face in his chest, closing my eyes. "No." I breathe him in. "You won't."

"Scarlet."

"Lose the mentality that you owe anyone in this world a thing, Lance. Not least the person who knows your story. We owe each other that much, don't we?"

"I owe *you* my entire life."

I lean back, scowling at him. He has no idea. His mother just walked by him as if he were a stranger after seven years of not seeing or speaking to him. "And *you* deserve it—your life. A good one."

His lip curls as he fingers a wayward strand of my hair. "You have that look in your eyes."

I lift my chin. "What look?"

"Like you're ready to go to war."

"You can't throw your heart at the feet of anyone you think deserves it and then expect me not to fight for it."

"I don't expect it."

"Exactly my point. You need love? You have it. You need family? We're right here. Traditions and ideals are great, lovely even, but it's also bullshit. Life isn't what it gives you in luck or DNA. It's what you make of yourself despite it." I search his eyes. "Lance Sullivan *is* your DNA, and that man has the shittiest luck, but the choices he makes for the people he chose—the people he loves, the way he cares despite people like her"—I nod in the direction of the house—"the way he loves in a way he's never experienced himself... Lance, it makes you so much more."

He stares down at me, his eyes heavy and glossy. "We define luck differently, me and you."

"How so?"

He gives me an upside-down smile, looking toward the house. "Well, I met you for starters." He brings his eyes back to me. "And you gave me the most precious piece of us. If that's bad luck, build me a ladder. I'll spend the rest of my days passing under it if it means I get more pieces of you."

"You'd walk under a ladder for me?" I smile.

I die a little inside when a full smile cracks his mouth, and he looks away. "For the rest of my days."

I purse my lips, trying to ease the ache in my cheeks. "I'll add superstitious to the list then."

He rolls his eyes and feigns frustration. "I was trying for romantic."

"You have a way to go to get to romantic."

"Three drains, will that do it?"

"Not the three drains," I say sarcastically.

"Uh-huh." His grin widens, and I can't help but want to keep it permanently on his face. "Tell me it does it for you. I'll search out every manhole in the country."

"Sorry, you'll what? Whose holes?"

"Shut up." He pulls me back into his chest.

I laugh. "That truly is the most romantic thing I've ever heard."

"You make it impossible to win," he grumbles into my hair.

"Weak competition."

I peer up at him when he stays quiet, finding him gazing out across the lake.

"What are you thinking?" I ask, hoping he'll let go of

everything he carried with him up the hill and enjoy the next week away with us all.

Lance shrugs. "How I never felt like I had a home until you showed me this place."

I swallow the wave of emotion inching up my throat, his honesty making my heart ache. "Hey," I say, waiting.

When he peers down at me, I force a reassuring smile. *I meant every word.* "You okay?"

He doesn't answer right away, the question answered in an unspoken understanding that passes between us. *Not really, sunshine.* "Yeah." *But I will be.*

TWENTY-THREE

Lance

You need love? You have it.
       You need family? We're here.

Her words bounce around my mind like a rogue ping-pong ball as I watch her sleep on the chair opposite me, Waverley curled up at her side. We've been in the air for over six hours. When we arrived at the airport, we found out we'd be flying alone. Nina and Mason weren't coming. Nor Elliot and Luce or Charlie and Lissie. They stood us up.

You need family? We're here.

I shouldn't need to be told. The fact Scarlet's words resonate so deeply is proof enough. Because I do know. There's not been a time since meeting the guys where I've not felt supported by them, that I've not known they'd have my back regardless of the consequences.

To ignore that fact and act like I don't have a family is an insult to them all.

You need love? You have it.

This one I'm not so certain of. Waverley doesn't know me. She loves me, in a way, but she doesn't know me well enough to love me the way she one day will. And Scarlet, I can see the fear in her eyes, feel the push back every time her gaze holds for five seconds too long.

I need love, and she tells me I have it, but not in the way I want it.

I want *her* love.

All of it.

Leaning forward in the seat, I pull out the letters I stuffed into my shorts pocket. I tear into the envelope and pull out the paper.

Lance,

Whether this letter finds its way to you or not, today, sat in this bed, cut open and stitched back together, empty, I need to write the words.

Ink to paper.

There so much we think we need in life to survive, and yet I think if we stopped and truly thought about it, our list would be a lot shorter. It's that question people ask, 'your house is on fire, what do you save?' It's a stupid question. Everything you could save from a fire can be taken at the hands of something just as terrifying.

My house is on fire, what am I going to save?

Nothing. Let me walk into the flames.

I'm going to lose her, Lance.

There's nothing I can have and love and hold that won't leave me, and now she's gone, too. I loved her so much, before I even knew who she was—before I'd ever know who she was, I loved her.

She'd wriggle inside of me, and I'd think it was the most magical thing. I had that time with her, I'm thankful for that.

I named her Waverley. They barely even caught it as they whipped her from the surgeon's arms and wheeled her from the room. I shouted it. I screamed it over their chatter. I needed them to know it despite the chaos.

It didn't mean a thing to a single one of them.

I'll be here until she isn't. What I am after that, I don't know. But this feeling, the empty, lonely feeling gnawing at my gut all over again, I can't bear that feeling anymore.

I'm sorry I failed her, Lance.

Truly.

Scarlet.

Lance,

I'm scared. I'm not sure I've ever felt more alone, like I don't even have myself.

Every day seems like survival, and each time I climb into the hospital bed, I win. But there's no prize, there's no happiness, or light, or excitement to wake up to tomorrow.

We have a daughter. Her name is Waverley Sullivan.

I planned to add a middle name when she arrived, but I couldn't think of anything after everything that happened, and I had to have her registered.

She doesn't have your dark hair, and I don't know if she has my eyes because they're taped closed. She's so small and fragile, sometimes I pray she'll sleep a little longer, just so that I don't have to watch the skin move over her tiny bones when she's awake.

They told me to prepare to lose her, and I did. When they took her from me, I mourned her. I told myself it was happening again, that life does this and there's no way of saving her and to let her go.

She was going to leave me, too.

But she didn't.

She's here. An innocent little life squeezing my finger in her strong fist, asking me to give her something I can't.

Because what happens when she does eventually leave me?

I don't think I feel what I'm supposed to be feeling as a mother, and it terrifies me. Even when I try, it feels like I'm doing it wrong.

Nothing is how it should be, but I can't find it in myself to fix it.

I don't even know if it can be fixed.

Not when I'm the one who's broken.

Scarlet.

Lance,

We're home. I didn't write for over a month because I didn't really have anything to say. Anything I did say would be selfishly about me, how I feel, how I'm broken. Not the little girl who has been fighting and fighting to be here, to stay here.

It's not gone unnoticed.

Her tiny heart sings to me.

Begs the cold parts of me to warm.

I can barely look at her.

There's been these moments where I almost think it's stupid, and I'm on the cusp of telling Nina how it is—how it feels inside. Anything to make her understand. But then I look at her and Ellis together and how she is with Waverley, and I know it's just me, and she'd never get it.

Like tonight, she came to our room and bathed Waverley. She kept asking me to do things, getting the towel and washing Waverley's neck. But I didn't want to do those things.

It kills me to look at her, physically hurts my chest to hold her skin to skin.

And that's why I can't tell Nina, why I let her climb into bed every night and hold me while I cry myself to sleep, why I let her get up in the night to feed our baby. Because telling her out loud that I can't do this only confirms what a monster I am.

I'm a coward for so many reasons, but choosing not to love our baby, mourning her before ever giving her *a chance in that hospital, that's what damns me to the world.*

I'm a monster and a coward, and I'm scared because if I fall for this little life in my hands, if I love her and lose her, I won't survive it.

I hate myself for it.

Scarlet.

My tears seep through the paper, making the ink bleed and run down the page. I snap my eyes up to where Scarlet and Waverley sleep opposite me, so at peace. Their love is pliable, there's no doubt in my mind about the kind of mother Scarlet is to our girl. It's a bond that could never be written.

To think she ever doubted it herself…

Only confirms the monster I am.

I stand from my seat, leaving my crutch, and sweep my hands under her body, lifting her into my arms. Waverley stirs, her eyes cracking open before lazily falling closed again.

"Lance?" Scarlet rasps, as I carry her to the back of the plane where a bedroom is located.

"Vinny, could we get a minute?" I ask, and he rises from the desk, collecting his jacket from the bed and slipping from the small room.

"Lance," Scarlet tries again. "Your leg."

Keeping her close, I gently lower her to the ground.

"You're crying," she notes.

I swipe at my face, my chest feeling like it's cracking in two. "Tell me you don't believe a single word on these pages."

She frowns, her delicate face screwing up as she sees the

letters I hold in my fist. "Ave's birth," she says. "I'm sorry. I don't fully remember the words I wrote, Lance. You had me at my most raw once I knew you weren't reading them."

"Scar," I whisper, my throat catching. "Baby."

She shakes her head, eyes filling fast. "Don't feel sorry for me." A tear escapes, the next one falling almost instantly. "What Ave went through was so much worse."

"You don't have to be brave for me," I promise, wiping the tears away. "You give *me* that. No matter how much it scares you to say it out loud."

She nods, looking up at me with so much vulnerability in her gaze. She's on the cusp of breaking, her chin trembling.

"You're not a monster, Scar—"

"Lance—"

"You've never been a monster."

I take her weight when her head drops, and she sags forward, her sob muffled as it seeps into my chest.

And I know that it'll leave a mark. Maybe not one you can see, but it will be mine and not hers anymore. I'll carry it for her.

"You're not a monster," I say again. "I'm so proud of you. Of who you were then and who you are now. I've never been prouder of anything or anyone than I am stood here right now with you."

She fists my T-shirt, and I sink to the ground with her in my arms, my own tears falling with hers.

"Tell me you don't believe those words," I beg.

She sinks further into my chest.

"Tell me, Scar."

I force her back, taking her chin and lifting her blotchy

face to mine. "Tell me you're not a monster, that you know it."

She tries to curl her head down, but I hold firm, giving her my eyes, letting her see. "Scar, please."

"I know—" She fights for breath as she nods. "I know I'm not a monster."

I pull her to me again, letting her sink into my hold as I lean back against the end of the bed. Relief surges through me, but I already know that it won't last.

There are parts of Scarlet that are broken. It's why she won't love me again, why she struggles to love anything anymore.

I don't blame her.

I certainly don't think she's a monster, but I don't have to accept it.

"Infinite," I whisper into her hair. "You don't have to believe it, you don't have to fight for it, but know that I won't ever stop showing you. Ave—your family, they aren't going to leave you. Not ever. I'll die before I break that promise to you, Scarlet. If you choose to believe in anything, believe in that."

"I'm so sorry," she cries. "I tried. I tried so hard to fight it."

I shake my head, rubbing my hand up and down her spine as my hand brushes the back of her neck, into her hair. "You don't have to fight anymore, sunshine. I'm here."

She eases back, her eyes red as she looks at me, tracking the dried tears on my cheeks, the sincerity I know is harboured in my eyes. When her mouth dips to take mine, I suck in a breath, not expecting it. It's been weeks since I kissed her in the shower. Since she let me take a little back.

I've waited patiently, knowing she needed the time she asked for. Every night that she's climbed into my bed, I've hoped, prayed, that she'd see.

I could wait.

I would wait.

The kiss is short. A tender, too brief brush of the lips that leaves me chasing her mouth with a kiss of my own. This one deeper. Firmer.

As I ease back, she reaches up and touches her lips, as if she can still feel me there.

I tuck a loose strand of her hair behind her ear, head tilting as my thumb traces her temple.

I'm not sure I've ever known anything more precious than this woman. The way I can look at her and feel a half step from home.

"I love you with my whole fucking soul, Scar."

TWENTY-FOUR

Scarlet

"It was sneaky. Ave's gutted the kids aren't coming out, too."

Nina hums in reply through the phone while my eyes roam the length of the horizon.

"Did Lance really not know?" I ask, still wondering if he was in on it.

"He had no idea, but that piggy-tailed, love monster you call a daughter who you feel so very sorry for..."

"Ave knew?"

"Ave *is* the mastermind. To the point Charlie had to book elsewhere for the week because Lis was desperate to get away."

"What about you guys? What about your time out?"

"Scarlet, please, you say it like we don't live the lives we do. We have whatever we want whenever we want it. I don't *need* a holiday."

I sigh. "You won't come out?"

"And save you from yourself? No."

Turning my back to the ocean, I lean against the balcony and peer into the kitchen where Lance is making dinner with Ave. He's topless, hobbling around on one leg, his smile scrunching up his cheeks. "He's too easy to fall for, Nina."

"Fall for." She chuckles. "I'd say we're past falling."

"You know what I mean."

Now it's her turn to sigh. "You can spend time with him, heal whatever you need to, and not cross the lines you're not ready to. You don't have to give anything you're not ready to."

"I know that."

"Then enjoy the break. Enjoy his company."

But what if I want more?

What if things feel like they're changing?

I turn away from Lance and Ave, finding the view at my back less ovary-exploding. "You know the time before I got help—after Ave's birth."

Nina stays quiet on the other end of the line, giving me a brief pause.

"Before you helped me, and we spoke to the doctor, I wrote about how I felt in the letters to Lance. I didn't think he was reading them. I can't even remember what I wrote—"

"I read one."

My heart sinks. "What?"

"I always told myself I wouldn't bring it up unless you addressed them, just out of respect. But I can't stand here and pretend I don't know what you're talking about. I mean, I don't know. I only know my experience of that time, Scar. But you left it on your desk one evening, and Ellis got a hold of it. When I took it from him and was packing it all away, my eyes caught on one too many words, and... Scar, they weren't words I could ignore. I'm so sorry."

Shame burns in my stomach like acid. Nina saw me at my worst. She was the one who helped me speak up and get the help I needed, but the thought of her reading what was in my head at that time, that she, like Lance, read anything from that time... "I was horrible to you. Awful at times."

"You weren't," she rasps.

"I wouldn't have got through it without you, Nina."

"I know."

I smile sadly, a tear slipping down my cheek. "I love you."

I hear her sniffle, but her words deliver me the dimple I know dances on her cheek. "I love you, too."

A large, heated hand settles on my back, easing around to my ribs as his scent wraps the rest of the way around me. "You're crying," he says, quietly enough Ave won't hear. "Everything okay?"

I place my hand on his, melting inside when he rolls my hand, letting his thumb dust down and around my cuticle.

"It's good that he knows," Nina says softly. "Not that anyone needs reminding, but he should see and appreciate the incredibly strong woman that you are. And, Scar, your words may have broken my heart back then, but I never thought less of you. You have to know that. Watching you fight your way up off the ground and become a mother made me the proudest friend on earth. You give that man what *you* want to give him this week, nothing more and nothing less. More would be for him. Less isn't fair to you."

My teeth clamp together in a bid to stop the knot in my throat from snapping. "I'll call you in a couple of days."

"Text me later," she rushes out, and I know she's smiling again. "I love you."

She hangs up, leaving me with a million scattered thoughts and a man at my back who seems to warm me from the inside out.

I turn to face him, finding his eyes narrowed carefully on me. "Who made you cry?"

I slide my phone into my dress pocket and smile. "Nina."

He frowns, his head tilting a little. "You can't make me hate her when I only just started to like her."

I chuckle and push him back by the chest, thankful for his obvious attempt to cheer me up. "It's happy tears."

He captures my hand in his, fiddling with it. "I've never understood those."

"You've never had happy tears?"

He shakes his head. "When I think of happy..." He pulls on a loose strand of my hair. "I think of you. Of wildflowers and late nights and early mornings. Of quivering aspen trees and cheese."

"Cheese." I bite my lip to tame my smile.

He remembers that?

He shrugs, smiling with me. "There's not a ton of happy I can look back on, sunshine, but that summer with you was the best of my life."

I divert my eyes away from him, not knowing how to handle the effect his words have on me. "Where's Ave?"

"She went to help Vinny set up at Elliot's place."

"He's not staying with us?"

"He didn't want to intrude. Just said he'd be here if we need him."

We'd never normally use Elliot's lodge for so few of us visiting. Even when we had more bodies than beds, we made it work up here in ours.

"They're meddling." Lance confirms my thoughts. "That doesn't mean I expect anything from you. Just spending this time with you and Waverley is enough. More than enough."

My eyes drift from his handsome face to his thick neck. His bare chest and toned stomach...

"Baby Lowell, you can't look at me like that whilst I'm stood here making promises to you."

Baby Lowell. My stomach dips, butterflies fluttering up from the depths. It's been too long. "I didn't look at you like anything," I say, stepping around him and into the lodge.

I hear him snigger, making a smile grow on my face as I head through the kitchen and down the corridor toward the stairs.

He's being patient with me, respecting my boundaries, giving me time to—

I'm nearly at my room when my thumb dips low and instinctively brushes my right ring finger, my stomach sinking when I find it bare. I hold it up, my finger free of the ring.

I lift my left hand.

My eyes drift closed, the ring, the statement it makes, causing my heart to pound in my chest.

Inside my room, I slide the pale purple stone adorning my ring finger off and unclasp my necklace with a slight tremble in my hands, sliding it onto the chain and fastening it back around my neck.

Nina's right, I might not be able to fall for Lance again, but I can fall harder, deeper—forever.

I lost myself when he left me. I lost myself when I thought I lost Ave. I can't keep falling.

Because one day, I won't be able to get back up again.

I'm lay on my lounger, thinking about the hospital, my colleagues who I'm stretching thin by being away, and the patients I'm not there to treat, when water rains down on my abdomen and breasts.

"Mummy, come swim with us!"

"Ave," I groan, pushing up my sunglasses to rest on my head. I stare her down, her toothy grin spreading wider and wider.

"Were you sleeping?"

"No," I tell her, swinging my legs over the seat. "I was just resting my eyes."

The last few days have seemed to fly by. Ave has spent every second with Lance, the two of them making every memory they can think up, crossing them off their list one by one. I've left them to it, not wanting to take a second of their time away from one another. Most of my days are spent sleeping in the sun or making them both food.

We've barely seen Vinny.

It's been a long time since I've been able to get away and actually relax on holiday, and with Lance here, telling me with a look that he's good, he's got it down with Ave, I can't help but want to make the most of it.

"Will you swim with us?"

"Yeah, just give me a minute." I stand and stretch, my body rippling in the best way.

"You're burning, Mumma," Lance says, pulling himself up on the edge of the pool and stalking toward me, wet and tan and hard all over. "Where's the lotion?"

Ask me something else.

Ask me the number of muscles visible on Lance's stomach. The length of the diagonal lines that disappear into his swim shorts. But don't ask me where the lotion is.

"I'll get it. It's in my room."

"Watch the floors, Waverley," Lance calls after her, drawing my attention to her dripping feet skirting through the folded back doors.

"Don't run!" I add.

I turn and grab my cover-up from the lounger, slipping my arms through. Before I can pull it all the way on, it's tugged away from me, followed by my body as hard muscle meets my soft belly. Lance palms my ass, his other hand at my chin as he closes the space between us and demands a hard, wet kiss.

He pulls back before I can protest, before I can suck on his lip and ask for a little more.

I squint up at him in the sun, my body wet from his.

"Look at me like that again, and I'll fuck you so hard you'll beg me to ship our daughter off to boarding school so that I can have you any place, any time no interruptions."

"That's never going to happen."

He lifts a hand and pinches my nipple. "Try me."

I chuckle despite the burning ache at my core, the seriousness in his stare when we both know he's bluffing chasing away my sleepy haze.

"I got factor twenty and fifty."

Lance holds my eyes until Ave is at his side. He looks down at the ground and takes a step back, doing a lousy job of covering his growing cock in his shorts. "I just need to go make a call." He rushes off into the lodge.

"Want me to help do your back?"

I smile down at Ave. "Yes, please, baby."

Once I'm topped up, we get into the pool, leaning over the edge and staring out at the ocean beyond.

"Mummy, can I ask you something?"

I peer over at her, instantly focused, ready. "Of course. Anything."

She rolls her lips, picking at a loose tile on the edge of the pool. "If you were going to tell someone you loved them, how would you do it?"

My brows rise in surprise. "Oh," I say, not expecting it. "A boy?"

Her teeth break her smile, and she nods as she says gleefully, "It's Dad."

"*Oh.*" I drop my head back and giggle. "Oh, Ave."

Her face drops. "I know I've not known him long, but—"

I pull on her arm, turning her body in the water and pulling her in close at my side. "Ave, you don't ever explain yourself. I wasn't laughing because I thought it was silly or too soon. I was laughing because I thought you were going to say something else. I'm sorry."

"You don't think it's too soon?"

"Not at all." I remember the moment I fell in love with Lance myself. Some would call it an infatuation, lust, maybe a little crush back then. But that night at the gala on the dance floor, our first night together, it wasn't any of those things. I fell for him, and everything promised in his eyes, when he begged me not to leave. I knew somehow, with the wild beat of his heart, I knew. Even if it took me the entire year that followed to let it mean anything. "It's never too soon to tell someone you love them, Ave. If it's how you feel, you should always tell them."

"What if he doesn't say he loves me back?"

"Sometimes loving someone can be really scary. It's big feelings and makes you feel a million different emotions on top of the good ones. But you know what the best thing about love is?"

She watches me, waiting.

"You don't get to pick and choose who you give it to." I tap her chest. "Your heart does the hard work for you. Tell me, why do you love him?" I ask.

She slips out of my arms, clinging to the edge of the pool and dipping her head back in the water. "He makes me laugh."

I nod. "You make him laugh, too. What else?"

"His hugs make me feel really safe."

An ache tightens my throat. "That's really special, baby."

"And sometimes, I want to be with him, even when I'm sleeping."

I smile. "Well, as someone who's spent the last month watching the two of you, who knows you both pretty well, I'd say the chances of your dad loving you back is moon and stars and beyond kinda high."

She straightens, her hair sticking to her shoulders. "You do?"

"I do."

Her eyes light up. "Will you help me tell him?"

I marvel at her happiness. "Of course I will. What do you have in mind?"

"I want to cook for him."

"Okay... tonight?"

Nerves flutter over her face. "I'm scared."

Concealing my smile, I look back out over the ocean. "You have that pretty dress Auntie Luce made you. It would be perfect—"

"Yes! I could wear it with my new sandals from Nanny Nes. Will you plait my hair? Can we eat out here on the terrace?"

"Sounds perfect to me."

"*Arschbombe!*"

We both wince as Lance enters the water, splashing the sides of our faces. "Arse what?" I clear the water from my face as Lance surfaces with a grin.

"*Arschbombe.*" Ave laughs. "It means *ass bomb* in German."

I look back at Lance. "What are you teaching our child?" Flattening my hand, I drag it across the water, scooping it up and splashing it into his face. "And will you be more careful on your leg?!"

"She taught me!" he swears, moving closer despite the onslaught of water.

"Uncle Elliot taught me," Ave promises. "Can we do handstand competitions? On the count of three we go! One, two—"

The three of us dunk under the water, swimming down until we can flatten our hands on the floor. Ave seems to open her mouth and panic, sucking in air. She rises to the surface.

I glance to my left and find Lance still at my side. He seems to glower at me before locking his leg around mine, dragging it to him. Effectively pulling me from my handstand.

As I push up toward the surface, his hands dance up my thighs, my stomach.

"A draw!" Ave whines as we both surface. "Let me practise. I ate water down there." She dips down again, her toes barely peeking out of the water.

Lance swims to stand at her side, helping her keep her legs straight until she comes up again, takes a gasp for air and goes back down.

I watch as he grins, running his hand through the soaked black strands of his hair.

Nobody should look this good wet.

"How was your phone call?" I ask, inching back until my shoulders rest against the wall. "Not something that could wait until you were home?"

He shakes his head without looking at me, his eyes remaining on Ave under the water. He taps her ankle, and she swims up. "That was my longest yet!" she squeals.

Lance high fives her before she swims off down the pool, heading for the giant unicorn float at the other end.

"It was short but sweet. And it would've been highly inappropriate to wait until I got home. Painful even."

I try to hold back my smile as he swims toward me. "It didn't last very long?"

I feel his eyes on the side of my face. "No."

"Doesn't sound like a very intimate phone call."

He turns away from Ave, facing his body out toward the ocean. His shoulder brushes mine. "There's nothing intimate about my cock in my own hand while I think about the feel of you wrapped around it, sunshine. Sucking on it. Dripping down it." I don't dare look at him. "That's not intimate? Am I getting that right?"

"That's right." I compose myself before turning my head toward him, finding his cheeks tinted red. I can't help but bounce my eyes around his face. "That's just a man with a dirty mind jacking off in a bathroom. It makes sense, though." I shrug. "You never could last long when it was me under you."

"I don't remember you ever complaining." He looks over his shoulder before inching closer, his mouth ghosting my ear as he reaches out and tugs on the ring that dangles from the end of my necklace. "And, baby, I jacked off in your bed, not a bathroom. If you're going to make my dick hard, you're sure as fuck going to let me lie where you sleep when I come for you."

My heart trips over itself, my chest working faster as a scarlet flush covers it. "You're too much," I mutter, side-eyeing him.

He runs his hands through his hair as he relaxes back against the pool. "You make me this way."

I push off from the wall, making sure to put my ass in the air as I swim under and surface again, creating a distance between us. I push my hair back, clearing the water from my face. "So, it *was* a good phone call?" I ask, playful.

His smirk is pure promise as he lazes in the heat of the sun. "Fucking lovely, sunshine."

TWENTY-FIVE

Lance

I'm barely out of the shower when there's a knock on my bedroom door. Wrapping my towel around my waist, I head over and open it. My smile is instant. "You're spoiling me."

Scarlet stands on the other side of the threshold, freshly showered and wearing a long, black, holey, see-through contraption that makes my balls ache. Her lavender hair is pulled high, twisted in a bun.

She licks at her glossy lips, her eyes fighting to stay on my face. "I just came to tell you to dress up tonight. Wear a shirt."

I tip up my chin. "Why?"

"Just do it," she snaps, not taking my shit. She looks over her shoulder.

When she turns back to me, I cock my head for her to come inside, smiling.

"No," she whispers, but doesn't move.

I grin and step over the threshold, wrapping one arm around her waist to secure her to my body as I lift her, carrying her inside. I shut the door behind me.

"Lance, Ave needs me."

"I need you," I whisper against her temple, placing her down. "To listen to me. To be close. Just for a second."

She sighs, her body relaxing.

I ease back, letting my eyes explore her face. And holy fuck is she beautiful. "You remember when I told you you're the personification of life."

Her eyes shine up at me, and then she gives me a nod.

"Well, I think what I meant by that is everything in it." I trace her hair line with a lone finger, eyes trailing the motion. "The sun comes out, and I think of you. The moon and stars, they're yours. Beauty, grace, light and dark." I straighten the ring that hangs between her breasts. "Love." I lift my eyes to hers. "I can't seem to grasp a single thing in this world without thinking about you."

"Lance—"

"You look stunning, Scarlet." Everything I've wished for and more than I'll ever deserve. "A better man would ask before kissing you." I take her lips with my own, my eyes closing when she melts into me. When her mouth opens for me, I slip my tongue inside.

The second our tongues touch, Scarlet pushes me back, chasing my mouth until I'm against the door. I groan, feeling my cock pulse as her teeth drag across my bottom lip.

Unhinged, I turn us, putting her to the door and reaching into the slit in her dress to lift her leg around my waist.

Bending my knees, I grind up, her swimsuit-covered pussy dragging over my towel covered cock.

"Lance." She grips my neck, sensing my need and moving with me.

I kiss her again. Harder. Telling.

You don't stop kissing me.

And suddenly, it becomes messy, messier than I planned when I pulled her into the room. I knew I'd kiss her. I knew that within the first three seconds of pulling open the door. But this... the towel dislodges from my waist, my cock bobbing free and hard. I'm so fucking hard.

Scarlet rubs herself against me over and over, the friction from her bathing suit making my body coil tight.

Close.

Too close.

I break the kiss, trying to find focus on her as I pull back. "Shit."

Her hand dips between our bodies, wrapping around my cock. And if it's not the best feeling in the fucking world.

I close my eyes, letting the feel of her hand on me settle in my bones. I've needed this for too long. Dreamt of it. Of her.

"You'll look at me when you come for me."

I snap my eyes open. Her own eyes fluttering, heavy, filled with desire. She pumps my cock, squeezing me just enough to make my balls draw up. She dusts her thumb across the head, spreading the precum that leaks out. I widen my stance, one hand on the door above her head and the other I let roam, from her ass to her waist, to her tits, and then up to her neck. I squeeze when she tightens her fist around me, but she squeezes harder, and I drop my head forward, nuzzling her shoulder instead. "Scar, baby, please."

She flicks her tongue over the skin just below my ear before sucking. "What do I get?"

I fight the urge to screw my eyes tight, keeping my gaze on her. "Anything."

Her eyes sparkle with delight. She leans in, her nipples hard and teasing against my chest despite her bikini top and dress. She lifts her free hand and smooths it down my face. My cock somehow gets harder from the extra contact. "Come for me, Lance," she whispers softly. "And I'll let you lick me clean tonight."

My body jerks, hips rolling up into her fist as she works me up and down.

I come in a rush, covering my stomach and her hand. It's the second time I've come because of her today, within a matter of hours, and it doesn't get any less fucking good. If anything, it feels better.

I crave more.

Need more.

I twitch in her hand, and she palms my cock, stroking up the length as I soften.

Leaning back an inch, I peer down at her hand wrapped around me, then into her eyes.

Those eyes.

Fuck, those eyes.

I'm gone. Ruined. "You fucking own me," I whisper, breath ragged. "You know that?"

Her answering smile tells me she does.

Scarlet

I avert my eyes when Lance spots us and stands from his chair, my stomach churning with anticipation.

The sun's setting, lanterns lighting up the outside dining area and cliff tops as a warm evening breeze dusts over the lodges in a gentle caress. Ave and I set the table ourselves this afternoon, picking flowers on our walk to use as a centrepiece.

Reaching for Ave's hand, I give her a reassuring nod, knowing she's nervous. When I look back up, I can't help but gawk at the man adorned with the most breathtaking, genuine, full smile.

There was a time I'd have given anything to see that smile on his face. Some days I'd have to work for it; the ones when he'd come home from work or after visiting his mum and need topping up.

I remember walking into his hospital room only last month, not knowing if I'd ever see him smile fully again.

"Daddy looks beautiful, Mummy," Ave says, tugging on my hand.

I go to look down at her. I at least try. But my eyes are glued to him. "Yeah," I murmur, swallowing. "He does."

We walk the rest of the way to the table, Lance taking a half step as we near. "Girls."

"Hi, Daddy." Ave waves awkwardly, not the only tell she's nervous if her slick hand in mine is anything to go by.

With one hand behind his back, Lance drops to one knee in front of her, squinting his eyes. "Miss Sullivan, it can't be."

Ave's smile could light a village. "Auntie Lucy made me this dress."

He pulls his arm from behind his back, revealing a fresh bouquet of pink roses. "You know, I bought these flowers for you thinking they were beautiful, but you just made them the third most beautiful thing I've looked at all day."

I see her eyes shine, and Lance looks up at me, his face so handsome my stomach twists.

"The third?" Ave eventually asks, playing right into his hands.

"Well, you're the first—by a mile."

She giggles. "Then what's the second?"

He tilts his head at her, his smile coy as he leans in and whispers in her ear.

Ave's eyes widen and then instantly flick up to me. I look away smiling, and I hear, feel, Lance's deep chuckle in places I'd never give him the satisfaction of knowing about.

"I cooked for you," Ave tells him, taking his hand and pulling him to his feet. She guides him to the table, not waiting for him to pull out her chair as he tries to before she climbs up and waits for him to sit.

"You cooked for me?" he repeats, giving her his undivided attention. "What did you make?"

I make my way around the table, sitting on the other side of Lance and opposite Ave.

"Steak. Mummy said it's your favourite. We made dessert, too, because the steak was really boring to prepare."

"I can totally see that," he agrees, pinning me with a look as his tongue darts out and swipes at his full bottom lip. "I've actually been looking forward to dessert all evening."

I shake my head in warning, my face flushing hot at memories of him naked, hard, and begging, the promises I had him make.

"Wine?" Ave asks, reaching for the bottle. Lance intervenes, taking it from her and pouring us both a glass and her some fizzy.

We eat our food as the sun slowly sets, the three of us lost in a constant stream of conversation—and confessions from Ave about the number of tiles she's peeled off the pool and hidden in her bedroom. It's relaxed. Real.

It's what I think a family should be.

We're mid-dessert when Ave stands, using her napkin to wipe her mouth in an act far beyond her years.

I'd smile, tell her with words, but she's well aware of how proud I am of her.

She flickers her eyes over Lance, quickly dropping them to her pocket. "I wrote some things down that I wanted to tell you."

Lance looks at me in question, and then at Ave, placing down his spoon with his smile still spread wide. "What's that?"

She pulls out a folded piece of paper and clears her throat.

"Okay..." She blows out a long heavy breath. "Daddy, I used to ask Mummy all about you when you were gone. I didn't know who you were or if you'd even like me. I thought you'd be like someone I didn't know when we finally met, like my first day at school all over again." She looks up at us smiling. "But you turned out to be everything Mummy promised you would be." I side-eye Lance, finding his smile long gone, fist clenched at his mouth, and his eyes shining. "She told me you'd come back and love me. She said your heart was bigger than anyone knew, even you, and that there was room with—for me." Ave smiles, rolling her lips as she sways, tripping over her words. "I don't know if I fit in there like she said I would, or if you do love me." She rushes over the word, catching my heart on fire. "But I do know that you fit in mine. I've always been a bit silly, and I think I was so scared of you not loving me that I didn't think about how much I might love you. Mummy, you told me that love can be really scary at times, and I think you're right, but Dad, since you came home, I don't feel that scared at all. I even tried sleeping without my lamp on last night." I gently swipe a tear from my face, dropping my other hand to steady Lance's bouncing knee under the table. "She also said that you don't get to pick and choose who you give your love to, your heart chooses, but I know that I'd choose you, Daddy, even if my heart didn't."

Lance is up before Ave can even get the last word out, scooping her off her feet. He holds her against his chest, tucking his face between her shoulder and neck.

I already know he'll never let her go.

Ave's arms wrap around his shoulders, clinging on for dear life as she squeezes her eyes tight together. When she eventually sits back, she has to coax the six-foot-three teddy bear's face from her neck. "Daddy."

He submits, lifting his head. Ave palms his cheek, and my throat catches as he leans into her, knowing what it does for him, how with just a touch he can be brought back from the darkest of places.

"You have tears," Ave says, wiping them away with a frown on her face. "Mummy..."

"It's okay, Ave," I tell her. "They're happy tears."

Lance twists his head to look at me, and I give him the best smile I can muster despite the tears lining my own cheeks.

You deserve her love.

You deserve the world, Lance Sullivan.

With a fleeting glance my way, he puts his forehead to hers. "Waverley, there's nowhere to fit. You are my heart. From the second I met you, and every moment since, it's been the rest of the world against you. I love you." He kisses her nose. "Even when you're a bit silly."

"You love me back?" She grins.

"I love you back times the biggest number possible."

I watch my little girl light up from the inside out. Years of unknown, of waiting, and she has her daddy right where he should be. I never doubted Lance's ability to love her. I knew the dad he'd be. And now I get to watch the two of them make and mend one another.

They deserve this.

I don't know two people who deserve this more.

"Scar," Lance says, cocking his head. "Come here."

I stand hesitantly, pulling my dress straight before walking to them. "Is your leg okay?"

Lance just smiles at me, shaking his head. Wrapping an arm around my waist, he pulls me into his side with them. Ave loops an arm around my neck.

Emotion lodges in my throat, and before I can swallow

down the feeling overcoming me, I cry, burying my face into Lance's chest.

The feel of them both so close, of their limbs around me, around each other. The smell of them. Their warmth.

"Girls," Lance says, his voice steady. When I don't look up, he takes my chin, lifting it. He tilts his head, that knowing smirk I've missed dusting his cheeks. "Happy tears?" he asks.

I nod, and he kisses my forehead before brushing noses with Ave, making sure he has her attention, too.

He looks between us both. "This is forever—no matter what. We fight, I love you. You don't agree with me on dad stuff, I love you." Ave chuckles, and he smiles before sobering his features, looking down at me. "We struggle for forgiveness... I love *you*."

I'll love you regardless, he tells me without words.

"This is the bestest day ever," Ave says, dropping her legs from Lance's waist and standing. "Can I finish my ice cream now?"

"Go for it," Lance tells her, not letting me go.

He smiles down at me, his eyes watching as if he knows all that's in my head and understands it when I don't.

With Ave busy at the table, he leans in to place a light kiss at the corner of my mouth.

He doesn't say anything else, letting his hand brush my abdomen as he rounds me and heads back to the table.

And with him goes another piece of my heart.

TWENTY-SIX

Lance

Some would call my day perfect, the best even—Waverley did. But I know that until I'm done with Scarlet Lowell tonight, it won't be enough.

She's in her bedroom when I find her, her hand working the clasp of her earring free. I stand just inside the door, knowing she's noticed but chooses to ignore me. I was too much at dinner. Maybe not for Waverley. In fact, I think it was exactly what Waverley and I needed. Her words stole a piece of me I never knew I owned.

I promised myself there and then I'd never let her question my love for her again.

I know what it's like to fight for the love of a parent, and Waverley won't ever know that pain.

"You need something, handsome?" Scarlet asks.

I push off from the door, pulling my hands from my pockets as I approach her. When I'm at her back, I pull her hair off her shoulder and kiss the smooth skin beneath. "You know, you almost look too good to spoil."

She peers up at me in the mirror, a hesitant smile lurking.

I trace her jaw with my finger until I reach her ear. "Almost," I rasp.

I work the other earring free, dipping my head to place a kiss just below. Her skin is warm, sweet from her body wash and perfume. I run my nose up the length of her neck, my eyes drifting closed. My palms smooth up her thighs, over her dress, my fingers dipping and dragging over her skin through the holes. "I *love* this dress," I tell her, gathering it in my hands and inching it up her legs. She lifts her arms when it reaches her waist, helping me remove it.

I toss it to the ground, my eyes already on the long length of her back.

Dropping my hand, I run my finger over the cheek of her ass.

Goose bumps trail.

Can I want to rush this, desperate to taste her, and want to make it last all night at the same time?

Heart thudding, I lean into her and wrap my arms around her body, holding her, the smell of her shampoo reminding me of a million moments just like this one. "Tell me I can have you tomorrow."

She twists her head up to look at me. "Lance..." she whispers.

"I know." I force a smile. "I know."

Pushing up on her tiptoes, she palms my cheek, bringing her lips to mine. Her kiss is slow, an apology, maybe. But it's enough—fuck, it's enough.

Even if it's all she'll ever give me, it's enough.

I tug on the string of her bikini top, the material going slack at her breasts. I gently pull it free of her arms and let it drop to the floor.

Her nipples are hard, and I let my eyes roam them greedily in the mirror as my cock grows stiff behind my shorts.

"Touch me." Her head drops back to my chest, a moan falling from her lips. "Please."

I skim my fingers from her hips to waist, watching as goose bumps ripple over her body. "Where?" My knuckles dust up the sides of her breasts and back down again.

She frowns, lips part. "Everywhere."

I pick her up and carry her to the bed, laying her down.

"Do I get to have you naked, too?" she asks.

I kneel on the mattress, popping a brow as she makes herself comfy on the bed. I can't help but get distracted by her body. "You want to undress me?"

She watches me down the length of her torso as I tease the band on her bikini. "Maybe later."

I smirk, wetting my lips as I tug her bottoms free, dragging them down her legs. I revel in the sharp intake of breath that leaves her once she's bare. Completely bare to me.

My hands trail down the smooth skin at her waist, curling at her hips. Instinct forces my eyes closed at the feel of her, but I fight them open as I look down at her pussy.

My thumbs spread her open. And then I groan, low and deep in my chest. "I apologise for the man I am after this." I flick my eyes up to hers. "I've been starved for seven years too long."

My head dips, and she gasps.

The first taste of her reminds me. The second fucks me up a little in the head. And the third—

"Lance," she sings.

She fucking sings.

I lose myself in the sounds that leave her, groan and hiss with every roll of her hips, every slash of my tongue, lapping at everything she gives me.

I remember what she likes, the way she'll grip the sheets if I suck and kiss down her lips, the twist and nips at her clit, the pressure behind the flat of my tongue.

Her hands find my hair at some point, snaking in, clutching the roots, my neck. I suck harder, grinning against her slick flesh when her thighs clench the sides of my head. "I fucking love it when you do that, sunshine."

"I'm... fuck, I'm—"

I slide a single finger into her, and her mouth drops open, back bowing as she forces her hips down the bed. "You're as greedy as I am," I mutter, pulling my finger out and sucking it into my mouth. "You'd take me so fucking good right now. You're dripping for me."

"Lance, please." I lift my head to watch her. Her cheeks are flushed red. "Please. I need you to..."

I grin, catching the wetness shining on the end of my nose with the back of my hand. I don't make her finish her words. Instead, I dip my tongue low, fluttering over her open-ing, teasing, before leisurely moving north. I slip two fingers into her, her whimper making my cock twitch as she clenches her pussy around me.

She wants me.

She wants my fucking cock.

"More."

I add a third finger, slow, watching as she takes them. "Fuck." I dip my head and suck her clit between my lips, pumping my fingers in and out.

Her knees capture me, hips driving up.

And then she comes around my fingers, pussy rippling and tightening as I lick and suck and kiss. I let her ride it out, her hips bucking and rolling with each lick. When I gently slide my slick fingers out of her, she whimpers.

I grasp her thighs, smearing the stickiness across her silky skin as I hold them open.

Her pussy glistens under the lights.

I drop my head, groaning as I lick up the length of her and swallow.

I rise on my knees, my hands trailing up her thighs. "Baby," I say, too throaty, not missing the desire in my voice, the need. There's no way Scarlet doesn't hear it, too. I lean myself over her, a hand beside her head and the other trailing the length of her body—hip to breast. I keep our bodies apart, my cock too hard to even think about giving in to the space between us.

The thought of not having her like this again, to have and to hold and to love every day for the rest of my life... "You could break me, and I'm pretty sure I'd crawl back in pieces asking you to do it again."

"I don't want to break you." Her voice falters. With her hands woven in my hair, she pulls me down for a firm but short kiss. "I'd never hurt you intentionally, Lance."

She kisses me again, groaning into my mouth when I

cover her breast with my palm, her nipple hardening between my splayed fingers.

Our tongues lick and tease, deep and slow. Her hands work on the buttons of my shirt, popping one after another in quick succession. I help her pull the shirt from my shoulders, the cuffs tearing when I rip them free of my wrists. Before I can even discard it, Scarlet has my shorts unzipped, her hand dipping into my boxer briefs to pull out my cock.

My eyes close at the feel of her hand wrapped around me.

I cup her face, using my other hand to lower my shorts, pushing them past my knees and feet. When her hand glides down the length of me, I curse, demanding her lips in another kiss.

Both naked, I lower myself over her. My cock settles in the line of her pussy, and it's warm and wet and all things fucking perfect.

I reach for her leg, grasping her behind the knee and lifting it to my side. I rock into her once, the head of my dick steamrolling her clit.

She drags her mouth away, dips back in and sucks on my bottom lip, and then lifts her eyes to mine. I can feel her heart thumping against my chest. "Have me," she breathes out, gaze searching. "Have me tonight. I'll figure out tomorrow when it comes."

I swallow as something unravels inside of me. Lay here with Scarlet beneath me, caged in my arms. Telling me to... "Have you?" I repeat.

"In every way that you need me. Just like I need you." She rolls her hips, gasping at the friction. She reaches between us, squeezing her breasts. "Love me like it's the last time, and fuck me like it's the first."

Her words make my chest burn, a firework going off in my stomach, sending a million sparks soaring through my veins. I groan, nuzzling her hands away and sucking on a nipple.

I grind against her pussy over and over, revelling in the feel. Of all the nights I lay with my cock in my hand, imagining the ways she could make me come. Of all the ways she did make me come.

With the sweet stickiness gathered between Scarlet's legs, coating me, I only have to angle my hips back and low, and the tip of my cock settles at her entrance. Our mouths hang open, lips together, frozen like our bodies as we teeter on the edge. "Which first?" I say, panting.

Her eyes darken, and before she can tell me with words that she wants me to fuck her, I sink into her pussy.

But *love* is fucking something and even when you want it to be nothing, it's everything.

Scarlet's moan grounds me, brings me back down to earth with a thud that mirrors my heart. I ease out of her, our hands a tangled mess as we grasp for one another, and I'm so to fuck with fucking her, I look into her eyes and slowly, inch by inch, sink back inside.

It's torture, yet I relish every second of it. I shake my head, settling down to lie over her as her hands thread through my hair. "Later, sunshine." I kiss her, holding her face as our mouths move in unison. I rock forward, knowing I'm as deep as I can go but needing more. "I promise I'll fuck you later."

Because this isn't a fuck like the first time. Not even close. It's skin to skin. Stolen kisses. Deep primal need between two people in love.

Even if she can't admit it.

Her hands roam my back, and I gather them up, entwining our fingers and lifting them to the pillow as my knee pushes her thigh up the bed, putting me deeper.

My brow meets hers, and I stare down at her, her heart thumping steadily against my chest. I screw my eyes tight, never wanting this to end. "Your heart's pounding."

"So is yours," she whispers, then kisses me.

I smile and wet my lips. As I lean back on my knees, my cock slides out of her, leaving it twitching and bobbing and Scarlet whimpering. I move down her body, dipping my head to kiss the underside of her left breast.

Hopelessly fucking wild.

I trail my nose over the words.

As I move back up her body, I enter her, sinking in inch by inch, watching as she takes me.

I wrap her up in my arms, rocking and grinding deep—too deep, desperate to find the mark I know I once left on her soul.

Scarlet

I lie on my side, tracing Waverley's name that's etched on the inside of Lance's bicep. Lance is lay on his back, his wide chest rising and falling in a gentle motion. "Did you ever think about what your children might be called?"

He opens his eyes, dropping his head to his pillow to look at me. "I never believed I'd have kids. My mum and dad put me off for a lifetime."

I huff a laugh, curling my hand around his neck and pulling myself closer to lie nose to nose. "I used to think about it all the time. I saw myself with lots of children. A house full."

"And you had names for all of them?"

"I had a list." I grin at him, and he stares at my mouth, as if memorising it. "It's probably at home somewhere."

He takes my hand, linking our fingers despite how close we already are. "Why'd you even ask?"

My stomach coils tight, the image of his strong body on top of mine, thrusting into me. I flick my eyes up to his. "We didn't use a condom."

"And so you're asking me if I know what I'd call my kids?"

I chuckle, not realising how creepy it sounds.

"That's me level crazy, Scarlet," he says. "I'm almost proud."

I squeeze his hand, leaning into him. "Stop. I obviously started at *Shit, we didn't use a condom* and then ended up at *I wonder if Lance ever had baby names picked out.* There was a whole ton of overthink in between."

"Sure, sunshine. I'm surprised you didn't lie with your legs in the air for ten minutes after."

I can't help the silly giggle that leaves me. "What do you know about it?" I tease.

"Enough." He twists our legs together. "Now, tell me these names."

"I don't even remember them." I try to ease the adrenaline rushing through me. "And I don't want any more children."

He narrows his eyes on me, his voice softer when he asks, "Will you tell me why?"

"Because..." The memory of the screen at my face, the lack of feeling as they cut into me. I'll never forget that day. How I felt. The sense of loss. "The day Ave was *born* should have been the best day of my life. But do you know how many times I've told someone that the day she was *taken* from me was the worst. It wasn't happy or exciting or special. It was tragic. It defined the twelve months of our lives that followed. I'll never put myself or anyone else in a position to go through that again."

First, I lost Mum. And then Mase. My best friend—my dad. The love of my life—Lance. And my sweet baby who never gave up on me even when I gave up on us both—Ave.

Coldness seals around my heart like a locket, sizzling away at the burning heat Lance put there only minutes ago.

God, I can't do that again.

"Hey." He takes my chin, forcing my eyes up. "Hey, don't do that. You don't want any more kids, I'm good. You want ten then I'll give you eleven. But don't shut me out. Please, Scar. You promised me tonight."

I see the plea shining back at me in his eyes along with understanding. And sorrow. And regret.

"Lance, for a man who's known such little love, you sure know how to give it." I turn into his touch, kissing his palm. "I hope one day you let more than just me see the man you are. You'd surprise a few."

"I don't care about anyone else. Just you and Waverley."

"Why do you only call her by her full name? There isn't anyone who uses it anymore."

"Ave doesn't mean a thing to me. Waverley means the world."

I nod, lost in his eyes. "I'd hate it if anyone else used it now," I whisper in a daze. "It's her name, and I'd hate it."

"Don't try to make sense of it. It's okay to be a little crazy over the things that mean something to you." He kisses my neck. "I revel in it whenever I'm near you."

"Hmm." I let his lips roam to my jaw, nipping and sucking, before guiding his head up so I can look at him again. At his eyes. "You look tired, Lance."

A soft rumble vibrates in his chest, his lips curling. "I'm fine. I'll sleep tonight."

Because he's in bed with me?

Even after what happened in the shower back at home, I still shared his bed, more for me than him if I'm being truthful.

I'm not sure when it happened, when the need flipped. Maybe it didn't at all if the red diluting the whites of Lance's eyes tell a story, but at some point, the footsteps padding on the floorboards to his room became heavier, desperate, seeking out the contentment his company brings me. Something we both seem to crave from one another.

I don't want to need anyone. To rely on a single person to survive.

"I'm sorry," I tell him. "I was worried with the rooms being so much closer here... it's so new for Ave even having you in her life without seeing us..."

"Shh." His lips brush mine. "I went seven years without you. The fact I'm even here on this island, in this lodge with you..." He kisses my jaw, dipping for my neck again. "Fuck, I could do this all fucking day, though."

I purse my lips, tilting my head back to give him better access. "Of course you could. Physical touch is your kryptonite."

The scruff of his jaw scratches my throat as his mouth stretches into a smile. "Scarlet, Scarlet, Scarlet," he chides. "You're supposed to be smart."

I chuckle, closing my eyes as his hands and lips explore further. He nuzzles my chest, biting before licking the underside of my breast. Something in me soars when he leans back and looks at my breasts, almost boyish.

I can't help but feel robbed of the years we lost. The majority of his thirties stripped away not just from him but me, too.

"I slept on these that night in the shower. I've missed them."

He stares at them, hands palming their heaviness while his fingers tease across my nipples.

I look down at him, at his hands, my nipples hard. "I think they missed you, too."

When his eyes lift, he grins, and for a second, I let go of the lost time. The what wasn't, what was, and what could've been. Those seven years were the best and worst of my life.

Instead, I take his smile, and I pretend there's not missing parts, not a smile I missed, or a tear I couldn't wipe away.

"If you promised me you wouldn't remember tomorrow, I might think about telling you I love you tonight."

He smiles smugly, his tongue poking out between his teeth. "I ain't promising you shit, Baby Lowell."

"I'm awful, aren't I?"

He rolls us, putting me on top and straddling his waist. I lean over him, my hair creating a veil around us. "No. Not even a little bit." He looks at me as if he knows I'm close, as if he doesn't care at all that I'm a coward. He has his line cast and can feel the tug on the other end. The fight of his life is almost in touching distance—because I am close. "You're perfect. *You're* my kryptonite."

And I don't deserve you.

With tears forming in my eyes, I bend and take his full lips.

Lance takes my hips and pushes me down his body, far enough back I line up with his erection. "Ride me while I appreciate your tits, Scarlet."

TWENTY-SEVEN

Scarlet

Whenever I'm at home and I reminisce about being here at the lodges, I always think of these moments. It's not the sun blazing down on the lounger as sweat sticks to my warmed skin, or the evenings spent around the fire pit or the dinner table. I love all of those things. But when I think back, I think about this.

The sun's slowly rising over the cliff top, the view uninterrupted thanks to the open doors and glass balcony panels.

It's a promise to me.

I wait all night in the darkness for the sun to come up and bring back the light. Everything is a little less heavy, clearer in the sun's presence.

Lance must have opened the curtains and doors. No matter how much time has passed, he still remembers all the little things. And I know by the heat still warming the mattress at my back that he left me only a short while ago, knowing Ave could walk in here at any minute and find us together.

Locks on the doors would be really helpful on mornings like this.

I smile at the thought, reaching for my phone so that I can add it to my notes. But as I reach out my hand, it slaps back to my chest. I frown, lifting it.

The sun breaks the cliff's edge as goose bumps pebble across my skin. I sit up, my eyes immovable from the ring on my left ring finger, the necklace still looped through its belly.

"I love you," I whisper, testing the words as my stomach twists into knots. "I. Love. You."

I slide it from my finger, letting it hang around my neck again. Then, with shaking hands, I reach for my phone.

I text Fran.

Scar: Can I see you when I'm home?

I pull up my Notes app and quickly add *locks* to my ever-growing to-do list, then drop my phone to the sheets I'm tangled in and sigh, a tear sliding down my temple.

I'd give anything to be just a little bit normal.

After showering, I slide on my favourite pink bikini and pick out the dress I've been saving, not sparing myself a second glance in the mirror as I head toward the smell of food cooking in the kitchen.

I hear them before I see them. "It's burning."

"I'm almost done."

"Dad..."

"I—" I hear a huff. "I don't know which I did last."

"Did you not keep the last strand in your pinkie? Remember that's the key."

Curious, I lean around the kitchen door, peeking into the room.

Ave is sat up on a stool, a YouTube video playing out in front of them which I can't quite make out. Lance seems to step away from Ave's back, hot-footing it to the sandwich toaster that's smoking on the other side of the kitchen.

"Told you," Ave deadpans. I can sense her smirk from here without even seeing her face. "Maybe we should try a ponytail today."

"No. You asked for braids."

"Turns out you're terrible at them," she sasses.

I smile as he sticks the spatula under the smoking sandwich and tosses it onto the counter. "It's my first time."

"Hmm. Ever made a cheese toastie before?"

"Waverley," he warns.

Her shoulders shake as she watches him. "I'll find a how to guide for dummies. They do a step-down version for beginners."

Shaking my head, I step into the room. "You're cruel, Ave."

They both turn to look at me.

"Morning, Mummy," Ave sings sweetly.

I tug on the messy, half-done braid that's slowly unfurling as I pass her. "You can't fool me, girly." I make my way around the island, my eyes firmly, unashamedly on the man who can't help but stare back at me. His eyes drop down my dress, and I know the second he notices.

"You told her?" he asks, looking around me at Ave.

I frown.

"I haven't told her nothing."

"Told me what?" I ask.

"Nothing." He shakes his head. "It's just... that dress."

The dress I wore on the day he picked me up from the pharmacy.

"You look perfect. It's perfect, actually."

Not understanding but choosing to go with it, I reach over and pick up the mostly burnt cheese toastie off the side.

"Sorry. We were going to bring you breakfast in bed."

I lift it to my mouth and take a bite out of the least burnt part.

"Scarlet, I'll make you another one."

I shake my head. "I want this one."

"You're weird," Ave mutters from behind me, making me smile. I take another bite. It's not nearly as bad as Ave makes out.

"It's fine."

"She's lying. You're both as bad as each other."

Lance chuckles, his smile wide as he steps around me and goes back to doing Ave's hair. I pull out a chair and watch while I nibble on the edible parts of my sandwich.

Half an hour later, Vinny walks in through the double doors. "Morning."

"Hey, Vin." I smile.

He comes around to kiss the top of my head.

We've barely seen him this week, and it shows. Whenever we come here, he ends up running around after everyone else despite us all telling him it's a break for him, too. But the golden tan that makes his blue eyes gleam and the lightness around his eyes, tells me he's used the week to rest and recharge.

"Vinny, will you do my braids? Dad's terrible, and Mum's refusing."

Vinny's chuckle rumbles from deep in his chest. "I don't want to get into trouble, Ave."

Lance holds his hands up, letting go of his now fifth attempt. He's nearly got it to be fair. "Please help me." He eyes me. "We've got to get going anyway."

"Get going where?" I ask as Vinny takes his place and starts brushing Ave's hair.

"He's taking you on a date," Ave teases. "He even went shopping and bought you a new dress."

I look to Lance, his hands on his hips as he shakes his head at his daughter. He brings his attention to me. "Your dress is perfect, Scarlet. I'll take the other back."

I smile. "What date?"

He shrugs, his cheeks colouring as he flicks his eyes from Vinny to Ave to me. "I never really took you on a first official one."

So that's why he was looking at my dress.

"Will you come?"

"On a date?"

He nods, swallowing around an unnecessary ball of doubt that he seems to hold in his throat.

I bite back my smile, looking across the kitchen island at Vinny and Ave. Ave who now has a perfect French braid twisted in her hair. "We're going to head into the village for the day, if that's okay," Vinny tells me. "Thought we could meet you there for dinner tonight when you're done. One last knees-up before we head home tomorrow."

"What's a knees-up?" Ave asks.

"That's sounds perfect, Vin. Thank you."

He nods gently, helping Ave down from the chair and taking her hand. "A knees-up is like a get together..."

I stare after them as their voices fade out down the corridor, a heavy but warm ache pulsing in my chest.

I sometimes wonder if Mum sent Vinny because she knew Dad wouldn't have enough time with us.

"He's a top bloke, isn't he?"

With a watery smile, I look at Lance. "The best."

He moves around the kitchen toward me. "You look beautiful today."

"Thank you." My skin burns as he pulls me to his chest. I tip my head back, peering up at him. "Where are you taking me?"

"It's a surprise."

I purse my lips, refraining from kissing him. "I wore this dress for you today." I grin, and he smirks back, stepping away from me with our hands entwined.

He picks up a basket from the side, leading me from the kitchen. "I know you did, sunshine."

Butterflies flutter in my stomach as Lance shakes out the blanket and flattens it to the bed of the boat. I say boat, but the one-hundred-foot yacht that Lance has hired for the day would sink if it could hear me.

"This is beautiful," I say in awe.

Lance stands, gazing around the open water.

My attention is firmly on him.

He's wearing a white linen shirt with beige shorts and black sunglasses. His hair is styled in a perfect mess, as if he's run his hand through it and said done. His jaw is coated in the same dark stubble that brushed against the soft skin at my thighs last night.

He looks like he did when we first met, only older and just *more*.

I'm not sure I've ever been more attracted to a man.

"I have some not so burnt things in here," he tells me, a cheeky look on his face as he lays himself out on the blanket and reaches for the basket. "Waverley helped me pack this, so no judgement."

I sit down on the blanket, folding my legs under me.

Lance pulls out a bottle of champagne and two glasses, uncorking it and handing me a glass. "Thank you," I say, not drinking it right away.

He extends his hand toward me. "To a better first date."

I pull my glass to my chest before he can clink it. "I loved the first."

"So did I. But this one will be better," he says, leaning further and tapping his glass to mine. He takes a sip, and I follow, the bubbles fizzing on my tongue.

"Do you remember much from that first night?" I ask.

"Other than taking you out to dinner and getting knocked on my ass?" He chuckles, his eyes darkening as he meets my eyes. "I remember all of it. I kept thinking I should run. The second I knew you were too good for me, I knew I should go back the way I came."

"You didn't."

"I couldn't. You told me you didn't have time for me, that you'd fuck me but wouldn't give me a thing more. It was like a moth to a flame." He looks away from me, shaking his head. "I was ruined from the first kiss."

I stare at the side of his face. "I was never too good for you."

He twists his head back to look at me. "You were entirely too good for me. Still are now."

"Maybe in your mind that's true, but in mine, that's not how I see it. You pulled me out of that place when no one else could. And I don't just mean the estate. I was happy, but I wasn't living, not really."

He stares at me, and I know he knows it, too. "You'd have found a way out."

"Maybe." I give in, knowing he'll never agree. "But I'm glad it was you."

He smiles into his glass. "What do you remember from it? That first night."

I blow out a breath. "Not being able to walk home."

A proud look takes over his face when my cheeks flush, the both of us laughing.

"No, mostly I remember thinking the world was mad. This man was stood giving me pieces one after another asking for nothing but my time in return. You were kind to me, told me more than anyone had about themselves in years, and made me feel like the most precious thing on earth. I remember wondering where you came from, why you were still single, and how long I'd get before you'd leave."

"I had no intention of going anywhere."

"I know. I still hoped every day you'd stick around."

"You told me you only wanted one night." He smiles, calling me out.

"I lied to the both of us," I mutter. "And I took a hundred more nights after that one, too."

"I wish I told Mase," he says out of nowhere. "Sometimes I wonder if things might have been different if I had."

"Hmm," I ponder, revelling in the sun as it warms my face. "It's easy to look back and think about all the things we would have done differently. If I listened to my head instead of following my heart that first night with you, my dad might still be here. I likely would've been there that day and maybe I could've saved him, but I wouldn't know you. I wouldn't have Ave. Mase wouldn't be home."

He stares at me thoughtfully, his eyes full of regret. "I'm sorry I broke the promises I made that night, Scarlet. I truly meant them at the time, not knowing how hard I'd fall or how easy they'd be to break."

I give him a sad smile, then look out across the water, realising how much of a trance we've slipped into. "I'm sorry, too."

And I mean it. Lance may have broken his promises, but he did it protecting me.

I lean over, spotting the cheese block in the basket and pulling it out. "You brought me cheese."

"I know the way to my girl's heart."

He doesn't see my smile, too busy rooting around in the

basket. He fishes out a knife and then gestures for the cheese. "Thank you," I say, handing it to him.

"I have a question for you."

I sit back, closing my eyes. "I'm listening."

"It's about Bear."

I look across at him.

"How come he ended up at the house with you."

"Ave," I tell him simply. "From the first time she met him he just loved her. He was overweight and needed a place to run." I gauge the space between us, the basket keeping us separated. "It was one of those things that just made sense," I add.

"I'm glad, you know. That she knows them."

I let my stare falter on him, from the vulnerability on his face. "Me, too."

He gives me a small smile after a beat, instantly, purposely, lightening the mood. "If you want this cheese, you're going to have to come over here and get it."

"So very chivalrous of you, Mr Sullivan."

"I'm a confident man, not a chivalrous one. You've been eyeing me up over this basket for the last ten minutes."

Crap. "I've not."

"No?" He reaches over and feeds me a piece of cheese.

"Hmm."

Lance licks his lips, watching me. "Taste good?"

I nod, and he reaches for another piece. As I open my mouth, multiple pieces of cheese miss my mouth, two cubes falling into the front of my dress.

"Oh no," Lance mutters dramatically.

I chuckle as he moves the basket and pulls me closer.

He reaches for the front of my dress, peering inside. He looks up at me, a mischievous look on his face. "Don't worry, sunshine. I'm going to find them."

I tilt my head, my attention caught on his green eyes in this light.

How can anyone be this good-looking?

"Chivalrously," he starts, and I frown. "Lance plants his face into the slit in Scarlet's chest." Grinning, his head dips. "Lips as gentle as silk, they explore, hunting for the lost cheese."

I giggle, trying to get away. "You're an idiot," I tell him, running my hands through his hair as his mouth slows, matching his promise.

"If this was one of your books..." He runs his nose up my throat, and my breath catches. "What would happen next?"

His hand flattens on my waist, fingers grazing the underside of my bikini top through my dress. "She'd reach for the cheese knife and plunge it through his heart."

"A plot twist." He chuckles, nipping at my jaw.

"Uh-huh."

His large palm dips low, grazing my thigh before slipping under my dress.

I shake my head at him.

The moment he finds the piece of cheese at my waist, his eyes spark. He pulls it out and eats it.

"It's good, isn't it?"

He shrugs. "There's plenty of other things I'd rather eat."

"You're being dirty." I push his shoulder, and he catches my hand, smiling as he pulls me to straddle his lap.

"Sorry. I forget it's our first date." He brushes his thumb

over my lower lip, eyes lingering on the spot. "I should get to know you before I go putting my hand up your dress."

I pop a brow. "I'd say you know me better than anyone else."

"I do." I shift on his lap, and he shakes his head, grabbing my hips and grinding me harder. "I do, but I want to give you the best first date you've ever had. I can't leave anything on the table for when the next guy comes along."

"The next guy." I chuckle.

"I know." He grins as if finding it equally amusing. "You're fucking mine forever." He licks at his lips, proud, then tips his chin. "Aren't you, Scarlet?"

I lean over him, my hair shielding us from the rest of the world. It's just me and him. "I never said that."

My lips hover close, almost touching, when he whispers, "No, but you wore that dress today, knowing what it would remind me of."

"I might not say it with words some days, Lance, but you're in everything that I do."

"Kiss me," I beg, brushing my lips to his.

He lifts his chin, flirting with my mouth before bringing his hand to my face. He puts us chest to chest. "I love you, sunshine." He flattens his lips to mine.

And funnily enough, no matter how scary it feels, how badly I want and know I'll fight it, I want to be his forever.

TWENTY-EIGHT

Scarlet

We find Vinny and Ave in a tiny shack on the beach waiting for us as the sun dips low on the horizon, forcing the visitors on the island out to the beach to watch its descent.

Ave has the biggest smile on her face, bags of supplies from some of our favourite little shops on the island stashed at her feet. Vinny sits proudly at the head of the table, Ave and I either side of him and Lance next to Ave.

I can tell she missed her daddy today. She's not given him a second to breathe since we sat down, asking him a million and one questions.

Lance told her everything he could about our day, his eyes drifting to me every now and then and holding. And maybe I'm dreaming it, but I swear I can see him figuring me out. Can see him catch the moments my heart thaws little by little.

We eat unhurried, the conversation filled with Ave's chatter, laughing when she says something as out of pocket as always and listening in awe when she tells us something she learned today.

It's one of those nights that mean nothing to anyone else, but I know I'll never forget.

And I won't ever forget it.

"What's that?" Ave asks, pointing across the room.

I turn to look at what she's referring to, seeing a small casket being carried into the shack. "Ave, don't point," I tell her without looking back at her, my eyes transfixed as another casket is carried in right after, followed by a third.

"What..." I face Vinny, wondering if he knows what's going on, but he shakes his head, at a loss.

Do we leave? It seems rude to stay but disrespectful to get up in the middle of whatever this is.

Is it a wake?

Vinny spots a local, and friend, from the island and cocks his head for him to come over to our table. "Teva, do we need to leave?"

"No, no, you can stay. This is a celebration of life. Of love. You are welcome here."

"What happened?" Ave asks, leaning up in her chair to see better.

My eyes snap back, seeing a woman shrouded in what looks like a thick blanket, her head bowed over the smallest casket.

"A tragic accident. One of our own lost his life and two of his children's out on the sea. It doesn't happen often, but it happens." He nods toward the woman. "Mahana. She lost them all."

I stare at the mother, my eyes filling with tears as music starts to gently float around us. Songs sung for lives not lived. For a wife, a mother, who grieves the loves of her life.

I can feel the world already moving on around her, can feel the loss in her chest from the other side of the room.

I turn and stare down at my plate of food, feeling my hands start to tremble in my lap. "I think I'm going to go back to the lodge," I try to whisper, my mind lost to all the wrong things.

I need to pull back.

I'm going to go.

I can feel it.

"Scarlet," Vinny rasps.

I shake my head, closing my eyes. "I'm not feeling well."

"Scar," Lance tries, but I can't.

I can't.

"Mummy?"

The first thing I remember is the smell of Freya's perfume. She isn't here, and yet a distinct memory allows me to remember it as if she's wrapped around me at this very moment.

"Okay, Mum, they're taking the baby upstairs to neonatal. She'll get the help she needs up there."

I lift my head, trying, searching for her. There's no cries, no tears or screams. "Where is she?"

"They're taking her up to neonatal, darling, it's okay," Freya tells me. *"We knew if she came early, she'd need a little help."*

"Wait. It's Waverley. Her name is Waverley," I cry.

"It's okay, Scar," Megan tells me from my left. "I saw her."

"Go with her," I say. "Go with her, Megs. Her name is Waverley."

Megan nods, her eyes glassy. "I'll go."

"Freya, I didn't see her. I didn't see her. They said they'd show me her."

"I think she needed a little help right away." She looks over her shoulder before finally dropping her eyes to me. They're full of tears, her cheeks already streaked. I've never seen Freya with a hair out of place and yet her face holds so much angst, so much worry.

"Freya, what's happening to her?"

"I don't know right now. I'm sorry, Scarlet."

I shake my head, tears leaking into my hairline. "Oh god. No."

She puts her head to mine, her sweet perfume chasing away the sterile smell in the air. "Listen to me, darling, she's as strong as you are. She'll show them. You've done all the hard work, and now it's her turn, okay."

"Freya, I don't want to lose her. I can't."

"You won't."

I palm my chest to stifle the heavy, piercing pain that radiates beneath, my fingertips tingling. I shake my head, my next breath coming up short.

"Waverley wasn't breathing when we delivered her. She was taken to our specialist unit and given immediate care."

I push back my chair, not being able to look at Ave or Lance or Vinny as I rush from the shack. I look from left to right as white spots invade my vision.

Home.

Get home.

I run for the road, tears leaking down my face as I make my way through the village.

"We managed to get her heart beating again, but she's in a very critical condition."

My sandals repeatedly slide out from under my feet, and I reach down, frustrated, trying to pull the straps from my ankles. I shake my foot to kick them off, my hands too unsteady to undo the buckle.

"Please, prepare yourselves."

I stumble, catching myself before an elderly woman can reach out to me fully. "Sorry. I'm... sorry," I tell her, bumping into someone at my back.

Squeezing my eyes tight, I sob, covering my mouth as I reach down blindly for my shoes. I quickly find my bearings and take off up the hill toward our lodges. I don't stop running the entire way home, not until I can no longer hear the sounds of their songs or the memory of the day they took my baby.

The soles of my feet burn against the cool tiles when I reach the lodge, bloody spots marking the pale stone. I frown down at the mess I've made, and then go straight to the sink, wringing out a cloth. Dropping to my knees, I wipe the tiles, scrubbing, my eyes focused on each smear that disappears.

When I'm done, I look around the terrace, knowing I need to go and get my phone.

Call someone.

I find it in my bedroom.

> Fran: Yes. Let me know a day, and I'll work around you, or I can jump on a call before.

I sit down on the bed, my heart racing.

I try to ease my breathing, knowing I need a scrap of composure before I call her. I have a missed call and voicemail from Annie, and I press play on autopilot.

"Scarlet, it's me. I'm just checking we're good to have you back in on Wednesday. To say we've missed you is an understatement. I hope all's well at home. Great news for Lance last week. I presume you sent him packing already." She chuckles, and I frown. "The disappointment on that man's face when I told him how well everything has healed and that he could manage at home on his own. You'd think it was a child having his favourite teddy bear taken from him. He really is looking good by the way; I'd totally understand it if you haven't sent him anywhere but your bed." She chuckles again. "Anyway, we can discuss this and everything I've missed over coffee on Wednesday. Travel safe, lady."

"Scarlet." I look up as my name rings out in the distance.

Lance lied to me?

"Scar!"

I stand and walk through the lodge, stopping in the middle of the lounge when Lance appears on the terrace. The second he spots me, his shoulders sag, and he starts toward me. "Scar. Fuck, I couldn't get up the hill. There's blood—"

"Did you lie to me about your leg?"

His face drops, steps faltering. "What?"

I take him in, his leg. All the days he's been walking around here without his crutch. "Did you lie to me about your leg? Did Annie tell you that you could go home?"

He steps toward me, and I wrap my arms around myself, simply looking up at him.

I feel so cold.

So empty.

"It was a little white lie. Just one I knew we needed."

"Why?"

He drops his brow to mine. "Because I knew you were close."

I shake my head, not even trying to understand. "Close?"

He smooths a hand down my face. "I needed a little more time with you. Just to see."

"To see what?"

"If you still love me like I think you do." His green eyes deepen. "I couldn't leave you when you were so close. We worked too hard—"

"I don't." I shake my head vehemently. "I don't want to love you. I can't."

He steps back, his face transforming right before my eyes.

And with that step, a weight seems to lift from my chest.

"Don't say that." He frowns, placing his hands on his hips. "Scar, please let me explain this properly later. You're bleeding."

My eyes follow his, my feet filthy and bloody. "You lied to me."

He stares through me as if not hearing me—or not wanting to. "Let me clean up your feet."

I let my eyes lock with his green ones as they search my own, a pain in them I know lives somewhere inside me, too.

I knew you were close.

"I'm sorry if I upset you. I should have told you the truth."

I do love him like he thinks I do.

And it's terrifying.

It's too much.

All of it.

Everything.

"Scar, come here."

"You came to live with us because of your leg, and it was an opportunity to spend time with Ave. It's been perfect for the two of you. I'm so happy for you both, and I'm glad that you're healing."

"Scarlet," he grinds out.

I nod, a lightness chasing away the dark. That terror ebbing away. "Ave's really excited to get a room set up at the house. We'll figure out the logistics of her going between the two of us."

"What are you saying?" he snaps. "Scarlet, I know you love me."

You can't choose your family, and it's the truth, you can't. "I can't. This is my choice."

"And it's fucking stupid. I'll make you see. I'm not going to leave you."

Something sparks in my chest, like a part of me remembers and wants to believe it. "You promised me that before. You promised me that and look what happened."

"And I meant it. I meant it to the point I put a bullet in another man to keep you!"

My eyes screw tight. "Don't say that."

He grabs my arms, putting us chest to chest. "Look at me."

"When the sun sets, and you start to forget me, remember every second you fell in love with me in this meadow."

My eyes drift apart, his beautiful face coming into focus. "I never forgot a second of it. I never will," I promise, a tear catching me off guard as it slips down my cheek.

It couldn't have been any better.

No matter how tragic my mum and dad's story was, I get it now. Stood here with Lance, the love of *my* life, I understand my dad's last words.

"I can prove it to you. Let me, please. We can do this."

I shake my head as I gaze up at him, images of the woman in the shack flashing in my mind. "Mum told me I was strong. In her letters. That I'd be strong for the people around me, but—" I feel my chin wobble and roll my lips, pleading to him with my eyes to understand. "I don't want to have to be strong anymore," I whisper. "I can't love you and be strong."

"But I won't leave you."

Everyone leaves. "Lance, let me go."

"No. No, Scar, stop it. Don't do this."

I push out of his arms, looking up at him. "When we get back on Monday, I want you to go home."

TWENTY-NINE

Scarlet

The look on Lance's face when I told him to go home doesn't leave me the entire trip home. I closed my eyes for the majority, hoping to fall asleep, but with him on the other side of the plane, his pain like an invisible thread tugging on my heart, I couldn't.

I wanted to take the words back the second they left my mouth. Not because I didn't mean them. I did in that moment, after what I witnessed in that shack. But because hurting him is the last thing on earth I'd ever want to do.

It's like putting a hand to an exposed hob.

You wouldn't do it because it's wrong.

He didn't try to come to my room after I told him I wanted him to go home, and I didn't expect him to.

When the sun came up, and I was lay on the bed alone the next morning, as the light rushed in, I knew I'd been cold. That

I'd seen those caskets and spiralled. I can still feel the churning in my stomach at the thought, the need to run a million miles from anything and anyone who holds the power to hurt me.

And yet I know the fact I haven't eaten since, and the sickness I had early into the flight, is because I've caused *him* pain.

Lance doesn't deserve that, and I can't stand it.

When Vinny pulls up to the estate, Lance wakes Ave up, taking her hand and walking her into the house.

I watch them with an aching, heavy heart.

"Is there anything I can do for you, Scarlet?" Vinny asks, unloading the last of the suitcases.

Can you fix me?

"No, Vin, you should go rest. It's been a long two days of travel."

He nods, still watching me. "You know where I am."

I give him the best smile I can find, waiting for him to leave before I head for my parents' garden. I sit down between the two headstones, looking out across the meadow and hilltop in the distance.

I'm not sure if I prefer sitting here in their garden or looking down on it from the hill.

"I don't want to be a horrible person," I say after a while. "It feels like a lose-lose situation. I can love him and lose him, then become a version of myself I know I can't come back from again. A version Ave doesn't deserve to witness and remember. Or I can let him go, and I hurt him. I become the woman who refused to love him." I stare at the sun, sending the world into a burst of white when I look away. "I hate myself either way, but I know that I'd hate myself more if I hurt Ave."

I lie back on the grass, closing my eyes as my hands settle on the grass.

"I thought I was getting better, guys. Like I almost let him back in."

Maybe I need time.

What happened in Bora Bora really messed with my head. I'm not sure I've ever been so triggered—even after some of my worst shifts at the hospital.

I sigh. "I have to apologise to Lance, but I'm scared." I'm scared to even look him in the eye.

I sit for over half an hour contemplating all the ways I could say sorry.

We spent a week together in one of my most treasured places on earth, and I ruined it all with a rash handful of words which I know came from a place of pure fear.

I lie, trying to figure out what my mum would say if she were here.

"I should probably call Fran."

The thought has me slowly standing.

I touch each headstone as I leave, making my way through the garden and toward the steps to the house. The front doors are already open, the estate oddly quiet for the early evening.

Nina and Mase are normally home by now, and I pause briefly, wondering where they are.

I'm just crossing the threshold when Lance starts down the stairs with his bags.

Everything—including my heart—seems to come to a halt.

Everything but him as he continues past me on his way toward the door.

"Lance," I rush out.

He stops reluctantly, stepping back a step and kissing my forehead. He doesn't give me his eyes, keeping his lips on my skin. "Thank you for everything you've done for me these last few months."

I open my mouth to speak, but he slips away from me before I can even catch a look at his face, taking the steps before I can think, before I can stop him.

"Mummy, stop him!"

I snap my head around to Ave, her tears heavy streaks down her face. "Ave, baby, I—I..."

I hear Lance's car start up in the garage, thoughts of whether he's allowed to drive, of going after him, of the fear of what I'd say if I did... the car rumbles its way out of the drive.

"Why did you let him leave? He was so happy, and now he's sad. Why doesn't he want to be here anymore?"

I shake my head as my heart bleeds in my chest. "Ave..."

"What did you do?" she cries. "What did you say to him?"

I stare at her with wide eyes, her hurt threatening to swallow me whole. *Ave. Focus on Ave.* "Baby, we're tired. We can put on a film and get some tea, have an early night. We'll figure it out tomorrow, okay?"

She flops down to the stairs, her hands covering her face.

I quickly wipe the tears that have fallen and rush to her, wrapping her in my arms.

Lance has gone.

He's gone, and it's all my fault.

"Did I do something wrong? He wouldn't tell me. He just said he had to go home because he wanted to. That's all he'd say, but I could see how upset he was."

I close my eyes as her body shakes with her sobs. Of course he wouldn't put the blame on me. "No, Ave, you didn't do anything. You're perfect. He loves you so much. It was me," I tell her. "I told him it was time to go home."

She leans back, the distance harrowing as she frowns up at me. "Why?"

"I told you he wouldn't be here for long, baby. I said—"

"That was before. I thought—" She hiccups. "I thought you were going to fall in love, and it could be like this forever."

My chest caves, opening up like a cavity and letting in everything I fight to keep out. "Ave, please, I'm sorry."

The front door creaks open, Nina appears in the doorway with one of Freya's glass trays covered in foil. Mason steps in after her, followed by the children.

Nina pauses when she sees us, quickly handing the tray off to Ellis. "What's going—"

"I want to be on my own," Ave yells, standing, her tears still falling.

"Waverley," I plea.

"I hate you for sending him away!" I cover my mouth with my hand as she runs up the stairs, a sob catching in my throat as I gasp. "Leave me alone!"

Before I can fully turn, Nina's arm is already around my neck, the other wrapping around my body. I see Mason hastily take the stairs after Ave, his face a mask of fury.

"Okay, so, you've told him you can't love him and sent him to the house that was left for him. I want to know something, and it's a hard question, so take your time," Fran says.

I pick at the blanket I'm sat on, the laptop propped up on a pillow at the end of the bed. "Go on."

"How would you feel if something happened to Lance now? Now that you've verbally put these boundaries in place."

A hole opens up in my chest.

She smiles softly. "I have a few things. You keep saying that when Lance leaves you, but there's nothing written in the stars that says he's going anywhere. Let's try to soften this mentality and the way you process it. We can circle back and work on it again, so don't worry. It's absolutely normal to revert to past habits after a triggering event. Secondly, you've said multiple times that you don't want to love Lance, that it scares you, and that you were close to telling him on your date that you do. This was also what you led with when I asked you to explain to me what happened."

I nod, wondering what she might say next.

"If I refer to your rundown of your trip, you told me that when Ave wanted to tell Lance that she loved him, you gave her the advice that you don't get to choose who you love." She looks down at her notes. "Your heart chooses for you."

"I did."

She smiles. "Scarlet, you've worked so hard to be where you are today. I have to admit I'm surprised you came to me with this. I'm glad. Always glad and happy to help, but honestly, you're not 'broken' like you say you are. In fact, I think it's quite the opposite."

"How so?"

"Well, I'm starting to think this fear of attachment and abandonment comes out of selflessness. You might not think you can handle the loss, but you have," she points out. "I'd be willing to put my house on you getting through far worse in all honesty. I wonder how much of the conflicted feelings come down to not the fear of loss, but the person you are after it. The fear of the burden you'd put on the people around you if you stumble. You had to carry a lot more than what was fair when your dad was sick. You gave up a lot and lost relation-ships because of it. Could it be the knowledge of that burden that scares you?"

I swallow, staring at the screen.

"I think anyone in your situation, who's suffered loss like you have, would be feeling very much the same." She jots something down. "Think about this for me. Loving Lance out loud or quietly won't change the fact you love him. Your face when I asked you if something happened to him how would you feel told me a thousand stories. Pushing him away won't make it hurt any less if the unthinkable happens."

I blink, eyes burning at the harshness of her words.

"I know that's a lot. We have plenty to work through here."

"I think I need some time to process."

"You want to stop for tonight?"

I wipe at my face. "I think I need to."

She nods, brows lifting. "You've not cried in all the sessions we've had."

"I tend to save it for after."

She smiles down at her notepad, her eyes catching on her notes. "I want you to practise something for me. I know you have a lot of support at home, so I think with a few conversations, it's possible."

I sit up, ready to take on her feedback. It's never failed me, after all.

"Whenever you go to do something for anyone else in your household, I want you to go to your to-do list—mental or written—and cross something off it first. I know it's ridiculous to you, and it's not a sustainable measure as a working mother, but take time to think about your needs before you handle everyone else's. Sit with the list, figure out what you need, and then do it."

"I already know I won't." I force a smile.

"Humour me and try. I think you'll be surprised what topping up your own cup can do for you and the people you love."

I schedule another appointment with Fran for three days from now, knowing we really do have so much to go over. By the time the appointment comes around, I'll have agreed with her, wanted to fire her, and come up with a million reasons why she's wrong.

It's a process, but I'm pretty sure she likes me.

THIRTY

Scarlet

"This seat taken?"

I lean into Mason as he sinks down next to me on the stone steps outside the house, closing my eyes when his arm wraps around me like a blanket.

"You've been out here for hours."

"Hmm. I'm thinking."

He toes the piece of chalk left behind by the kids. "Did you catch a call with Fran?"

I nod. "It was brutal."

Mason chuckles. "You always say that." Silence settles, the comfort of his warmth at my side and just being here with him making everything feel a little less shit. "I spoke to him earlier. He's home."

No, he isn't.

"He shouldn't be driving. He'll lose his licence if he gets caught."

"I told him that, too."

I squeeze the sleeve of my cardigan when my eyes burn. "I don't know what I'm doing, Mase."

"Then we're all fucked," he says, and I know he's smiling. "I probably should've sent my wife out here."

I shake my head, slipping my arm around his waist. "No, I'm glad it's you."

My brother tenses before holding me tighter.

"How do you do it? How do you love Nina like you do—the kids—without fear of something happening. You almost lost Nina once."

"I physically couldn't not," he says simply. "It doesn't feel like an option. I met her and knew she'd be it for me."

"I think that's why this feels so wrong. No matter how much I don't want to, I can't not."

"What holds you back?"

"The idea of him leaving again." I roll my lips. "Everyone leaves, Mase."

"Lance didn't leave."

I frown.

"Not by choice," he adds. "He did something I didn't. He was here for you when I wasn't." He shrugs as if it's simple. "You let me back in."

"You're my brother."

"And I treated you like shit. Has Lance ever treated you so poorly?"

I shake my head.

He reaches for the piece of chalk, writing Lance's name and then mine beside it, dividing it with a line down the middle and adding a tally under Lance's name.

I chuckle and push into him. "You're such a softy these days, it's gross."

"Give me the worst thing Lance has ever done to you."

"I don't know... he ghosted me for a year once."

"Worse."

"He ghosted me for seven years and never read my letters."

He adds two tallies under my name for that one.

I think on it. "He told me he'd take it back. Everything we had."

Another tally.

"But I think that was just him hating himself for hurting me and wishing he hadn't."

Mason sighs in defeat. "I'm not rubbing it out."

I smile into his shoulder.

"Now give me some good things."

"Mase, this is ridiculous. There are a million good things."

"I don't know them. Tell me."

I shake my head and smile. "He used to drive out here after work every day. He'd spend the night with me just to drive all the way back at stupid o'clock in the morning. And he'd always find time for Dad, too, checking if he needed anything." I look up at Mase. "He cared about Dad."

Mason smiles. "What else?"

"He never gave up. Even when I pushed him away. I was horrible when Dad died, said some really awful things."

"Yeah, me, too," Mason says.

"He always listened to me, to what I wanted, and he

stayed away when I asked him but never let me be fully alone."

"I have one. One you don't know about."

"What do you mean you have one? You didn't know about us back then."

"I know what an asshole I was to you. So did he." He pulls in a lungful of air before releasing it. "I signed the house over to you when I was in the midst of losing Nina." He holds me tighter when I flinch. "Lance came to my office one evening, and I was preparing the papers for Charlie. Had the original deeds there ready to send off."

What?

I have to force my words past the bitter lump in my throat. "What did he do?"

"He took them and never gave them to Charlie. He knew how badly it would hurt you to have me step away from this place completely. He did it for you."

"When was this?"

"Around the same time shit hit the fan with Jasmine. He told Nina that he buried them on the estate."

He continues to exceed every one of my expectations. "I had no idea."

He leans forward, adding four tallies. I stare at them, knowing the scales will always tip in his favour. He's one of the best men I've ever known. I've done worse to Lance than Lance has to me.

But... "He still left me, Mase. It doesn't change that fact."

"Wait here." Mason stands, heading back into the house.

When he settles back down beside me, I see he has one of

my mother's diaries in his hand. "There's an entry you should read. It's to me, but I think it's better suited to you."

His frankness has my mouth dropping open. "You read Mum's diaries, the entries she wrote to you?"

"I'm getting through them." He flicks through the pages of her life as if he's done it a million times before. "Nina reads them to me mostly. I find it easier for some reason."

I swallow, nodding even though he isn't looking. The nights I spent with Lance, my mother's diaries spread out as we learnt her. Shared her life together.

My eyes swim with tears before he can find the entry.

"Here. This one." He starts before I can stop him. "My darling boy." He smiles, and I know this is it. So many things helped heal the man at my side, his wife and children being at the top of the list, but that smile, that's because of our mum. "I'm not sure how good your father will be at giving the talk on love. I could put my trust in him to do it right and tell you to trust him... or I could tell you my experience, what I've learnt from it, and maybe if you ever need it, it will help you.

It's not easy. It's not always fair. You'll want to run from it as much as you'll crave it at times. You especially, Mason. I can already see the walls stacked around you. The fort you'll build around your empire and heart.

By now, you know about my mother and father. When they cut me off, I told myself the safest possible route was to never let anyone close enough again. Life then put your dad in front of me and dared me not to love him. He was the first man to ever love me, and I stole his heart quickly. No matter how long it took me to give him mine, he never once asked for his back.

It took me too long.

I knew I loved your dad, but I fought it.

I think my biggest fear for you, Mason, is that you'll be too busy building the walls back up around your heart to notice that the one person who loves you is trying to climb over.

I know it's scary. I know you love me and will lose me and that will stay with you. But don't let it make decisions for you. I have weeks left of my life. Weeks, Mason. If you ever fall in love and wonder if you should tell that person who's holding your heart, if you can be brave enough to let them in, know that if I could go back, I'd have told your dad from that first moment, that first day, in an instant.

The idea I could've had more time hurts worse than the fear of what loving him means tomorrow.

Hindsight is a beautiful, wonderful thing, so take it. Take my life and my mistakes and promise me you'll let them in. Let them love you like you deserve to be loved and love harder than the fear of anything else. It's the only and best advice I can give you.

There are two loves I've done right.

Two hearts I allowed to catch me from the first beat whilst they lived within me.

Two loves I don't regret or wish I'd done differently.

If I could love you and your sister from that first beat all over again, I wouldn't change a thing. No matter how much it's going to hurt when I'm gone.

Don't need this advice, darling, don't read it ten times over. Take it from me and love. Be loved. Be happy and silly and free from fear.

Love. With your whole heart. Before it's too late, and you regret it. There are no do-overs in this life.

Thank you for making it so easy to love you.

Forever, Mum."

Mason stares down at the diary, his smile wide. "What a woman."

A sob escapes my throat, tears breaking the dam and falling without restraint.

"Hey." He pulls me to his chest. "It's okay."

It's not.

I'm so selfish.

Mason stays with me on the terrace for as long as it takes for my tears to dry up, sharing with me some of his favourite entries Mum gave him.

When the rain comes, and I eventually get up and head into the house, I make my way to the kitchen.

Nina is at the kitchen island on her laptop. She's wearing her dance clothes, which tells me she'll be heading downstairs to her studio at some point this evening.

Without needing to say anything, I make a cup of tea and sit with her at the counter, staring at the huge bouquet of flowers in the middle of the table. "Those flowers are huge. They're yours?" I ask.

She nods in my periphery, her eyes on the side of my face.

"They're ridiculous and beautiful." They might be the biggest bunch of flowers I've ever seen. "What did Mase do?"

Nina chuckles from beside me. "Not Mase. They arrived whilst you were away." She stands, shutting down her laptop and reaching for her pre-workout. She stops at the stack of letters on the counter just inside the door, flicking through them.

"You heading downstairs?" Mason asks as he appears in the doorway, not missing the chance to run his hands over his wife's body.

"Uh-huh," Nina mutters, still looking through the letters.

"Hmm. Let me grab a glass of my favourite, and I'll come watch."

Nina smirks, dipping her head into his kiss when he goes for her neck. She finds what she's looking for and places it on the island, pushing it toward me. "Come on, you needy man," she tells Mase, giving me a warm, reassuring smile before leaving.

I reach for the small rectangular card, frowning as I flick it open.

For the nights I couldn't hold them.
And all the ones you did.

I stare at the card for a long time after Nina and Mase head downstairs, the silence in the house reminding me of another time when I had nothing but the empty walls surrounding me.

So much has changed since those days. I have my family here now—all of them. I can't help but wonder if I'd have any of those things if it wasn't for Lance.

He kept the deeds.

He gave me Ave.

I reach for a flower, pulling it from the arrangement and lifting it to my nose.

The man never stops.

I'm not sure he even knows how, and I sure as hell know I don't deserve his love.

I make my way upstairs, passing Ave's room with a heavy heart and tears in my eyes.

She's never spoken to me that way in her life. I know that she was hurt and probably confused and scared seeing Lance leave, but hearing those words come from her, after everything we've faced, it was like a hot iron through the chest.

I pause when I get to Lance's room, my feet dragging the closer I get to my own. There's a stack of parcels on his bed, snagging my attention. I wipe at my cheeks and step into the room to get a better look.

Sitting on the bed, I pull the closest box to me, the tape already torn open.

Inside there are books. At least twenty. I reach for the next box and find it just as full.

In the third, I find gold lettering.

With no idea what they are or where they came from, I leave them on the bed and make my way to my bedroom.

I go through the motions, showering and changing, before pulling back the covers and slipping between the bedsheets.

Tears fall in rivulets down my cheeks the entire time.

I'm tired—beyond tired from travelling—and I know that sleep is exactly what I need. No matter how badly I want to lie here and make sense of everything in my head tonight, getting sleep and facing it all with a fresh head in the morning is the right thing to do.

But I can't sleep because nothing is right, and Lance isn't here.

I think about Ave. I think about her and what she said and how I can fix it.

I think about my mum. I think about my mum for a little while longer than normal.

And I think about him.

I think about him until I know how fucking stupid I am that I climb from my bed, pull on my boots at the front door, and head for the city.

I'm almost there, the rain lashing down on my windscreen, when my car engine light comes on, and it judders to a stop.

Lance

The clock reads two forty. I should be asleep after two days of travel with no sleep. Seems impossible after I left the only two people I give a shit about in a house over an hour away.

They feel too far.

If this is it, if this is how it has to be, I'll sell the house. I'll move closer to the estate so that I can see Waverley.

I can't do odd evenings and weekends. I need to see her every day.

Scrubbing at my face, I sit up in the stupidly large bed as I look around the room.

Everything about Elliot's house is over the top. From the chandelier when you walk through the front door to the sofa and chairs in this main bedroom. It's cold and unnecessary, and nothing like home.

Home is where they are. A house down a little lane, covered in ivy and filled with our memories.

I can be here, live here, but it won't ever be my home.

Pulling back the covers, I stand, wincing when my leg jars. I reach for the TV remote, angry and pissed off at the world as I launch it across the room. "Fuck."

I run my hands through my hair, my mind a carousel of thoughts—all of Scarlet.

I hate myself for being angry at her. That I told myself, and her, that it was enough, when it isn't.

My whole life I watched my mum fall at the feet of my sisters whilst I fought for her love. If I didn't have my dad, his love, who knows the man I'd be today. Regardless of him, it wasn't enough. It's never been enough, and I resent my mum for it even to this day. For the days I needed her so badly, and she wasn't there. When I'd need advice or just a hug, and she couldn't give it to me—fuck, she could barely even see me most of the time.

I gave her everything she could possibly want and need because I didn't know what else would satisfy her, and even then, it was thrown back in my face.

Somehow, I found a group of people who abolished all the bullshit. Who, from the second I left college to today, took me as I was and am, Scarlet more than any of them.

Not one of them ever asked for a thing in return.

Scarlet loved me, but I lost her. No matter my intention or need in that moment seven years ago, I took her away from myself.

I finally found it—love, and I fumbled it.

I shouldn't be angry. But I am.

At her.

And at myself.

Because I'm pretty sure Scarlet does love me, even if she doesn't want to, and I can't just be here and take that.

I won't.

I walk to the entrance of the house with little thought, swiping my keys from the sideboard.

THIRTY-ONE

Lance

The rain is pouring on my windshield in heavy beats, the road ahead barely visible in the dark. I take the roads slow despite how quiet they are. It was only weeks ago I was taken out on this very road.

No one is stupid enough to be out here tonight.

I try to make sense of why I'm driving the roads to the estate, not knowing what I'll even say to Scarlet when I get there. Can I just slip into bed and pretend the last week never happened? Will she send me away again?

I don't need a big grand confession of her love for me.

I don't need an *I love you*.

I just *need* her.

A car at the side of the road catches my attention, and I squint, trying to get a better look. "The fuck is anyone doing out at this time of night?" And in this weather.

I slow as I near, spotting a figure dash out from around the back of the car and into the front seat.

I sigh, knowing I should at least get a look despite the fact they haven't bothered to flag me down.

When I pull over in front of the car, my eyes drop to the Mercedes badge and then the number plate.

"What the—" I pull open the car door, and in a panic, Scarlet seems to do the same.

With the rain pelting down, I take in her soaked clothes, her pink cheeks. My eyes widen. "What are you doing?"

She shakes her head. "I couldn't sleep!" she instantly yells back. "What are *you* doing?"

"You couldn't sleep? So, you think dancing around on a road I was almost killed on in the fucking rain is a good idea?"

"Stop yelling at me. I was coming to your place."

"My place?" I ask, dumbfounded. "Then why are you stopped at the side of the road and soaked through?"

"The car." She thumbs behind her. "It wasn't as charged as I thought." She doesn't look at me. "I didn't bring my phone and was checking the boot for a coat so I could walk."

My eyes bug out, and I turn, unable to even look at her. I run my hand through my soaked hair. "I can't... I can't believe you thought it was a good idea to walk this road. I can't—"

"Why are *you* out here?" she snaps back, and I can tell she's shaken up by the way her voice cracks. "Where were *you* going?"

"Where do you think I was going?"

"I don't know."

Yes, you fucking do.

I watch her grasp at straws, her brow pinching together. "Maybe... maybe you had needs you needed seeing to."

My tether all but snaps. "Yeah, Scar, because you didn't fucking nail me to the ground by the balls the second we met. You think women exist in my mind outside of you? 'Cause they fucking don't."

"I know that." She shakes her head as if it's stupid, water dripping from the soaked strands of her hair. "I'm sorry."

"Sorry," I repeat.

She nods, eyes lifting to lock with mine. A small smile teases the corner of her mouth, one she tries so fucking hard to fight.

Fuck.

"Did we just have our first fight?" she asks.

"Yeah, and I'm that pissed at you, we're likely about to have our second. Get in the car."

She makes her way around my car, slipping inside.

I slide into the driver's side, watching her hands smooth over the seat at her sides. "I'm getting everything wet."

I focus back on the road, turning the car around and heading back the way I was coming from.

We don't talk to one another as we pass through the city, my brain going over every scenario that didn't happen but could've.

Scarlet's smart. Maybe one of the smartest people I know. To think she got in her car, knowing it was low on electricity, and then drove without her phone... "Why would you get out of the car? Why not wait until someone passed and flag them down?"

She sits quietly at my side.

"Why didn't you wave me down? You were going to let me pass. Surely you knew it was me?"

"I got out because I didn't feel like sleeping in my car in the middle of nowhere, and I wasn't going to wave down a stranger either. When you came around the corner, I kind of froze. I didn't expect it to be you."

"Yeah, well, same," I snap.

"Can you not be angry at me about this?"

I force my attention away from the road, regretting it the second I lay eyes on her. Her face is still flushed pink, her hair dripping. "If something happened to you, Scarlet—"

"It didn't."

"It could have."

"I'm sorry, Lance."

I clench my jaw, knowing she means more than just risking her life by walking in the rain on the shittiest road I know.

We pull into Elliot's drive and rush into the house, both of us wet through. "Go shower. You need to warm up. I'll get you something dry to put on." I head for the laundry room where I found a stack of fresh towels when I arrived earlier.

When I come back out, Scarlet's still standing in the middle of the hall, a puddle of water forming at her feet, and shivering all over.

"You need to get out of those wet clothes," I tell her, handing her the fluffy towel. "You know where the bathrooms are."

"I was on my way here for a reason."

"You can use the en suite in the main bedroom if you prefer. It has body wash but no shampoo."

"Lance—"

"I don't need to hear you tell me you don't love me again, Scarlet." I close my eyes, feeling like a complete asshole. I really did plan on slipping into her bed tonight, hoping we wouldn't have to do this again. "Please."

I know that she loves me, but if she tries to explain all the reasons she can't and won't, she might just finish me off tonight.

"That's not why I came..."

I turn and start up the stairs, knowing I'll say the wrong thing and hurt her if I stay.

"I'm just scared," she calls to my back, and I slow before coming to a stop. "Aren't we all a little bit? I'm terrified of falling in love with you, Lance."

I swallow, staring at the shitty chandelier hanging in front of me.

"I couldn't watch you fade to nothing in that hospital bed, and yet I knew I'd fall a little if I fixed you. I knew that having you close to me on the estate would kill me inside every day that I fell in love with you all over again, but I did it anyway." I take a step back and turn, looking down at her. And the tears that threaten in her eyes almost bring me to my knees. "I did it anyway because it's what we do. It's what stupid humans do over and over again even though we know the risk. I don't want to love you or my brother or my friends or my job or even my child because I'm scared I'll lose every single one of you." She goes to step forward, but I move first, taking the stairs until we're chest to chest. Her eyes soften as she stares up at me. "But you need me. Mason needs me. The girls need me. People *need* me." Her voice wavers. "Ave needs me, Lance." A tear rolls down her cheek as she reaches for mine. I melt into her touch. I always will. "I knew the risks, and I fell regardless. For all of it."

"Baby," I whisper, dropping my forehead to hers.

"I never meant to hurt you—"

My jaw goes stiff. "You told me to go home. This isn't my home, Scar. This is a million miles from home."

"I know. You belong on the estate. You belong with us."

I frown, eyes burning. "You mean that?"

"I can't promise the person I'll be because of it, but I do love you, Lance. I've never stopped. I hate that I made you think for even a second that I didn't. That I was so afraid—a coward—to live it. That I still am."

I chuckle despite the ache.

Taking her face, I lift it up. "Sunshine, I know what it is to not be loved." I brush my thumb over her full bottom lip. "This isn't it."

"You'll never not know it," she says desperately, stepping closer. "I could never not."

"I know," I whisper against her temple. Because it's in everything that she does. The dresses she wears. The songs she plays. The walks we take around the estate. Choosing to sleep in a shitty chair just to know I can sleep, too. I tuck a piece of wet hair behind her ear. "You've been telling me for weeks."

She nods.

"I love you, too." I lean in and kiss her.

"I'm so sorry," she whispers, pulling back. "For every-thing I said—"

"No more apologies." I take her hand and pull her back to

me, wrapping an arm around her shoulders to keep her warm. Our foreheads meet and hold. "I love you so fucking much, Scar."

Her stare stays fixed on my own, and in this moment, I know that this is it.

This is us.

Forever.

"Where do we go from here, Lance?"

My brow furrows against hers. "Probably therapy."

Her gaze falters before she laughs and pushes against my chest.

I wet my lips, dusting my nose against hers as I smile. "Home, Baby Lowell. Even if it takes us a lifetime to get there. We make it a promise, no matter what comes at us, to always make it home."

THIRTY-TWO

Scarlet

My feet ache, I'm drained beyond comprehension, and I have six hours left of my shift.

Lance has been officially home for three weeks. When we told Ave it was going to be for good, she reacted exactly as we knew she would.

She was ecstatic.

I came back to work a day later, and to say the transition after so much time off has been hard would be an understatement. I feel different. I have Lance now. Ave has her daddy. It brings less guilt over working long hours—no matter how badly I want to be at home with them.

It means Nina isn't left with a house full of children, and tea on the table when I get in, and a bath run with candles, and a body that keeps me awake past respectable hours of the night whilst it worships my own.

Work at the hospital hasn't gotten any harder. What I leave at home just got a million times better.

"I need a coffee." I sigh, pushing back from the desk. "Anyone else?"

Mia and Annie look at me as if I'm crazy.

The cafeteria is busy, and we join the queue, shuffling forward every couple of minutes.

"We should get a machine in the break room," Mia says.

Annie turns and shakes her head. "We tried it in my first F1 year. It was used for a month, and nobody cleaned it."

"I think I like the walk down here, too. For five minutes, we're just a couple of women in a queue waiting on coffee."

"Hmm," Mia agrees. "We definitely come more when you're here."

"I won't apologise." I chuckle. "I know you love the gossip."

"Do you have any?" says Mia.

I shrug. "I actually have nothing."

"Has that gorgeous man put his ring on your finger since the last time?"

I've woken up or watched Lance move his ring four times in the weeks since he came home. Each time I switch it back. Not because I don't want to marry him, I do, but it's kind of become a thing.

"He actually hasn't. It's been over a week and nothing."

"He's probably given up," Annie says. "You're so mean."

"If you say so." I smile, moving forward in the line. "Do you ladies have your dresses picked out for the ball yet? Annie, did you get the time off?"

"I'm trying."

Annie has made it to just one of the memorial balls I've hosted, always working overtime or unable to get cover. It's almost impossible to plan it around my own shift, let alone all the people I care about.

This year, I *need* her there.

"This one feels special. I want you both there, okay?"

"You know I'll do my best."

"I don't know how you do it, Scar. You work and plan and mum and barely even break a sweat," Mia tells me. "I swear you're supersonic."

"I'm honestly dead inside this week, so, shh. I fell asleep mid... you know... last night."

They both turn their eyes on me.

"What?" I say, shrinking back.

"You do realise we don't get any?" Mia retorts.

I chuckle, and Annie's lip twitches. "Like none at all. And you're out here falling to sleep on that god of a man?"

"I made up for it this morning before I left for work."

"Ugh, you make me sick with jealousy."

"Hmm, I woke up and realised my patient's sick had splattered my trainers yesterday," Annie says, wincing. "We're living very different lives outside of those doors, you know."

My phone vibrates in my pocket, and I fish it out.

Lance: Scarlet?

Scarlet: Yes, Lance.

Lance: I love you.

Lance: Indefinitely.

My smile is instant.

"Jesus," Mia mutters. "We don't even want to know."

I text back and pocket my phone. "Don't be salty."

"No," Annie says. "We're not. It's good to see you smile." Mia gives me a look that matches Annie's words. "You deserve this."

"Thanks, girls."

Lance

"Imagine writing a book about sex and putting a flower on the cover," Mason deadpans. "How do they know it's that kind of book and not one about gardening?"

I chuckle, unboxing another load of books and placing them on the table. "Scar says it normally means something to the story."

"I guess you can market a flower," he ponders, looking around the soon-to-be-finished library. "But there's like a lot of flowery shit here." He gestures to the stacks of books Scarlet has collected over the years.

"She bought the discreet ones so that your dad wouldn't ever know what she was reading. I've managed to find a lot of the originals since, so she has both now."

"Two of the same book?"

I shake my head. "Some come with hardcovers or special covers." I walk to a row of shelves. "These four books here," I say, pointing. "All the same book."

Mason looks horrified. "How much does she spend on books?"

"Nothing. Scar would never get all the editions. But I've seen her looking at them before, so I presumed she'd want them in here."

"Reading is supposed to be a healthy habit."

"Trust me." I smirk at him. "It's a perfectly healthy habit."

He holds up a hand to stop me. "I get it."

We continue to unpack the books, Mason very surprisingly sticking to the system I set up, making sure to categorise the books in sub-genre, keeping series together, with the authors being in alphabetical order. It took me days to figure out a system that works. I could have done a-z with authors and their multiple books, but Scarlet always was a mood reader, and I think she'd prefer having them in genre order.

I had the room leading off from Anthony's sitting room gutted whilst we were in Bora Bora. Scarlet could have walked in here at any point in the weeks since we've been back, but between the hospital, my spontaneous scheming, and the fact Scarlet rarely comes in here anymore, keeping her out in the evenings has been easy.

"She's going to live in here," Mase muses. "Ave, too."

"Waverley will be allowed in this room when she's fifty, and I'm senile," I tell him, unboxing a raunchy book with a naked-chested man on the cover. "We'll keep the door locked."

"Yeah, agreed. You really bought all of these?" He picks up the classics I found years ago before I knew I wouldn't be here to move the library myself. "Must have cost a fortune."

"Pocket change to you, Lowell." Stepping around the table, I clear my throat. "I have something to ask you."

He opens the book, frowning. "What's that?"

Pages rustle as he flicks through, pausing every so often to peer down at a chapter heading.

"I want to marry your sister."

His eyes lift to mine.

"I know I've not long come back into her life, and I know I hurt her." I hold his gaze, needing him to know how serious I am. I may have had Anthony's blessing, but I was a different man then, and Mason is the man of this house now. "She wants to be with me, and that's a blessing in itself. I'll worship her for the rest of my life regardless of a ring on her finger. But I love her, and I'd be the proudest man on earth to get to call her my wife."

Mason places down the book.

"No fight will ever be big enough. No one else could ever be good enough. She'll always be first—her and Waverley before anything else. She's my world—my home." I scrub at my mouth before putting my sweaty hands on my hips. "Your dad once told me I'd have his blessing should I need it. If you'll let me, Mase, I want to marry your sister so that I can spend the rest of my life trying to be half the man he thought I was."

Mason chuckles quietly, a little taken aback.

He steps toward me. "You me and both," he says contemplatively. "You want my blessing, Lance?"

I tighten my jaw, not realising how badly I need the right answer from him.

He throws his hands out at his sides and shrugs as if it's

obvious. "You have it. Of course you have it. Scarlet would be lucky to have you, and so are we."

My brows lift, and he grins.

"You thought I'd say no?"

"No. I just never thought you'd ever think yourself lucky to have me as a part of your family."

"Well then, you're as fucking stupid as you look because you've been a part of this family for a long time now."

He goes back to unpacking the books, unaware of the feeling whispering beneath the skin on my chest. "Thank you, Mase."

His eyes lift to mine, head still bowed. "Thank you for asking. It means a lot."

I nod. "Any advice?"

Mason smiles, starting a new row with the classics. "No advice. I'm still fucking up three times a week. I wish you all the luck in the world, though."

Scarlet

If I could wish for one thing for all of the children in this world, it would be for them to have the safety and freedom to run.

I remember the feeling. The wind on my face as I'd try, with all my might, to keep up with Mason and Elliot. Early mornings, mid-afternoons, late evenings. We'd run through the fields from one home to another with no idea of the time, only the sun to dictate our path. And we wouldn't look over our shoulders or care for anything else in the world.

Nothing was bad back then.

Only good.

"This is so much fun!" Elsie squeals, her voice jarring with every bump we hit.

I hold her tight on my lap, the little girl inside of me gleefully smiling along with her as Lance speeds up the caddy, pulling the broken, plastic half barrel we found and attached with rope, along behind him.

The rest of the children all run alongside us, their happiness reminding me how damn lucky we are.

"Faster. Faster," Elsie chants.

Lance looks back at us, laughing when I shake my head "no" at him.

We're supposed to be setting up the last of the lanterns for the ball tomorrow, but with all of the children here this weekend, including Nessa-Anne and Chloe's children, it was easy to get a little sidetracked out here on the meadow tonight.

I can hang the lanterns once they're in bed—after memories have been made.

Somehow, maybe lost in translation, Lance doesn't catch my "no," speeding up the caddy and pulling Elsie and me at a pace Lucy would lose her sweet little mind over. "Lance!" I yell.

"Faster!"

"Elsie, no," I scold, not helping the ache in my laughing cheeks. "Oh my god."

"Faster!"

I feel every mound of mud as if it's a rock beneath my ass, thumping and bashing against the plastic barrel. Still, I can't stop the rush of endorphins the feeling of being so silly and reckless brings me as we fly through the meadow.

When Lance eventually comes to a stop, he jumps out of the caddy and jogs back to us, helping Elsie out before reaching down a hand to me.

"With Elsie on my lap?" I ask. "Lucy would kill you if she could've seen."

He gives me his beautiful full smile. "She loved it."

I avert my eyes, agreeing that Elsie absolutely loved it but not wanting him to think he's right. "Not that fast again," I warn.

Lance holds his hands up, smirking as I get up with a wince. "It's my turn anyway," he tells me.

"I'll drive!" Ellis shouts, running for the caddy.

"No, you won't," I call after him, catching him up just as he slides into the driver's side. "Ellis—"

"I'll be super careful, Auntie Scar, please. I know how to drive it."

"He'll be fine," Lance shouts as he seats himself in the broken barrel.

I slide in next to Ellis. "Go slow and stay away from the others. Ave, take your cousins over to the gate and stay there," I call.

We wait for them to gather before Ellis starts through the meadow, a cheeky smirk pulling at his lips. "Auntie Scar, if I hurt him, how much trouble would I get in?"

I raise my brows, lip twitching. "A lot." I shake my head. "Don't give me that look, Ellis."

He chuckles, putting his foot down. The wheels spin, and I'm jolted back before the caddy takes off across the grass.

"Ellis!"

I hear Ave and the kids cheering at the gate and turn, finding Lance holding on for dear life as he's pulled behind us.

Good god. "When you get to the hill, turn around and head back."

"Okay."

"Make sure you slow down," I tell him as we near. He starts to turn, and I frown. "Ellis... slow. Slow. You need to—"

I flip around in the seat, just catching the moment the barrel tips, and Lance goes bouncing and rolling across the grass.

I cover my mouth, partly to hide my laugh.

Ellis turns us around fully and heads back, coming to a stop beside Lance. "I'm soooo sorry."

Lance lies in the grass looking up at the pink sky. "I think I'm broken."

Ellis looks across at me and nudges my side. "That was for you," he whispers, jumping out of the cart and walking across the meadow to his cousins.

Biting my lip, I look down at my poor, broken man. "I'm presuming you are actually okay and can move?"

"Just, sunshine. Just." He sits up, using the caddy to pull himself to his feet.

He gingerly slides into the driver's seat, wrapping his arm around me and pulling me close. As we pass Ellis on the way back to the children, a rumbling laugh echoes off Lance's chest. "He likes me, you know."

I smile. "Yeah, I think he does."

When Lance drives right past the kids, their faces drop

before they all start running for us, I turn around to watch them, relishing their joy.

"I have something to show you."

I don't bother looking up at Lance. "Better than this?" I ask, my heart warming when Ave reaches for little Poppy's hand to help her keep up.

"No," Lance says. "Nothing beats nights like this. But I think you'll like it."

THIRTY-THREE

Scarlet

I don't like surprises. In fact, I hate them so much I focus more on the layout of my home in my head than the excited ball of energy growing in my stomach as Lance guides me, hands covering my eyes, through the front door.

"Don't peek."

"I'm not," I tell him, picturing the hallway that leads off to the different rooms. I frown as I'm led toward my dad's old sitting room. "What's in here?"

"Scarlet, I said don't look."

"I'm not looking. I can just tell." Even if I did lose track of my feet, I'd know the smell of this room anywhere. "It's not Dad, is it?" I chuckle.

"That's some pretty morbid humour."

"If we don't laugh, we'll cry."

He leans into my back and dips his mouth to my neck, nibbling at the sensitive skin under my ear.

I squirm, smiling.

I've barely slept the last couple of weeks. Between planning for tomorrow, keeping secrets, and being back at the hospital, I've not had a chance to fully enjoy having Lance back here for good.

Don't get me wrong, I've enjoyed him when I can, but not in the way I've wanted to.

We cross the room and halt at the door to the study.

My dad stopped using his home office when we were young. Whether that was because of memories he didn't want to relive lingering within the walls, or because he'd simply work from wherever he was in the house, I don't know. But I always presumed it would be a room for Mason one day. He was the one who took on the business and at such a young age. He deserves to have the space eventually—when he's ready.

It's why I left it untouched all these years.

"Are you ready?"

I frown. "No." If it's not for Mason... "Is it a library?" My brows lift. "Did you move it?"

"Scar!" I hear his hands slap to his sides.

I open my eyes and turn to face him. "Sorry." Reaching for his T-shirt (that's covered in mud from his excursion across the meadow), I pull him closer, looking up at him as I flutter my lashes. "I don't like surprises."

He shakes his head, putting a hand on the door above my head as he towers over me.

I grin, biting on my bottom lip as the smell of him surrounds me.

I need him.

"You're a pain in my ass."

"You moved the library?" I murmur, my voice already sounding a little heavier.

He reaches behind me and twists the handle, taking my weight when the door swings open. I turn in his hold, my jaw dropping when I see the room.

Pushing Lance's hand away from my stomach, I step forward, my eyes darting from the floor-to-ceiling shelves to the rows and rows of books.

It takes me a moment, but with each inch of the room my gaze passes over, I realise everything that was here before is still here now, my dad's desk being a focal point in the room. It sits below the window and is littered with books, a candelabra lit, creating a soft, warm ambiance in unison with the open fire.

My eyes grow watery as I run the tips of my fingers along the spines of countless books, making my way around the stacks until I reach the heavy armchair my dad once lazed in.

I blow out a shaky breath, not expecting *this*.

"Lance... this is..."

"Your brother helped me. He didn't have any issue with you having the space."

I tilt my head as I find focus on him, not being able to utter how thoughtful and sweet it is that he considered it.

My toes curl on the rug underfoot, and I peer down, finding the same patterns I crawled across as a baby spread across the hardwood.

"This is insane. Beyond perfect." I spin in wonder, shaking my head as I notice my mother's mirror mounted above the fireplace, her picture, our pictures, set proudly on the mantel below. "You thought of everything."

"Come see this," he tells me, ushering me to some of the shelves.

There are bookshelves built into every wall, but here, like it's the heart of the room, the shelves sit deeper.

Lance pulls out a book or a diary, I realise. "The originals and the ones your dad had rebound. I made copies of the originals with your mum's personal letters and Mason's all included. So, you can read with cheese and wine and not worry about ruining them."

I stare at the side of his head as he smiles at the diary in his hands. "There are some incredible stories in here. Ones Mase said you haven't read and need to. I swear your mum would have been an author worthy of these shelves if she were still here today." I swallow, my gaze lost to him. "And then this one." I don't look at what he's reaching for. I can't. I'm too in love with him. "This one is ours." When his head twists toward me, eyes meeting mine, his smile fades. "Hey."

I shake my head. "I'm fine."

"You're going to cry."

"I'm just a little overwhelmed." I take the diary from him, pulling myself together. "What's this one?"

After a beat, as I flick open the page, I realise. "This one is ours," he tells me again.

"My letters."

He leans against the shelves, letting me look. "They're raw and hard and never should have needed to be written, but they were." He takes the bound book that's filled with my letters and places it back on the shelf. His gaze settles back on me, and it feels so permanent, so forever, I can't help but want to drop to my knees and pray for it. "I'll finish reading them one day. Probably in here, curled up with you, I hope."

I stare up at him in awe. "That sounds like something I'd like very much."

He grins, pulling me to him by the neck. "Yeah?"

I nod. "I can't believe you did this. It's nothing like what I'd have managed myself, and it's beautiful. It's thoughtful."

And he knows it.

Thought went into every detail of this room, and it shows.

It's not just a library filled with books. It's my dad's study, my mother's memory, my haven, and generations of history stuffed between pages of books that I know I'll read over and over until I no longer can.

"We split it into two sections. Your mum's classics and yours." He smirks at me as he leans to reach for a book further down the shelf, picking out one of my smutty books. "Then there's the sub-genres."

I listen in wonder as he proudly lists off each one and how he's arranged the books.

Pushing up onto my tiptoes, I cut him off with a kiss.

He smiles as I pull back. "You've not even seen the best bit yet," he tells me.

"What's that?" I whisper, hovering close.

Lance steps out from between the shelves and me, making his way around the room to the door.

He clicks the lock into place.

"I was thinking... if we're going to live with your brother, we're for sure going to need a place we can get lost in for a little while where no one can hear us."

"Oh..." I watch with a sly smile as he walks to the shelves in the very corner of the room and reaches to pull out a large book that's high on the shelf.

I frown as he opens the thick hardcover, and I make my way over. "Wait, is that a box?"

"This all started with a girl not having anywhere to hide her toys—"

My eyes widen when he lifts out my vibrator. "How did you find that?"

"You didn't do a very good job at hiding it."

"I didn't expect anyone to go looking."

His teeth break his smile, sinking into his bottom lip. "Did you use this while I was away, sunshine?"

I take it from him and look up at him. "Of course I did. I'm not a saint."

He seems to like the answer. "Will you show me?"

"Show you?" I frown.

"The last time we used it together it was your first time. You've had seven years of practice since. I'm sure you've only improved your masturbation skills in that time."

"My masturbation skills? You make it sound like a science experiment."

He chuckles, stepping up to my feet as he peers down at me. "Sorry, if I'm not being clear. I want to watch"—his hand curls around the side of my thigh—"as you fuck yourself with your vibrator, Scarlet. I want to listen, smell, *feel* you as you look at me in the eyes and come all over it. I want to see." His lips catch my own. Not a kiss, but a tease as he speaks against them. "I want to see the pleasure you gave yourself on the nights I couldn't. I want to dip my tongue inside and taste what you did to yourself. And then I want to sink deep enough that I can feel the blood pumping through your veins."

I swallow as the tips of his fingers graze my underwear.

"I want to watch you come for me, sunshine, and then I want you to come around me. I want you harder. More. All for me. As real as it gets. But mostly, I want you to remember the dissatisfaction, to resent it, so that I can sink deep inside of you and remind you exactly what *we* are."

I don't blink as he reaches up with his free hand to push my hair back from my face. "Fuck." He chuckles. "I can still make you blush."

He can. There's a fire burning at my core from his words, sending flushes of heat licking out in all directions. "This is cheating, though," I manage, still grasping the vibrator in my hand.

He tips his chin as if to humour me. "How so?"

I move my hips, letting his fingers dust over the front of my underwear. My lips part as I take a shaky breath. "I'd normally need lube."

The blacks of Lance's eyes seem to dilate. "You're wet."

I tip my head back when he drags his thumb over the cotton covering my pussy. "Yes!"

Before I can anticipate the next swipe of his thumb, Lance's hand drops away from me.

I whimper.

He smiles, taking hold of my chin. "Go and lie on the sofa."

Giddy with anticipation, I practically skip across the

space between the shelves and the sofa, the vibrator clinched in my grasp as I lie back on the cushions.

"I've never seen you this eager for my cock, sunshine. Should I be worried?"

I wait as he rounds the sofa and stands above me, his face a mask of desire.

"Depends," I mutter.

His eyes narrow as I lift my hips and shimmy my underwear down my legs. "Depends on what?"

I stuff the damp cotton into the pocket of his jeans, then drag my hand across his erection, squeezing. "How well you can fuck me after."

Hunger spreads through me as Lance glares down at me, his bottom lip pulled between his teeth. "Will you ever lose that mouth?"

I don't answer because I know he doesn't expect me to, and because I know he'd be lost without this mouth.

He walks the length of the sofa to my feet. "Sit up."

"No please?" I tut playfully, fiddling with the vibrator buttons until it turns on.

"Sit up," he repeats.

I rise into a seated position.

"Take your dress off."

I roll my lips and drop the vibrator to my side, doing as he asks and removing it. My bared skin turns feverish as the fire licking inside of me is married with the heat from the flames that dance below the mantle.

I ease back onto the cushions, my nipples pebbling.

I drop my dress to the floor.

Lance takes his time, fingers trailing up my leg, eyes

roving my body, before he bends, hand settling against my butterfly-filled stomach as he gently kisses my forehead. "Thank you, Scarlet."

I reach for the pulsating vibrator, not breaking our stare. Arching my back under his light hold, I leisurely drag it up my inner thigh.

I gasp as Lance's hand flexes against my stomach as he steps away.

"I need to see," he tells me, looking down at me from the end of the sofa. "Pretend I'm not here and show me."

As I reach the lips of my pussy, I angle the vibrator and let the head roam from bottom to top, just like I normally would.

The only thing I change, the only thing I cannot physically do differently, is my eyes. I keep them open when I'd normally close them.

I'd close them and think of Lance teasing me with his tongue as I'd let the pulsating head settle against my clit. I'd think about his tongue dipping and slashing into me over and over as I gently slip the tip inside a little.

I moan, lifting my free hand to palm my aching breasts.

Lance is heavy-eyed where he stands, watching the vibrator that I grasp barely penetrate me. He rolls his lips as if to silence himself, the soft plump skin left with a shine when he frees them.

"Lance."

He ignores me.

It's not enough.

I need him.

I can't have him stand over me and watch me and not touch me. I'll go mad from need. "Please, Lance. Touch me."

When he only frowns down at me, almost pained, I give in, pushing back into the cushions as I ease the vibrator deeper.

I whimper.

It's hard and cool against my warmth and nothing like how Lance feels. Nothing like what I want. The only saving grace is the pulsating of the silicone as it brushes over that sweet spot inside of me.

My mind drifts to Lance, eyes focused on him. I imagine his strong body over mine, imagine the warmth from the fire is him, rocking and grinding my hips deep into the cushions. I imagine his hand on my waist, teasing my breasts, his thighs against the backs of mine as he takes another inch, more and more.

"Lance..."

He clenches his fist, and I close my eyes, dropping my head back as I circle my hips and drive them down as my hand drives up, not able to get the vibrator deep enough, hating that it's fake and vibrating and not him.

Knowing I need the pressure at my clit, I twist to lie on my stomach, not caring if Lance can't see. I slip my hand between my body and the sofa and rock down and deep against it, using the tips of my fingers to hold the vibrator firm.

And then I think of him.

I think of him behind me. Fucking me. Fingering me. Licking me and sucking... I think of him watching me, just like this. I look at me from his point of view. I think about his cock and how hard it is. I think about him stroking it, coming from watching me.

"Lance... Lance... L-ance." My mouth parts, my limbs going stiff as an orgasm shudders through me, my body convulsing from the aftershock of each vibration as it continues to pulse.

My heart pounds, sweat tingling over my skin.

I lift my hips, widening my legs to gently pull the vibrator out of me, not able to handle the sensation any longer, but as the tip is all but free, a large palm covers the back of my hand, pushing it back in.

"Lance, I can't." I fist the blanket draped on the back of the sofa.

"Your pussy is gleaming, Scarlet. You always this wet for your friend?"

I shake my head, my hips driving down as Lance slowly grinds the fake penis deeper. "No. It's you."

He eases it out and lifts my hips.

My own breath catches as his flutters through the slit in my lips. "What's me?" he asks, knowing I can feel him whispering right there.

"Lance."

"You're incoherent, Scarlet. Use your words."

"I need you."

He slides the vibrator back in, and I hate how much I love it. Hate that I'm so close to coming again. "You need more?"

"Yes," I moan, but it comes out muffled. I lift my head from the pillow. "Yes, I need *you*."

His mouth is right there, ghosting my slickened skin. "I know you do."

I want you to remember the dissatisfaction.

I whimper and moan as he fucks me over and over with the vibrator, his own need bleeding through as he watches, grunting and groaning at my back.

I imagine the view he must have and spread my legs wider, pushing back into his grasp to meet his thrusting hand.

"Lance... you. I need you. *Please.*"

"*Fuck.*"

I close my eyes, knowing it's only a matter of time.

And with each inch he pushes into me, I'm edged closer and closer to orgasm, only held back by the knowledge that he's ready to snap. That I could push and have him inside of me.

"Let it go," he groans.

I shake my head. "I want you."

His hand wraps around my throat, pulling me up from the sofa and temporarily cutting off my air supply. My hands cover his out of instinct, my back meeting his solid chest and abs. A strangled moan passes my lips as he works the vibrator between my legs. "Give me something to lick up, something worth me devouring."

The changed angle ruins me, the pressure around my neck just the right amount as Lance slips his thumb inside of me and forces the vibrator to rub against that spot he knows by heart inside of me.

My body coils tight, the orgasm coming quicker and making my thighs ache as I kneel.

I drop backward into Lance's chest, his heart thudding against my back just as aggressively as my own as he takes my weight. I roll my head, spent, and look up at him, chest heaving.

His hand unfurls from around my throat, dragging down between my breasts and stomach. Needing more of him, of our connection, I nudge his jaw with my nose, letting my lips skim his stubble.

Lance dips his head to look down at me, his eyes dark and heavy.

And then he slides the vibrator out of me.

I grasp his forearms, my nails biting into them as I hold my breath. I hear a thud before Lance's other hand is on me, his arm wrapping around my body. My lips part, so close to his own as we remain together, eyes locked.

He closes the space and tenderly kisses me. "Bend over, Scarlet."

He supports me as I lower back down to the cushions, keeping my hips in place until my face is flat to the pillow. Flattening his palms, he smooths them around to my ass, stretching each cheek out and up.

I clench and squirm, the feeling of being spread out and raw for him whilst he refrains from touching me making my pussy ache.

I can feel how wet I am. Can feel the stickiness coating my inner thighs.

The sofa dips and creaks as if he's leaning in. The antici-pation as I wait, knowing a dart of his tongue passing his bottom lip would have him touching me.

He lets out a breathy chuckle, the warmth of it making me whimper. And then his mouth covers my heat, and it's as if he's starved.

I sink into the cushions further, my back arching as Lance's tongue dips inside of me.

And because this man knows me—my body. Because he's aware I'm a trembling mess from the orgasms he's already given me, he licks up, fluttering across my sensitive skin before trailing hungry kisses back to my clit. His teeth graze, nipping and teasing, as he pulls my thighs further apart, seemingly desperate to taste more of me.

He slides a finger inside of me, and I cry out, grinding down onto his mouth and hand until he hits the spot he's looking for. Heat erupts at my core, my heart becoming wild in my chest. I try to pull away as it takes over, his mouth relentless as he pins me in place, holding my hips firm as he goes harder with his fingers.

He growls against me whilst I shake and tense, only withdrawing his fingers once I'm limp on the sofa beneath him.

"Baby, turn around."

I can't.

I can't move.

"Scar."

I crack open an eye, my heart echoing deep into the cushions below.

When I don't make a move to turn, he does it for me, laying me on my back. He smiles proudly down at me, his cheeks full, making his eyes wrinkle.

It's my favourite smile of his.

After everything he's been through, from a boy to a man, I can't help but want to protect that smile forever.

He reaches over the back of his head to pull his T-shirt off.

My eyes can't help but hungrily trail the length of his torso. "Lance," I whisper, shaking my head "no."

His smirk remains as he unbuttons his jeans. "One more."

I bring my knees together, closing my legs. "I can't."

He pulls his cock out, stroking up the length of it before pushing against my shins to tilt my hips back. I watch as he bends, licking through my slit before I can realise what he's doing. "Lance!" I cry, my legs trembling.

He kneels over me, unlocking my ankles to split my legs so that he can settle between them. He plants a hand on the pillow beside my head. "You don't want my cock, sunshine?" he asks as it bobs, trailing my abdomen. And I know that he means it.

If I say no, this ecstasy ends.

"I can't come again," I warn him.

"You need me to be gentle?"

I nod.

He lowers himself over me, taking my lips in a deep kiss. When he pulls back, his eyes are closed, one hand in my hair as the other reaches blindly to guide himself to my entrance. "I'll try."

My breath catches as he sinks into me, his lips not hesitating to capture mine. He snakes his tongue across my bottom lip, wanting in. I open to him, wrapping my legs up and around his waist to bring him closer.

And as he rocks forward, control melting away, a growl reverberates from deep within his chest. I can't help but revel in his weight as he falls heavy onto me.

It's a weight I'd happily drown in.

I want you to remember the dissatisfaction, to resent it, so that I can sink deep inside of you and remind you exactly what we are.

"Don't be gentle with me, Lance," I pant. "I want to feel it all... please. Let me feel it all."

"Scar."

I tilt my hips up, recoiling when a tremor sucks him deeper.

He growls and grinds down, circling. "*Scarlet.*"

My mouth drops open, not being able to stop it as another orgasm rattles me to my core.

"Fuck," he roars, drawing back the slightest bit before driving back in. "Yes. Fuck, yes."

I continue to ripple around him as he grinds deep and hard, knees dug into the sofa with each lunge forward.

I cling on, my body screaming out at me to drag it away from his blissful torment as my heart wildly dares me to stay, wrapped around him for a lifetime.

As our sweat bleeds into rivers and the world ceases to exist around us.

As he takes that little bit more of my soul.

I cling on.

THIRTY-FOUR

Lance

It's clear from the moment I crack open an eye that Scarlet isn't in bed with me. Disappointment has me reaching out a hand, smoothing over the cold sheet.

I was worried it would be impossible to get her into bed last night, her need to make everything perfect for the ball keeping her out on the grounds until past eleven o'clock most nights this week. Fortunately, her legs had long given up on her by the time I picked her up from the sofa in the library and carried her upstairs, promising to help her finish the final touches first thing this morning when she complained.

You'd think we didn't have our friends and family here to help us.

We do.

Megan flew home last week and has been holed up here since. Lucy and Elliot have been over daily, Elliot taking the week off to help in any way needed. And Charlie and Lissie have been staying in the lake house to be close by.

It's been a long week of trying to make everything exactly how Scar wants it to be, and I'm fucking ruined.

I sigh into my pillow before sitting up and scrubbing at my face.

Only when something smooth and cool grazes my cheek, I pull my hands away, looking into my cupped palms at the gold band that hugs my ring finger on my left hand.

I flip it over, frowning.

"The fuck."

The ring is thick, the polished surface flawless.

I snap my gaze up, my heart falling through my ass when I find the white bouquets of flowers Scarlet and I have spent the week putting together littered around our bedroom.

Tossing back the covers, I stand from the bed, walking to our wardrobe where a tuxedo is hung on the door, a card tucked into the pocket.

I pluck it out, hands shaking. My heart...

> *I know I don't make this easy but...*
> *Will you be hopelessly fucking wild with me, Lance?*
> *This time, forever.*
> *You know where to find me.*
> *Your sunshine. x*

I lift a hand to rub across my chest as I read the words over and over, the sound of the string quartet already playing somewhere close by finally registering.

Without a moment's hesitation, I head for the shower,

making sure to take my time as I wash, shave, and trim my beard.

The tuxedo fits me inch perfect, the inside lined with lavender silk.

When did she do all of this?

How did she hide it from me?

Once ready, I take one fleeting glance at myself in the mirror and make my way from the room and down the landing, running my hands through my hair as a ball of energy churns in my stomach.

I take the stairs, looking around the silent house with no idea where anyone is.

You know where to find me.

I swallow and smooth my hands down the front of my tux, my heart feeling like it could break through my chest at any minute.

Pulling back my shoulders, I reach forward, dragging open the heavy wooden doors that lead outside. The moment I spot the figures on the hilltop, the kids running, I smile.

I take off across the terrace, walking on shaky legs for the first field. As I near Ellis's garden, the hairs on the back of my neck stand on end right before I spot Mason in his bests, stood with a drink in hand at the gate.

"You're late," he tells me, a smile growing.

I stop, my throat growing tight. *This is it. This is really happening.* "I was only just invited," I tell him.

He downs the last of his drink, emotion swimming in his eyes as he nods for me to keep going.

I stare past him into the garden, not being able to see shit but knowing.

She's in there.

I know she is.

I walk backward a couple of steps before pocketing my hands and stalking through the fields and up the hill.

When I reach the top, breathing eludes me, and I come to a stop.

Our flowers decorate the lakefront, a small number of chairs set either side of an aisle that leads to the dock.

"Uncle Lance!"

I snap my head to the right, catching Sammy running for me. I pick him up, searching behind him. I see Ralph and Ellis, but no one else. "Hey, mate. Lads," I say to the boys.

"You're late," Ellis tells me.

I chuckle. "Your dad said the same thing."

He narrows his eyes on me before stuffing his hands in his pockets. "You look like you're going to cry."

"Rib me for it all you want, mate."

I see a small smirk slant his mouth before he pulls his hands back out and awkwardly offers me a handkerchief. "It was one of Pap's," he explains, shrugging.

I stare down at it, at the gesture. "Thank you, Ellis."

He takes Sammy from me, tipping his chin as he steps away. "You're still a pussy."

I snigger and pocket the handkerchief.

And then I make my way toward the people waiting at the lakefront.

To Elliot, and Charlie, and my mum and sisters.

To Vinny, and Stan, and Ellis, and Sammy, and Ralph.

It's not a lot of people, but it's the only people we care about.

When I reach where my mother sits with my sisters and the children, she stands, stepping forward to hug me.

Without thought, I wrap her up in my arms, taking everything from the moment that I can.

"I'm happy for you, love," she whispers.

My jaw goes taut as I breathe her in on a deep lungful of air. "Thank you, Mum."

When I pull back, I look down at my sisters, Chloe and Molly. My eyes burn at the absence of Nessa-Anne, and I hate that part of me for caring.

But fuck her.

I choose to turn toward my family instead.

The people I chose.

And when I do, I'm met with the widest, happiest grins on their faces that I think I've ever seen them wear.

"Motherfuckers could have warned me," I tell them.

Elliot steps forward first, taking my hand and pulling me in for a hug. "Where's the fun in that, Sullivan?"

I push him back, walking the rest of the way to where Charlie stands beside Stanley Dukes—Vinny's younger brother—who seems to be holding a book and papers.

"I took it upon myself to be your best man," Charlie announces. "I didn't have the stiffest of competition, but I'd like to think I've done you proud."

I tap the bottom of my fist to the centre of his chest. "I'm sure you went beyond expectation, Charles."

He nods once, a silent, heavy promise he made and kept and keeps.

I turn to Stan, his broad shoulders barely contained in his

suit. "Dukes, you look more nervous than me," I say with an emotion-filled chuckle.

"I have the pleasure of marrying you today," he explains. "I apologise in advance."

Everyone laughs.

The string quartet quiets, the song changing. I turn as Elliot moves in front of me, ushering the children into their seats.

I look to the hilltop, waiting.

Her girls come first. Lucy, Megs, and Lissie.

I'm good with her girls.

It's Waverley who comes next, hand in hand with Nina as Bear bounds along at her feet, who threatens to make a lesser man out of me.

I pull my lips into my mouth, biting down before letting them go. I do it over and over, my eyes not leaving my daughter as she looks around.

And I know how nervous she will be. How she will have caused chaos all morning and been excited and ready right up until it was time to go, and then she'd have gone quiet.

Lucy pulls my attention away, gently touching my hand and giving me a smile that I can't quite return as she passes by.

Megan stops in front of me, pulling me into the biggest hug. "She looks fucking divine."

I do smile then, waiting as Lissie looks from me to Charlie to me again. She winks before taking up place next to the girls.

When I face forward again, Waverley is just letting go of

Nina's hand, completely out of rhythm with the music as she runs to me, leaping into my arms.

I put my face in her neck, breathing her in and letting her light me up. "Hey, baby girl."

"Hi, Daddy."

"You look perfect."

She leans back, holding my face. "So do you."

My eyes shine, but I don't care. I don't care because I know that she's coming next. I know that no matter how many days and nights I went without the woman who makes my world right, no matter how often I told myself she deserved more, someone else, a life without me in it, I know that after today, I'll never go a day without her by my side. So, I don't give a shit about any tears that fall.

Because they will be happy ones.

And fuck if I've only just learnt how good those can be.

Scarlet appears on the hilltop, pausing with her brother in arm as they turn and look back toward the house. Toward their parents.

I bow my head and mutter low and quiet, *"With my life. I'll love and protect her with my life."*

When they eventually face us, making their way down the bank to the aisle, I wonder if I've ever felt more lucky, more grateful in my whole entire life.

She's beautiful, her dress held up at her neck by a thick band, the material fitted to her every curve as it trails her body and the path she walks.

She's perfect.

"So perfect."

As they near, I see Scarlet's smile, so sure and full. I shake my head and chuckle. "Sunshine."

"Sullivan."

She stops a foot away from me, and I can't help but eat up the space, regardless of Mason at her side. "A better man would wait to put a ring on your finger before kissing you."

She grins, holding up her left hand, showing off the lavender diamond adorning it.

I lean in and kiss her. I kiss her gently, slowly, and as if she is mine forever.

When we eventually part, Mason proudly steps forward, putting Scarlet's hand in mine. "We don't tend to do conventional around here." He turns to take whatever Charlie passes him, handing it straight to me. "It's from the three of us."

Frowning, and presuming *the three of us* are him, Charlie, and Elliot, I pull the papers from the envelope, reading the words over and over as I blink at them in confusion, disbelief, of what they mean.

"Lance..."

I peer up at Scarlet.

"It's not official. You have a choice. But I wear my name with pride because it means more than just family to me, and I'm pretty sure it means just as much to you, too. It's the one thing I had when there was nothing else. It's home. It's unconditional. I know that being Mrs Sullivan would make me just as proud. But if you'll have us..." She gestures around her. "Will you take our name along with your own?"

I drag my gaze down to the papers, the documents adding Mr Lance Lowell-Sullivan and Mrs Nina Lowell to the deeds for the estate.

"I don't—" I shake my head, my heart feeling funny.

"This is home, Lance. It always was and still is and will forever be *your* home."

I stare at her, not quite sure if it's all real.

It can't be real.

My eyes dart to Mason, his small nod a promise, assurance. "Has a ring to it, doesn't it?"

I scrub a hand across my mouth, reading the document again. "Scar..."

"Do you need some time?"

I frown. "What? No. No, I don't need time. I just..." *What the fuck?* "Are you sure?"

She smiles. "It's like the only thing I'm sure of. You deserve this, Lance."

Do I?

"I get to change my name, too, Daddy," Ave tells me, bouncing on her feet.

"Waverley Lowell-Sullivan." I grin over at her. "Sounds like a queen's name."

"Fitting." Charlie coughs under his breath, earning a glower from Waverley in return.

I hand the papers back to Mason before settling my stare on Scarlet. I take her face in my hands, smoothing my thumb over her deeply blushed cheek. "God, I love you, Scar. I didn't think I'd get to stand here like this with you in this lifetime and yet look at us." I smile. "You gave me a second chance, and I have no idea why. You're the most kind, loyal, selfless person I've ever met, and it's easy to throw those words around in moments like these, but I know for a fact there isn't a single person gathered around us who would disagree. My life began when I met you and was made when you had our daughter. Even if I didn't know it. And now, today, I devote it to you both. For as long as there's air in my lungs, I'm yours, and I love you. I can't promise you our time will be perfect. I don't think I'd want it to be. But I know that every second of the life we'll share here on this estate, the walks we'll take, the books we'll read, the parties we'll have." I pull my lip between my teeth, hiding my smile as I remember her spread out for me on the sofa. "The nights we'll steal"— Scarlet turns her head in my hand, kissing the palm—"will be remembered for a lifetime. By us, our children, and maybe one day their children." I nod. "I'll take your name with pride, my sunshine, but know that nothing will ever come close to what being by your side through this life, being your husband, means to me."

Scarlet's smile is watery, and I mirror it as she reaches up to blot at the corner of her eye.

She looks from me to Stanley. I follow her gaze, realising he's stood before us, waiting.

"No one is going to know if we don't follow it," he says, holding up the papers. "You guys are doing great."

Scarlet chuckles, turning back to face me. "My heart's going wild," she whispers.

I kiss her forehead. "Mine, too."

She blows out a shaky breath and steps closer to my chest, looking up at me. "It feels pointless telling you all the ways you amaze me, but it's our wedding day, and it's kind of the done thing." Everyone chuckles at her words, and she frowns, hands shaking in mine. "That came out wrong."

"Sunshine, talk to me. Forget about them."

She rolls her lips, locking our eyes. "You won't believe me, that's all I meant. You never have believed what I wish you would." She tilts her head. "You are loved, Lance. By me and so many others around you. I remember meeting you and thinking you were the hardest-faced man in the room. Turns out you are."

I feign hurt, bringing my hand to my chest as if she's shot me.

She smiles. "Fortunately, you picked me to share all you hide behind it. And, Lance, what a man you are. I'm so proud of you. I'm certain your dad is proud of you, too. I remember you asked me on our first night together, right here on this lake, if I thought my mother would hate you." She smiles as laughter rings out. "And I told you I wish I knew." She pauses, and I know it's because it hurts that they aren't here. "Well, she's the woman who knows every word of our story up until this point. I gave her the best and worst of us over the years, not leaving out a single wild beat." Her eyes fill as she smiles, voice whispering. "I don't know if she hates you. I wish I did." She nods, and I catch a tear. "But I can only take what's in my heart and in my soul and trust that she loves you as much as I do. That she sees the man you are to me, the friend you are to Mase, and the father you are to Waverley, and knows exactly what you hide from this world. You are good, Lance. You deserve my love and every bit of love you get. You may not believe it, making these words pointless today, but I mean them, and I'll spend the rest of my life showing you how much."

My brow dips to meet hers, our smiles wide—forever. "Fuck, I love you."

There's a shuffling of papers as Stan clears his throat. "I can see we've already exchanged rings," he deadpans, making us both laugh as he flicks over the page. "Ah, here." He scans the text. "You may now kiss the bride."

"My *wife*," I correct, grinning as I take her face in my hands. "I can kiss my beautiful wife."

And I do.

THIRTY-FIVE

Lance

"So, what, I can't call you Sullivan anymore?" Elliot asks, slowly walking the length of the dock at our backs with his hands stuffed in his tux pockets. "Lowell-Sullivan seems excessive."

"Nah, I'm still going to call him asshole," Mason says from beside me, knocking my shoulder as he hands me the cigar we're sharing.

"I like Lowell-Sullivan," Charlie tells me. "It's professional. Would look good on a building." He pops his brow at the suggestion.

My eyes settle on the water below us. "I want to get back to work. It's on the cards, and I've spoken to Scarlet about it a little."

"Do you want your position back at the Ellis and Frey, or are you thinking about starting something else? We can back you if you need a hand getting something off the ground."

I shake my head, handing Charlie the cigar. "No. I have no plans." I swallow, rubbing my hands down my thighs. "I have some things I need to work through first. Heavy, messed up shit..."

They go quiet around me, Elliot eventually taking a seat on the edge of the dock next to Mase.

"I've struggled a little at times, if I'm being honest, lads. Since being released."

"Even now?" Elliot asks. "I mean, the first few weeks it was pretty obvious."

"Expected," Charlie adds, handing me his drink.

"Yeah. Even now." I take a sip of the amber liquid, remembering my promise to make it to bed fully conscious tonight. "I've had my accident and Waverley to keep my mind busy for the most part, but there are things not so easily forgotten."

"Do you want to talk about them?"

"I'm not sure I'm ready to."

My friends sit in silence, but I can hear their minds racing, all trying to find the right thing to say. "I have these dreams—or nightmares, I suppose. They seem to shit me up the most. Brings it all back."

"Have you thought about speaking to someone about them?" Charlie asks.

"Yeah, Scarlet's suggested it a couple of times after her own sessions. I get the feeling she doesn't want to push."

Mason clears his throat. "I've never mentioned it." He looks between us all. "But both Nina and I have dipped in and out of therapy throughout the years. Talking therapy," he clarifies. "But they have a ton of methods."

"There's a whole load of options," Charlie agrees.

"I think in my mind, talking about it could make it worse. Like I don't want to be waking up next to Scar sweating or clawing the sheets, you know?"

"We've all been there, mate." Mason huffs a humourless laugh. "She'd rather you get the help you need than bottle it up."

"I know." And I do.

"Well, I'm a pretty perfect man and not the best voice of reason for this conversation." Elliot breaks the silence that's settled, making us all chuckle. He reaches across Mase and grasps my shoulder. "But if you ever need someone to talk to or a safe space to just be for a while." He nods. "You just ask for it."

"Hear hear," Mason agrees, wrapping an arm around my neck and pulling me closer.

I see Charlie nodding out of the corner of my eye. "I'm glad you've mentioned it to us, Lance."

I twist my neck to look at him, not mustering the words that I want to.

Because although I can't say it, I really am thankful to have them.

Charlie's face transforms into a rare smile, his eyes flicking between each of us. "Fuck, who'd have thought it, boys." He tips his chin. "Wasn't sure we'd get here at points."

Elliot snorts. "I was sure it was all over on that jet ski. I won't lie."

I tip my head back and laugh, feeling the heaviness melt away.

"To the boys," Mason says, reaching for the glass and taking a swig.

Elliot follows, lifting the glass. "The boys."

He passes it to me, and I take a sip and then hand it to Charlie. "The boys."

Charlie drains the glass.

Scarlet

We're on the dance floor when my husband and his groomsmen find us. They disappeared over an hour ago, Lance telling me he'd be back soon as he fought to break his lips from mine.

Ave, of course, demanded Lance dance with her the second she spotted him. I'm not sure I've ever been as in love with them as I am today.

It was the night I got caught in the rain on the way to Elliot's that I decided to make the memorial ball something more.

Our wedding day.

I didn't bother changing the guest list, having only asked the people most important to the family to the ball anyway.

To say our guests were shocked when they arrived to find us married is an understatement.

Mia and Annie both made it, their shared happiness hitting me square in the chest as they showered me in their unrelenting love and support.

Everyone who's here is happy for us today.

I'm happy for us.

"Mrs Lowell-Sullivan."

I spin, finding Nina approaching me on the dance floor.

"A dance, please, if you will."

I pull her close, our arms tangling as we cling to one another. "Anything for my favourite sister-in-law," I gush.

She giggles, turning her head to look at me. Her eyes look glassy, like she had one too many glasses of champagne. "You fucking rock, you know that." She kisses my cheek hard. "You're probably the most beautiful bride I've ever seen."

"I'm pretty sure you've told all of the girls that on their wedding days."

"Shh. Let me love you."

I chuckle, holding her tighter as we sway to the music. "I can't ever put it into words what it means, you know," I tell her over the music. "Thank you, Nina," I add, my voice softer.

"What for?" She frowns as she pulls back.

"Lots of things." I roll my lips as emotion builds in my throat, my mind throwing me right back to that first night when Mason brought her home to meet Dad and me. The way she pulled up at the kitchen island, told we were going out for my birthday, and then never left me alone after it. "Your kindness, patience, and love." I smile. "But mostly for not letting me fall."

Her arms go slack at her sides, her eyes shining with tears. "Scar," she warns.

"I know. Let's not cry anymore today."

She grasps my arm, stopping me when I try to pull her back to me to dance.

Her brown eyes search mine, her own vulnerabilities

reflecting right back. Because we both might be a million miles from where we once were, but the journey can't be forgotten, and our scars will forever be marred and remembered for what they are. "Always always, yeah?" she tells me.

"Always." I nod.

She steps into me, letting me hug her as we sway to the music.

"Girlies, I feel left out," Lucy squeals, forcing her way into the hug. "You're not going to ditch me now you're legally sisters, are you?"

"We'd never, Luce," Nina tells her, wrapping an arm around her.

Megan slips her head between Nina and me, and we split apart, smiling as she joins our circle.

I look around for Lissie, spotting her already dancing with Charlie. "Lissie!" I shout.

Charlie's glare is instant, and I give him the finger when Lissie doesn't think twice about ditching him.

"He said you're a real lady, Scar."

I dip my head back and laugh, cuddling into her the second she's close enough. "It's my wedding day, I can get away with it."

The song changes to *There She Goes* by The La's, and as I look around at the women who got me to today, who will dance with me into tomorrow, I can't help but feel a sense of immense security.

Because good men exist, we sometimes find the very best of them, but good girls?

Those bitches are for life.

THIRTY-SIX

Scarlet

"If I take it off, it will all be over!" Ave whines, flopping back to the bed in her dress.

I follow her, dropping my head to the side to smile at her when my own dress settles across the comforter. "Today was a good day, huh, Ave?"

"The best." She hugs my arm, kissing the back of it. "He's going to stay now, isn't he?" she says, hopeful.

I take her hand lying between us on the bed, squeezing it tight.

"Forever," Lance mutters from the door.

Lifting my head off the bed, I take him in, the tuxedo I had made for him doing all the things. I roll my eyes, over the top, just like Ave would.

He walks to us and lies down on the other side of Ave. "Even when you don't agree with me on dad stuff, remember?"

She gives him a toothy grin. "I remember."

"Good." He kisses her forehead, reaching an arm above her head to smooth the backs of his fingers over my temple. "I love you." He looks down. "Both of you."

"We love you, too, Daddy."

I readjust my head on the bed, staring up at Waverley's ceiling as the celebrations outside continue, knowing there's no place I'd rather be than here with them.

We lie silently, Lance's thumb dusting my cuticle as the sun finally dips beyond the horizon, waiting as the moon illuminates the sky, smiling as the stars shine.

And it's not terrifying or earth shattering to watch the darkness slowly settle over us—

"Mummy, you can turn the light out now. We don't have to be afraid anymore."

Because tomorrow the sun will rise.

The End.

Grand Lies

(Mason & Nina's story)

Grand Love

(Mason & Nina's story)

The Grand Pact

(Elliot & Lucy's story)

Pre-order **The Grand Duel** (Charlie & Lissie's story) on
Amazon now!

AFTERWORD

Thank you so much for reading!
If you enjoyed The Grand Ruin, please consider leaving a
review on Amazon.
Reviews are so important to authors!

Want to be notified about future book releases of mine?
Sign up to my Newsletter via my website
www.jchawkeauthor.com

Come join my Facebook reader group for a first look at sneak
peeks and teasers. This is a PRIVATE group and only people
in the group can see posts and comments!
Hawkes Hangout - JC Hawke's Reader Group

ACKNOWLEDGMENTS

To my three loves, thank you for always being my biggest supporters. For showing me love and family and never letting me veer too far off the track when I get a little wobbly. I love you forever.

To my sisters and cousins, all of you, because without you, there'd be no meadow to run through or play sleeping lions in, no baby birds we'd rescue and nurture, games of catch out played, or barrels we'd attach to cars so that we can be dragged over the fields at Bodbrane. I stole moments of our childhood for this story, and I'm so glad that I did. They were a joy to write and relive. Thank you.

To Mum and Dad, for not only selling my books to everyone you know and meet but for being you. I love you endlessly.

To Jess, for always being that person. You went from being some girl on insta I talked authoring with to being my best friend. I couldn't go a day without our bitching and moaning. And I couldn't do this without you. LY.

Katie and Billie, thank you. For your support and friendship. I know I ask A LOT of questions LOL, but I know you love me and I love you right back. I can't wait to continue this journey with you both. Let's get that writing retreat booked!

Jodie, thank you for always making me look like I know

what I'm doing. JC HQ would be a lot less together without you.

My betas, Jess, Shells, Billie, Amy, Jo, Rach, and Gem. You guys are the best, and I couldn't do this without you!

To Sara, for not only fuelling me with the greatest playlists but for coming along on this journey with me. You connected to Lance and Scarlet as deeply as I did, and for that, I'm forever grateful.

And to my readers, You're the most special of them all (shh, don't tell the others). You put trust in me and my books time and time again with no clue if they're going to be any good. So, for picking this book up, or maybe all of them, thank you.

You're making my dreams come true!

Until next time,

Stay Wonderful

xo

ABOUT THE AUTHOR

JC Hawke is an author of contemporary romance. She lives in the South-West of the United Kingdom with her husband, two curly haired daughters, and beagle woofer.

Printed in Great Britain
by Amazon

42020363R00243